# ZOMBIE YOUTH
## PLAYGROUND POLITICS

**H.E. Goodhue**

**To all my loved ones, no matter where you are.**

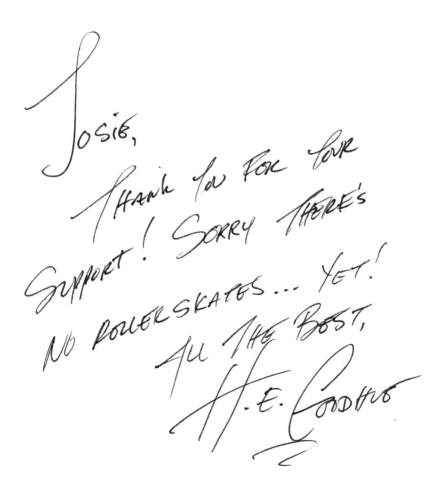

Josie,

Thank you for your support! Sorry there's no roller skates... yet! All the best,

H.E. Goodhue

# PLAYGROUND POLITICS

A throat-tearing scream raced through the school at the pace of a heartbeat. The shellacked cinderblock walls did little to dampen the terror entwined in the scream, rather echoing it further through the building, spreading more fear and confusion.

Five minutes earlier, everyone in the Montville Regional School Complex heard the tinny announcement of, *"Teachers please hold your rosters. All teachers hold your rosters."* It was another Lock Down Drill, no more serious than an announced changed to the school lunch menu. The classrooms were closed, lights off and students and teachers huddled in the far corners in well-practiced silence. Everyone at Montville Regional had assumed the call for a school wide lock down had been nothing more than another of the numerous monthly drills that were conducted in the post-9/11 and Columbine world of education. They had slowly risen from their work and laughed until their respective teachers silenced and shuffled them into a corner away from the small, glass and chicken wire windows that centered their classroom doors.

The students and faculty were used to the principal or vice principal rattling the doorknobs, or pushing on the doors in comical attempts to portray the necessity of taking refuge from an intruder. Montville had seen its share of problems and even faced down a real one or two, but there had never truly been a need to lock down the entire school complex from an intruder. For the students and staff, Lock Down Drills held the same level of effectiveness as a 1950's bomb drill; simply something to give people the thin veil of security to hide behind. They all knew that they were no safer from an intruder hiding in a corner than they were hiding from a Russian A-bomb under a cheaply made desk. And everyone at Montville knew they were no more likely to have a real A-bomb dropped on their school than they were to have an actual intruder.

But with the echo of one throaty, primal scream, the students and staff were snapped out of their complacent stupors of false suburban safety and thrust into a world where the realization that they could be harmed, possibly even killed, was more real than any of them cared to admit. This was not a drill. Something was truly and profoundly wrong.

● ● ●

*Seven hours before...*

Gone were the days of the little red schoolhouse. All across the East Coast, former farming communities were finding themselves overrun by the pharmacological revolution and all of the annoying, newly rich worker ants that cropped up with each new factory. The already flattened fields, perfectly suited for building, were being snatched up by developers to make more prefab McMansions, all of which were given commercially trendy street names like Wanders' Way; as if in some way to entice the drones to abandon their hectic city lives for the quiet wonder of the newly created Agro-Suburbs.

These communities experienced a population explosion that could easily double or triple their towns overnight. Services had to be rapidly expanded to meet the ever-growing needs of the community. Schools, once quaint and welcoming, were replaced with massive brick complexes with state of the art facilities and all the charm of an asbestos factory. Towns consolidated grades and schools into larger and larger complexes, literally creating schools within schools, all in the name of saving tax dollars.

Once two laned country roads were widened and expanded to make way to accommodate the now overwhelming morning rush hour, but as quickly as lanes could be built, they were jammed and soon the casual calls of the cows were replaced with a disconcerting concert of car horns and curses. And at the epicenter of this dissonance, was exactly where Sam Williams found himself Tuesday morning.

Sam leaned his head against the thin glass window of the bus and squeezed his eyes shut, in a vain attempt to shut out the insanity unfolding outside of the school bus. He used to look forward to the bus ride to school; it was a chance to talk to your friends without adults around, but with the coming of the new school year and the switch to the newly opened Montville School Complex, Sam had realized the noisy peace he had once enjoyed was no more than a distant memory. He had spent every morning for the last month sweating on a cheap, green vinyl seat of the school bus, while the mid-morning traffic surged around the bus. Sam wondered why no matter how much the town dumped money into their new school, none of it ever seemed to go towards better busses that did not have seats held together with duct tape or reeking of years of stale butt sweat.

Sam wished that the driver would just ram the cars out of the way, but the bus's lack of maneuverability and wide turning radius kept the driver, Wally, from making any progress forward. Within minutes of entering the fray, the bus would quickly become a yellow boulder in the middle of shiny metal rapids that angrily surged around it. And like a boulder, the bus hardly moved an inch. Sam imagined after centuries, the bus would be eroded and the children inside swept away in the insane rush surrounding it.

"Stop dreaming about your mom naked," Joey Potts laughed, snapping Sam out of his thoughts. Joey had been Sam's friend since kindergarten, but that did little to stop Sam's groaning at Joey's over-sexualized jokes. Joey's mind had seemed dirty enough in kindergarten, but now with the boys being thirteen and in eighth grade, Sam imagined that they could shoot an episode of Hoarders there. Every word out of Joey's mouth had something to do with girls, sex, or both, and while Sam, in truth, thought about those things as well, he hardly had the energy at seven in the morning to talk about it.

"I wasn't dreaming about my mom Joey. I was only wondering how long it would be before your palm hair grew in and you went blind," Sam chuckled.

"Everyone needs a hobby," Joey shrugged after checking the inside of his hands for errant hairs.

The bus lurched forward into a space recently vacated by a maroon Toyota mini- van and began to make a little progress forward. Sam and Joey continued their light-hearted exchange, but fell silent as the bus pulled up to its final stop on the route to Montville. This was both the high and low point of the ride for Sam, and Joey could not help but laugh out loud as he saw the expectant look on his friend's face.

The doors swung outward with a gentle hiss and Sam watched silently as she got on to the bus. She was Alice Shah. Her family moved here a year ago after her father had been transferred to the new J&J plant, and while Sam detested most of the changes brought to his town by the drug companies, he had to admit they were not all bad.

Alice was totally different from all the other girls that Sam had grown up with. The local girls all seemed cut from the same cloth and one-dimensional. Sam honestly had a hard time telling them apart. Alice was taller than most of the girls, but she was not gangly. Rather puberty seemed to be suiting her just fine and her slender silhouette was never that far out of Sam's mind. More important to Sam, she was smart, but not nerdy, good at sports, but not butch, and above all, Sam loved the way her eyes looked when she casually smiled as they passed in the hall. Her eyes were a shade of brown that Sam had never seen before, something like a cane sugar brown flecked with gold. He had been assigned to her lab group last year, and almost failed science because he spent more time studying Alice's eyes than the experiments. He would have gladly sat sweaty on a bus for the rest of his teenaged life to get a chance to talk to Alice or simply steal a glance. But above all of the usual teenage boy interests that drew Sam towards Alice, it was her confidence that he loved. She never seemed to be unsure of herself, like so many of their peers. Alice carried herself with a silent strength and she never backed down when a classmate or teacher questioned her. And somehow, to Sam's amazement, in spite of all of these stunning attributes, Alice never appeared to be arrogant. She was nice to all her classmates and never tried to rub their faces in her attributes. Sam had never had a crush before, but with Alice, he understood perfectly well why it was called just that. Thoughts of her constantly pressed down upon him and weighed on his mind the minute he let it begin to wander.

Alice knew little of Sam's feelings or how he thought about her, but she suspected that there might be spark waiting to be fanned. She had always been a good judge of people and could usually figure out what someone was after, even before they said it, but in truth, she had actually never stopped to think that any of the boys would or could take an interest in her. Intelligence and ability had always isolated her from her peers and seemed to intimidate all of the boys. None of the boys seemed capable of speaking to her without making some comment about being a brain or trying to regale her with pointless stories of touchdowns. Alice would have loved for someone to stop trying to put her on some ivory academic pedestal and just ask her what she thought of last night's episode of *The Bad Girls Club* or latest Ryan Gosling movie. She longed to be viewed as normal, but her father, *the doctor*, did not seem capable of accepting normal. Saturdays were not for movies with friends, let alone a boy. No, Alice's weekends were reserved for enrichment tutoring, traditional dance classes, piano lessons, meetings of the Future Doctors of America Club and traveling soccer. There was no way her parents would have ever let her talk to any of these boys, but in truth, Alice was not really interested in talking to any of the boys in her classes, except for one: Sam Williams.

Sam was so awkward and would often trip over his words when they worked together in science class last year, but instead of finding it annoying, Alice loved it. She felt Sam was different from the other boys. He never tried to impress Alice with the usual teenage stories of strength or sports prowess. Sam always approached Alice as an equal and treated her like a person, not a challenge to conquer like the other boys or a china doll like her father. Sam was completely different from any boy Alice had ever met, but she could never tell him that. What difference would it make? Her parents would never allow it. So Alice had resigned herself to secretly love Sam Williams and found the ride to school on the humid, stale school bus to be the happiest fifteen minutes of her day, because at least there she could play by her own rules and be her own person. But maybe, just maybe, there was some way she could let Sam know. She had finally convinced her parents that she needed a cell phone, for safety reasons obviously, and they had actually given one to her. But would Sam even want to talk to her? Maybe he was just being nice and she had mistaken it for interest! Unlike many challenges in her life, Alice was unable to solve this one, but she had grown tired of waiting and wondering. She would rather know one way or another, and if she failed, she failed. And as all the thoughts rumbled through Alice's head, she climbed the stairs into the bus to the happiest part of her day where she could steal glances at Sam or smile at his awkward waves.

Joey was snapping his fingers next to Sam's head. "Dude wake the hell up. Jeez man, you stoned or something this morning?"

Sam slapped Joey's hand away and took the opening to deliver a devastating titty twister. "My bad man. I couldn't hear you so I had to turn the volume up."

"Bastard," Joey hissed while rubbing the area of Sam's attack. "Next time, I'll give you something to grab with your mouth."

"I'll make sure to bring my tweezers and magnifying glass," Sam laughed, but cut it short as Alice approached the empty seat in front of him.

"H-hey Alice," Sam stammered and instantly tried to cover up, "You, uh ready for that test today in science?" *Smooth*, Sam internally chided himself. Why the hell couldn't he just talk to her like he did in class? Why was it so difficult here? And as if in response to his unspoken questions, Joey chimed in.

"Hey Alice love what you're doing with your hair," he smiled obviously content with his operating skills.

Alice smirked briefly at Joey and turned her attention back towards Sam, "Yeah Sam, I guess I am, but you get that stuff so much better than I do. I really wish we could have studied together or something." Alice knew that half of what she had just said was a complete lie; she was top of the class for every subject, but she really did wish Sam would ask her to study with him. It was the only way her parents would let her see him.

Sam blushed, "That probably would've helped me more than you. Well, I'll see you in class."

Alice started to speak, but stopped herself, "Yeah, see you fifth Sam." As she turned to continue down the aisle, a folded square of paper slipped from her stack of books and lazily wafted towards Sam.

Sam's eye's widened, maybe there was a God and this was his way of telling Sam to go for it. Maybe this was fate giving him a push towards Alice. Almost reflexively, Sam's arm shot out to grab the errant sheet of loose-leaf from the middle of the aisle. As Sam started to lean back into his seat, a heavy push caught his arm and propelled him face first onto the dirty, rubber-ridged aisle. Before Sam knew what was going on, something huge crashed down on top of him and a collective gasp echoed through the bus.

Sam rolled over trying to see what had just landed on him while still clutching Alice's paper, but before he could see for himself, he had his answer.

"You dumb shit," an overly deep voice growled. Sam closed his eyes for a second and wished he were anywhere other than where he currently was. Of all the people for him to trip, literally an entire busload to choose from, and it had to Chris Kelly.

Chris Kelly was in the same grade as Sam, but that was where all similarities ceased. Chris had been left back numerous times, so while many of his classmates were dealing with the onset of pubescent awkwardness, Chris had moved into the deep-voiced, thinly bearded, angry phase of life known as full blown teenagehood. And while Sam was not a small or sickly kid, he was eclipsed by the height and mass of Chris, all of which presently sat on top of him.

"Hey Chris, sorry man. I didn't see you there," Sam offered apologetically.

"You tripped me," Chris said somewhere between an accusation and a question. He seemed slightly perplexed by the current situation, having gotten used to his peers steering wide of him, but the inquisitive expression on his face quickly passed and a cloud of red anger seeped across. "You *friggin' tripped me* Williams?" He shouted as he grabbed Sam by the collar and hefted him from the floor.

"Dude, it was totally an accident," Joey tried to interject, but only succeeded in getting his face palmed and being pushed back into the seat.

Sam knew what was next, but tried to smooth it over, "Chris, my bad. I'm clumsy. Total accident. Never happen again."

At this moment, Wally caught a glimpse of the situation in his angled safety mirror. "Hey you two stop screwing around. You wanna slow dance, save it for Saturday night." Sam winced at Wally's remark knowing it would do nothing to assuage Chris's anger.

Chris's grip tightened and he pulled Sam closer to his gritted teeth. "Later," he hissed as spittle flecked his chapped lips and then he released Sam and made his way to his honorary spot in the back of the bus.

"Shit," Sam muttered as he slumped down into his seat next to Joey. In that moment, Sam was sure that both fate and God must be real, and that both must absolutely hate him.

● ● ●

The school day seemed to slow down and stretch, painfully extending every minute. And while Sam was almost thankful that the day seemed to be delaying his meeting with Chris Kelly, he almost wished he could just get the beating over with and move on.

The bell chimed its two rounds of a three-tone synthetic xylophone song; the students would almost reflexively fill in the missing third round while they moved down the hall. As Sam moved through the seething mass of students, he wondered if maybe there was some Pavlovian reason, known only to the administration, that the bells never seemed to finish, only so that the students could.

The rush of students in the halls pushed Sam closer to his next class and he instinctively moved to the right and slipped out of the flow and into the classroom. Alice turned as Sam walked in and smiled, but something about her smile struck Sam. She looked almost apologetic, almost sorry to see him. Had he really made that big of a fool of himself on the bus earlier today? Or maybe Alice was just offering an early condolence for the injuries he was sure to have later on. But Sam tried to put this out of his head and slowly picked his way through the minefield of backpacks to take his place at the lab table across from Alice. Sam tried to put the awkwardness of Alice's hello out of his mind and concentrate on the fact that he had a chem test. No teenage boy that had ever walked the Earth, could pass on a chance for a good round of self-loathing over some mistake made in the presence of a cute girl, and Sam was no different. His ears burned with shame and he could feel the prickly heat dancing up and down his neck and back. He was sure that his typically fair complexion had transitioned nicely into one resembling an over-ripe strawberry.

The other students filled in around Sam, the test was distributed and he blindly circled answers and filled in equations. Failing this test was not going to be the worst part of his day, but Sam still chided himself for not being able to focus. He kept glancing over his shoulder at Alice only to find that she was staring back at him too, and every time accidental eye contact was made, she would quickly offer the same sad smile and look quickly away. Each time this gauche social dance played out, Sam could feel another piece of his self-image shrivel and die.

*"Way to go this morning!"* he chided himself internally, *"Really a good way to get her to notice you by tripping some cro-mag and letting him sit on you!"* Now Alice's smile, something that used to make Chris's guts turn to melted butter, was causing him more pain than anything Chris had planned for him.

The same half- hearted tone resounded and before Sam knew it, chemistry was over and he was moving one more period towards his inevitable beating at the hands of Chris Kelly. Head down, hands in the kangaroo pocket of his hoodie, Sam moved towards the door, but something in the pocket brushed his hands. It was the folded piece of loose leaf that Alice had dropped on the bus. With everything that had happened, Sam forgot to give Alice back her work. *"Even that you can't do right!"* Sam's angry interior voice scolded, but his berating was cut short by the fact that Alice seemed to be waiting by the door, and not only that she seemed to be looking at Sam, she must have known that he had the paper. Sam figured he had probably kept her from handing in some homework, something she never missed, and now she was waiting to rescue it from his sweaty grip. Clumsiness aside, Sam figured he really had no chance now.

"Hey Sam," Alice said hesitantly, "Did you, uh, find um, a paper on the bus this morning?"

Without thinking, Sam blurted out, "Yeah, I'm sorry. I should have given it back so you could hand it in." His hands shot out of his hoodie pocket and thrust the now wrinkled and creased square of paper towards Alice. Her tan skin turned a shade of crimson and she started to speak, but was cut short by Sam's attempt at damage control
"Just tell me what teacher the homework was for and I'll tell them I had it. That it wasn't your fault." A look of confusion clouded Alice's face.

"Uh, Sam, no that's ok," she paused, "You didn't look at the paper, did you?"

Completely confused Sam shook his head dumbly, "Nah, I didn't. I was gonna give it back, but, well, you know. I'm sure you saw." He frowned.

Alice decided to take control of this situation and pushed Sam's hand and the folded square of paper back towards him. "Yeah, I saw. He's such an idiot. But, um, maybe you should hold onto that."

Even more confused than before, Sam's mouth hung slightly open, "Wha...?"

Alice smiled, but this time the awkward, apologetic one was gone. In its place was the gut melting radiant smile that Sam looked forward to every morning.

"You're literate, right Sam?" Alice said jokingly, "I mean I'm gonna feel really bad if we're in the same classes and you can't even read."

Sam felt as if he had entered an alternate universe where another Sam and another Alice were having a completely different conversation and he was totally lost.

"Yeah," he said as his brow knitted together, "I read, I mean I can read."

Alice's eyes brightened with a hint of mischief, "Glad to hear it. Maybe you should read that." And with that, her smile brightened even more and she ducked into the throng of students surging towards their next class.

Numbly Sam unfolded the square of paper. He had no idea what had just occurred or what Alice was even talking about.

The paper unfolded and with it some sense of reality crept back in; Sam looked down to see what Alice wanted him to read. Why would she want him to read her homework? Did she really think he was that dumb? That he needed to copy hers? But his questions were cut short as he looked down to see a short phrase written in the middle of the paper in Alice's precise looping script.

There written carefully on the paper Alice had written:

*Sam,*

*Call me sometime. I'd really like to talk to you more than just on the bus.*

*Alice*

And there underneath her name was her phone number.

Now Sam was sure that he fallen into some alternate universe. There was no way that Alice actually liked him. No way he was that lucky, but in spite of his attempts to prove his inner fears of loser status, there it was written clear as day.

The bell sounded and Sam was now late for gym class, which meant running laps, but he could not have cared less. Chris Kelly be damned, as far as he was concerned this was now the best day of Sam's life.

• • •

*The usually glib banter that passed as morning news reporting was somewhat more reserved. The anchors on CNN and MSNBC put aside their potshots and celebrity reports to relay a story breaking on the BBC. Even Fox News abandoned its typical apoplectic diatribe on the Left to run the story.*

*"Outbreaks of illness are currently being reported throughout the United Kingdom, as well as all major cities in France, Germany and Spain. Unconfirmed reports are coming in from as far as China and Australia, but the true scope of the situation is yet to be determined." The reporter paused and wiped her brow, "Very little is known, but it appears that a virus or disease of some variety, attacks the nervous and circulatory systems resulting in sudden stroke or cardiac arrest. Victims complained of flu-like symptoms, reporting complaints such as headache, nausea and fever. It is recommended that anyone displaying these symptoms contact a relative, friend or lift company to provide them with transport to the nearest hospital. The authorities are asking that citizens do not attempt to drive themselves in the event of an incident while operating a vehicle."*

*The reporter paused and swallowed hard as the cut away shots began to roll. Regardless of the city, all the scenes appeared the same, overwhelmed paramedics were loading ambulances as fast as they could pull up to office buildings, apartments and retirement homes. Large numbers of heart attack and stroke victims were being taken away as the police tried to maintain some sense of order on the streets.*

*The BBC reporter shifted uncomfortably and continued, "As of right now, all that is known is that the outbreak appears to be affecting older citizens. Reports of victims range in age from twenty to eighty. There have been no reported or confirmed victims under the age of twenty."*

*More scenes were displayed showing French police trying to maintain order outside of numerous hospitals. Masses of people had panicked and were trying to force their way into the emergency rooms. As the camera zoomed in, a few tangled bodies could be seen wrapped around the legs and under the feet of the mobs. The station quickly cut the live feed and returned to the reporter, who currently looked waxen with large creases of stress and anxiety breaking across her brow.*

*"Authorities are asking all citizens to remain calm and assure us that the situation is under control. A joint task force of national health agencies led by the European Centre for Disease Prevention and Control has promised answers soon, but is suspending international travel until further notice. Currently, there have been no reported incidences in the United States, but the CDC has been placed on alert and is in close communication with European agencies."*

● ● ●

Spying his little brother smiling like an idiot, Mike Williams ducked into the boys' room and waited for him to pass. Quietly he slipped out and fell into stride behind Sam, who seemed lost in reading a scrap of paper over and over again. This was the perfect opportunity. Mike's prey completely unaware and unguarded left no chance of failure. Success was guaranteed.

Sticking his index finger into his mouth, Mike covered it in a thick, slick coating of saliva and could not help but grin. This is what being a big brother was all about.

As the spit laden finger entered his ear, Sam shrieked more from surprise than the actually grossness of the event. He had been completely unaware of everything as he made his way down the hall towards one of the four gyms at Montville. Reading the two short sentences and ten single digits contained within Alice's note were the only things that mattered to him, and that had left him totally unguarded for a vicious Wet Willy from his older brother Mike. But even the rapidly cooling viscous saliva that now encased his entire left ear canal could do little to wipe the smile from Sam's face.

"What's that little man?" Mike asked as he made a half-hearted attempt to snatch the paper from his brother.

Sam protectively tucked the note behind his back. "It's a note from Mom and Dad letting me know that you were adopted. That's why I was smiling."

Mike smirked, "Please. If anything, I was so wonderful that they decided to try and have another, but after the disappointment of you they quite trying."

Both boys began laughing. This exchange was a well-rehearsed set of lines that they often threw at one another, but never meant. Mike definitely capitalized on his role of older brother and light-heartedly tormented Sam whenever he could, but neither doubted the devotion of the other, which was exactly why Mike had been looking for Sam in the halls.

"Hey man, I heard about the bus this morning from Joey," a slightly apologetic look crossed Mike's face, "I'm sorry I couldn't give you a ride this morn, but coach is running friggin' two-a-days."

Sam shrugged, "Not your fault Mike. Chris is a douche bag." In fact, Sam had momentarily thought that the whole Chris Kelly situation was Mike's fault. If he had been around to give him a ride to school, this never would have happened, but then again, if he had not been on the bus maybe Alice would have never given him the note.

Mike smiled, "Look I got another practice after school, but I see that dildo in eighth period study hall. You want me to say something to him? Threaten to smack him around a little?"

Sam mulled Mike's offer over for a few seconds. He knew his brother would make good on his offer if he was asked to, and that Mike was maybe the only person in the entire school that Chris would think twice about fighting. Years of football and weightlifting, not to mention his tireless training in Kali and Ju-Jitsu, had left Mike a lean six foot two pile of muscle, so maybe a few words from him would keep Chris at bay? But Sam declined. Mike was a senior and next year would not be there to hold his little brother's hand, so Sam figured he needed to find his own way on this one, regardless of how tempting the offer was.

"Nah, it's cool," Sam said, "He's so friggin' dumb he'll probably forget by the end of the day or find someone else to beat up."

Mike shrugged, "Ok little bro, but offer stands."

As the two brothers made their way down the hall, the intercom system beeped loudly, signaling an announcement. Mike and Sam paid it little attention, there was always some pointless message being conveyed; this surely was no different.

*"Teachers please hold your rosters. All teachers hold your rosters,"* resounded through the school, echoed in every classroom and hallway. Mike cut a quick glance to Sam and shrugged.

"Probably just another stupid Lock Down Drill," Sam remarked plainly.

Mike agreed, "Yeah, probably should get a move on to the gym." But before the boys could move further down the hall, the guidance counselor, Ms. Woodland spotted them passing by her office.

"Boys! Boys," she fired off in rapid succession while waving her hands nervously at her sides, and slightly hopping up and down causing her elongated pinched face to turn a bright shade of crimson. Mike thought she looked like an angry wounded bird. "Boys, this is a Lock Down. You must clear the halls. Get in here!" Both boys laughed dryly. Ms. Woodland was so over-reactionary. Everything was a crisis, which was exactly why all the students had stopped going to see her. Of course, she would get this worked up over a routine drill. They had at least one of these pointless things a month. But as the boys slowly made their way towards the Guidance Office the front doors of the school were thrown open and two paramedics rushed past, wheeling a stretcher and carrying what looked like a large red toolbox.

"Ok, ok, Ms. Woodland," Mike stammered, just beginning to understand the seriousness of the situation, "We were just..." But before he could finish his next sentence, a scream echoed from the administrators' offices across the hall. It appeared that a fight was taking place in the office. The vertical blinds were drawn and thrashing violently against the windows, but the outline of four people could be seen struggling with a fifth that appeared to be on the floor. Before anyone could react, a body was slammed into one of the large glass windows that made up the front of the administrators' office. Mike, Sam and Ms. Woodland all shared an equally confused and scared look with one another and quickly hurried into the Guidance Office where they locked the door.

"I don't think this is a drill," Sam whispered weakly. Neither of his companions thought his comment needed a reply.

● ● ●

Mrs. Rachel Williams had always enjoyed being a stay at home mom. She kept a beautiful home, raised two good boys and had a happy husband. By all measures, she felt like a success.

But today was different. Today Rachel hated being alone in her house. She was sick. Her stomach was churning in burning knots and her head felt like it was about to split in half. As she lay in bed watching reruns of daytime talk shows, Rachel silently cursed her husband Gary for getting her sick. She had no idea how he went to work with the flu, but that was Gary she figured. He always worked hard to take care of his family. After which, she immediately felt guilty for having spited him moments before. She hoped he was feeling better and was happy that somehow the boys had escaped the flu this time.

● ● ●

Moments before the Lock Down was instituted, Bev Jennings happily typed away at her keyboard in the main office of the Montville Regional School Complex. Sure, she was supposed to be updating the student files, returning phone calls, editing Mr. Carson's monthly Principal's Newsletter, basically doing anything other than updating her Facebook page with pictures of her grandson, but she dared anyone to tell her otherwise. Not only was she known to all staff members as the Dragonlady, she was retiring at the end of this school year, so let them write some letter for her file. Like it would matter in June when she danced her considerable girth through the double front doors and right into a retirement, soaked in the irony of Skinny Girl margaritas and ice cream.

"Bev," Mr. Carson bellowed from his office, "Bev! Now!"

Bev rolled her eyes and shifted in her chair. "Fat bastard," she muttered, "Probably wants to place a third lunch order."

In truth, Mr. Carson was of equal size compared to Bev. Both had achieved the level of obesity where gender seemed to disappear and they were simply categorized as "human" but each was convinced that the other was larger than them.

"Bev! Damn it where are you?" Mr. Carson growled. She quietly smiled to herself when she heard his chair groan as he attempted to heft himself out and up, only to collapse back into it. She was not going anywhere until he said the magic words.

Finally, swallowing his pride, Mr. Carson cooed sarcastically, "Oh, Ms. Jennings. If it's not too much trouble might I please have a word?"

Bev reached her thick fingers underneath her office chair and pulled the pneumatic lever that pitched the back of chair forward and assisted her in the process of standing. The short walk from her desk in the front of the office to Mr. Carson's door would have been cleared in mere seconds by any other staff member; three minutes later, Bev stood slightly swaying and out of breath in the door of the principal's office. Her ankles were swelling with each passing moment. This had better be quick.

"Why yes Mr. Carson? How can I help you," Bev smiled hiding her true feelings and thoughts just barely. Contempt was plainly written across her face.

Now that Mr. Carson finally had her attention his demeanor shifted gears back to his usual rancorous tone. "Now Bev, I have a question for you," he snarled.

The smile faded quickly from the secretary's face, "Of course Mr. Carson, I'll go get the delivery menus." She mimed a half turn just to add a little more salt to the wound she was so fond of opening.

The broken veins in Mr. Carson's nose and cheeks flushed from their usual light red to a fiery shade. Small beads of sweat began to percolate through pores of his nose. Bev smiled. She had definitely hit a nerve.

"No," Mr. Carson hissed as his lower chins vibrated with rage as they attempted to pull themselves over his dominate first chin. Bev thought it looked like his neck was attempting to swallow his head.

"What I want to know is why," Mr. Carson paused to breathe, "Why the school's email would be used to send advertisements for your daughter's massage services?" Venomous acid dripped from every word, but Bev was unphased.

"Oh, oh that," Bev paused, "Well I figured the staff would be stressed with the beginning of a new school year, so I was just trying to raise morale. You know, be a team player."

"And you felt including the picture of your daughter straddling the massage table was warranted and appropriate?" Mr. Carson was barely keeping it together.

Bev hesitated for a moment and considered that maybe, just maybe, that had been a little overkill, but quickly dismissed the thought. "That's just good advertising Mr. Carson. If you're worried about getting an appointment I can put in..." Her words trailed off and her demure expression seemed frozen on her face for a few moments before one of intense confusion took hold. Even Mr. Carson seemed to notice.

"Bev? Bev? Bev?" his voice rose with each repetition, "Are you ok?" But no response was offered. Bev had slumped against the doorframe and was trying to say something, but the words seemed stuck in her throat, which she was now desperately clutching at with thick, sausage like fingers tipped in deep purple nails. She clutched so intensely that Mr. Carson observed one of her press-on plum talons fly free from its perch and land on the carpet.

Mr. Carson got out of his chair as fast as his mass would allow. He quickly lumbered around the desk and was at Bev's side. His knees protested, but he knelt down anyway and pressed two fingers against his secretary's neck. There was no pulse.

"Nurse!" Mr. Carson bellowed, "Call the nurse and an ambulance!"

In the adjacent office, the vice principal Ms. Oakes, heard the cry of her boss and rapidly punched 9-1-1 and then, as per district policy, issued a Lock Down order for all staff and students.

● ● ●

*Millions of Americans found their normal daytime television broadcasts suddenly cut to run news coverage from one of the big three in American reporting, but regardless of the station, all carried the same message. Not since 9/11 had all the channels been blocked out for news feeds.*

*The small television Bev kept tucked under the corner shelf of her desk was streaming a story from CNN. Anderson Cooper's normally cool and collected affect seemed shaken to its core. His immaculately quaffed silver hair was messed and looked as if he had been grabbing fistfuls of it before broadcast. His shirt appeared rumpled, as if he had just lost a wrestling match and his eyes appeared heavy and bloodshot.*

*"America," he paused, "Seems to have encountered the same difficulties that are now besieging Europe." He knew he was putting it lightly, but prided himself on professionalism and did not want to inspire panic in the populous.*

*"While initial reports from the CDC are conflicting, it appears that the illness that has befallen numerous adults in all major European countries has now been found within our borders." He paused and continued, "Earlier today, I traveled to some area hospitals and attempted to speak to ER doctors. Their reactions were troubling to say the least. Can we please show the footage?" Cooper seemed to be genuinely asking for permission and his anger was evident when it was apparently denied.*

*"Look Frank," his cool facade had cracked and he yelled at someone off camera, "I don't give a shit what they told you! This is America! Play the damn tape!" He slammed his palms down on the desk causing his CNN coffee mug to jump a few inches into the air before landing haphazardly on its side. The mug listed back and forth for a few seconds before Cooper seemed to notice it and gently set it right. The screen cut to black for a few*

*seconds and then began to stream what he had recorded only an hour before.*

*At first, the tape appeared to be nothing more than another of Cooper's typical guerilla style reporting stories. He was quickly weaving his way through the ER of some hospital while the cameraman struggled to keep up. Anderson grabbed the shoulder of a young doctor as he ran past and attempted to ask him a few questions, but the man quickly shook his head "no" and took off towards an incoming ambulance. Anderson turned to the camera with a concerned look on his face. "Obviously, the situation is a dire one. There appears to be no one who is able to provide any answers or information, but we..." He paused and turned towards a loud argument that was unfolding near the ambulance the young doctor had rushed to meet. "Let's make our way over and see what is unfolding," Cooper continued as he picked his way through a seemingly endless supply of patients.*

*The cameraman followed in close pursuit of Cooper and swung the lens back and forth across the ER as they made their way. All the rows of plastic chairs were filled with people clutching their heads or swaddling their stomachs protectively. An air of panic was clearly visible, but none of the patients seemed to be taken in for treatment. Maybe the back examination rooms were all full the cameraman wondered as a middle-aged man in a wrinkled business suit grabbed his bent elbow. The camera inadvertently swung down to capture the man's face. It was creased with pain, and sweat was pouring from his brow at an unbelievable rate.*

*"Please," the man pleaded weakly, "Please get a doctor. I'm, I'm..." but he could not finish his sentence. He doubled over and clawed at his stomach. A weak moan escaped his lips, which was immediately followed by a violent torrent of pink tinged vomit that spattered the cameraman's legs and feet. Blood leaked slowly from the man's mouth as he struggled to lift his head and mutter a weak apology. Before the cameraman could react, Anderson had blindly grabbed him by the other arm and pulled him along towards the confrontation erupting between the young doctor and two National Guardsmen.*

*The doctor was standing at the door trying to wheel a stretcher past what appeared to be two National Guardsmen. Cooper quickly made his way towards the men.*

*"There appears to be a military presence. I think I can see three Hummers parked outside, but I'm not sure what is going on."*

*The doctor began to push past the Guardsmen with the stretcher, upon which an elderly patient lay. She was a frail woman with stringy gray hair and it appeared that she had succumbed to whatever epidemic was now unfolding.*

*"Look," the doctor pleaded, "She only just passed as the ambulance pulled in. There's still a chance to..." But the soldiers shook their heads. "Please!" the doctor pleaded.*

*Anderson tried to intervene, "Gentleman, surely you understand the importance of this poor woman receiving the medical care she desperately needs. Time is of the essence. You must allow this man to do his job!"*

*One of the soldiers grabbed the stainless steel runners on the side of the stretcher, "We got orders to lock down this hospital. Orders state no one else is to be taken in until further notice. CDC's ordered home site quarantines based on information obtained from Europe and the ECDCP." Both Anderson and the doctor looked confused. "But she's already here!" the doctor's voice cracked as he slammed his fist down on the stretcher.*

*The soldier gripped the doctor's arm and pushed the stretcher back the way it had come. "Put her back in the damn ambulance and take her home!" At this point, the absurdity of the situation seemed to leave the other soldier who noticed that the entire debacle was being filmed. His hand quickly shot out and attempted to grab the lens of the camera.*

*"Give me that friggin' thing!" he shouted, but Anderson quickly pushed him away with a well-rehearsed move and put a good five feet between the camera and the soldier.*

*Turning to his cameraman, Anderson acted as if he were going to add some comment or remark, but his eyes widened and he simply shouted, "Run!"*

The few seconds of footage that followed were filled with shouting voices and shaky scenes of the floor tiles and pounding vomit soaked shoes, but right before Anderson and his cameraman pushed through a set of double doors, the camera swung back up and briefly caught a shot of the soldiers and doctor. It appeared that the elderly woman had awakened and was attacking the soldier that had pushed the stretcher. The doctor and other soldier were struggling to pull her off, but she seemed to be attached to the hand and arm that had grasped the stretcher.

"My God," Cooper gasped as the camera zoomed in, "Was she biting him?" Then the screen went black. After a few moments the feed returned to an even more distressed Cooper, now slumped at his news desk.

"When it was realized that we were there, we were contacted by the CDC and told not to air the footage," he weakly shook his head, "They sent someone to the CNN offices to recover it, but my journalistic integrity would not allow them to bury this story, so I copied it." His eyes began to glisten. "I really don't know what I just showed you folks, but I feel like you had the right to know what's taking place out there." He shrugged, almost apologetically. A loud bang was heard from somewhere off set and Anderson looked towards what was sounding like rushing feet and shouting.

A defiant look flared in Cooper's eyes. "I'm not sure what is going on America, but I'll do my best to continue to bring you the truth," he swallowed hard and appeared to be at a loss. The shouting was getting louder and an obvious argument was erupting somewhere in the studio. After an uncomfortably long pause, Anderson pinched his brow and continued, "For the first time in my life, I am at a loss for words, so I will sign off tonight with a quote from another famous journalist Edward R. Murrow, 'Good night and good luck."

The screen went black once again, but this time Cooper did not return. The loud pitched whine of dead air and Technicolor bars were all that could be found on any channel.

The staff in the office of the Montville Regional School Complex missed most of the story as they struggled to assist two *paramedics with loading the body of Bev onto a stretcher. They were told she apparently had just suffered a massive heart attack.*

● ● ●

The screaming in the front office eventually died down and left Mike, Sam and Ms. Woodland enshrouded in an uncomfortable silence. After hearing such disturbing noises and seeing what they did, it was almost unbearable for the three to remain quite, but no one dared to move. Each thought the breathing of the others was getting too loud, that whoever was in the office would surely hear them, but in reality, there was hardly a breath taken between the three.

Ms. Woodland, finally finding the silence excruciating, spoke first, "Boys, I'm not sure what is going on here." She paused to consider her next course of action, "But I think it's best if we stay right here and wait for help to arrive."

Neither boy felt like arguing. Sam, who was huddled halfway under the guidance counselor's desk poked his head out and said, "Don't you think we should call the cops or something?" No one reacted, but Mike took out his cell phone and opened it, casting the room in an eerie blue glow.

"I don't have a signal," Mike whispered, "Check yours."

The other two quickly retrieved their respective cell phones and reported the same.

Ms. Woodland arose from the floor and quietly crossed the room towards her desk. Sam pulled himself further under. She grabbed the phone, pressed "9" and almost broke into tears when she found that there was no dial tone.

Turning to Mike, Ms. Woodland croaked, "It's not working either." Her words trailed off as she let the receiver fall uselessly to the desk. Sam jumped at the sound it made above him and stifled the urge to cry out.

Sensing that the situation had just gone from bad to worse, Mike attempted to gain some sense of control. "Ok, ok, ok," he repeated involuntarily while he attempted to collect his thoughts, "It's gotta be some kinda attack or something. Like a national emergency or terrorists or, or,.. I don't know, or maybe some crazy student or something."

Sam poked his head out from under the desk, "Jeez, Mike why not fricken aliens too? This doesn't make any sense. Did you hear any gunshots? And if it were any of those other things why the hell were the paramedics here?" Sam had always maintained a more analytical mind than his older brother. Even in crisis, he was always able to remain calm and logistical. Mike always sought an answer, tried to fit the broken puzzle pieces together into some kind of disjointed picture. Sam accepted that there may be no logical answer and just moved forward with whatever facts were known.

Mike shook his head, "Yeah, I mean no. I didn't hear anything and you're right about the paramedics, but then why don't the phones work?"

But before anyone could answer, the lights in the hallway flickered and went out. A few emergency lights kicked on, but the hallways were largely filled with deep satiny shadows. All three collectively held their breath, almost sensing that the situation was nowhere near being over, that in fact, it had just gotten worse.

Heavy footsteps could be heard slowly moving across the hall from the administration's office. Mike was the first to react. "Quick," he hissed, "Everyone back behind the desk." Sam, who was already there, pulled himself tighter into the corner to make room for the other two.

A loud, wet *thwack* hit the small rectangular window that was offset to the right of Ms. Woodland's office. The noise repeated a few more times and the door rattled violently, but no one dared see what was making it. Eventually, the slow footsteps could be heard moving down the hall towards the gym.

After what felt like an eternity, Mike poked his head out from behind the desk and peered through the dimly lit office at the door. "There's some crap all over the window," he reported, "I can't really see outside." Mike retrieved his cell phone from his pocket and pushed a few buttons until suddenly the room was lit up in a blinding white light. "Flashlight app," he answered before anyone could ask.

Mike slipped out from behind the desk and shielded most of the light's glare with his head, but as he got closer to the door, he lifted it to inspect the window. Mike doubled over and dry heaved.

Ms. Woodland whimpered weakly. Sam climbed over her and peered over the lip of the desk. "What the hell is it Mike? What happened?"

Mike could not find the words to answer, but held the phone up to illuminate the small window for his brother. Sam gasped at what he saw. Blood was smeared across the small window in long drawn out handprints obscuring the view, but moving closer to the window Sam's eyes widened as he saw that it was even worse.

Without taking his eyes off the door, Sam held his hand out towards his brother. "Gimme your phone." Mike silently handed over his phone to his little brother. Moving it closer to the window Sam gagged as he saw crudely cut red chunks mixed with the blood. In one corner he was pretty sure there was a ragged strip of skin slowly making its way down the window. There appeared to be a few hanks of peppered hair that were matted with blood and slowing the flesh's progress. Mike had moved beside his brother and was equally as shocked.

Somewhere from underneath the desk, Ms. Woodland clutched her head and let out a low moan. She whimpered, "Oh boys. This, this stress is too much for me." Through the open space at the bottom of the desk, the boys could see that the guidance counselor had apparently lain down on the floor and curled into the fetal position. She rocked back and forth with her hands pulled up over her face.

"This is just too, too much," she muttered, "All this stress is giving me such a stomach ache and I think my head may just split." Neither Sam nor Mike paid Ms. Woodland much attention; she was always such a drama queen.

● ● ●

Alice could not believe that she had actually gone through with her plan and given Sam that note. Sure, she was confident and driven, but this was a totally alien landscape she was trying to navigate. Plus, maybe a girl being so forward would put him off? Had she insulted his machismo by being so direct? "Male egos," Alice muttered as she made her way to gym class. To make matters worse, her plan had gotten Sam in trouble with Chris Kelly. Alice never could figure Chris out. He seemed like he actually could be a nice person, but he was just so determined to make sure the world was scared of him. Alice suspected it had more to do with him being scared of the world. She had seen this with her own father. He was terrified of the world and used money and snobbish behavior to keep it a bay, but all he really accomplished was making himself look like a bully to his daughter. She detested the arrogance that her father used as a weapon any time her mother got out of line, and how he seemed to think that he always knew what was best for Alice without ever asking her. Alice swore she would never marry anyone like her father; she would never allow any man to dictate her life. Maybe that was why she was willing to take a risk and give Sam the note. Sam was the polar opposite of her father. He was smart, but did not feel the need to use that as a means of validation or to put other people down.

"Hey Alice," Joey shouted from the doors leading into the gym. Alice waved back. There was no way he would ever end up in one of her classes other than gym, so Alice actually looked forward to being around "normal" students, even if it was only for forty minutes of poorly organized sports. Besides, Joey was annoying and some days down right perverted, but Alice figured he was harmless and Sam was friends with him, so that had to count for something.

"Hey Joey," Alice replied as she got closer to the gym, "What's the sport du jour?"

Joey's face twisted into a knot of confusion, "Du jour? I dunno maybe we play that fourth marking period. I think today is volleyball."

Alice smiled, "Thanks. See you in there." The two went to their respective locker rooms.

The gym at Montville Regional was really more like four gyms in one. There were enough bleachers to handle a D1 college basketball team and facilities that would make the Olympics envious. Alice found it all to be a bit much, but figured that if the school could benefit from the influx of pharamacon tax dollars so be it; even if the school was really built more as a gold leafed middle finger to the surrounding towns instead.

"On the lines," Ms. Kozlov screeched, "Today we're practicing bumps." She palmed the entire volleyball in one hand, fingers flexing as if she was contemplating popping it.

Joey raised his hand, "I'm sorry Ms. Koz, you said we were working on bumps?" Alice could see that he knew exactly what he was doing, and had to kind of admire that he was willing to take on the Russian Bear to get a laugh from his classmates.

"Joseph Potts," Ms. Kozlov growled. It sounded like her vocal chords were wrapped in sandpaper and nicotine. "Yes, we will be working on bumps. Why don't you ever listen?"

Joey smiled, "I was just concerned Ms. Koz when you said we were practicing bumps."

"And why would that be Joseph?"

"Well, because you forgot about the pumps, too."

"There is no such move in volleyball. These two do not go together Joseph." Ms. Kozlov clearly had missed the early 90's hip-hop revolution and Joey was more than willing to offer a lesson.

"Not true Ms. Koz," Joey had stood up, "It's a well known fact, the legendary volleyball player, known as one Mr. MC Hammer was quoted as having said 'pumps and a bump, pumps and a bump. We like the girls with the pumps and the bumps." Joey had gotten to his feet and currently had his hands on his bent knees and butt pushed out, which has moving in slow circles aimed at Ms. Kozlov.

Ms. Kozlov waited for Joey to tire and the laughter to die down and the minute he straightened up, she whipped the volleyball at full force into his gut. A hollow sound reverberated through the gym that Alice was unsure of origin.

It could have been the ball, but just as easily could have been Joey's stomach. He doubled over, but still continued to laugh.

"Not a fan Ms. Koz?" Joey wheezed from the floor.

Ms. Kozlov's response was simply, "Laps. Now." Then she retrieved the volleyball as it slowly meandered across the gym floor, and began running drills with the rest of the class. After Joey had regained his ability to breathe, he took off at a slow jog around the indoor track that encircled the gym. By the end of the year, Alice figured he would be ready for the New York Marathon.

Alice got in line and waited for her turn. The students were alternating throwing the ball up for a partner or bumping it near the net, all the while Ms. Kozlov growled from the side that they were slow and weak. The kids seemed to simply tune out their angry gym teacher and go through the motions.

Every few minutes Joey would jog past, flex his arms and growl, "Strong like bear," which would cause Alice to laugh and miss the volleyball. On his last lap, Alice had laughed so hard that she completely missed the fact that her partner had thrown the ball and as she looked up it came crashing down squarely on the bridge of her nose.

Alice's eyes immediately began to water and she sucked in gulping mouthfuls of air, but overall she was ok. It hurt, but it was the kind of pain that, for some strange reason, made you laugh instead of cry. Through watery vision, Alice could see Ms. Kozlov lumbering over mumbling in a thick accent, "American childrens...all so soft."

As Alice was pulled from the floor by Ms. Kozlov's thick hand, her vision began to return to normal, but as she took in a deep breath and exhaled, a thin trickle of blood ran down from her right nostril and spattered the front of her t-shirt. Alice gently touched her fingers to her nose and looked at them. A little blood, nothing serious she figured.

"Back to bumps," Ms. Kozlov commanded the students, but was cut short by the high-pitched tone of the PA system.

"*Teachers please hold your rosters. All teachers hold your rosters.*"

Ms. Kozlov groaned deeply, "Ok childrens. Move it!" She pointed towards the weight room in the back of the gym. It was the only place in the gym, other than the locker rooms and coaches' office that could be sealed off and locked. "Silence!" she bellowed as Joey danced his way into the weight room. Then Ms. Kozlov turned off the lights and locked the double doors as the students moved into the far corner.

● ● ●

*A robotic voice came on after a loud drawn out siren sounded on the television tucked away under the secretary's desk. In the commotion that occurred after the paramedics arrived it had been knocked onto its side, but had still remained on.*

*"This is not at a test," the voice stated flatly, "This is not a test. This is the Emergency Broadcast System. Quarantine has been issued for all counties within broadcast radius. Road travel is suspended. Remain calm. Officials will provide assistance shortly." The message repeated before the loud alarm began droning again and the message continued its pointless lie, but no one in the administration office seemed to be troubled by the broadcast.*

*Milky, cloudy eyes turned towards the television, but had no means of comprehending what they were seeing. A thick fist, missing its thumb angrily crashed down on the television shattering the box and caused a short that blacked out half of the school. The hefty form then turned and lumbered through the open door of the principal's office.*

*The noise of the television breaking roused two more bodies that slowly lifted themselves from the sticky blood soaked carpet. Swaying slightly, the two began to move towards the doors, further smearing a thick clotted snail's trail of bits of ragged flesh, entrails and blood with each dragging step. One of the bodies, hardly discernable as female, stumbled in its pair of heels. Its ankle rolled outward and broke with a sickening snap. The pale skin near its ankle bulged momentarily and then shredded into tangled ribbons of flesh as the jagged ends of the fractured bones lacerated the skin from the inside.   It paused for a moment, but did not seem to notice that its foot had turned inward at a ninety-degree angle and continued forward at an uneven pace into the hall.*

● ● ●

Chris Kelly had never cared about school. It had never served a purpose and did not look like it ever would. Honestly, the only reason he continued to show up was he was at least guaranteed something to eat for breakfast and lunch through the free lunch program; that was the only time being poor had ever benefited him. Otherwise, living in Montville, with all the new money flooding in, was extremely difficult for Chris. He knew that he was often ridiculed by his peers and had spent a good deal of his adolescence pretending to ignore snide remarks, only to cry himself to sleep at home. Lord knows his mother never offered any comfort, she was usually too whacked out on booze and pills to even form a sentence, let alone offer a kind word and when she was awake, Chris just wished she would pass out again. There was never a father to offer a shoulder or provide the silent strength he was supposed to; Chris's mother had never even mentioned who his father was and would often completely ignore the question when he was younger, and still cared enough to ask it.

So from an early age Chris had learned that the only one he could count on was him, and that school simply served as a means of obtaining food, no more important than the drive-thru at McDonalds. He could never figure out how his teachers expected him to focus on meaningless things like variables and spelling, when he was worried about the next time his mother would try to put a cigarette out on his back. But eventually Chris grew bigger and his mother's drinking worsened and she just began to pretend he was not even there, which by that point suited him fine.

Chris knew that none of the snobby rich kids would accept him. Knew they all viewed him as gutter trash. He was never going to be invited to a birthday; no parents would ever allow him to take their daughter to a dance. So much of the life that he saw his peers take for granted was denied Chris, simply because his mother made bad decisions and was broke. He never asked to be born poor, never asked to be the son of his mother, but he figured life had little concern for what he wanted. He had also figured out that he would never have his peers' friendship, so at the very least he figured he would have their fear.

From an early age, Chris put effort into getting bigger and stronger than any of his peers. In elementary school, he did endless amounts of push-ups and pull-ups when he came home from school and once he entered middle school, he began going to the high school and lifting weights. He entered his freshman year of high school two years older than anyone in his class and bench-pressing over three hundred pounds.

Auto Shop was the one class that Chris cared enough about to go to on a regular basis and not because he was particularly fond of cars, but more so because Mr. Parks was the only teacher that treated him like a student. All the other teachers seemed to be tolerating him until he did something big enough to go to jail, but Mr. Parks was different. Chris would never call him nice, because in fact he was not. Mr. Parks was a mean spirited little ass on his good days, but what Chris respected was that he was like that to everyone, so in Auto Shop, Chris felt like he belonged, that he was part of the group. Mr. Parks had developed such a reputation for nastiness that aside from a few token Vo-Tech kids, some dumb football players and some weird kid with a well-manicured mini-afro named Ronnie; Chris was one of the only students that had remained in the class on a consistent basis.

Chris stared at the massive engine block that hung in front of him. He had just lifted it out of an old rusted out 1950's Willy's Jeep. The engine looked like something that had been salvaged from the bottom of the ocean and was leaking from numerous places Chris knew it should not be. Getting this thing to fire up again would take a miracle.

As Chris began to check the plugs and gaskets, figuring he would start with the most obvious, albeit unlikely, causes of the leaks, something in the corner of the auto shop caught his eye.

Two of the larger football players had Ronnie pushed up against the wall. Chris looked over to Mr. Parks, who either did not see or care, what was going on. Ronnie was obviously distressed by the situation and was stuttering rapidly and pacing back and forth within the small area afforded him, while the other two laughed and taunted him. Chris decided to go see what the hell was going on for himself.

As he got closer, he heard the larger of the two kids say, "Doin' it wrong huh? Think-you're-friggin'-smarter-than-me?" Each word was punctuated with a jab to Ronnie's rib with the butt end of a large screwdriver.

"No-No, not what I was saying," Ronnie stammered as he looked towards the door hopefully.

The two meatheads seemed to enjoy tormenting the smaller student and Chris figured they had no intention of letting him go easily.

The smaller and evidently nastier of the two leaned in towards Ronnie and said, "Sure you did Ronnie. That's exactly what you said. Just admit it and we'll let you go." Chris thought his voice had all the sincerity of a snake. "Just say it Ronnie. Go ahead, come on now. Say it and we'll let you go."

Ronnie mumbled for a few moments and then nervously stammered, "I was just saying that you had the wires wrong...that's all...that's all. The polarities were connected wrong at the battery. That's very dangerous."

The smaller of the two turned to his friend, "See there Tim, he admits it. He says that you're a dangerous retard." The shoulders of the bigger one tensed and Chris knew what was coming next. But he was not going to allow it.

"So now I'm a retard huh?" the bigger one taunted, "How the hell can a friggin' retard call someone else a retard? That just don't seem right?" He moved to draw his arm back, but Chris had arrived behind him and clamped his hand around the back of the neck of the one called Tim. With his other hand, Chris grabbed a fistful of Tim's letterman jacket and yanked him backwards.

"What the hell," Tim said trying to turn around.

Chris's fingers tightened and his knuckles popped. The skin under his fingers began to turn white as his hand squeezed the blood out. The smaller of the two made a move towards Chris, but his momentum forward was quickly stopped as Chris's large black boot landed on his solar plexus and sent him reeling into a pile of bald tires.

Chris calmly kept his grip on Tim's neck and asked, "So what exactly are you and that pile of afterbirth doing over here?"

Tim, refusing to allow his machismo to be questioned, spat, "What the hell do you care? We pickin' on your boyfriend?"

Chris laughed for a second, which bothered Tim more than anything, and then turned his boot sideways and brought it heavily down onto the back of Tim's knee. Tim's weight betrayed him and he immediately collapsed to the floor. Chris pushed him forward and put his boot square in the middle of Tim's back and looked at Ronnie.

"You ok man?" Chris asked.

Ronnie still stunned, simply shook his head "yes."

The smaller one tried to untangle himself from the tires, but Chris turned and simply said, "Stay there." The threat was understood and the smaller one sunk back onto the pile. Chris turned his attention back towards Tim.

"Alright douche, here's how it's gonna go," he said matter-of-fact, "You're gonna apologize to Ronnie and you'd better make it good, cuz if he doesn't believe you, I'm gonna take a hammer and break your knee cap. And let's be honest rich boy, you and I both know that ain't really gonna change the direction of my life much, but it'll seriously fuck up yours." Chris reached over to the workbench and picked up a heavy clawed hammer. "Got a choice there Timmy. Good bye scholarship or good bye pride." The hammer twirled slowly in Chris's hand.

The fight went out of Tim and he went slack on the floor. "I'm sorry Ronnie," he sounded like a four year old caught stealing cookies, "Please forgive me."

Chris pushed his boot down harder, "Man, that didn't sound sincere at all. You need some motivation." With that, Chris reached down and grabbed Tim by his ear. "You know, it only takes something like seven pounds of pressure to rip off a human ear? Gonna be real hard to run the ball with no sense of balance." Chris smirked at Ronnie, who was still unsure what was happening.

"Ok! Ok!" Tim yowled, "I'm sorry! I'm so sorry! I was being a douche! You were right! Ronnie, please, please forgive me!"

Chris raised his eyebrows towards Ronnie, who responded, "Uh, ok, sure."

Twisting Tim's ear one more time to make his point and then letting go, Chris said, "You're lucky Ronnie is such an understanding guy, but I'm not quite so easy." He leaned in towards Tim and sneered, "I see that shit again and there'll be no talkin'." Chris thrust the hammer into Tim's chest.

About this time Mr. Parks had wandered over and looked at the four students for a moment and then turned to the project car, "Which one of you retards reversed the wires running to the battery? It's friggin' color-coded. You want the damn thing to explode?"

Ronnie was the first to respond, "Uh, Mr. Parks, sir," he raised his hand, "That retard was Tim." Chris swore he saw a smile cross Ronnie's face for just a second as Mr. Parks mercilessly reamed Tim for his mistake.

On the way back over to his engine, Chris stopped and motioned for Ronnie to come over. "Why do you put up with that crap?" Chris questioned.

Ronnie shrugged, "I don't know. They're just like that. I don't understand it." He paused and then continued, "That's why I like machines, like cars, they're easy to understand. They make sense. People don't. You can fix a car, but not a person."

Chris smiled, "Well, you got me there. People definitely do not make sense, but look man, anything like that happens again you tell me. I can't stand those friggin' rich boys."

Ronnie was still unsure of his new friend, but responded, "Yeah, uh, ok. Thanks Chris."

"No worries," Chris mumbled as he turned back to the engine, "Now I gotta figure out what the hell is wrong with this thing."

Ronnie's brow knitted together and he was silent for a moment. "Did it leak?"

"Yeah, like a hooker in a room full of rich guys," Chris responded.

Unsure of the analogy, Ronnie leaned in, "What about the oil? Did it look kind of white?"

Chris shrugged, "I dunno." But saw that Ronnie was right when he pulled out the dipstick. "Yeah, man. It's all nasty and looks kinda like butter."

Ronnie looked for a few more seconds, "Water pump is broken, leaked into the engine and messed up the oil. You need a new pump, oil and gaskets."

Chris almost laughed out loud, "Man, you really do know cars, huh?" But before Ronnie could respond there was a shrill whistle from the PA system followed by, *"Teachers please hold your rosters. All teachers hold your rosters."*

Mr. Parks looked irate from the announcement and made no move to follow procedure. As he mumbled something about wasting time, the lights in the auto shop went completely black and everything was enshrouded in darkness.

● ● ●

Mrs. Woodland had stopped complaining and now was silent underneath her desk. Sam turned to his brother, "Thank god," he whispered, "I think she finally whined herself to sleep." Over the last forty minutes, the boys had thought they might go insane if the guidance counselor did not stop moaning about one physical complaint or another.

"Seriously," Mike returned, "Like a little headache matters? Look outside, hell, just look at the damn window. There's Columbine Two going on out there and she wants an Advil." As the boys let out an uneasy chuckle, they heard Mrs. Woodland shift from under her desk. It appeared to be no more than her simply rolling over in her sleep.

Mike pressed his ear to the door and listened. "I haven't heard anything out there for close to an hour. Don't you think the cops or fire department or someone should be here by now?"

Sam conceded that his brother had a valid point, "Yeah, I'd think there'd be something. Plus I haven't heard any gun shots or explosions, so I don't think this is some pissed off student."

Heavy feet scrapped the carpet and knocked loudly against the counselor's cheap metal desk. The loud bang startled both boys, who spun quickly around to face the sound.

"What the hell?" Mike muttered, "Mrs. Woodland? You ok under there?" She gave no response, but seemed to be awake because she was clearly visible moving around under there.

Sam took a step towards the desk, "Maybe she's dreaming or something?" But even he did not believe it.

Mrs. Woodland shifted a few more times and groaned loudly as she rolled over onto all fours.

"Jeez," Sam whispered loudly, "She must have one hell of a headache."

Mike was not so sure, "Mrs. Woodland? You should stay there if you're not feeling good. Just lay back down." Something about the situation was making Mike uneasy and he wanted Mrs. Woodland to just lie back down and not come out from under the desk. "Just stay there Mrs. Woodland," Mike almost pleaded, "We'll let you know when help gets here."

Mrs. Woodland let out a long, drawn out moan and began to struggle to her feet. The boys could see her shifting around and beginning to stand. In the darkness of the small cramped office, Mike and Sam saw Mrs. Woodland's shadowy form unroll itself, but she was not coming out like a normal person and she had yet to respond to either of them. They could see Mrs. Woodland's bowed back sway for a moment. It looked like she was trying to touch her toes, but she suddenly shuddered and swung her head up violently, completely unaware of the fact that she was still half way under the desk.

As she suddenly tried to stand, Mrs. Woodland crashed the back of her head into the underside of the desk causing it rise a few inches and her body to sprawl out underneath. She lay there unmoving.

If the circumstances had been different, both Sam and Mike would have laughed hysterically at what they had just seen, but they found themselves standing there, unsure of what to do and wrapped in an almost painfully uncomfortable silence.

Sam's eyes were wide, "What the hell, Mike? What the hell was that all about?"

Sensing his brother's fear Mike tried to exert some level of control before hysteria set in, "She's just sick Sam. Probably just knocked herself out or forgot where she was or something...I mean, well, I guess."

"We should see if she's ok, right?" Sam asked tentatively.

Mike hesitated, but then took a step towards the desk and knelt down by the small opening in the front center. "Mrs. Woodland," Mike reached out and poked her exposed hand, it was ice cold, "Mrs. Woodland you need to come out from under your desk...uh, please?" Her hand moved slightly. "Mrs. Woodland?"

The icy hand withdrew under the desk and Mike turned away to speak to his brother, but as the words began to form, Mrs. Woodland's hand shot out from under the desk and latched onto Mike's wrist with a vice like grip. The counselor's hand tightened even further and began slowly pulling Mike's arm under the desk.

"What the hell!" Mike yelled as he braced his shoulder against the desk and pulled away from Mrs. Woodland. "Let go! Let go!" But she silently pulled Mike closer and closer towards the small opening.

Dumfounded, Sam suddenly snapped into action and grabbed Mike by the shoulders and pulled backwards, but Mrs. Woodland's other hand shot out and gripped Mike's arm by the elbow and yanked him violently to the floor. As he fell, Mike's forehead met the hard edge of the desk and stars swam through his vision. He could feel himself starting to pass out, but fought against the blackness that was creeping into his vision. As Mike collapsed to the floor, Mrs. Woodland let out a low guttural growl and pulled his upper body under the desk.

Sam quickly leapt over the corner of the desk and almost came down on the lower half of Mrs. Woodland, but ended up straddling the guidance counselor, who wriggled and growled underneath him. Sam grabbed her by the shoulders and pulled back. "Mrs. Woodland! Stop! Stop!" She showed no response to his pleas, but instead turned her head and tried to bite Sam's hand.

Mrs. Woodland's teeth gleamed in the dim glow of the emergency floodlights, Her lips curled back and she gnashed her teeth trying to find purchase in the soft flesh of Sam's arm.

With Mrs. Woodland's attention turned on Sam, Mike was able to slip out from underneath the desk. He could feel the warm trickle of blood running from the gash that had opened above his brow. Mike shook his head and as his vision began to clear and the ringing in his ears silenced, he could hear his brother screaming for help.

"Mike! Mike!" Sam yelled now more concerned with what was going on in the office as opposed to the rest of the school. "She's trying to bite me!" Sam screeched from behind the desk.

Without thinking, Mike grabbed the edge of the desk and flipped it over onto its left side scattering the phone, papers and computer across the floor. He could hardly believe what he saw before him. The only thing Mike could equate the situation before him to was a professional wrestling match spun completely out of control. Sam was sitting in the middle of Mrs. Woodland's back holding her by the shoulders, all the while trying to avoid the guidance counselor's repeated attempts to bury her teeth in his arm.

"Mike!" Sam bellowed.

"Mrs. Woodland," Mike said angrily, "Last time. Stop now you crazy bitch!" The final warning was offered more for his own sake than Mrs. Woodland's. Mike knew that whatever was going on, this was not going to end well.

"Stop talking damn it!" Sam screamed, "Just help me!" He had to release Mrs. Woodland's left shoulder to avoid being bit and she used the opportunity to roll onto her back and buck

Sam off of her. Sam tumbled backwards into the wall and onto his butt. Mike stepped over the guidance counselor and grabbed his little brother by the collar of his shirt yanking him to his feet.

"Move, now!" Mike commanded and Sam quickly backed towards the door. Mike grabbed one of the cheap chairs that used to sit harmlessly in front of Mrs. Woodland's desk and began to hold it in front of him like a lion tamer.

Mrs. Woodland slowly arose from the floor and clumsily got her feet under her. Swaying for a few moments and then raising her face towards the boys, she released a hungry snarl that caused ice to run through their veins. Her hands extended towards the boys with her fingers hooked like talons and slowly, ever so slowly, she took a step towards them. She wobbled after two or three tentative steps, like a toddler first coming to an understanding of its own mobility. Then the steps became slightly steadier and she advanced across the office.

"Mike," Sam said weakly, "What the hell is wrong with her eyes?"

Following his brother's question, Mike looked up from his chair and into the eyes of Mrs. Woodland, which appeared to be awash in a sea of spoiled milk. Slow clouds with a sickening yellowed hue swam through her eyes, almost obscuring their natural color completely, except for a slightly darker, gray disk dilated to an unnatural size in the center of each eye.

"Open the door," Mike commanded, but noticed that Sam was already trying.

"It's locked! It's locked!" Sam yelled as he repeatedly shook the door. Mrs. Woodland was almost on them. "Where's the keys? Mike the keys!"

Mike swallowed hard and groaned, "I think she had them in her pocket."

● ● ●

"This isn't part of the usual protocol," Ronnie whispered in an almost mechanical voice. He and Chris had moved to the high steel benches that surrounded the table at which they had previously been working. Mr. Parks did not feel the need to have everyone huddle in the back corner as long as they followed his directive to, "Shut the hell up and sit the hell down!"

"What are you talking about?" Chris whispered, "This is just another stupid drill."

"Not true, not true," Ronnie droned, "I read the school protocol for Lock Down Drills and they are not supposed to do fake blackouts. It's dangerous and could lead to someone tripping and then a lawsuit."

Even in the dim light of the auto shop Ronnie could see Chris's mouth hanging open. "Where the heck did you find that out?" Chris asked.

Ronnie rocked slightly on the stool causing it to scrape back and forth on the two legs that had lost their castors. "It was online," Ronnie stated plainly, "After a Board of Ed meeting they post the minutes online. You can read pretty much anything about the school online and this should not be happening."

Chris thought about what Ronnie had just said and he had the very unsettling sense that he may be right, but before he could ask another question, one of the large double doors leading into the auto shop scraped open. The dim light of the emergency floods filtered in through the open door. Mr. Parks evidently did not feel the need to follow that rule either.

"What the hell is going on?" Mr. Parks asked the silhouetted figure that had stumbled in through the doors. "This wasn't in the announcements." Mr. Parks was obviously pissed, but no response came from whomever it was that he was addressing. The figure moved closer, as if to whisper.

Chris leaned over to Ronnie and whispered, "Probably some d-bag from the office checking on Parks, cuz he never does this crap right. Looks kinda like Oakes." Ronnie remained silent. The slightly crooked, duck-like posture definitely appeared to be that of Ms. Oakes, but something about the choppy movement of her steps was deeply unsettling, yet indefinable.

The figure moved closer and Mr. Parks took a step forward to meet them half way. Mr. Parks leaned in to the figure's ear,

"Why the hell didn't Carson send out an email?" But still no answer was given. "Ms. Oakes?" Mr. Parks questioned with more than a little fear in his voice, "Are you ok?"

The figure leaned in, as if to answer and slowly turned its head. Mr. Parks screamed as teeth were buried deep into his neck. The blunt nature of the human teeth did not allow for immediate cutting, but the continued pressure of the jaw muscles pressed them further into the meaty flesh of Mr. Parks' neck, puncturing the skin and causing a large spray of vibrant blood to leap sideways. His scream cut through the large auto shop and reverberated off the corrugated metal panels that compromised the roof.

Chris was already out of his seat and moving towards one of the project cars, an old Ford F350 that Mr. Parks had brought in from somewhere. Chris quickly flung the door open and climbed into the cab, where he flicked on the headlights, then pulled them back to engage the brights. The auto shop was filled with a blinding light and Chris could now clearly see the vice principal, Ms. Oakes standing in front of the classroom with Mr. Parks behind her. Mr. Parks had stumbled to the large white board and was trying to stay on his feet, but Chris could see him holding the side of his neck and gasping like a fish. There was a loud squealing sound as Mr. Parks slowly tried to remain standing, but slid sideways leaving a bright red trail of elongated, bloody handprints across the white board before he collapsed onto the floor.

Not registering what was truly occurring because the obvious answer was too awful to consider, Chris was convinced that some mysterious injury had happened in the dark. Ms. Oakes probably was in shock from seeing all the blood, which must be why she had not moved or spoke since the high beams were switched on.

With a few large strides, Chris cleared the distance from the truck to the front of the classroom. "Ms. Oakes," Chris said quickly, "Grab some of those rags. We need to put pressure on his neck." But Chris knew he was probably already too late. There was a massive pool of thick, murky blood working its way across the concrete floor away from an unmoving Mr.

Parks. "Oakes!" Chris shouted, "Friggin' move you dumb cow! Wake the hell up!" The vice principal shifted her weight and slowly shuffled in a circle to face Chris, and that is when he saw that it looked like she had broken her ankle and some fragments of the bone were showing. But even more disconcerting was the fact that she appeared to be chewing.

A large wad of raw flesh was slowly rolling in Ms. Oakes' slightly open mouth as she shifted it back and forth between her teeth. She swallowed. Her tongue broke from between a mouth that looked as if it had been attacked by dogs. The upper lip was swollen and looked like a bloated red grub, but the lower lip was clearly missing its middle section. The remaining outer corners of the bottom lip hung in two tattered pieces on either side of Ms. Oakes' mouth. Her tongue protruded from behind stained teeth, and thickly hung for a moment before delicately tracing the outline of the destroyed mouth and collecting the thick, coagulated clots of blood that caked Ms. Oakes' face. Chris immediately gagged and felt his knees go weak.

Stumbling backwards, Chris tried to regain his ability to move. Every fiber of his being told him he needed to run, told him to get away from this thing that used to be his vice principal, but the fear was clouding his mind and overriding his primal instincts. Ms. Oakes advanced on Chris as he clumsily back peddled. She was not moving fast, due to the fact that she had completely turned her ankle inward and was walking on the mangled side of her foot and one black high heel. She appeared slow, but the steady clip-clop of her tortured steps was closing the small distance between them. Finally, Chris's instincts kicked in and he spun on his heel to run, but the massive amount of blood on the floor caused him to spin in an almost graceful pirouette before crashing heavily to the floor.

Chris immediately pushed himself up from the tacky floor and began to crab walk away from Ms. Oakes. "Anytime now guys," Chris called to the other students, but no one answered. "Help?" Chris said weakly as Ms. Oakes emitted a feral gurgling from her blood-choked throat. Chris's back came up against a far wall; he had nowhere to go and for some reason, could not get to his feet to run. Fear had paralyzed him. Chris was used to winning confrontations through fear and intimidation, but it was obvious to him that Ms. Oakes was feeling neither of these. In fact, when he looked into her wrecked visage, the only feeling that was evident was hunger, a deep seeded primal hunger. Ms. Oakes groaned and bent forward on stiff knees to bring her face towards Chris's. Long, stringy threads of gore leaked from her mouth and landed thickly on the front of Chris's t-shirt.

Ms. Oakes snarled and opened her mouth wider than Chris thought a person should be capable of doing. She leaned in, growled and snapped her teeth. They clicked together and sounded as if they might crack, but she did not seem to notice.

Having shut down the major control center, the primal drive of Chris's reptilian brain took control and commanded that he bring his heavy booted toe into the soft skin between Ms. Oakes' neck and chin. His boot buried itself a good four inches into the vice principal's neck, but aside from a few stumbled steps, she did not appear to notice. No pain registered in his attacker, but Chris found enough time to climb to his feet. He spread his feet and prepared for the next attack.

Suddenly, a loud, hollow *thunk* echoed through the auto shop and Ms. Oakes fell heavily to her knees. A mildly confused look momentarily replaced the animalistic one of hunger and she pitched forward onto the floor with a drawn out groan. Her blood did not run nearly as much as Mr. Parks', but still, thick black tendrils wound their way from a massive wound on the back of her head and commingled with the cooling pool of what used to be Mr. Parks' life. Chris stared wide-eyed and open mouthed at the large concave hole that had collapsed the back of Ms. Oakes' head, unable to make a move or form a word. The entire situation was too much to process.

Ronnie emerged from the shadows behind where Ms. Oakes had only moments ago stood. In his hand was the heavy hammer that Chris had hefted before to threaten Tim. Ms. Oakes lay at his feet and did not move.

"Holy shit!" Chris exclaimed as he gasped for air, "You friggin' killed the VP?"

A confused look crossed Ronnie's face, "Killed her? That wasn't Ms. Oakes." He looked down at the corpse crumpled before him, as if to confirm, "Nope, not her. And besides she was already dead." He nudged the mangled body of Ms. Oakes with his sneakered toe. She did not move.

"What are you talking about Ronnie?" Chris almost screamed, "Dude that's her right there." Chris pointed at the body, "Right friggin' there with a giant hole in the back of her head, from where you smashed it with a damn hammer!"

Looking at the hammer for a few moments, Ronnie looked up and calmly replied, "She wasn't Ms. Oakes anymore. It was the only way to stop her from getting you. Everyone else ran away."

Chris could hardly believe the conversation he had fallen into, "What the hell do you mean *she wasn't Ms. Oakes anymore?*"

"She was a zombie," Ronnie stated coolly, "She was going to bite you."

Pretty sure that his savior was insane, Chris ventured a question, "How the hell could she be a zombie? How could you know that? Shit Ronnie, that stuff ain't real man. There's no such thing."

Almost in response to Chris's questions, Mr. Parks moaned loudly and shifted on the floor. "Wait! Just wait!" Chris cried as Ronnie stepped forward with the hammer raised high over his head.

"He's a zombie too, now Chris," Ronnie hesitated, "He was bitten."

Hardly fighting the panic in his voice, Chris said, "Damn it Ronnie! They're sick or something or hurt, but they are not zombies."

Mr. Parks got to his feet and released a low growl that gurgled from the gaping wound on the side of his neck; torn flaps of skin vibrated slightly on the wound's ragged edges. Ronnie motioned towards the wound, "And how is Mr. Parks alive right now with that kind of trauma. Sickness or not, he has lost too much blood to be up right now and growling. Look at his eyes Chris." Chris turned quickly to see that Mr. Parks moved into a deep crouch, as if making ready to leap towards Ronnie. Instincts took over again.

"Hammer! Now!" Chris yelled. Ronnie tossed it to him and using the momentum of the throw, Chris brought it crashing down on the bridge of Mr. Parks' nose. The grizzled old teacher was knocked backwards, but quickly recovered. He righted himself and squared off with the two boys. The shattered remains of his nose hung from a stringy bit of flesh and Chris could clearly see the interior of Mr. Parks' nasal cavity. There was no way Mr. Parks should be up and about right now and Chris knew it.

"Head, Chris, his head!" Ronnie commanded, "You have got to smash the brain!" Before Chris could question, he found himself burying the claw end of the hammer deep into his former teacher's skull. He wrenched it back and forth a few times, freeing it from Mr. Park's now split skull.

"That should work, but I don't think he was a zombie." Ronnie appraised.

Chris was almost relieved for a second, but then the thought that he had just killed his auto shop teacher began to set in. Before Chris could completely fall apart, Ronnie spoke again.

"I don't think Mr. Parks was a zombie. He moved too quickly. He was probably a ghoul," Ronnie said flatly.

The hammer fell heavily from Chris's trembling hand to the floor. "How did you know? I mean, shit! Shit Ronnie! Zom...zomb..." He could not bring himself to say it.

Ronnie looked at Chris. "I told you, the internet," he said plainly, "You can read about anything on the internet."

Chris scoffed, "Ronnie, I'm not talking about some loser fan boy site. Jeez man, we may have just murdered two people and you're justifying it with something you read written by a fat guy in his mom's basement?"

An offended look crossed his face and Ronnie replied, "No, not some fan site. The CDC published a report on what to do during a zombie apocalypse. They even have videos on

YouTube. A hammer was rated very highly for close range zombie attacks."

As much as Chris did not like what Ronnie was saying, it did make some level of sense. Ms. Oakes had been chewing on what looked like a chunk of Mr. Parks' neck and how the hell else would Mr. Parks have gotten up after losing all that blood? "Alright, Ronnie," Chris muttered, "What else did the CDC say to do about the, uh, the zom...the things?"

Ronnie thought for a moment, "Well, the government said we should stick together. We should find other survivors and organize. Try to find shelter somewhere safe."

Handing another hammer to Ronnie and picking up his own, Chris moved towards the doors, "I can't friggin' believe this and I'm pretty sure we're going to jail, but let's go." The two boys stepped through the double swinging doors and into the shadowy, deathly silent halls of the Montville Regional School Complex.

● ● ●

"Joseph! Shut up!" Ms. Kozlov hissed. She had kept the students locked down in the weight room for over forty minutes now and even she was beginning to feel a little antsy. The fact that there had been no sign of the administration or police was not good. And to make matters worse, the power had gone out, killing the air conditioning and it was becoming unbearably hot and malodorous within the confined space of the weight room.

Joey shifted over on one of the benches and whispered to Alice, "What the heck do you think is going on here? No drill has ever gone on this long."

In the weak light that trickled in, Alice could see that Joey was concerned. His eyes were wide and pupils dilated. It looked like he might lose it at any minute. "It's going to be ok," Alice said assuredly, "Whatever is going on, I'm sure it's being handled. Besides we're safe in here."

"I told you to shut up children!" Ms. Kozlov bellowed. Alice could see the lines of panic etched into her gym teacher's face. For all Ms. Kozlov's toughness, she seemed to be falling apart just as fast as the students. Alice sensed that the entire situation was on the verge of spinning out of control and that no one was trying to stop it.

"Joey," Alice whispered, "Whatever happens, just stay with me ok? I feel better not being alone." She had just lied. Alice could just have easily been fine on her own, but she sensed that Joey needed something to draw strength from, so she played on his teenaged male ego.

A weak smile broke through Joey's tightly pulled lips. "Ok," he said, "I'll make sure we're okay, Alice. Don't worry."

A figure crossed through the doors and moved into the center of the gym floor. It looked left and then right, but apparently decided whatever it was looking for was not there and moved back towards the doors. For a fleeting second, it passed through a pool of light cast from the emergency floods and Ms. Kozlov thought it appeared to be wearing the uniform of a paramedic.

Moving closer to the doors and pressing her wide face against the small window, Ms. Kozlov almost shouted, "Childrens! I see a medic out there. Things are going to be ok. Stay here and be quiet until I return." The students shifted uncomfortably in the dark, but before anyone could speak, Ms. Kozlov had retrieved her ring of keys and unlocked the door. She silently slipped out and relocked the doors, just in case.

As soon as their gym teacher was out of the weight room, the students began shoving each other and vying for a spot at the two small rectangular windows. Alice and Joey had pushed their way to the front and peered out into the gloomy gym. Ms. Kozlov was quietly walking towards the paramedic, who appeared to be trying to exit the gym, but could not quite figure out how to work the handle.

"Joey," Alice said breaking the silence, "Something's not right. It just doesn't feel right. Why wouldn't the rescue workers know where to look for us? Shouldn't they know that kind of stuff?"

Joey shrugged, "I dunno? Maybe he's just confused or didn't know?" They both held their breath as they saw Ms. Kozlov raise her hand to get the attention of the medic.

"Hello?" Ms. Kozlov said, unsure of the situation, "We are here. Hello?" The medic turned to face her and that is when the ravenged landscape of his abdomen was visible.

Ms. Kozlov gasped and took a few steps backwards. She was sure that what she was looking at had at one time been a paramedic, but the creature snarling before her surely offered no help.

The medic stepped forward and titled his head sideways, as if unsure of Ms. Kozlov, perhaps wondering why she would be foolish enough to walk up to him. The medic's uniform hung in ragged strips of fabric from his shoulders and swayed slightly as he took another step forward. The middle section of his shirt had been ripped apart and hung open, exposing an empty cavity where his intestines had once rested. Even in the dim light, Ms. Kozlov could see a few tattered inches of large and small intestines swinging to and fro inside the opening. The entire front of the medic's uniform pants were caked with gore, bits of flesh and what appeared to be his own innards. Bloody handprints painted his entire uniform, giving him the look of a nightmarish kindergarten teacher. A few jagged bite marks were visible on what remained of his exposed stomach and the reek of popped intestines, bile and excrement overwhelmed Ms. Kozlov, causing her to gag and her eyes to water.

Holding her hand to her mouth Ms. Kozlov began to sprint across the gym towards the relative safety of the weight room. As she fumbled in the pockets of her wind pants for her key ring, the medic broke into a full run across the gym. She could hear his heavy steps slapping against the gym floor and closing the distance between them.

The students watched in horror as the ragged visage of what used to be a symbol of comfort and help leapt onto their teacher's back.

● ● ●

"Stay behind me," Mike commanded as he thrust the chair legs into Ms. Woodland's sternum and gut. She doubled over from the impact, but otherwise made no sign that she had felt any pain.

Sam pressed his back against the door and reached behind to fumble with the doorknob. "We need the keys! We need the keys!" He shouted.

Mike pushed the chair into Ms. Woodland as she advanced again. She showed no signs of stopping. "Tell me something I don't know Sammy," Mike spat through gritted teeth. He slammed the chair legs one more time into Ms. Woodland, trying to knock her down, but he had panicked and did not pay attention to where he was aiming and hit Ms. Woodland in the face. One of the cheap castors had been knocked loose in the scuffle, leaving behind a jagged chrome tip, which had sunk deeply into the left eye socket of the guidance counselor. Mike's stomach flip-flopped as he looked at the damage he had just caused. It was clear that Ms. Woodland meant the boys no good will, but Mike had not prepared himself to really cause her any permanent physical damage, let alone impale her with a chair leg.

"Oh shit, oh shit," Mike sputtered, "I'm sorry! I'm sorry Ms. Woodland."

Sam looked over his brother's shoulder and saw what had just occurred. "Holy crap Mike!" Sam yelled, "What the hell was that all about?"

Mike still shocked, stammered, "I...I didn't mean to. I was just trying to..." As his words trailed off, the boys were horrified to see Ms. Woodland slowly push herself up from the floor.

A good third of the chair leg had broken off and now stuck straight out from Ms. Woodland's destroyed ocular cavity. A slow trickle of slimy, milk colored liquid leaked slowly from where her eye used to be and down onto the front of her tweed two-piece business outfit. She made no attempt to pull the offending piece of metal from her eye; rather she seemed to have no concern of its presence in the least. A wild sound erupted from her throat as she reared back her ruined face.

Sam saw the shock settling across his brother's face. "Mike," Sam yelled, "Mike stop staring and help me find a way out! It's not your fault! Something is very wrong here! It's not your fault!" Mike hesitantly shook his head back and forth, but Sam could slowly see thought returning to his brother's eyes.

Grabbing the partially destroyed chair from the floor, Mike looked over his shoulder and shouted, "After I move, find something heavy! Break the windows!" With that, Mike propelled himself forward with the chair held out in front. Halfway across the office, he collided with the rushing Ms. Woodland and the momentum of the two, buried two of the remaining chair legs deep into the gut and thigh of the guidance counselor. Mike almost vomited, but forced it down and followed the chair and Ms. Woodland's path to the floor. Pushing the chair down with all of his strength, Mike climbed on top of it and pinned Ms. Woodland to the floor. She struggled and thrashed, snarling at Mike and trying to push the chair backwards, but Mike held his balance and tried not to think about what he had just done or was currently doing. With her leg and gut pinned to the floor, Ms. Woodland could do little more than a pathetic sit-up, but she showed no sign of giving up the fight.

"Hurry up Sam!" Mike commanded from atop his shaky post, "I don't think this is going to last very long!"

"I'll just grab the keys while you have her pinned," Sam offered, "It'll be faster."

Mike had already thought of this. "No, don't friggin' touch her. We got no idea what the hell is going on here. Just break the damn window!"

Sam could see Ms. Woodland bucking violently from underneath the chair. Blood was slowly, but steadily covering the carpet beneath her. She spastically thrashed back and forth and tried to pull her impaled leg free. It looked like she was willing to rip through the tendons, muscles and flesh of her own thigh just to get free. But Sam had little time to consider this and began searching the destroyed office for anything heavy enough to break the window, but it was impossible to see what was available.

Grabbing whatever was nearest, Sam hurled the boxy computer monitor at one of the large windows adorning the front of Ms. Woodland's office. The window cracked, but the monitor shattered into a thousand useless pieces.

"Keep trying!" Mike screamed as he almost fell from his perch atop Ms. Woodland.

Sam turned frantically in a circle, looking for anything with some weight. In the dimly lit gloom, something sparkled and caught Sam's attention. His hand immediately shot out and grabbed the object. Looking down at his hand, Sam realized that he had grabbed the paperweight that had sat on Ms. Woodland's desk. It was no bigger than a softball and he vaguely remembered some cheesy phrase etched into the front that said something like, *"Counselors do it cuz they care,"* but he had no time to consider the sexual undertones of this message and smashed the paperweight into the window where the monitor had previously hit.

The crack widened and crept across the window with each blow, but the glass would not break. Sam's knuckles and fingertips were beginning to bleed from his repeated blows, but he pushed the pain from his mind and continued to strike the window. Eventually, a large shard of glass fell free and as quickly as Sam's hopes were raised, they were completely dashed to the ground. In the dark, he had not noticed that the windows spread across the front of the office were made of the old safety glass from the 1970's. Chicken wire was sandwiched in the middle of the glass and no matter how much he smashed, there was no way he was getting the wire out, it was set directly into the metal sills.

"Mike," Sam's voice trembled, "Windows aren't gonna work. There's chicken wire in the glass."

"Shit, shit, shit," Mike hissed, realizing that his brother was right. The administration and guidance offices were located in the older part of the school. Montville had simply expanded upon the old high school and aside from some paint and carpet; this section had not been updated in the renovation. He angrily stamped his foot down, not realizing what he was doing and drove the jagged chair legs a few unsettling inches deeper into Ms. Woodland. Mike recoiled with the realization of his action, but Ms. Woodland remained unphased.

The chipped and bloodied paperweight fell away from Sam's hand. "I gotta try for the keys," he murmured and before he could object, Sam was down on the floor trying to get his hand into the pocket of Ms. Woodland's slacks. Her anger seemed to increase as Sam got closer and she whipped her body back and forth causing Mike to hold onto the back of the chair.

"Just hurry!" Mike yelled, as the chair tipped back and he lost his balance. He tumbled to the floor and landed hard on his back. Sam quickly rolled away from Ms. Woodland, who was now attempting to get up, but finding it difficult with the chair legs impaled into her leg and stomach. Sam rushed over to help Mike off the floor.

"What the hell do we do now?" Sam asked frantically as Ms. Woodland rolled over onto her side and stiffly got up. She took a few stilted steps forward, but could not truly make any progress with the chair sticking out of the front of her.

Mike stepped in front of his brother and thrust his heavy sneakered foot into the center of the chair, but Ms. Woodland would not fall down again. Mike kicked a few more times before he gave up. "Sam," Mike said sternly, "Just stay behind me, ok?"

Both boys prepared themselves for the worst, they were either going to be killed by a deranged guidance counselor or have to kill her themselves. They did not relish the idea of either option. As Sam pushed himself harder against the door, he could have sworn he felt the doorknob move ever so slightly, but he was not sure.

Suddenly the door began to shake violently as someone or something tried to pull it open. "Someone's trying to get in," Sam reported in a panic, "What if it's another one like her." He tried to peer through the small window, but all the gore smeared across let him see, was a dark shape moving outside.

Mike thought for a moment. "Screw it," he said, "Let it break in. It saves us the time and at least we'll have a chance then." The two moved to the side of the door and waited. It continued to shake, but they heard the unmistakable jingle of keys on the other side. Mike quickly delivered a kick that sent

Ms. Woodland stumbling back a few steps. "Help us!" he screamed, "Open the door!" Sam tried to peer through the window he had cracked, but it was too dark in the hall to tell who was out there.

As Ms. Woodland closed in again, the door swung open. With no concern for who or what was on the other side, Mike and Sam rushed through and into the hall, ending up in a tangled pile with whoever had been on the other side.

"Ay Dios mios ninos," someone mumbled from underneath Mike and Sam. They shared a quick confused glance and looked down to see who had opened the door. A crumpled, slate gray set of coveralls squirmed, trying to pull itself free from under them. The boys leapt to their feet and grabbed the man from the floor. It was one of the custodial staff, the name "Hector" was emblazoned on the left side of his coveralls in tight, red embroidered script.

As Mike was about to thank Hector for letting them out, Ms. Woodland sprang forth from her office and tackled Sam to the floor.

"Get her off me! Get her off me!" Sam screeched as Ms. Woodland gnashed her teeth mere inches from his face. Hector moved in a flash past Mike and kicked Ms. Woodland in the ribs with a heavy steel-toed work boot, sending her sprawling across the floor. Mike marveled at the strength the little man seemed to possess. With no hesitation, Hector jumped over Sam and continued after Ms. Woodland, swiftly drawing a heavy pipe wrench from his belt.

Ms. Woodland quickly recovered and dropped into a defensive stance and snarled. Her teeth clacked and bit at the air, as if promising the same to Hector's flesh if he came close enough. Seemingly oblivious to the bloodied one-eyed danger in front of him, Hector continued towards her. Ms. Woodland howled one more throaty, coarse time and then sprang forward towards Hector, who simply side stepped the attack. As he moved, Hector brought the wrench up in a wide arc and shattered the teeth that had just threatened him. The force of the blow dropped Ms. Woodland to the floor and before she could recover again, Hector collapsed her face inward with one final devastating blow.

"Zombi," Hector muttered and turned back towards the boys. "You ok?" He asked them with a heavily accented voice, "No bites?" Both shook their head "no."

Collecting himself from the floor, Sam offered his gratitude, "Uh, thanks. How'd you know what was wrong with her." He motioned towards the decimated corpse of the guidance counselor. In truth, both Sam and Mike had thought that their predicament was something outside the realm of rational explanation, but neither had considered that it had been torn from a page of George Romero's notebook.

Hector shrugged and knelt down beside Ms. Woodland's corpse. He grabbed a handful of her skirt and cleaned off his wrench. It was then that Mike realized that what he had previously thought was rust coating the tool, was actually bits of gore and caked blood. This was clearly not Hector's first kill of the day.

After the wrench had been cleaned to his liking, Hector placed it securely into his belt. "Zombies, my friends," he motioned towards Ms. Woodland, "You have to get the brain to stop them."

Mike shook his head, as if trying to deny what he had just heard, "How the hell could she be a zombie? That crap isn't real. Maybe crazy, maybe sick, but she was not a zombie."

Hector shrugged, "Believe what you will my friends, but she was a zombie and there's plenty more around. We need to move."

Hesitantly Sam questioned, "But how the hell would you know? I mean that's just horror movie stuff. It's not real. No one believes it."

Exasperated, Hector offered a brief explanation, "You children all seem to think that every person you see is as simple as their job." The boys flushed, but he continued, "I was not always a janitor. My people in Peru have known about these things, but many just dismissed them as stories. But some know that there are places in the jungle that you do not go, because the dead wait for the living there and they are always hungry. Sometimes people would come looking for riches or adventure and ignore the warnings of natives, dismissing them as foolish or ignorant. But when I was a young boy, one of these explorers made it back to our village, and my grandfather, the village shaman, was called to help him, but it was too late. He had a bite on his arm and died soon after, but he didn't stay dead. The villagers held him down and my grandfather beheaded him. He had the same eyes as Ms. Woodland and all the others I have seen."

Sam and Mike stared wide-eyed. "But how could this be the same thing?" Mike asked, "I mean, that was all the way in the middle of the jungle."

"We never knew the reason," Hector replied, "Some believed it was greed, that these people had traded their spirits for money or that they were angry spirits that couldn't rest, but most believed it was a sickness." Hector could see that his actions and story had disturbed the boys, "When I first saw what my grandfather did, I did not understand either. I was sick from it and angry, but he explained that the man would infect the village and that he had to be killed to save everyone. I never thought I would see it again or at least I hoped I wouldn't."

Sharing a look of equal concern and amazement, Mike and Sam silently agreed to go along with Hector's version of history until something more plausible presented itself.

From somewhere in the school a scream resounded, shattering the silence Mike and Sam had momentarily enjoyed. Hector turned towards the direction of the gym and withdrew the wrench. A weary look in his eyes, Hector motioned, "Let's go amigos." The three set off in the direction of the gym.

● ● ●

Moving silently through the halls, Chris and Ronnie encountered no more of what Chris had categorized as "things," and Ronnie vehemently insisted were zombies. Passing a few darkened classrooms, they could hear shuffling inside and desks being slowly pushed around, but heard no voices. They assumed that either there were live people inside and they were better off staying put, or that whoever had been in there had become one of the "things" and there was no reason to open the door and let them out.

Rounding the corner, the two came upon the Commons, a wide-open lounge-like area set up for senior students to relax in during their study hall or free periods. There were large round tables in all states, some flipped or broken and others simply looking like the occupants had gotten up to use the bathroom. There were open books, backpacks and food strewn about the area, but it otherwise appeared to be empty.

Ronnie paused to survey the area, but Chris had no desire to do so. "Come on man," Chris whispered, "We gotta keep moving. We're close to the exit by the main office." But Ronnie did not move.

"There's something in here," Ronnie said through the side of his mouth, "Stop moving and listen." And there, ever so quietly hidden underneath the dull ringing of the silence, Chris heard it, a noise. But he could not say what. Remaining silent, the two continued to listen, but worked their way slowly around the perimeter of the Commons. The noise continued, but they were not sure from where. It seemed to be emanating from somewhere in the center of the Commons, but was not an easy sound to explain or place. As near as Chris could figure, it sounded like stalks of celery breaking, followed by another indefinable noise, but regardless of whether or not Chris could place it, the sound made his skin crawl. Some primal urge was screaming at Chris to run, that something was extremely wrong here.

"Look," Ronnie hissed, "There behind those tables." Chris followed to where Ronnie's trembling index finger pointed and there behind a flipped over table, he could see a low shadow moving. He was not sure what he was looking at, but for some reason it reminded him of his two dogs eating.

Chris quietly reached out and tugged at Ronnie's shirt, "Just keep moving man." But as he took his next step, his foot came down on an empty soda can that had rolled from one of the flipped over tables. The crunch of the can was slight, would not have even been noticed on any other day, but to Ronnie and Chris, it felt like someone had just sounded an alarm and fixed a beaming spotlight on them both.

Whatever was behind the table immediately stopped, looked up, greedily sucked in air and clicked its tongue. It was pulling scents and tasting them the same way a snake would. Through the shadows, its tongue could be seen darting out, lapping at the air and then sloppily being sucked back into its mouth.

The low shadow slowly rose off the floor. It was large, at least the size of a man, but it moved on all fours with a hunched back taking a posture not unlike that of a wild boar. As it sat back on its hunches, Ronnie could see it holding what appeared to be a shiny stick between its hands. His eyes widened as he watched the creature snap what it held between its hands into two parts, and begin to suck on one of the jagged splintered ends. A nauseating sound echoed through the Commons as the creature grated its teeth against the bone, and hungrily slurped the marrow from the inside and then tossed aside the scrap.

"Is that a friggin' bone?" Chris asked, fighting the bile that surged up into his throat. Ronnie did not respond but kept inching around the outside of the Commons. Chris followed, hoping, even though he knew better, that whatever was in the middle of the large room had not heard the sound of the soda can crushing.

Having finished gnawing and sucking on both fractured fragments, the boys saw the creature's attention turn back to the jumbled mass that lay in front of it. As they moved further around they could now see behind the flipped over table, behind which the creature huddled. There was a tangled mess of body parts strewn about on the floor before it and it was tearing at the flesh and gristle to get to the bones inside, which it would then snap and hungrily slurp at before returning to render more flesh in its greedy search for more bones.

Having made the turn, Ronnie and Chris were almost clear of the Commons. They kept their backs pressed close to the walls and silently shuffled towards the main office, but as they came upon the final leg of their painfully slow journey, a slight breeze meandered down the vacant hall and gently drifted past the two boys. Chris hardly seemed to notice and kept moving, but Ronnie suddenly froze and swallowed hard. "I think we should run," he whispered loudly. Chris turned to see the creature's head rise from behind the table and its tongue lash out. It had picked up their scent. Before, the overwhelming stink of death and decay that lay before it had masked the two boys, but now it had found fresh prey. Grabbing the table with one hand, the creature sent it spinning across the Commons area and turned its attention towards Chris and Ronnie. A low growl rumbled from deep within its chest. The boys turned to run, but the creature had already broken into a loping sprint across the room.

● ● ●

The journey through the vacant hallways felt painfully slow for Sam, but Hector had insisted that they move slowly and carefully. He stopped at each room and checked for survivors, but they had not found any. All the group had come across so far were bits of half- eaten faculty and students, and large puddles of gore, bits of innards and blood. They remained silent as they moved from room to room with Hector in the front, wrench in hand, Sam in the middle and Mike walking backwards in the rear to watch for any movement.

Coming upon one of the art rooms, Hector froze in his tracks. It was dark inside, but a slightly darker shadow could be seen shuffling through the gloom. "One's in there," Hector motioned.

"Just close the door," Sam said hopefully. He had already seen enough violence for his lifetime, let alone the day.

But Hector shook his head, "You leave one and then there will be three to deal with and then twenty. We put down whatever ones we find, so we don't have to worry about them making more."

Mike nodded, "He's right Sam. If what Hector says is going on is true, then we can't leave any of these things wandering around."

"Ok," Sam acquiesced, "What do we do?" But Sam already knew what was coming and had begun to look around for something heavy. Hector motioned towards an overturned janitor's cart that lay a few feet down the hall.

"There boys," he motioned to the cart, "Mike, something heavy. Sam get a broom or anything with a long handle."

Hector silently stood guard outside the door while Mike and Sam quickly rummaged through the janitor's cart. Mike came back brandishing a small cat's paw and Sam had picked up a broom handle with what looked like a paint scrapper duct taped to the end. Hector told him it had been used to get gum off the floor.

"We move in quietly," Hector whispered, "With our backs to the wall. Be careful, there might be more than one in there. When we get close, Sam you push it against the wall or down onto to floor and keep it there. Mike, we go for the head. Ok?" They both nodded and the group silently slipped into the art room.

Whatever was in there did not seem to notice that the group had moved around beside it. It simply swayed and groaned, shuffling in a small circle near the front of the room. Coming around the side of one of the worktables, Sam could see that whatever was in the front of the room used to be Mr. Simmons, the art teacher. Through one of his tattered pants legs, Sam could see that the majority of flesh was missing from his right leg, causing Mr. Simmons to move in slow concentric circles. His right arm appeared to be torn off and the dull nub of bone that was his elbow poked out from the lump of mangled flesh that remained.

"Now," Hector bellowed, and Mr. Simmons let out a loan moan turning slowly towards them. Sam rushed forward with the broom handle and crashed it into the chest of the bloodied former art teacher. With a weak leg, Mr. Simmons was easily pushed to the floor, where he struggled against the paint scraper that pinned him. Sam's eyes involuntarily pulled shut as he felt the tip of the paint scraper begin to dig into the flesh underneath with each rocking motion that Mr. Simmons made. Mike and Hector quickly moved around Sam and silenced Mr.

Simmons' groaning. As Sam opened his eyes, it was hard to believe that the red and black stain that spread from the neck had once been a head. Hector and Mike cleaned their weapons and moved back towards the door without saying a word, somehow knowing that there was nothing worth saying at this point, and no words to even try to explain their barbaric actions, but both knew that they had to do what they had just done.

Nearing the open door, footsteps could be heard pounding down the hallway in their direction. "Something's coming," Hector said as he stepped in front, "Move to the sides and be ready." As the footsteps got closer, Hector leapt forward tackling whatever was running down the hall. Sam and Mike followed closely behind; ready to dispatch whatever the janitor was wrestling to the floor.

"Get the hell off him!" Chris yelled, as he kicked Hector in the ribs and knocking him off Ronnie. Dazed for a moment, Hector sat sprawled on the floor. Chris moved towards him with a hammer raised menacingly.

"Wait! Wait!" Sam yelled, "Stop! Stop!" The hammer hung in the air for a minute, Chris still unsure, but then relaxed it at his side.

"What the hell man?" Chris said looking at Hector, who had gotten back to his feet and looked sufficiently pissed off about having been kicked. Ronnie had moved back, slightly behind Chris.

"We need to go. Right now," Ronnie said emphatically.

Sam, Mike and Hector had moved behind Chris and Ronnie forming a semi- circle. Mike spoke first, "Chill, we know shit is out of control and the last thing we need right now is a pissing contest, so Hector I'm sure you're sorry for tackling...?"

"Ronnie," Chris and Ronnie said in unison.

"Right, I'm sure Hector is sorry for tackling Ronnie," Mike looked to Chris, "And I'm sure you're sorry for kicking Hector in the ribs. So let's just cut the shit and see what's going on in the gym. People might need our help."

Chris looked concerned, "We're not going to the gym. Why the hell would you go looking for any of those things?"

"Zombies," Ronnie corrected.

"Ok, thanks Ronnie. Zombies," Chris said uneasily, "Why would you go looking for more zombies? We're getting the hell out of here and finding somewhere safe."

Hector chimed in this time, "Because if there's even one left there will be more and soon enough, it won't matter where you're hiding, it won't be safe. Who knows, maybe it already isn't."

None of the others had considered that whatever was going on could extend beyond Montville, and that maybe outside of the school was even more dangerous and out of control than inside. A collective shudder rippled through all four boys. Chris was about to answer, but a low growl turned everyone's attention to the darkened end of the hallway that Chris and Ronnie had just run down.

Ronnie began shifting back and forth uncomfortably, "We need to go, we need to go." He had already started moving down the hall away from the noise.

"What's down there?" Hector asked, hardly hiding the panic rising in his voice, which completely unsettled Sam and Mike. A low shadow emerged from the darkness and slunk back and forth across the hall in a slow zigzag pattern. Every few steps it would stop, lift its head and sniff the air.

The group slowly began walking backwards away from the creature. As it passed through one of the pools of light cast by an emergency floodlight, all saw exactly what was pursuing them. Even Ronnie and Chris, who had previously seen some of the creature, gasped when they saw its full form.

The creature paused in the yellowed pool of light and sat back on its haunches. It appeared to have been human at one point, but the skin on its face had been shredded and peeled back, exposing the muscle and bone underneath. The darkened sockets of its face held no eyes, only the tangled remains of the nerves that had once been attached. Long, ragged gouges radiated away from the sockets like crudely drawn suns. It looked as if the creature's eyes had simply been scratched out. The meaty lump that centered on its face spoke testament to the fact that a nose had once been there, but now all that remained was a darkened, glistening knob of flesh haphazardly hung above the exposed openings of the nasal cavity. Each greedy breath the creature inhaled and exhaled caused the small chunk of flesh to dance fitfully in the opening. But perhaps the most disturbing aspect of the monstrosity before them was its mouth. The teeth, having been ruined from gnawing bone, were broken off at various angles and lengths, creating a mouth that was chaotically lined with tiny, yellowed daggers tinged with pink. The creature's tongue would periodically protrude, lap the air, then its nasal cavity and return sloppily to its mouth.

Hector crossed himself a few times, but refused to take his eyes off the creature. "I think it tracks by scent," he whispered, "Just keep moving slowly towards the gym." Everyone nodded and shuffled a few more steps down the hall. The creature seemed to have not noticed them yet, but still moved in their direction. They all knew it was a matter of time before it caught their scent. Then Ronnie sneezed.

For a few seconds everything seemed to freeze in the hallway. No one, including the creature moved. Then all hell broke loose. The creature snapped its head in their direction and inhaled deeply. Sam was sure he saw a wicked smile spread across the monster's destroyed mouth, right before it broke into a full sprint down the hall towards the group. Moving on all fours, the creature covered ground quickly and before anyone could react, it was closing in on them. Hector pushed the boys behind him and braced to the attack.

The creature was within ten feet of Hector and sprung forward like a lion preparing to take down prey. Hector silently murmured a prayer and raised his pipe wrench to meet the attack.

Suddenly, the creature's side buckled and it fell onto the floor. It lay there momentarily, snarling and struggling to get back up, but Sam drove the paint scraper deeper into the creature's body and pushed it back to the floor. His hands whitened as they twisted around the broomstick, and small bits of foam flecked his lips and the corner of his mouth through gritted teeth. The others surprised by Sam's attack hesitated only for a few seconds and then fell on the creature with their blunt instruments. When they finally stopped and stood panting in a circle around where the creature had previously struggled, they saw all that remained was a tangled mess of meat and broken bones, but nothing that was in the least bit identifiable as human. Somewhere from within the knotted pile of glistening meat, the tattered remains of a cornflower, blue pinstripe tie poked out. Everyone's eyes tried to miss this detail, but none could deny that this creature had at one time been a teacher, coworker or even friend.

"Come on," Hector motioned towards the gym doors. Everyone moved, but Sam was still pushing the blunt tip of his makeshift spear into the torso of the creature. He did not appear to be blinking.

Mike walked back to his brother, "Sammy, let go. Com'on man, let go." He placed his hands on the broomstick, but Sam pulled tighter.

"Let go," Sam hissed as he turned to face the others. Something burning in his eyes made them take a step back.

"What the hell is wrong with him?" Chris asked no one in particular, "He infected or something?"

Sam's eyes widened and a frightening rage rumbled through them. Voice shaking, Sam said, "You all were going to let him die." He was pointing at Hector. "He stood to protect you and you were going to let him die?" Sam was shaking. Up until this point, Sam had been a relatively passive member of the group, going along without interjecting much of an opinion, which was why everyone was that much more shocked by his current disposition. But something had snapped within Sam. He could find some way to deal with what was going, could come to terms with what they had to do to survive, but he was unwilling to sacrifice anyone. Something inside of Sam insisted that they must cling to at least the most basic semblances of humanity and at its core; he felt that meant taking care of each other. No one was expendable or to be taken for granted.

"It's ok," Hector offered, "I made my own choice."

"No! No! It's not ok!" Sam was almost screaming, "We don't leave anyone behind! We all get through this together. There's no heroes, no cowboy bull shit! We stay together!"

Ronnie stepped forward, "He's right. The CDC report on the internet said…"

"Not now Ronnie," Chris said placing a hand on his shoulder, "But Sam is right. Nobody does any hero crap, cuz then we gotta deal with another thing…zombie…whatever. We play this safe and that means sticking together." Sam finally relaxed and his shoulders sagged as he placed his foot on the torso of the creature and wrenched the paint scrapper free.

Everyone agreed and silently moved together through the double doors into the dimly lit gym.

● ● ●

Alice and Joey watched in horror as the paramedic clung to Ms. Kozlov's back. She screamed and flailed her arms backwards, trying to knock the man off her back, but he would not come loose.

"We gotta help her," Joey said, although even he was unsure of the idea. Most of the other students had moved into the corner and were crying quietly or staring blankly at the ground between their feet.

Alice agreed, "I know, but what is going on out there? Why is the paramedic attacking Ms. Kozlov?"

Joey shrugged, "I don't know and I really don't care." Joey turned away from the door and began searching the room. As he picked up a dirty towel, he heard Alice gasp.

"There are more Joey," Alice's face was pressed tightly against the small window, "It looks like five more just came in."

Returning to the window, Joey watched as five more figures slipped in through the gym doors at the far side of the gym and quietly work their way towards the gym teacher.

Ms. Kozlov continued to turn in tight half circles, swinging the paramedic violently back and forth, but his fingers were firmly knotted into her hair. The paramedic appeared to be trying to bite Ms. Kozlov'z neck, but was finding it difficult with her throwing him about.

Suddenly, Ms. Kozlov seemed to have gotten an idea and ran backwards into the closed wall of bleachers. A wave loudly rippled through the stacked seats, but one of the paramedic's hands appeared to come loose. A large hank of hair was clutched between his fingers. Ms. Kozlov took the opening to grab the man's free arm and fling him over her shoulder and into the gym floor. A wet slap reverberated through the gym as the man's face met the hard wood floor and his teeth scattered like dice across the shiny surface.

Panting for a moment, Ms. Kozlov turned and ran for the stacked bleachers. She grabbed hold of the exposed space between the seats and began climbing towards the top. Joey could see the wounds on Ms. Kozlov's back weeping blood as she struggled to get higher.

The medic lay still for a moment, but quickly got back to his feet and rushed towards the bleachers. He stopped at the bottom, as if trying to figure out what to do next and then began to beat his fists angrily against the bleachers. Ms. Kozlov refused to look down and continued to the top twenty feet above the gym floor, and collapsed onto her back in the small space between the uppermost seats.

Joey turned to Alice, "We gotta do something now before that lunatic starts climbing." And almost as if cued, the two saw the paramedic place a tentative foot into the bleachers and begin to climb. He made it a few feet up, lost his footing and crashed to the gym floor, landing on his back. But no sooner did Joey turn away to continue searching, did the paramedic get to his feet and resume climbing.

Shaking the bar across the door angrily, Alice shouted, "Grab something heavy Joey. We have to get there before those others do!"

"Help me push this!" Joey yelled as he began to move the weight rack slowly forward. Alice rushed to help him and a few more students joined in, seemingly shaken out of their shock with the presentation of something to do.

The rack clattered against the doors, spilling plates and denting the door, but not opening it. "Again!" Joey yelled pulling the rack back. This time the rack hit full force into the doors and everyone could see them bulge outwards a few inches. Pulling it back again Joey pressed his back to the far wall. "Now!" He screamed as they rushed the doors. With a deafening crash, the rack broke the lock and swung the doors open.

The paramedic stopped for a second and turned towards the sound. In the gloom of the weight room, he spied far easier prey huddled in the corners and clumsily dropped from the bleachers landing in a predatory stance.

Joey scrambled over the top of the tipped weight rack and was the first to see that the paramedic had ceased his climb. "Oh no! Oh no!" Joey stuttered as he back peddled away from the door. "He's coming here!" Panic immediately surged through the weight room and students that were seemingly comatose sprung to life and ran screaming for the door. Many tripped over the overturned rack and twisted or broke their ankles, only to be trampled by their fellow classmates.

There was no way to close the door, now that it was clogged with injured students and spilled weights. "What do we do now?" Joey asked.

"Quickly, help me pull the injured people out," Alice commanded as she began to drag away one student. Joey arrived in time to grab the foot of one student just as the paramedic grasped her arms.

"Help me!" Joey shrieked, but he could already feel the girl being pulled from his grip. Alice grabbed hold of Joey's waist and pulled backwards with all her might. The girl's shoe slipped off in Joey's hand and sent both of them sprawling to the floor. The screams of the girl echoed through the gym as the paramedic sank what was left of his teeth into her neck and tore her throat out.

Both Joey and Alice quickly jumped up from the floor and moved away from the door. The bloodied body of the girl lay atop the tangled pile of weights and injured students, but there was no way to get to them. The paramedic sat crouched on top of the entire pile, lording over his prey and greedily chewing on the ruined remains of the poor girl's throat.

As Joey moved backwards, he stumbled over something on the floor and cursed quietly. Looking down he saw a ten pound weight plate that must have rolled away from the rack when it crashed. Joey slowly reached down and grabbed the small plate, wrapping it in the grimy towel he had previously found and twisting it to form a makeshift mace. He hefted the mace a few times in his hand to make sure the weight was secure.

"Stay behind the Ellison Machine," he said to Alice, but she made no move to follow his directions.

An angry look broke across Alice's face and she said calmly, "No time for gender stereotypes Joey." Looking over, he realized that Alice had followed his lead and created her own towel mace and was preparing to attack. "On three," she whispered.

Joey never heard the countdown, never remembered slowly saying the numbers. His mind simply skipped over the countdown to what he knew was a bad and dangerous idea and before he knew what was going on, he felt the heavy end of his mace come crashing down on the back of the paramedic, as it blindly chewed on one of the injured students.

The paramedic was dropped onto his stomach with limbs splayed out in all directions, but Joey could see that he was still trying to get up. Joey moved forward to strike again, but lost his balance and tumbled backwards off of the rack. As he fell, he saw Alice leap over the rack with the mace arcing high overhead. The plate wrapped within her towel came down squarely between the paramedic's shoulders and a sickening crack resonated through the gym. Alice panted for breath, and was about to turn back to Joey when she noticed that the paramedic was pulling himself once again over the rack and towards the student he had previously been snacking upon.

"What the hell?" Joey muttered, "There's no friggin' way this guy should still be moving."

Shuddering at the grotesque scene unfolding before her, Alice prepared to strike the paramedic again.

"Go for the head!" A voice bellowed across the gym, "The head!" Alice looked up to see the five figures racing across the gym, but the momentary turning of her attention was all that the paramedic needed.

A cold, strong hand grasped Alice's ankle and pulled it forward. Her balance thrown off, Alice was dropped onto her back on top of the rack. The various little steel pegs painfully jabbed into her back, but she had been fortunate enough that they had missed her head. Pain radiated from everywhere, but Alice did not have time to dwell on this. A slow, but persistent, hand tugged her further across the rack and out of the room.

Kicking out blindly Alice struck the paramedic in the face, but he continued to drag her forward. Once he was close enough, he wrapped his mouth around the toe of Alice's shoe and bit down. She could feel the pressure squeezing her bones, the thick rubber and lack of teeth made it difficult for the medic to puncture her skin. Sitting up, Alice felt her shoulders being grabbed and she was suddenly pulled out of her shoe and back into the weight room. Both Joey and Alice watched in horror as a group of five people fell upon the crippled paramedic, who was dumbly chewing on a running shoe. The medic's body bounced and writhed, as the five men beat upon it in time with a primal beat only they could hear. When the assault was over, Alice and Joey looked up to see a sweaty, out of breathe Sam climbing over the tangled mess before them.

"Hey guys," Sam wheezed, "Are you…"

Sam's words were suddenly cut off as Hector pushed past and entered, wrench hanging menacingly at his side with a thick string of gore slowly leaking from it. "Who's been bit?"

● ● ●

Catching what little luck was left in the day, it turned out that Alice had not been bitten. Her foot was bruised, and she was sure a few of the smaller bones had been broken, but the paramedic's few remaining teeth had not found purchase in her flesh. Even Ms. Kozlov, after having been coaxed down from the bleachers, was battered and frightened, but for the most part was ok. Her constant flailing and judo throw had kept the paramedic from finding time to bite her. Still, ragged wounds ran down her back and slowly wept blood into the waistband of her windpants. Using what few clean towels could be found in the weight room, Joey and Alice tended to her wounds.

After checking over the other survivors, Hector and the others shared a quick recap of their stories, as well as their zombie theory. The majority of people within the weight room remained in a state of catatonia and seemed completely unaware or uncaring of what they heard. None of the younger victims appeared to be reanimating, but Hector insisted that they make sure, just in case. None of the others had the stomach to crush the skulls of the already dead students, so Hector silently moved around the pile of weights and students, bringing his wrench up and down repeatedly. With each dull crack, everyone's stomach filled higher and higher with an icy, greasy sludge, even Hector's.

"Zombies? Are you serious?" Alice asked skeptically, "How is that possible?"

"Look," Sam said holding his hands up, "I'm not saying I know one hundred percent what is going on or why it is happening. We're just going with what works." Alice looked unconvinced.

"Zombies don't seem possible, I'll give you that," Joey interjected, "But how is everything that happened to that medic and him still trying to eat you possible? I mean, you paralyzed him with that hit to his back and he didn't even wince, never even made a sound. And still, he was going after you. I'm no expert, but that looked like a friggin' zombie to me."

Alice turned to Ms. Kozlov, looking for a voice of reason or perhaps some support, but was surprised by the gym teacher's reaction.

"Russian folktales of taxims and fiends lurking around graveyards have been told for as long as anyone can remember," Ms. Kozlov said, "My grandmother would tell us stories about them coming out at night to eat dead bodies or children. We always thought it was just a story to make us come home on time, but now I am not sure." Ronnie nodded approvingly.

"Ok," Alice sighed, "Let's just go along with the whole zombie thing until we figure out otherwise. It'll probably be better for people to put a name to what's going on, even if it is zombie."

Mike, Chris and Hector were speaking off to the side, but seeing that the others were in agreement, rejoined the group.

"Good," Mike said, "Now that we're all in agreement, we have to figure out what to do next. It doesn't look like help is coming anytime soon, so we gotta hunker down here and wait it out."

"But what about our families?" Joey asked hesitantly, "We have to let them know we're ok. Wouldn't we be safer out there anyway?"

Sam was about to agree with Joey, but Mike put a hand on his shoulder and whispered, "Sam, Mom and Dad will be ok. They would want us to be safe. We gotta do that for them before anything else." Sam nodded weakly.

"We'll get to that Potts," Chris said, "But who the hell knows what it's like out there? It could be even worse. I say we check out the school, find food, make sure it's safe and then worry about checking in at home."

"Chris is right," Ronnie added, "The CDC report said we should find shelter and fortify it."

"Where the heck would you learn that from?" Alice asked incredulously.

"Internet," Sam, Mike, Chris, Hector and Ronnie all said in unison. Then they set about making their plan.

● ● ●

Before anyone could break off to attempt their own tasks, Ronnie had insisted that they secure the gym so that they had a safe place to fall back to and deal with the other surviving students. The majority of students in the weight room had run the minute the door was forced open. About half of those students had tripped on the rack and were trampled by their classmates, only to have their throats torn out by the paramedic. Those that had made it past the rack and paramedic, had run for the back door and streamed out of the school to supposed safety. Only about five or six catatonic students remained, quietly mumbling incoherently to themselves and rocking back and forth. Everyone figured it was best to just leave them where they were for the time being and quietly moved the corpses into a darkened corner of the gym.

"The CDC report said that it's important to have secure shelter with supplies," Ronnie continued, "We need to make sure the gym is safe before we do anything else." The sudden rush and focus that comes with having a plan tugged at everyone, making them jittery and reckless, urging them to quickly accomplish something, even if they were unaware of what, but that urge was a dangerous one and they knew it.

"We need to take things slowly," Sam added, "No one rushes off to do anything without someone else there. But Ronnie is right, we need to secure the gym before anything else."

The others nodded in agreement and set about checking the doors into the gym. The windows were located above the bleachers, so they were at least twenty-five feet above ground level. All and all, the group figured the gym was a pretty good spot to set up as home base. It was easily defensible, having only a few doors and high windows, as well as large bathroom facilities and a lot of space.

Ms. Kozlov was steeled through the hope of a plan and quickly began moving to the doors and locking them with her set of keys. She looked tired and winced with each movement, but she was strong and would not allow the gashes on her back to take her out of action.

As Joey and Ms. Kozlov were checking the last door, an exterior one that opened into the parking lot, they caught a glimpse of movement. There in between the cars they could see a figure moving up and down the rows.

"Someone is outside!" Joey yelled and the others rushed to see. Through the small windows they could see that there were about six figures moving through the parking lot towards the school.

"Maybe it's help. They look like they have on police uniforms," Ms. Kozlov added hopefully, but she knew better than anyone that they could not trust a uniform anymore. The choppy and stilted movements of the figures clearly marked them as more zombies.

As they got closer, the group could see a small mob shambling towards the school in a relatively close-knit circle. What had at a distance appeared to be disciplined, well-trained movement, now could be seen for what it really was. One zombie in the middle, whom the others had seemingly attacked, had his long, ropy intestine tangled around the necks and waists of the other zombies and was acting as an anchor. As they attempted to pull away, the intestine would flex and recoil drawing them back into the group.

"I think I'm gonna puke," Joey muttered, "That's the most disgusting thing I've seen all day and that's saying a lot."

"They must have gotten tangled when they were feeding," Chris offered as a possible explanation.

"Why are they coming here?" Alice asked and then they saw the answer. A few shadows moved under the cars, crawling away from the tangled mob that slowly pursued them. Someone from the school must have tried to get to their car and run into the zombies. Now panic was causing them to stupidly scuttle under the bellies of the parked cars in an attempt to escape the zombies.

"We gotta help them," Sam demanded, but no one moved. "What the hell are you waiting for? We need to get out there!"

The others exchanged a few glances before Hector spoke up, "Sam we don't know what else is out there. We could put everyone at risk by going out there. Who knows what might get in?" Everyone else remained silent.

"You're just going to sit there and watch them get eaten? You can live with that?" Sam cast accusingly at all members of the group.

"We need to at least try," Alice said weakly, "If we go quickly, we can probably get to them and back here before those things even get close." The debate carried on for a few more minutes.

Chris, who had remained silent throughout the debate, spoke up, "Look, if it was any of you out there, wouldn't you want us to at least try. Ms. Kozlov open the door and then lock it the minute I'm out there."

"You're going?" Sam asked, "Wait a minute, we should go out as a group, it'll be safer."

"Yeah and slower," Chris replied, "I can get out there and back much faster on my own, than I can with all of you tagging along. Just open the door and be ready to unlock it when I get close." Sam could not understand why Chris, who seemingly delighted in making other people's lives horrible, would be willing to risk his own life for whoever this stranger was. The entire thing seemed out of character.

Ms. Kozlov slowly turned the key in the lock and gently pushed the bar to open the door. Chris slipped past and sprinted towards the parking lot before anyone could say anything else.

● ● ●

The cool autumn air burned in Chris's lungs as he tore across the walkways towards the parking lot. The early fall sun had begun to set, painting the parking lot in a strange wash of purples and oranges. There were long shadows everywhere, but Chris refused to stop and think about what might be hiding out there. He needed to remain focused, single minded on his task. Anything that happened along the way there, would be handled as it occurred. Trying to think too far into the future would have paralyzed Chris with the insurmountable amount of "what-ifs" that permeated his current plan.

The hula hooped zombie mob was moving closer to whoever was trapped under the parked cars, but each one tried to move in a different direction, only to be sluggishly pulled back by the knotted intestine, which considerably slowed their progress. Chris was sure he saw movement in other parts of the parking lot, but he forced himself to have tunnel vision. All he saw was the shadow under the car, the zombies and the occasionally glimpse of his hammer as his arms rapidly swung up and down.

Hitting the curb at full speed and almost belly flopping onto the pavement, Chris ran straight for the car under which the shadow currently moved. "Here!" Chris yelled, "Over here!"

A hand reached out from under the belly of a nondescript tan economy sedan and was slowly followed by another. "Hurry up!" Chris screamed, as he got closer to the car.

Approaching the car at full speed Chris was unable to slow himself, and slammed into the rear passenger door causing the car to gently rock. He reached down and grabbed the shirt of the person underneath and turned to run. A weak whimper caused him to look back as he ran and he realized he was basically dragging the poor girl across the pavement.

"Get up! Get up now!" Chris demanded, as he saw the mob turn towards him. The obvious sight of prey seemed to spur them into high gear and all began to collectively shamble towards them. A chorus of guttural moans danced through the silent parking lot, echoing off the steel of cars and pavement.

"We gotta move," Chris said, a little more kindly, "Come on. I need you to get up." The girl pulled her feet under her and stood; she appeared, strangely enough, to be dressed as a dancer. Her tights were torn and bloodied from crawling under the cars and a long scrape ran down the middle of her back from where she must have forced her way under a lower vehicle, but Chris did not see any bites. Her eyes were large and glassy, like something from a fish market, but they were slowly beginning to clear and show signs of life again.

"Time to go," Chris said, reaching out and grabbing her wrist. The two ran as fast as the girl's battered legs could carry her and did not stop until they collapsed onto the hardwood gym floor. Chris lay for a moment panting, but jumped backwards as the zombies slammed into the door and pounded on the small windows. They had only been a few steps behind.

The horde continued to bang on the doors, but slowly shambled away as everyone moved further back from the door.

"I think they follow movement and sound," Ronnie offered, "So eventually something else catches their attention and they go away, kind of like a toddler."

"Yeah," Mike added sarcastically, "Toddlers that want to eat you."

The girl sat on the floor and pulled her knees tightly around her with her arms. Her closely cut hair sat in tight curls, but a few spots stood in rough spikes from where oil had worked into it from the undercarriages of cars. Small bits of gravel and glass had dug into her flesh and had tiny wells of blood pooling around them causing her mahogany skin to almost sparkle. Chris thought it would almost be beautiful if it were not so awful. Everyone was keeping their distance, not knowing if she had been bitten and would change.

"I didn't see any bites," Chris said, sensing everyone's reservations, "Besides she's our age and none of them changed." Chris motioned towards the tangled mess in the doorway of the weight room. Everyone took a few tentative steps forward.

"What's your name?" Alice asked gently.

Staring for a moment, as if unable to comprehend what had just been asked, the girl finally responded timidly, "Amelia. Amelia Barrows." Some sense of reason and life was beginning to return to her dark eyes and her breathing had returned to normal.

Hector leaned past Alice. "Were you bit Amelia?" He asked kindly, but with full intention of doing what needed to be done if she answered incorrectly.

Amelia shook her head, "No, they tried, but they couldn't get under the cars because they were so tangled. It was awful."

"What were you doing out there?" Chris asked.

"I was trying to get out to my car. When the Lock Down started, we were all in the studio out back and then the lights went out. Mrs. Ortiz, our dance teacher, started gasping and fell to the floor. It looked like she was suffocating or having a heart attack or something, but she was way too young for that. She was like only twenty-seven. We tried to help her and a bunch of the girls went to find help, but then we heard screaming," Amelia shuddered but continued, "They were screaming so loud and then there was nothing. Only a few of us left were there and we could hear that Mrs. Ortiz had stopped breathing.

One of the girls, Abby, tried CPR, she said she was certified. But as she blew into Mrs. Otriz's mouth she woke up and, and..." Tears welled in Amelia's eyes, but she took a deep breath and forced the story forward, "Then Mrs. Ortiz bit her. She woke up and bit Abby. She tore off her lips and Abby feel back screaming. It was terrible. She had no lips and kept screaming and screaming for what seemed like forever, but then Mrs. Ortiz attacked her again. We were all too scared to do anything, but I hit her. I didn't want to, but it looked like she just kept biting Abby and I had to help her. I didn't mean to hit her so hard, but I panicked and grabbed the leg from a stretching bar that wasn't up. I hit her, but she didn't stop and then she came at me. I tripped and she lunged at me and the..." Amelia was struggling to get the next part out, "And when she came down, the bar went up through her chin. Abby was, was..." Amelia vomited violently onto the floor and then just shook her head, as if refusing to acknowledge her own story.

Alice put her arm around Amelia, "It's ok. I mean, I know it's not, but we've all seen things like that today. We've all had to do awful, awful things." Amelia rested her head against Alice's shoulder and everyone could visibly see her body relax. All the hours of stress and horror seemed to rush out of her and she quietly began to weep.

"What were you doing out there anyway?" Chris asked, "Why didn't you stay in the building?"

Amelia lifted her head and Chris could see her eyes were shot with small veins and tinged a violent red, but Amelia answered. "I was trying to get to my car. I couldn't stay in that room. Everyone else had run and the only thing left in there were the bodies. I just couldn't stand it anymore and ran through the back door. I wasn't thinking. I should have remembered that my keys were in my jeans in the changing room, but I just couldn't think straight, ya' know? So I got out there and realized I didn't have my keys, but I saw a group of police officers out near the street and ran to them, but when I got there, they were all those things and they were eating one, but he got up too. Then they came after me, so I hid under some of the cars and tried to get back towards the school. And then I heard you yelling for me." Finally finishing her story, Amelia seemed to collapse into herself and tucked her head between her knees and sobbed loudly. Alice tightly pulled her against herself and gently rocked her like a child.

"Come, let's get you cleaned up," Ms. Kozlov said lifting Amelia off the floor, "I have clothes you can change into in my office." The three women made their way towards the gym teachers' office at the back of the gym.

"The water should still work in the bathrooms," Hector called, "The gym is part of the old building and still runs off of the old wells. It'll be cold, but it'll work."

Amelia weakly waved her hand in a gesture of thanks and allowed herself to be steered into the office.

With the girl gone, the remaining group members turned towards Chris. "What the hell was that all about?" Sam asked, "I thought we agreed no hero stuff?"

"Yeah man," Mike added, "I'm glad you saved that girl but who knows what could've happened out there?"

Chris shrugged, "I dunno. I guess I know what it's like to be abandoned and left on your own. It sucks." And there it was with Chris's simple explanation, everyone understood why he had to save Amelia. So many people had abandoned him in his life that he could not stand to see it happen to anyone else. Whatever had happened to Chris in life, he could not stomach the idea of someone being totally and hopelessly alone; the exact feelings he had for most of his life.

"Fair enough," Hector said, "But we need you around here amigo, so no more rushing off to save the pretty ladies, eh?" Chris nodded. He knew what he had done was completely reckless, and he also knew that he had to do it.

● ● ●

After a half hour, the three women returned from the office. Amelia wore baggy sweatpants and an oversized t-shirt, both emblazoned with the Montville Regional School logo. She still appeared a little shaken, but she looked a lot better than when Chris had brought her in. Alice walked slowly next to her and gently sat her down on one of the bleachers that had been pulled out.

The group gathered in a loose circle around Amelia, filling in random spots in the bleachers. Everyone appeared to need a little bit of space, perhaps to be introspective or perhaps just to take a break from the reality in which they currently existed. The horrors of the day had bound all members together, but also threatened to tear them apart if they did not take periodic breaks from it. None of them were ready to acknowledge that the world was completely falling apart, but the presence of the other members was a constant reminder.

Never completely understanding group dynamics or social cues, Ronnie blurted out, "We need to get supplies." Everyone was shaken out of their respective cocoon of self-reflection and brought back to the excruciating situation in which they currently found themselves.

Hector rose from where he had lain down on the bleachers and cracked his back. While rolling his neck in small circles he muttered, "We need to deal with the facts of this situation and that means admitting and coming to terms with a few things." Everyone looked up.

"Alright man," Chris said wearily, "Where do you wanna start? That the world has ended? That zombies ate everyone we used to know? That we're basically trapped in the friggin' gym?"

Hector shrugged, "Yeah, all of those and also the fact that it doesn't look like anyone is coming to help us anytime soon. You all saw what was left of those cops out there. We have to assume that most others are like that too. All we know so far is that whatever is going on, seems to be affecting adults, so that means that everything and everyone we would be counting on for help is pretty much gone."

"Well thanks for that happy thought," Mike spoke up, "But we also need to acknowledge that we survived. For whatever reason, we're still alive and I think we can all agree on staying that way. But Hector is right, there is no help coming, so we gotta help ourselves. We know those things are outside, so we have to assume that they are at least all over town. But who knows, this could be the whole state or country even. For the time being, it seems like we're safest here." He looked over at Amelia, Alice and Sam, "I know that we all want to get home to check on our families, but we're not doing anyone any good rushing out there unprepared. We have to get things settled, make a plan and then go see."

Sam sat up, "Ronnie you said there were plans in that fake CDC report, right? So let's start there. What do we need?"

Ronnie detailed the basics of the CDC plan for a zombie apocalypse, and for the most part it was little more than the same supplies needed for a hurricane, earthquake or terrorist attack. They needed food, water and medical supplies, all of which they could find in abundance around the school.

"Those are all good ideas Ron," Chris said, "But we gotta add a few things to the list, like weapons and transportation."

"We should stay sheltered, the report said so," Ronnie stated matter-of-factly.

"I'm not arguing that," Chris replied, "But we can't assume that those things aren't going to come back or that there aren't more of them in the school. I'm not gonna face a whole group of them with only a crappy hammer. If there were cops out in the parking lot, that means cop cars, which means guns."

"We'll be more likely to shoot ourselves," Sam added, "We can't just go running around like Rambo."

"Don't knock Stallone," Joey quipped, "That's where I got the weighted towel idea from."

"What the hell are you talking about?" Mike asked.

"Ya' know that movie when Sly is in jail and working on that old mustang. He beats the hell out of that guy with a weight wrapped in a towel."

"Seriously Joey?" Alice asked shaking her head, "I don't know if I would have followed you if I knew your idea came from a Sylvester Stallone movie."

"It worked," Joey added sullenly.

"You can all debate 80's Stallone movies later," Chris said exasperated, "Point is, we need to arm ourselves with something other than tools. And I'm also not gonna squirrel up in here and not have a way out if we need one. I say we back one of the smaller busses up to the outside doors just in case we need to make a quick exit. I also think we should get our hands on those guns."

Everyone had to admit that the idea of an escape route and a few guns was not a terrible one, but they all agreed that only those with experience, like Ms. Kozlov, who taught rifles in third marking period, or Hector, who had grown up around guns, should carry one, at least for the time being so that nobody shot themselves in the foot. Chris reluctantly agreed.

With the list of supplies finally agreed upon, everyone once again became antsy and jittery with the prospect of some course of action to take, but they were also exhausted. Large, swollen, rings hung empurpled beneath everyone's eyes and despite the large amounts of adrenaline coursing through all of them, a periodic contagious yawn was passed from one to the other.

"Sun's down," Hector said looking at the high windows, "It'll be too dark to see in the school anyway. We should rest."

Ms. Kozlov had already begun to drag out a few gymnastic tumbling mats from the supply closet. "They are not pretty, but they smell better than the wrestling ones," she said.

Everyone collapsed onto the mats, with their respective mauls close at hand and tried to sleep. And while at first everyone was sure they would never sleep again, the exhaustion that invariably follows an adrenaline dump slowly pulled each one off into a fitful night's sleep.

● ● ●

The morning sun broke through a few cottony clouds and lazily worked its way through the wide gym widows and across the highly polished floor. Everyone had been up before light had broken, but no one was quite ready yet to begin another day in the new world in which they now lived.

Sam lay on the blue tumbling mats and absent- mindedly pulled at a spot where the cheap vinyl was beginning to peel. Looking out through the high windows, Sam could see the sun climbing higher into the bright cerulean sky. The thought that the rest of the world remained seemingly unaffected by the horror unfolding around him niggled at Sam. How could things seem so normal when they were absolutely not?

"It's hard to watch isn't it?" Alice whispered from nearby.

"Huh?" Sam said startled, "What'd ya' mean?"

Alice continued, "It's hard to watch the sun rise, see the sky blue with birds flying in it and realize that the world continues to turn regardless of what's happening to us."

"Yeah," Sam admitted, "I could just as easily be watching the same thing through my bedroom window. But I know that's probably never going to happen again."

Alice chuckled a little, "Yeah and getting ready to get on the bus and trip Chris again."

Sam felt the heat roll across his face as he blushed, "You couldn't just stick that note through the vent in my locker could you?"

Laughing a little more loudly Alice quipped, "Oh come on. I couldn't make it easy for you. What fun would that be?" Soon enough, both Sam and Alice were laughing. It was nice to have a moment in the hostile world in which they had been thrust to be just teenagers again, to capture a few fleeting moments of the life they had taken for granted mere hours ago, before that ember was completely snuffed out and all they would be left with was the carnage and madness waiting a few steps outside. Then everyone else was up and it was time to start another day where the fear of pimples and pop quizzes, had been replaced with the all too real fear of being eaten.

The next few days became stagnant, and the hours swirled like so much filth trapped in the gentle ebb of a torpid pool. No one in the group seemed able to accomplish much of anything. A few more of the students had emerged from the weight room and dumbly stumbled around until they encountered an obstacle and shuffled the other direction. None of them had yet to speak and Sam found their mannerisms completely unsettling because the line between them and the zombies seemed so dangerously thin, perhaps it was for all of them.

● ● ●

Mike and Joey silently worked their way through the halls of the school. The early morning sunlight illuminated most sections, but a few watery shadows remained in the darker corners of the classrooms and offices. Joey had not necessarily been Mike's first choice for a partner, surely Hector, Sam or Chris could handle the zombies better, but Mike did have to admit Joey's attack with the weighted towel had been impressive, even if he had landed on his butt. The notorious towel hung limply from Joey's hand, swinging slowly, back and forth as he moved down the hall. His other hand was loosely placed on the handle of a squeaky cart the boys planned to use for moving supplies out of the cafeteria. Mike had taken point in front of their pushcart and brandished the steel rod he had found earlier. Both had done their best to rinse the gore from their weapons, but the blood seemed to be part of them now, almost infused with the materials and metals.

They had been given food detail and were making their way towards the massive cafeteria that rested in the center of Montville, but getting there meant going through almost half of the entire main building, an idea neither of the two relished. To further complicate matters, Hector had given them a large, flat pushcart with large shopping cart-like wheels that spun in every direction, but the one the boys wanted it to go in.

"It'll work better when it's loaded down," Mike assured Joey.

"It'll work better when it's not a total piece of crap," Joey retorted, "Seriously, this was the best one in the janitor's room? There was nothing else? What the heck do our tax dollars go towards?"

"Nothing," Mike said grimly, "At least not anymore."

"Gee thanks Debbie Downer," Joey replied, "Like I need any other reason to be depressed. Please give me some more good news. Like maybe that I'll be a virgin forever? That'll really brighten my day."

Mike could not keep the smile from his face. "Joey," he said seriously, "You were gonna be a virgin forever, long before any zombies showed up. You should just be happy that you have a better excuse now."

After lightly punching Mike in the arm, Joey resumed pushing the cart. Crossing through the Commons area, the boys came across dismembered remains of whoever had been partially eaten by the creature that had chased Ronnie and Chris only days ealier. The sickly sweet odor of decay slowly wafted through the Commons and filled the hallways. The absolute horror of the gnawed splintered bones, and haphazard piles of unidentifiable ribbons of tissue and mounds of meat caused both to hesitate. It had been terrible enough to hear Chris and Ronnie recount what the creature had been doing, but to view the carnage first hand in the stark contrast of the morning sun, was almost too much. Their minds struggled to make sense of it all and ultimately they silently agreed to pass through as quickly as possible and with no conversation.

Approaching the long hallway leading to the cafeteria, Joey paused to look out through the long row of doors that served as the main exit for bus loading. Hector had told everyone that most exterior doors were run off timed magnetic locks, so as long as the power was out, they could not be opened from the outside. That knowledge did little to calm the feelings of unrest that surged through Joey, as he watched heavy waxen hands monotonously bang against the glass. Each thud left a greasy smear on the windows, but it was difficult to tell if it was gore or grime. None of the zombies had been dead long enough to really begin to decay, but the flesh was beginning to shrink away from the fingernails, almost giving the appearance of claws. Each of the zombies that banged against the windows had entered the early stages of rigor mortis, and a rictus grin stretched tightly across each dull face giving the expression of sad, toothy clowns.

"Do you think they'll break through?" Joey asked.

Mike thought for a moment and considered that the banging had increased in frequency and force, the closer they had gotten to the doors. "I don't think so," he said unsurely, "The glass in the doors is double-paned and those zombies don't seem to be strong enough to break through that. The other ones we've seen might be able to."

Joey shuddered, "What about the classroom windows? If those are anywhere near the quality of our cart here, we're screwed."

Mike nodded, "True, but as long as they don't see us they don't seem to notice that kind of stuff. But we should probably take care of that right away. Maybe there's some plywood in the industrial arts classroom or stage area? But let's worry about getting the food first."

Joey turned away from the empty, pus-toned eyes that hungrily bore into him and continued towards the cafeteria.

"Not that I'm complaining," Joey said, "But why don't you think we've seen more zombies inside?"

"Once the power cut and the screaming started, I'd bet most people did what Amelia did and ran for the parking lot," Mike answered, "I looked outside this morning and most of the lots are practically empty, but I bet there's still more in here, so don't get careless." Mike poked at Joey with the end of his steel rod.

"Jeez, alright," Joey winced, "Just get that nasty thing away from me."

The doors leading into the cafeteria swung open easily. A few tables were overturned and chairs lay scattered about, but it did not appear that anyone, living or dead, was left inside.

"Leave the cart," Mike said, "We go slow. Make sure nothing's out here and then we check the kitchens, ok?" Joey nodded and hefted the twisted, stained towel in his hands. Wordlessly, Joey and Mike worked their way around the perimeter of the cafeteria, making sure nothing was lying in wait. As they returned to their point of origin, both breathed a collective sigh of relief; it appeared that everyone had fled the cafeteria and that none of the zombies had shambled in since.

A loud bang resounded from somewhere deep within the kitchen, shattering the small moment of relief that the boys had enjoyed. They immediately tensed and prepared to face down whatever was behind the brushed steel, double doors that lead into the kitchen from behind the steamers lining the serving stations.

Mike motioned towards the door and held a finger to his lips. Joey nodded and began to work his way around the serving station. Another loud bang echoed from within, causing Joey to let out a small squeal of surprise, which he quickly tried to cover up and hoped that Mike did not notice.

Approaching the doors from opposite sides, Mike leaned in towards one of the round porthole windows that centered each door. Most of the kitchen was painted in inky shadows, but the far corner, having a few greasy windows, let in some orange tinted sunlight. Two figures could be seen moving within the gloom and Mike silently pressed his face closer to the window in an attempt to determine what was going on.

"Don' come near me ya' filthy creature!" A thin figure screamed raising something large and round high overhead. The command was answered by a gravelly moan followed by another loud crash.

"Let's go. Someone's in there," Mike said, pushing the doors open. Joey swung his weighted towel one time to be sure and ducked in through the double doors close behind Mike.

Through the murkiness of the kitchen, Mike and Joey could see a conflict unfolding in the limited space between the obscure angular shadows of the kitchen equipment. A dull metallic *thunk* reverberated loudly throughout the kitchen, reflecting off of the numerous stainless steel surfaces.

"Hey! Hey! Over here!" Joey yelled.

"No ya' mule," a winded voice retorted, "Over here! Come and help me!"

Rushing around the corner of one of the long prep tables, Joey and Mike saw one of the lunch ladies bludgeoning another one with a heavy cast iron skillet. The pan was wider than the hoop of a basketball net and easily weighed over five pounds, but the woman was tirelessly raising it repeatedly over her head to smash the skull of the other lunch lady that lay collapsed before her. The moan emanating from the floor was definitely not the result of being hit over the head, rather it bespoke an ungodly hunger, one that Mike and Joey were rapidly becoming all too familiar with.

"I got the legs," Mike yelled, "Help her with the head!" Throwing himself forward, Mike wrapped his arms securely around the puffy ankles of the former lunch lady. He pulled back, but she had become slippery from crawling across the greasy floor and Mike's gripped faltered. His hands shot forward, attempting to grab the woman again, but he was only able to catch hold of her scuffed Shape-Ups, which slipped off her foot and sent him sprawling backwards. From his spot on the floor, Mike irritably threw the ridiculous shoe at the woman, hitting her in the back of the head with its oversized heel. It uselessly bounced backwards, but did succeed in getting the zombie to notice Mike.

The zombie rolled over onto its back; further staining the greasy maroon frock it currently wore. The longer it stayed down there on the floor the more it was beginning to look like a drowned slug, but Mike had little time to consider this as Joey stepped past and swung his weighted towel in a high arc. The zombie continued to slime its way closer and closer, but was suddenly stopped in its path as the weight came blurring down from above and connected with the back of its skull. The skillet had started a small fissure along the base of the skull where the weight caught the edge and split it like an over ripened melon. The zombie slumped forward on her forearms and collapsed with head turned to the side, slowly oozing bits of fractured bone and organic matter across the tiled floor and into one of the overflow drains.

Joey stood, legs spread over his conquest and looked at Mike. He could hardly contain his gloating at having been the one to finish the zombie.

"Did you see that?" Joey exclaimed, "Holy crap that was wild!"

The fact that Joey seemed to have enjoyed what he had just done bothered Mike more than anything, but then again, maybe that was Joey's way of dealing. Maybe he had to view the zombies as nonhuman so that he could do what needed to be done? Mike thought maybe he needed to heed Joey's lesson.

The former rules of civilization and society no longer applied to the world in which they found themselves. If they were going to survive, new rules had to be made and the first one was stop viewing these things as people. They were zombies and surely saw Mike as nothing more than a meal, so wasting his time pining for the person they used to be was going to serve him no purpose beyond getting eaten.

"Good shot boy," the thin lunch lady commended, "This skillet was too damn broad to crack the skull."

"Uh, thanks?" Joey said, "Who are you? Why are you still here?"

"See now Joey," the woman said shaking her head, "How come I can remember all your names, but you spoiled little children can't be bothered to know mine? That one on his bum over there, you're called Mike ain't ya'?" Both boys stood slack jawed, unsure of how to proceed, but the woman let out a deep, good-natured laugh that seemed too big for her slight frame.

"Elsie," she said, "And I been serving you children for years, but not one of you can be bothered to ask or remember my name, let alone say 'thank you'. I'd think you'd want to know who handled your food better than anyone, but maybe not, I guess?" The boys felt ashamed, while both could easily identify Elsie as the lunch lady, it was true that they had never bothered to learn her name and here she was, having served hundreds of children and she could easily recall theirs simply from the few minutes it took the serve them lunch.

"Stop beating ya' selves up boys," she laughed, "The child is yet to be born that has manners or sense. It's gotta be worked into ya' by life."

Mike had risen from the floor. "Sorry anyway Elsie," he apologized, "How the heck did you know to go for the head?"

"Yeah," Joey added, "We're having a hard time figureing out butts from buttons right now and you already knew. What gives?"

Elsie leaned back against one of the prep tables and finally put down her large cast iron skillet. "I know the sloppy work of a zobop when I see it," she said confidently, "And I know an out of control zombie when I see one too."

"Zobop?" Mike asked, now more confused than before he had even asked a question.

"Voodoo priest," Elsie replied, "Gotta be one with no sense to make this mess. I grew up in Haiti and most of the zobops are good- natured men, just trying to help out their neighbors, but every once in a while some jack-ass tries a spell and mucks it up. We've seen a troublesome zombie or two, but nothing like this."

"You've seen this before?" Joey asked in disbelief, "How come it's never made the news before?"

Elsie laughed, "Why would we want to let everyone know what goes on in our business? No reality shows der' and sure as 'ell ain't gon tell the news about another Belarivo showin' up at any parties." Seeing the confused look on the boys' faces, Elsie clarified, "Belarivo was a troublesome zombie. Refused to listen to the man that raised him. Kept showin' up at parties and mule that he was, wouldn't go back to rest in his grave. Ended up in a lead coffin under some boulders. But he was nothing like any of this."

"So zombies have been around for..." Joey began.

"Forever Joey," Elsie finished, "But not like this. Zombies were basically slaves used for hard work in cane fields and such, never going around eatin' anybody. This is something else, something even more evil than raisin' someone up to be a slave."

Mike nodded, "I don't think this has anything to do with making slaves, but I am getting that this whole zombie thing has been around a lot longer than any of us thought or at least everywhere but here."

Again Elsie laughed, "Mike, there's been zombies here too. Your people just didn't care to listen to who was telling the stories. First it was the Native American and then the African slaves telling tales bout zombies, but the white man never heeded tales that didn't come from his own mouth." Mike and Joey figured in light of recent events there was no arguing Elsie's summation.

"Why didn't you get out of here when everything got nuts?" Joey asked, "Seems like most people cleared out after the lights went."

"Believe me I thought about it, but then Sue started feeling ill and I didn't want to leave her alone."

"Sue?" Mike asked and Elsie pointed to the floor. "Oh," he said averting his eyes from Sue's split cranium.

"But you boys are still here too, huh?" Elsie asked, "Are there many of you left?"

"There's nine of us in the gym. We came here to get food and water," Mike replied.

"Well then let's get on with the shopping," Elsie said, "We got plenty here to last us for a while."

With Elsie's help, Mike and Joey loaded the squeaky pushcart with numerous pallets of canned and dry goods, as well as cases of bottled water. They now had enough food and water to last them for at least a week and plenty more in the pantries Elsie had shown them. As the three made their way back to the cafeteria, Elsie was shaken by the violence strewn about the hallways and splattered across the walls, but Mike and Joey noticed that she never faltered. Elsie was a woman forged in fire and a more than welcome addition to their small group.

● ● ●

The door leading into the main staircase clattered loudly behind Sam as he put his foot on the first step. The sudden metallic clamor shattered the silence entombed within the staircase and caused Sam to jump up the next two steps in surprise. Alice and Hector turned around with half smiles cracking their weary faces.

"You ok?" Alice asked with a chuckle.

Sam rapidly nodded, "Yeah, yeah. I'm good."

The three were carefully making their way towards the second floor of the school to, as Hector put it, "check for survivors," but both Alice and Sam knew that Hector was equally as interested in searching out the non-living as the living. No one believed that Hector actually enjoyed killing zombies; in fact, an expression of deep sadness clouded his face every time he did, but everyone knew that safety was his first concern and that meant clearing out the zombies.

The plan was a relatively simple one; they would quickly search through the upstairs classrooms and then make their way down the opposing stairs and to the Nurse's Office, located adjacent to the doors. Once they reached the Nurse's Office, they would search out any medical supplies that would be useful and then get back to the gym to regroup with everyone. The simplicity of the plan filled Alice with unease; nothing was ever as easy as it seemed and that sure as hell had been multiplied exponentially since the dead had risen to eat the living. But Alice also knew what doubt could do to a group, especially one as tenuously held together as hers, so she muted her concerns, gripped her weighted towel tighter and pushed forward up the stairs.

Immediately upon exiting, Hector was blind-sided by a zombie. Fortunately, it was one of the slower ones that simply shambled around looking for something to eat and not one of the more motivated ones that they had seen in the Commons or Gym.

"Maldito zombi," Hector gritted as he pushed it away from himself and into the corner. The zombie thudded into the wall and slumped onto its backside like a toddler learning to stand and walk. Hector quickly split the zombie's skull with a blow from his wrench, and by the time Sam and Alice realized what was happening, Hector was already cleaning off his weapon on the zombie's stained dress pants.

"Holy crap," Sam whispered, "I didn't even see that one."

Hector shrugged, "We gotta be more careful. I was lucky it was one of the dumb ones. If it had been like some of the others we'd have had a problem."

Nodding, Alice added, "Yeah. Well we'll take whatever luck the world's got left to offer. The Shamblers seem easy enough to deal with." She motioned towards the corpse in the corner.

"One at a time, sure," Hector replied, "But a group of those, what did you call them?"

"Shamblers," Alice replied.

"Shamblers, huh? Well a group of Shamblers would be even more dangerous than those ones we saw last night," Hector cautioned, "Many more mouths to worry about."

The upstairs classrooms were largely empty. The sun had not yet fully risen, so the darkness was thicker and painted everything in strange, distorted shades of gray. As they checked the last classroom before the staircase, Sam gasped when he saw a tall figure looming silently in the corner of the room. Rushing forward he released a stifled battle cry and brought his broomstick squarely down on top of the figure's head, collapsing it to the floor.

The dry bones of the model skeleton rattled loudly as they settled into a disjointed pile at Sam's feet. He jumped slightly as Hector rushed over to help.

"I think you killed him my friend," Hector chuckled, "Yup, killed him dead."

Alice laughed softly from the far corner of the classroom, trying hard not to embarrass Sam.

"Better safe than sorry?" Sam offered and everyone nodded in agreement.

Closing the door into the second staircase, Sam was far more careful not to allow the door to bang loudly. Immediately after the door quietly clicked shut, Sam was grateful that he had remembered to use caution.

Alice was about to whisper something, but Hector quickly held his index finger over his lips and tugged his ear. Everyone froze in place and listened. Somewhere in the pool of darkness that swelled around the bottom of the staircase, the group could hear at least one set of heavy steps shuffling through the gloom. The emergency doors located behind the stairs cast a dim light that just barely made the figures visible. There at the bottom of the stairs, were the remains of what looked to have been a student before it was greedily consumed. At least two zombies were pointlessly shuffling back and forth, having not yet pushed the door to free themselves. The remains of the student had been completely picked over. A few tattered shreds of skin and cloth still adorned the chewed body and a few random clumps of blood-matted hair still remained atop the mostly skeletal face, but otherwise, all bits of edible flesh and organ had been consumed, leaving behind little more than a puddle and pile that used to be a person.

Hector leaned close to Alice and Sam, "There's gotta be more down there. There's no way one or two of those things could eat that much, even in a night."

A troubling thought crossed Sam's mind, "What if there's another of those things that Chris and Ronnie saw in the Commons? They said it was eating a lot."

"I know," Alice whispered, "But from what you guys said, that thing had gouged its eyes out, so it must have been going off of smell and sound."

"Ok?" Sam said, not quite following Alice's line of thought.

"Which means if another of those was in here," Alice shuddered, "It would already know about us and I don't think it'd be waiting. The Shamblers seem to go off of sight mainly, and since we haven't been attacked yet, that's gotta be what's down there."

"Yeah," Hector agreed, "But who knows how many?"

Everyone hesitated for a few seconds, not really sure of what to do next.

"We can go back the other way and work our way over," Alice offered, but Hector shook his head.

"We're going to have to deal with whatever is down there sooner or later, so we might as well handle it now," he replied.

An obscurely lit outline moved in halting steps towards the direction of the group. It stopped, groaned loudly and slowly began to look around, it seemed aware that something else had entered the stairwell, but unsure of what. Sam stepped forward.

"I've got an idea for this one, but be ready cuz the rest are gonna be coming," he whispered, and then lay flat against the floor, peering through the railing. Hector and Alice nodded, not quite sure of what Sam's plan was.

Being on the landing of the second floor only put the group about ten feet above the zombies and Sam, sooner or later the Shamblers would figure out they were up there and begin clambering clumsily up the stairs. Sam wanted to use this to their advantage, but figured getting rid of one Shambler beforehand was probably a good move.

From his prone position, Sam watched the Shambler waver back and forth, trying to place the slight noises it had picked up on. Sam slipped one arm through the rails and with the other passed himself, his broomstick and paint scraper. The previous night Hector had sharpened the edge of the scraper until it cut his finger as he ran it across them, and Sam planned on putting that to good use.

With both arms through the bars, Sam raised the makeshift spear high above his head and let out an earsplitting whistle. The Shambler immediately snapped its stiff neck upwards and glared at Sam through hazy, chalky eyes. A loud moan echoed through the stairwell and other sets of heavy feet could be heard dragging through the gloom behind the stairs. Sam did not wait for the Shambler to move, and brought the point of the scrapper down full force into the left socket of the zombie. He felt it connect and split bone, but the Shambler stayed on its feet. The powerful reverberation through the handle caused Sam to lose his grip.

Seemingly unaware of the long spear protruding from its face, the zombie turned to make its way towards the stairs, but the broom handle was caught between two of the rails and banged loudly as it tried to turn one way or another unsuccessfully. The bouncing and dancing of the broom handle reminded Sam of the fishing line during a summer spent at the lake with his dad and Mike.

"Grab it!" Hector yelled, realizing there was no longer a need to whisper. He and Alice took positions at the top of the stairs, just as the first of six Shamblers rounded the corner.

Sam's hands flailed, trying to grab hold of the handle, but the zombie's shaking was making it difficult. The zombie paused for a moment, as if to consider its next course of action and Sam capitalized upon the momentary immobility, and wrapped both hands firmly around the broomstick. Once again aware of its predicament, the zombie began twisting, but Sam had taken control of its head, which left it with little control.

Hanging over the railing, Sam twisted the zombie to the left and right, banging it into the walls, but not really causing any damage. He turned to see how Hector and Alice were doing and watched them bludgeon the first of the hoard that was slowly closing in on them. The first Shambler had been walking ahead of the others, as if designated point and had been easy enough to handle, but Sam knew the next three, so closely grouped together, would be far more difficult for Hector and Alice to dispatch.

Suddenly, the broom handle lurched forward and Sam was dragged halfway over the railing. He dangled precariously for a few seconds, flapping his arms and trying to regain his balance, but the zombie below turned suddenly, whipping the broom handle in a wide arc and catching Sam on the side of the face. Alice and Hector watched in horror as Sam tumbled over the railing.

Falling, even such a short distance, seemed to stretch out and expand for Sam. The few feet that he traveled were accomplished in mere seconds, but to Sam it felt endless. The wondering about survival, the promise of pain and the knowledge of what waited below for him overwhelmed his mind and the conscious regard for time was erased.

As Sam considered that perhaps hanging over the railing had been a bad idea in the first place, he came plummeting down on top of the Shambler that eagerly looked up with a gaping hungry maw. The fact that the zombie had been looking up turned out to be Sam's first bit of luck, because as he painfully collided with the zombie's upper body he heard a nauseating crunch and felt its head whip back, as if in a car accident. Groaning flooded into Sam's ears and filled him with dread before he realized it was his own, and shakily pulled himself from the crumpled pile of Shambler that lay beneath him. Fortunately, his fall seemed to have finished what Sam had started with his spear and the Shambler was no longer moving.

Suddenly, the real world and all of his sense came flooding back to Sam, and he could hear Hector and Alice battling through the horde and attempting to reach them. Sam wanted to scream out, let his friends know that he was ok, but knew that would draw the other Shamblers and leave him cornered, so quietly he placed his foot on the chest of the twice-killed Shambler and pulled his spear from where it was securely lodged in an orbital socket. The spear came loose, but much to Sam's dismay, it did so in two pieces. His fall had broken both the zombie's neck and the handle of his spear.

Alice and Hector valiantly swung at the heads of the Shamblers that were descending upon them, but with them so closely grouped together, it was difficult to hit such a small target. Each swing landed, but they were falling upon the jostling bodies of the zombies and were essentially useless. Alice struggled to swing the weighted towel again and again, each time bringing it high over her head and towards the mob. Hector kicked out repeatedly, trying to knock some of the zombies away so that he could get a clear shot, but each kick only moved the front zombie a few inches back before it was pushed forward again by the one behind.

"Get out of here!" Hector yelled to Alice, but she violently shook her head.

"No," she screamed, "I'm not leaving you and I'm not leaving Sam!" One of the front Shamblers dove forward, but Alice sidestepped its clumsy attack and it collided with the step, cracking a few of its front teeth. It picked itself up from the floor and resumed its march forward.

Coming around behind, Sam could see that the Shamblers were closely packed together and could also see that Hector and Alice were beginning to tire, while the zombies, which had previously been held at bay, now slowly advanced up the stairs as Alice and Hector backpedaled towards the doors. Tightening his grip on the two broken pieces of his weapon, Sam crept silently up the stairs.

The horde was closely packed in as they jostled and grabbed for Alice and Hector, but one had been forced towards the back and was blindly trying to grab over the head of its companions, completely unaware of Sam behind it.

Sam had tucked the half of his broomstick, which still had the scraper attached, into his belt. With both hands, he raised the splintered end high over his head and brought the pointed end into the soft spot right behind the Shambler's knee. The flesh and thick tendons resisted, but Sam put his full weight behind the push and drove the pointed broom handle straight through and out the other side. Thick black jelly oozed from around where the broomstick had been driven through its knee, but beyond that, the zombie showed no sense of pain or discomfort from what Sam had just done. The sudden push caught the Shambler's attention and it slowly attempted to turn around. The stick having gone through the connective ligaments of its knee, left the zombie wobbling on one leg with little mobility and Sam feared that gravity might take over and it would just fall on him.

Before the zombie was able to turn completely, Sam grabbed both railings, reared his foot back and kicked the end of the handle that was still exposed with all his might. The crack of both bone and hardened wood reverberated throughout the staircase. Even the Shambler seemed to look down in confusion at the fact that its leg was facing the wrong direction. Sam leapt out of the way, as the crippled zombie rolled down the stairs and collapsed into a pile at the bottom.

With one Shambler temporarily dealt with, Sam turned his attention towards the four that remained. The noise and commotion had caught their attention, as Sam had hoped, and now they were turning to lumber towards him. They stumbled to get past one and then the other, but the narrowness of the stairs jammed them up, leaving them defenseless from behind.

Hector and Alice were shocked when one of the zombies suddenly tumbled down the stairs, like a hastily thrown bag of laundry, and even move shocked when they saw Sam leap from behind it. He had drawn the other four Shamblers away and gotten them to turn their attention towards him, which left the backs of their skulls completely open. Without a word, Hector and Alice set about splitting the two nearest skulls. The Shamblers collapsed on the stairs and their limp bodies wiggled a few steps down before an arm or leg became tangled in the rails and stopped them. One of the two remaining zombies turned to see what the sudden, hollow noise behind it was, only to have Alice collapse the front of its face with her tightly wrapped weight.

The one remaining Shambler had been too far for Hector or Alice to reach and with the other tangled bodies impeding them, they could not assist Sam. The zombie continued to trudge closer and closer to Sam. "Looks like he's mine," Sam mumbled and reached behind his back to retrieve the remaining end of his weapon. The zombie lurched forward, as if caught off guard by its own motion, and stumbled towards Sam. Arms outstretched and tripping, Sam thought the zombie looked like a clumsy child, but quickly dismissed that thought and held out the sharpened edge of the scrapper at a dangerous angle. His arms recoiled as the full weight of the zombie's body fell upon the edge and drove it deeply into the stringy flesh surrounding its windpipe. Sam had almost completely decapitated the disgusting thing, but felt the hardened resistance of the spinal column push back against the scraper.

Sam felt himself becoming light headed and anger suddenly surged through him. He viciously whipped the weapon back and forth inside the zombie's neck cavity, flaying flesh and spattering the walls with chunks of viscous gore and loose strings of flesh. The Shambler still pushed forward and grasped at Sam. The rage that had been unleashed was still burning fiercely within him, and Sam released the handle and grabbed the zombie by the spattered brown leather belt that encircled its waist. With his grip tight, Sam rushed forward in an upward sweeping arc and planted his shoulder into the zombie's gut while pulling the weight of it forward.

The zombie's head bobbled from side to side with no real amount of flesh left to hold the spinal column rigid. As it went over Sam's shoulder, the zombie's head was flung violently backwards only to crash into the concrete stairs, where it was split and its contents scattered across the floor.

The zombie that Sam had previously crippled writhed on floor, but was unable to rise to a standing position. Grasping the stairs, it began to haul its husk up the first few stairs and even though Sam saw it, he could not find it in himself to care or react. His eyes suddenly began to burn and before he could stop himself, he was crying and heavily dropped onto the stair upon which he stood.

Realizing something was wrong, Hector leapt the final stairs and landed next to the crippled zombie. Placing his heavy booted foot in between the Shambler's shoulder blades, Hector pushed its body flat onto the floor and quickly delivered a devastating blow to the back of its head. The Shambler finally stopped moving. Hector turned and looked back up the stairs to see Sam and Alice sitting next to one and other on the stairs. Sam had his head on his knees and Hector could tell from the way his shoulders were moving that he was crying. Alice had her arm wrapped around Sam and was pulling his head against her.

"I gotta check something out there," Hector lied, "You two give this spot one more look and meet me out there when you're done," and he slipped through the doors to wait quietly in the hallway.

Alice pulled Sam towards her. At first, he resisted and pulled away, but then allowed himself to be drawn into her. It was strange, less than two days ago, Sam and Alice had been fostering a secret love for one another, and now they found themselves embracing on a staircase littered with zombie corpses, but in some weird way it felt well practiced, almost instinctual.

"It's ok," Alice said softy, "None of us enjoy this. It makes us all angry."

Sam shook his head, "It's not that. That's not it at all."

"What is it then Sam?" Alice asked gently, "I know the past few days have been insane and we're all coming apart at the seams. Honestly, I'm amazed it took you this long. I'm surprised all the crying last night didn't keep you up."

"I just got so damn angry at those things," Sam replied, "I just lost it. I wanted to rip them apart. I wasn't even thinking when I was doing it, but then all of a sudden, I kept seeing my mom and dad instead of that thing." Sam pointed to the bottom of the stairs. "What if they got eaten or even worse, are like one of them now? Then what? Am I going to have to do that to my own parents? I'm not sure I could do it, but I could never just leave them like that."

Alice shuddered. The thought of what she might find in her house had been haunting her as well. "I've been thinking about that a lot too," she said, "I think that if we're going to check our houses we need to make sure that we're bringing someone else inside." She paused, "And if any Shamblers are there, then whoever's house it is goes outside and everyone else deals with it. I think we all need to make that agreement and stick to it." The thought that this agreement could mean that someone had to crush the heads of her parents was not lost on Alice, but she had decided before she even said it, that she would do it herself if she had to. No one she loved was going to spend an eternity wandering around until they had become so fetid and rotten that they could not move anymore. As graphic and unsettling as the idea was, Alice knew it was the right thing to do. It was a final act of mercy and love.

The anger had abated and Sam shook slightly, but quickly pulled himself together and stood up. "Thanks," he said offering Alice his hand, "I'm glad to know I'm not the only one that's on the verge of going crazy."

Alice laughed, but every word was gilded with sorrow, "It's not any of us that are going crazy, it's the entire freaking world. Everything is upside-down and we keep trying to figure the picture out, but I'm not sure we can. Logic and reason don't apply anymore. We just gotta keep doing the best we can."

With nothing more to be said, Sam and Alice moved down the stairs, over the corpses and through the doors. Hector simply nodded to both of them as they came through, but comically lifted his eyebrows when he saw that they were holding hands. Sam and Alice immediately blushed and released each other's hand, as if they had touched a hot stove.

"Come on," Hector laughed, "The Nurse's Office is right over there." The three moved in a tight group towards the door. The Nurse's Office had no exterior windows and was completely dark. A small amount of golden sunlight cut jagged lines through the partially open venetian blinds, but nothing was easily discernible within the office.

"I don't see anything moving in there. Let's just go in and get whatever we can," Sam said, unsure of his own words.

Using his master key, Hector slowly opened the door. Everyone's next breath was caught in their throats, anticipating the sudden rush of some horrible creature or the slow ambling promise of violence that the Shamblers carried. But nothing came. The light that broke through the doorway illuminated an empty office that appeared to be as it would any other day of the week.

"The nurse had been called down to the office before the Lock Down," Hector explained, "She must have locked the door and left. We should be safe in here." He took a tentative step into the office, but both Sam and Alice noticed that Hector had yet to relax his wrench. "It looks ok," he said and the other two entered.

The office was deathly silent, but fortunately was empty. Hector's summation of the Nurse's actions must have been correct because the group encountered no people, living or dead, inside.

"There's a bunch of Band-Aides, gauze and stuff over here," Sam said, opening one of the cabinets. Hector tossed him a small blue teachers' union duffle bag he had found under the Nurse's desk and Sam quickly dumped the supplies into it. "We need to find some medicine or antibiotics too, Band-Aides aren't really gonna cut it."

Alice had found a locked cabinet and was busily trying to pry the doors open, but was making little progress.

"Let me help," Hector offered and slipped the handle of his wrench underneath one of the handles. He forcefully pulled back and ripped the locked handle clear through the cheaply made door.

"I guess that'll do," Alice smiled and peered into the dim interior. There were numerous small orange and brown bottles organized in neat rows, each with a different label, student and diagnosis. There was an abundance of student medications for things like depression, ADHD, chronic pain and numerous other afflictions fretted over by hypochondriac suburbanite parents, who were concerned enough to have their children diagnosed and medicated, but never enough to make sure that they were home to see that the drugs were taken properly. But Alice figured that was just another parental responsibility abdicated to the schools and passed off under the guise of tax dollar accountability.

Alice surveyed all the bottles, "My god, there's stuff in here for some pretty serious shit." She turned a bottle of chemotherapy drugs over in her hands. Sam looked over Alice's shoulder.

"Jeez how can you even pronounce half these drugs, let alone know what they're used for?" Sam asked in astonishment.

"Well some of them I can't and don't," Alice admitted, "But my dad is..." Alice's voice caught in her throat and she swallowed hard, "My dad was...was a pharmaceutical engineer. He had tons of books about this stuff in our house and was always telling me about some new drug that hit the market. And every other Saturday he would make me go to these stupid Future Doctors of America meetings where they'd make us do reports on this kind of crap. He really wanted me to be a doctor, I guess."

"Is that what you wanted?" Sam asked, "To be a doctor?"

"I was never really sure," Alice said, "But at least taking the MCAT's doesn't really seem that scary anymore, and I'm pretty sure the lists to get into med school just got a lot shorter." She chuckled dryly. Sam tried to laugh, but the noise that came out was more of a wet rasp.

Hector came out of the back room carrying a case of saline bottles with a small box of insulin gently sliding back and forth on top. "There's more supplies back there," he said, "But I think we should carry what we can and leave the rest. If I lock the doors it shouldn't be a problem." The other two nodded and piled the rest of the pill containers into the duffle bag. Sam hefted it onto his shoulder.

"Back the way we came?" He asked and they started towards the stairs. As Hector turned to lock the door, Alice leaned over to Sam.

"Could you please hold this," she whispered. Sam turned expecting her to hand him her weighted towel. What he found was her hand outstretched with splayed fingers and a coy smile cracking the edge of her mouth.

● ● ●

For two days, there had been no sightings of survivors. A few zombies ambled around the grounds of Montville, but after a few sweeps it seemed that Hector, Sam and Alice had cleared most from the main building. Everyone knew they would have to eventually deal with the ones outside and attempt to close the gates leading onto school ground, but for the time being, everyone sat in dull food coma.

The whirl of the hand crank on Hector's hand-held radio was the only sound audible throughout the gym. Everyone had gathered around as he vigorously turned the tiny handle and charged the little box. With baited breath, he turned the dial. There was nothing, only the venomous hiss of silence and the void.

"So nothing new there," Chris said flatly, "We're still on our own. We knew that." Hector ignored Chris's cynicism and kept scrolling through channels. Nothing on FM or AM, even the Emergency Broadcast System had been silenced.

"That's an emergency radio right?" Ronnie asked. Everyone turned to face him.

"Yeah," Hector replied, "I usually just use it to listen to music and talk radio. I got the stupid thing during a fundraiser for the public station. Stupid thing never had good reception."

"Can I see it please?" Ronnie asked and Hector handed him the radio. Ronnie turned it over in his hands and began examining the switches. He quickly gave the handle a few rotations and flipped a switch on the side.

"...anyone...boxed in...Rangers Unit 87..."

Everyone's eyes went wide and their mouths hung agape.

"That sounds like a military broadcast," Ms. Kozlov whispered, as if afraid to speak too loudly and miss something.

"It's an emergency radio, so it can pick up locally broadcast government signals," Ronnie stated matter-of-factly. He kept turning the hand crank, "We need to get higher to get the signal better." Mike grabbed the small radio and quickly climbed the closed rows of bleachers until he reached the top. He turned the volume to its highest setting and pressed the radio against the window.

"*Repeat...Rangers Unit 87 is boxed in. We need immediate withdrawal. Anyone respond please, anyone respond. We are bunkered at the Municipal Center, but cannot push through the crowds. Vehicles are out of commission, food and ammo are low. Please respond. Over.*" The message repeated three more times before anyone else spoke.

"Sounds like a recording," Amelia spoke breaking the silence, "Could be no one there and just running on a loop."

"Or it could be that there's still some soldiers there," Elsie retorted, "At least there's a chance that someone else is out there."

Mike had climbed down and handed the radio back to Hector. "They're in the Muncipial Building, that's five miles from here. Might as well be in Antarctica. There's no way to get over there and you heard them, they're surrounded."

"Everyone must have gone there for a FEMA shelter or something," Chris said, "Can you imagine how many freaking zombies are there if there was any sort of medical shelter set up? Plus all the noise the guns must have made. I gotta agree with Mike, there's no way to get over there."

A debate broke out dividing the group over who thought it was worth a shot to at least try, and those who felt it was too risky. Hector had remained silent since hearing the radio transmission and appeared to be deep in thought. The arguments and reasons of the group sounded little more than static to him.

"Hector! Hey Hector!" Alice said waving her hand in front of his face, "What do you think?"

Hector shook his head, "Sorry, I was just thinking. If there's anyone still there it might be worth getting them or at the very least getting their supplies."

"Look, we were all ready to rush out and check our houses," Sam said, "Who's to say that they're any safer than the

Municipal Building? If we're going to go out there, we should at least try."

Nodding Hector added, "I don't like the idea better than anyone else, but Sam is right. And I think I know how we can do it."

● ● ●

Chris and Ronnie had already elected to find some sort of vehicle to make the journey to check houses. Initially, they had intended to go back to the Auto Shop, but Hector's suggestion had steered them towards the Transportation Building on the other side of the school grounds to retrieve something a little safer.

Hector, Ronnie and Chris stood just outside the doors of the gym, recently opened with Hector's Master Key.

"We'll stay right here and make sure the doors are clear when you get back," Mike said, and the rest of the group created a defensive half-circle in front of the double doors. Elsie remained inside with the few students who had previously been wandering around stupefied and worked on organizing food supplies, but even Ms. Kozlov joined the group. The gym teacher was bruised and battered; still winced when she stretched the scabbed gashes on her back, but she was ready to do her part. She brandished a club she had created by screwing three two-pound plates to the end of a bicep curl bar. Sam had followed suit and created one to replace his spear. He secretly hoped that no one would notice that he only had two plates compared to Ms. Kozlov's three.

Hector's plan was to cut across the back soccer fields and head straight for the Transportation garage. They would quickly deal with any zombies they came across and just keep a beeline towards the garage. Once there, they would find whatever vehicles had keys and bring them back. The others had offered to go with them, but Hector refused saying that they could move faster and safer in a smaller group.

The sun had yet to truly break the rise of hills outlining the horizon, but a deep purpled light had already begun to creep across the land and push away the darkness. Streaks of fiery orange and yellow cut ragged tears in the heavy gray clouds of dusk, but Hector had felt this was the best time to attempt to cross towards the garage. If the Shamblers worked mainly off sight and sound, as Alice had proposed, then they would have a difficult time discerning shadows in the weak early morning light. Everyone hoped if they moved slowly that they would not draw the attention of any of the Shamblers that were wandering the school grounds. No one wanted to talk about what they would do if any of the other creatures, that Ronnie had begun calling Stalkers, happened to be out there.

After having been wished "good luck," Ronnie, Chris and Hector set out towards the soccer fields. In reality, the trip was little more than a half-acre walk, easily traversed in minutes, but it felt like miles through hostile territory and everyone was more nervous than they wanted to admit.

As they got a few steps away from the gym doors a voice softly called out, "Wait, I'm going too." It was Amelia.

"No," Hector said, "I mean, no thanks. You're better off here."

Amelia held a weighted towel, similar to Alice and Joey's in her hands. "I'm going," she stated empathically, "You need a fourth person to watch your backs."

"It's not a good idea," Chris said, "You were pretty shook up a few days ago. Probably not a good idea to go back out there so soon." He could not explain why he felt the need to protect her, but he had felt responsible for Amelia ever since he had pulled her out from under the car; more than that, he had felt attracted to her, but chided himself for thinking of such stupid things when there were far more pressing issues at hand. Still he had found himself finding excuses to spend time with Amelia or always seemed to locate an open spot next to her during meal times. And as much as Chris tried not to overanalyze things, he could not help but notice that Amelia always smiled when he looked her way.

"I'm fine," Amelia said firmly, "There's no point hiding. The world is what it is and we gotta deal with it. So I'm going."

"It would be better to have someone looking in each direction," Ronnie commented, "Safety in numbers. The CDC report..."

Chris chuckled, "Ok, ok Ronnie I get it. You're both against us and we're not gonna win." A serious look crossed his face. "You sure?" He asked Amelia.

"As much as I can be," Amelia responded and fell into place beside Chris.

The group hit the small rise that led up to the soccer field. Thus far, there had been no sign of Shambler, Stalker or whatever other horrible living nightmare was lurking around. As they came over the rise, everyone heard Amelia gasp. There in the middle of the field was the tangled mob that had chased her through the parking lot.

Chris reached out to pull Amelia behind him, but she shook off his hand and spun to face him.

"I knew what I was getting into," she said coldly, "Let's deal with this crap and move on."

The tangled group of Shamblers in tattered police uniforms, seemed to have not noticed the small group working through the shadows of the high metal bleachers towards them. The large intestine that encircled them like a revolting hula-hoop had tightened as it dried in the sun. The elasticity of the intestine having diminished prevented the Shamblers from making any sort of progress in one direction or another, because the minute one would move it would pull the others tumbling down on top of itself.

"They don't look like they have much maneuverability," Ronnie commented.

After observing their clumsy movements for a few minutes, Chris said, "If I come from one side and get the nearest one to move, it'll trip the others and then you can come from behind and get them while they're down." No one liked the idea of Chris using himself as bait, but they had to get past the small mob and had to admit that his plan seemed the most practical. Chris remained in the shadows of the bleachers as the other three back- tracked and snuck around the small rise to get behind the zombies.

Silently counting down from three to one, Chris took a deep breath and stepped out only twenty feet from the nearest Shambler. It had gotten the intestine looped around its neck like a gruesome noose. The originally viscous gore that coated the intestine had dried, leaving large, gummy chunks coating the neck and face of the Shambler with cakey bits of things never meant to be on the outside of a human body.

Chris tried to think of something impressive or threatening to say to draw the attention of the mob, but all catch phrases seem to elude him and he simple whistled loudly followed by a "Yoo-hoo!"

The Shambler nearest to Chris unleashed an unearthly groan and took a few heavy steps towards him. Chris watched as the zombie stiffly extended its arms and hungrily gnashed its teeth. The heavy rope of intestine that looped around the neck of the zombie tightened as the other members of the mob became aware of Chris's presence and began trying to circle him. But with each step, the intestine pulled tighter and tighter, eventually reaching its capacity and refusing to yield any more elasticity. Comically, the nearest zombie was yanked backwards and tumbled headfirst into its nearest compatriot; throughout the entire plunge, the Shambler remained seemingly unaware of the fact that it was falling and it dully continued to grasp at the handfuls of air suspended before it. The sudden motion of the one zombie falling brought down the others on top of it, creating a writhing, moaning mass of tangled, bottomless hunger.

Seizing the moment, Amelia dashed over the small threshold and sprinted towards the collapsed pile of zombies at Chris's feet. Hector and Ronnie ran to catch up with her, but she was easily out distancing them with each stride. Chris looked up in time to glimpse a feral look burning in Amelia's eyes; this was personal for her. This was about revenge, about taking back the power that she had lost in the parking lot only days before. Chris knew better than to try and stop her, but as he felt the first fist of stiff fingers close tightly around the cuff of his jeans, he knew he could not just leave the kill to Amelia alone; there was no time for that. The zombies were quickly getting back to their feet and Amelia could be overwhelmed.

An equally wild energy coursed through Chris as he thought about Amelia becoming tangled in the mess before him, and he angrily pulled the hammer that was securely tucked into his belt. With one powerful downward blow, he crushed the right side of the Shambler's cranium, sending bits of blackened, jellied gray matter spattering across his boots and the faces of the other zombies. As he lifted his eyes from the ruined zombie at his feet, Chris saw Amelia leap a good four feet into the air and bring the weight plate crashing down into the middle of the back of the nearest Shambler. A crack louder than a gunshot rang out from the site of her attack and the zombie crumbled before her, but as she went to step over it and attack the next, its hand grasped the baggy sweatpants she was wearing and pulled her towards the ground.

Chris immediately went into action, leaping over the Shambler he had killed and bringing both of his heavy boot heels down on the head of the one that grabbed at Amelia. The Shambler's head split and spilled its contents across the ground like a rotted melon, but the sudden divide of the skull caused Chris to lose his balance and come crashing to the ground. His left ankle twisted at an unnatural angle, but Amelia was pretty sure it had not broken. Years of dance had made her privy to many twisted, sprained or broken limbs.

The remaining four Shamblers immediately focused their attention upon the easier meal and began dragging themselves and two dead companions towards Chris. Grabbing the tacky rope of intestine, Amelia quickly coiled it around her forearm like she was rolling a garden hose. The texture and smell of the thing made her eyes water and stomach churn, but she pushed those feelings down and focused on keeping the Shamblers away from Chris. With a good three feet of large intestine twisted around her arm, Amelia pulled violently back and stamped her foot down on the remaining slack. Chris watched wide-eyed as she held the four zombies in place and Hector and Ronnie quickly dispatched them.

Amelia extended her hand to help Chris from the ground and then realized it was slick with clotted blood, and quickly wiped both hands in the dewy early fall grass. Chris was still wide-eyed after having seen Amelia wrangle the four zombies with an intestinal lasso, but accepted her help up the second time it was offered.

"You ok?" Amelia asked, "It looks like you twisted your ankle, but nothing major."

Rotating his ankle a few times, Chris replied, "Yeah, its ok." And then added, "That was f-ing nuts."

Amelia shuddered, thinking about what she had actually just done, "I guess, maybe we're even now? It was pretty disgusting, but it worked and honestly I don't think there's any place left in the world to be girly or anything."

"Does this mean you're gonna start trying to take a leak standing up?" Chris joked and Amelia gave him a light shove.

The rest of the journey towards the garage was made in silence. Shadows of smaller groups of Shamblers could be seen moving outside the high wrought iron fence that circled the Montville School grounds. Embracing their overwhelming sense of arrogance, the school board had attempted to make school grounds appear as collegiate as possible, which meant brick pillars and a heavy gated, black iron fence. No one said so, but the entire group was now in full support of the school board having done so.

The garage was little more than a large steel hanger fronted by two large bay doors, one of which hung slightly ajar. Inside the group could hear something knocking around, a pointless clattering of paint cans and other materials.

Leaning against the door and attempting to peer through the darkness, Hector whispered to Ronnie, "You and Chris pull the doors open and I'll rush whatever is in there, catch it off guard." Everyone nodded.

The doors slid open easily enough on their heavily greased tracks and Hector rushed into the garage, but nothing was there. Evidence of someone or something having gone through the maintenance supplies was scattered all over the shop, but the culprit appeared absent.

"Be careful," Ronnie cautioned, "Could be a Stalker trying to ambush us. I definitely heard something banging around in here." The crash of an empty gas can caused everyone to involuntarily leap a few inches into the air and turn to face the noise.

"Hello?" A timid voice called out softly.

"Who's there?" Hector responded, "Come on out." Slowly two children emerged from where they were tucked away behind some supplies.

"What the heck were you doing back there?" Chris asked in disbelief.

A short blond boy stepped forward. He could not have been much older than nine or ten. "We ran from our school when the monsters came, but there were more out here, so we hid."

Amelia knelt down to the child's level, "What's your name sweetheart? I'm Amelia and that's Chris, Ronnie and Hector." Everyone waved for their respective introduction.

"Erick," the blond boy responded, "And that's my little sister Emily." The small girl waved from behind her brother and offered an unsure smile.

"What grade are you in kiddo?" Hector asked from where he leaned against one of the workbenches.

"I'm in third and Em is in kindergarten," Erick's eyes grew wide and watery, but he took a deep breath and continued, "My teacher got sick, a lot of them did." He covered Emily's ears, as if she were unaware of the situation, "She started eating my friends, so I took the extra key by the door and escaped." He released Emily's ears and continued, "Then I snuck down the hall to Em's class. Her teacher was..." he hesitated, "She was sick and asleep. I tried to get the other little kids to come too, but they were scared and then the other sick people ran in. Em and I got out through the back door." Emily began crying softly and Amelia moved to hug her, but Erick stepped in front of her, a hard look on his face. He hugged his little sister and  whispered her ear, "It's ok Emmy. It's ok." Amelia nodded and stepped back. She understood that Erick was not ready to trust them and that all he was doing was protecting his little sister.

"So you're telling me you ran all the way here from the K-4 building?" Chris asked.

"That's all the way on the other side of the property," Ronnie added for clarification.

Erick looked at both of them, still hugging Emily, and nodded. There was something hard in his expression, while the color of his eyes was light; there was nothing child-like left in them. Whatever else he had seen over the last few days had robbed Erick of his right to be a child. Chris marveled at the inner strength this little kid seemed to possess, but also was deeply saddened by the fact that he had needed it. This whole mess was hard enough for adults, let alone for a ten year old.

"Why didn't you try and go home or get into one of the other schools?" Amelia asked.

"We looked in the windows and saw more monsters," Emily answered in a halting tear-choked voice. Then she pushed gently away from Erick, "I wanted to go home to see Mom, but Erick said 'no,' cuz there was more of those monsters outside the fence."

"We couldn't go," Erick pleaded with his little sister, "It's too far of a walk Emmy." His sister sighed heavily, but did not continue arguing.

"You made the right choice little man," Chris said, "It ain't safe out there and you made a good move hiding in here. You saved your sister's life. That's all that matters right now." Erick smiled grimly, but nodded his head.

Amelia stepped next to Chris, "You two can't stay in here. There's no food, no bathroom and it's not secure. You've gotta come back with us. It's not perfect, but we've got the gym in the high school pretty safe. Please, Erick, just come back with us and then we'll figure out what to do once we're safe again. Just until your mom comes, ok?"

Emily and Erick moved away from the group and tightly huddled to discuss this new option. They were both young and scared and craved the security that came from an adult presence, but Erick was also careful about who to give his trust to and was not going to do anything that might put his sister in danger. But as he knew there was no other real option, there was no way they could stay hidden in the garage, and at least this way if anything did happen to him, Erick knew there would be someone else to take care of Emily. Besides, that Amelia girl seemed nice enough and Erick figured the others were probably ok too.

"Alright," Erick agreed, "We'll go with you, but just until our mom comes to get us." Even Erick knew that what he and Amelia had just agreed to was a boldfaced lie, that their mom was not coming, but he knew that Emily needed to hear that. She was too young to have nothing to put her hope into; so was Erick for that matter, but he had put everything into keeping his sister safe and therefore he let the lie hang out there in the air and bolster what little reserves Emily had left.

A loud bang resounded from the opposite end of the garage and Hector whistled loudly. "Time to choose a ride my friends," he said triumphantly having knocked open the key safe with his wrench.

"There isn't much," Ronnie appraised, "But I think the two Buildings and Grounds vans would be best. They're open in the back and have the protective steel mesh over the windows. That's an added layer of security."

Chris and Amelia agreed and began trying sets of keys until they had opened and started two of the vans that were within the large garage. Ronnie threw open the back door of one of the vans and began loading red plastic cans of gasoline into one. Amelia helped Erick and Emily into the back of the van Chris was driving, and climbed in behind them. As Ronnie climbed into the driver's seat of the other van, Chris noticed that Hector was not inside it. He rolled down the window and yelled, "Hey, where the hell is Hector?"

Ronnie shrugged, "Said there was something out back that he wanted and that he'd meet us in the front."

"Alright," Chris said and shifted the van into gear. As the two vans rolled to a slow stop in front the garage, a loud rumble could be heard working its way around the left side of the garage. Chris and Amelia exchanged unsure glances, unsure of what they were hearing or what Hector had gone to retrieve.

The growl grew louder and louder until Hector emerged from behind the garage, sitting high up in the steel basket that surrounded the controls for the large Caterpillar backhoe that he was clumsily maneuvering around the corner. Chris smiled and shook his head as Hector yelled over the loud diesel engine, "She ain't pretty and she ain't fast, but I figure we might need this lady's muscle." The three vehicles slowly worked their way back to the gym and stationed themselves outside the guarded double doors.

Everyone hooted and applauded when they saw the group returning with the new transportation and the cheering only got louder as Amelia emerged from the back with the two small children. Ms. Kozlov and Elsie quickly ushered them inside to be cleaned and fed. Erick and Emily noticeably relaxed as the two women doted over them. As the rest of the group watched some level of normality being returned to the two small children, none of them could deny that they too felt a small spark of hope flicker deep within the blackened chasm of their daily struggle for survival.

● ● ●

The radio transmission continued consistently for the next few days, but with no way of sending a response, everyone was left pointlessly listening to the looped message again and again. But it never did stop, and as Ronnie pointed out, that meant that someone must be keeping it hooked up to a power source, unless of course as Chris had pointed out, it could be playing over and over because everyone was dead and the Municipal Building simply had not lost power yet. Either way, everyone was hypnotized by the message and would gather around the small survival radio to sit transfixed by the repetitive pleas for help that most certainly was not going to come.

Whether the unit transmitting the message was alive or not, did not really change the plan that everyone had agreed upon over the past few days. They needed to go out there and check their families, and if they were out there anyway, they should swing by the Municipal Building and check on the situation. Best case scenario, they could find a military unit that might be able to offer some assistance or answers and worst case scenario, they would find everyone dead and try to take their supplies anyway.

No one relished the idea of arming children with powerful weapons, but as Chris had pointed out earlier and continued to do so, the old rules no longer applied and running around with crappy makeshift clubs was not going to cut it forever. They needed something more powerful, with greater range and more importantly, the ability to deal with humans, as well as zombies.

The sudden insistence by Chris and Amelia for guns was somewhat disconcerting for the other group members, but after the torches had shown up everyone began to agree. Night watch was a shared duty that alternated between everyone in the group, except for Erick and Emily, but Erick could often be found on the roof with whoever was on post that night anyway, so he ended up sitting watch more consistently than anyone else.

At first, there had been a few weak flames bobbing up and down throughout the carefully planned neighborhoods, and for a while everyone mistakenly wrote them off as small fires, nothing of any real concern. But by the tenth night, the torches had multiplied into a block long serpent with iridescent scales of fire that writhed through the darkened streets.

"Look at that!" Erick exclaimed wide-eyed. Chris and Amelia turned to look where he was pointing and collectively gasped.

"Holy crap," Chris said astonished, "There's gotta be forty, fifty people there!"

Amelia had moved over to the edge of the roof and was leaning forward over the edge in a pointless attempt to get a better view. "What do you think all those people are doing?" As if in response to the question, small groups began breaking off and entering houses. The shadows would emerge soon after and a torch would be hurled through the doorway or window.

The dragon slowly shrank and dimmed, but the flames that raged on either side of the street soon illuminated the darkened neighborhood. A shadowy mob stood in the middle of the road, partially hidden, but their numbers were staggering.

Chris and Amelia exchanged troubled looks and turned back to the scene unfolding a few miles away.

"Do you think they're coming to help?" Erick said excitedly, "Maybe it's help!"

Chris shook his head, "I don't think so buddy. I don't think so." He quickly hurried Erick off the roof and back into the gym to wake the others. Amelia kept post and watched in horror as the mob rejoiced loudly and writhed in the orange-tinged shadows that danced along the edges of the street.

● ● ●

After Chris had woken everyone in the gym, no one was able to go back to sleep. They all climbed the fire ladder at the back of the gym up to the roof and rushed to where Amelia sat with her legs listlessly dangling over the edge. The smell of burned wood hung heavy in the damp early morning air, but the flames had died down and the street was once again shrouded in darkness and obscurity.

"Where'd they go?" Mike asked Amelia, "What the hell is going on?"

Amelia replied plainly, "Both good questions Mike, but I haven't got the slightest idea. One second a huge group of crazy people are burning down an entire block and dancing in the street and the next they just pack it up and shuffle off in the same direction they had come from."

"They were heading that way?" Hector asked, pointing towards the southernmost edge of town, "What's up there? It's just woods and a few farms right?"

Elsie nodded, "Yeah that's all that's really over there."

"And that church at the top of Zion Road," Sam added, "What's it called, The Happy Day Connection or something like that?"

"The Pillar of Zion Communal Church," Ms. Kozlov corrected, "Some kind of born again Christian thing. But why would a church group be out there burning down houses?"

Everyone remained silent for a few moments and considered the question, but no one could formulate an answer that seemed to make any kind of sense. As the sun broke from behind the small mountains that surrounded the eastern edge of Montville, a blinding radiance stretched lazily across the evenly planned blocks and previously meticulously manicured lawns. Slowly everyone was able to take in the full extent of the damage. A full development had been burned to the ground and all that remained to greet the morning rays were the violent angles of twisted building materials and jagged blackened wood. Most of the houses had collapsed in upon themselves and fallen inward into the foundations.

"How would the houses all have fallen the same way?" Chris asked, "That seems impossible."

"That development, I think it's Glenn Knoll," Ronnie answered, "All the houses there are pretty much the same design, so if someone knew where to set the fire, like near the load bearing walls and beams, you could make that happen."

"How'd you know the development," Mike asked.

Ronnie stated flatly, "Cuz that's where I used to live."

A shocked sob caused everyone to turn around quickly. Emily had climbed the ladder and Erick was trying to keep her from coming forward, but she had heard most of the conversation.

"That's where our Mommy lives," Emily sobbed, "What about our Mommy?"

The women moved towards Emily, all wearing the same crestfallen expression, but Hector beat them to her and he swept both her and Erick into his arms.

"I know ninos," Hector whispered to the two children, "There's nothing left for us to do, but it's ok for you to cry. We'll stay here until you're ready." Hector sat cross-legged on the roof and held both of the sobbing children. Erick and Emily buried their faces into Hector's strong shoulders and their bodies shook, completely racked with grief.

"What are we..." Chris began to say, but decided against it and allowed the moment of silence to stretch a few seconds longer.

Hector looked up and a rage equally as destructive as the previous night's fire burned in his eyes, "We go out and check the rest of the houses today. Make sure all the vehicles are filled." Mike, Sam, Chris and Ronnie nodded and quickly moved off the roof to check the three vehicles. The remaining members of the group remained silent on the roof. Each pained sob that escaped from the children shredded into their souls and filled them with questions that no one dared asked, but all of them shared. What if there were worse things than zombies to worry about? They were bad enough, but monsters acting like monsters made a certain level of sense. Explaining the monstrous behavior of other humans seemed far more complicated and terrifying.

● ● ●

The vans rolled slowly along, engulfed in the acrid clouds belched out from behind Hector's backhoe. They had already checked most of the houses and found them to be empty or inhabited only by a random Shambler or two. Following their plan, no one entered their house alone and if they did find a Shambler, the resident left and the others quickly took care of it. Erick and Emily had stayed behind at the gym with Elsie and Ms. Kozlov; none of them had any family to check on. Erick and Emily's mother was nowhere to be found and the entire neighborhood was little more than cinders and ashes, so going looking for her seemed like a pointless endeavor. Ms. Kozlov and Elsie had both left their families behind to come to America, and there was no way of knowing what was going on in the next town, let alone another country, so they had offered to stay behind with the children. Ronnie, even knowing that his house had been burned down, insisted on coming. He wanted to see what was out there and compare it to projections in the CDC report. It struck everyone as odd that he was not more upset. Ronnie had snuck off to cry for a few moments, but quickly returned and seemed to be treating the entire situation in a cold analytical sense and bounced along in the seat next to Chris.

"The world is crazy," Ronnie stated, "It was before any of this happened, so why should I be surprised when crazy things happen?"

"I know man," Chris agreed, "But what about your parents? Aren't you worried?"

Instead of answering, Ronnie responded with a question, "Aren't you? Worried about your parents, I mean."

Staring forward into the swirling haze washing over the hood of the van, Chris shook his head, "Nah, I mean, I don't want anything bad to happen to my mom or anything, but she was a friggin' zombie long before any of this shit happened. But what about yours?"

Ronnie thought for a moment, "I don't know. I hope that they are ok, but logically I know that they're not. Best case scenario is they died quick, worst case is they died quick and got back up to wander around and spread whatever this is." Ronnie motioned out the window. Much of the town looked the same, but something was markedly wrong about the entire set up. There were no other cars moving, no children outside, no signs of the quintessential suburban life promised upon so much bulldozed farmland.

"Besides," Ronnie continued, "If my parents were dead or even if they were Shamblers, whoever burned the house down did me a favor. I should thank them."

Chris involuntarily shuddered, "You didn't see what I did last night, Ron. That was no mercy mission, those whack jobs were enjoying what they were doing. They were dancing around like it was some kinda celebration or something."

Both boys fell silent as Hector slowly plowed through a mob of about fifteen Shamblers that grasped at the backhoe. They had moved through a few groups like this, but nothing larger than twenty to thirty. No one wanted to admit that this seemed like far too few and if that was true, then where the hell where all the other ones?

"Alright," Hector's voice rattled through the CB hanging down from the van's roof. "Two more stops. This one is yours

Chris. Then Mike and Sam. After that, we make a beeline for the Municipal lot and see what's there. I'm still getting the radio signal, but haven't gotten any response on the CB channels. Be careful in there Chris."

"Thanks Hector," Chris replied into the receiver, "You do the same." Chris pulled the van onto the dry, water starved patch of yellowed grass that adorned his front lawn. It always amazed him that the grass could look dead, but still somehow grew high enough to hide the beer cans his mother launched off the rickety front porch. The second van pulled up behind the first and Mike gave the thumbs up from the driver's seat. Everyone slipped out the back doors and gently shut them, afraid to make too much noise. They quickly moved across the lawn and through the front door as Hector rumbled slowly down the street to bulldoze a few wrecked cars from their path towards the Municipal Building.

● ● ●

"My god," Amelia gasped. She stared wide-eyed at the chaos that surrounded her. The coffee table lay on its side, missing a leg and a half. There were random piles of dirty laundry and dog-eared pop culture magazines strewn about the living room. A threadbare couch and a duct-taped Ez-Boy recliner finished off the crack-house chic aesthetic that Chris's mother had gone for. "What do you think happened?" Amelia whispered, "Do you think something got in and chased your mom through here?"

A bitter laugh escaped Chris's lips. "Nah, place always looked like this. No matter how many times I'd clean up after she passed out, it'd always be back to this by the following day."

Amelia peeked through a slightly open door into an immaculately kept bedroom, "This one yours?"

Chris nodded and pushed the door open further, "Yeah, it was the only place I could keep clean in here. She gave up on trying to mess with my shit after I quit fighting with her about it. I think that's really what she was after, I guess." He quickly grabbed a duffle bag and began tossing clothes and other supplies into it. "Grab that bag and some of the stuff that's under the bed if you could," Chris asked Amelia.

"Sure, but what's under here?" Amelia asked as she pulled out a long plastic box with a blue snap lid.

"Just some old clothes," Chris muttered, "From when I was little. Thought Erick and Emily might need some stuff since…well, you know." Amelia immediately found Chris unbearably adorable and began sorting through the clothes and packing the smaller items. She was about to tell Chris just how cute she thought he was, but the others showed up in the doorway. A troubled look rested upon all of their faces.

"Uh, hey Chris," Sam began, "There's something banging around in the room off the kitchen. Ronnie's holding the door closed, but something's really trying to get out."

"That's the laundry room," Chris said, "Lord knows why the hell my mother would be in there. She never washed a damn thing." Chris dropped the duffle bag and started moving towards the door.

"Whoa, wait a sec man," Mike held his hand up, "If that's your mom in there, we'll take care of it. You stay here, that was the deal."

Chris shook his head, "Look, I don't care even if it is my mom. I'll deal with it either way. Any emotional damage caused by killing my mom's zombie won't be anything worse than what she had already done." He shrugged and slipped past into the kitchen.

"What are you doing here?" Ronnie asked, as Chris entered the dingy kitchen. "You should wait outside." Chris just shook his head and pulled Ronnie away from the door. As soon as Ronnie's weight was taken off the door, it immediately jumped on its hinges and shook. A dull thud slammed into the middle of the door.

Chris sighed and picked up a grimy meat tenderizer from the chipped countertop. A look of penitent resolve on his face, Chris opened the door and was violently thrown to the floor.

Two large Staffordshire Terriers swarmed over Chris, licking his face and playfully grabbing mouthfuls of his hair. Hearing the sound of Chris hitting the floor and then the skidding of claws across the sticky linoleum brought everyone else running into the kitchen where the dogs were happily reuniting with their owner. The larger of the two, a rust colored female with a white crest suspiciously eyed Mike. The other, a brindled, muscular male continued licking Chris's face, oblivious to the others having entered the kitchen.

"What the hell is…" Mike questioned as he skidded to a stop near the lopsided electric stove.

Pushing himself up from the tacky floor Chris laughed, "It's just Gozer and Zule. My mother used to lock them in the laundry room when she was pissed at them. Kinda lucky I guess, cuz there was kibble in there." The dogs had settled and were greedily lapping up a bowl of water that Chris had set out for them.

"What about your mom?" Alice asked as she petted the larger of the two dogs, a female named Zule.

"Oh her?" Chris muttered, "I was coming back to check on these two. I wanted to make sure they were ok, or at least that they had gotten out. Who the hell knows where my mother went, probably never left whatever barstool she was stuck to."

"That's touching," Joey sneered, "A boy and his dogs." As he began laughing, Chris delivered a punch to his arm that moved him two steps sideways.

After retrieving a few bags of dog food from the garage, Chris loaded Gozer and Zule into the back of the van with Amelia. They immediately began vying for position on her lap and licking her face. As Chris turned to close the door, he saw a shadow stumble past the low basement window and could have sworn he heard a low groan.

"You ready to roll?" Sam asked from the other van.

"Uh, yeah," Chris lied, "Just give me a sec to run down the basement and grab a couple of things."

A few seconds later, there was a dull *thunk* from the basement. Chris emerged with two heavy moving blankets wrapped around his arms.

"Everything ok?" Amelia asked as Chris got into the van.

"Huh?" Chris said; his eyes were glazed over, "Oh yeah it's ok. I went to grab these for the dogs. For beds." He reached back to pass Amelia the blankets and she could not help but notice a few blackish specks of what could have only been blood spattered across his fingers.

● ● ●

The vomit simply would not stop. For not having eaten anything near his normal amounts, Sam was amazed at the volume of partially digested food surging out of his mouth. A long string of yellowed mucus-laden bile slowly descended from his chin and swung pendulum like to and fro for a moment, before dropping heavily into the swirling soup of upset, that lazily circled its way around the circumference of the toilet bowl, which Sam presently rested his head upon. He had run headlong for the bathroom located just outside of his parents' bedroom on the second floor of the their house.

Upon entering the house, Sam and Mike had been relieved to hear nothing; just the silent creaks and shudders of an old house settling, but fortunately, there had been no heavy footsteps or groans. The silence had been a gift at first, a signal that their mother had not succumbed to this unexplained plague, but the longer they spent in the house the more unsettling the silence had become. What neither of the boys had wanted to admit, was the secret hope fostered by both that they would find their mother alive, maybe shaken and hungry, but ok. They knew that their father would have gone to work in the city shortly before all this had broken out and the likelihood of finding him was exceptionally small, but that did little to quiet the small voice of their inner children that longed for the comfort and support that came with the presence of a parent, especially a mother.

Chris and Ronnie had circled around the house from the outside, checking the back garage and shed for any signs, but found none and made their way back towards the front yard to wait with Hector. Mike and Amelia worked their way through the first floor of the house, collecting supplies and had ended up in the basement.

"My mom kept crazy amounts of canned food down here in the back pantry," Mike said as he ducked between the rafters.

"I never really understood why, but I guess it's a lucky break." He pushed open the thin, unfinished door, leading into the small room lined with rough plywood shelves that were packed tightly with neat rows of various canned goods.

"Jeez," Amelia said turning a can around in her hands, "You weren't kidding. There's like eight cans of lychees here. What the heck would you ever use that for?"

Mike chuckled, "Same question I asked when she brought them home, but they're actually pretty good. They're kinda sweet; some kind of fruit from China or Hawaii or somewhere, but I thought maybe Erick and Emily will like them. Let's just load everything into these boxes and sort it later." The two loaded the rest of the supplies in silence and took turns making trips upstairs to pass the boxes off to Chris and Ronnie.

The final step on the staircase creaked loudly as Sam stepped down on it. "Wow," Alice laughed, "That is seriously the loudest step I have ever heard. Didn't that bother your parents? That'd drive me crazy."

Sam retreated into his memories for a moment. "Yeah, it's pretty loud huh?" He said, "But Mom never let Dad fix it cuz she said it always let her know when Mike or me got home. Said it was how she knew when it was ok to go to sleep."

Alice smiled and bounced her foot a few times on the creaky step. "Your parents sound really great," she paused, "I would have loved to have met them."

"They were pretty cool," Joey added, "Didn't even really get mad when me and Sam almost burned the shed down." Alice raised her eyebrows, but Sam could not respond. The words began to form in Sam's mouth, but he swallowed heavily and nodded; the thought of happier days with his parents would crush him, if he allowed himself to think that might never happen again. He turned from the top of the stairs and moved towards the closed door leading into his parents' bedroom.

"Hey Sam," Alice said, trying not to let her voice rise too high, "Maybe you should let me open that? You know, just in case." She regretted having to say those words, but knew that the truth needed to be said.

"No," Sam said plainly, "It's ok. I'll see, besides I don't hear any movement in there. If she is...is a..." Sam could not bring himself to say it. "Whatever it is I'll handle it." Alice noticed that his hand trembled as he reached out for the doorknob. When the tips of his fingers lightly brushed the cool, black marble knob, his hand involuntarily jerked back as if shocked or burnt. But Sam quickly shook off his nerves and forced himself to turn the handle, opening the door.

The sealed room immediately emptied its trapped contents into the hallway, filling it with an overwhelming putrid odor that caused both Sam and Alice to gag. A small outline was visible on the left hand side of the bed, lightly outlined by the thin white sheet that lay over it.

"Oh Sam," Alice said with tears welling, "I'm so sorry."

Sam's body trembled and shook. He felt like a chill had settled into his bones and he could not get rid of it. There was a god-awful mix of anger, sadness and relief washing back and forth through his stomach, churning everything and tying flaming knots with his guts. Sam tried to respond, wanted to hug Alice, wanted to say that he appreciated her kind words, but the only thing he seemed capable of doing was throwing up.

Clutching his stomach and with wide eyes, Sam ran around Alice and into the nearby bathroom where he began violently vomiting into the toilet bowl. Sam knew that Alice was standing in the doorway, could sense that she was there unsure of what to say.

Hacking a large wad of blood tinged mucus into the bowl, Sam gripped the cold edges and forced himself up from the floor. He grabbed a fistful of toilet paper from the nearby dispenser on the wall and wiped his eyes and mouth. As he turned to toss the balled waste paper into the bowl, he caught a glimpse of himself in the mirror. He was ragged, eyes rounded in large, purple, half- moons and bloodshot. He needed to keep it together; he was far too close to falling apart and could not let that happen. If Sam fell apart, where would that leave Mike? No, he needed to keep it in check so they could go through this together. He was not going to leave Mike dealing with his own grief, and that of his little brother.

Sam tried to move past Alice and back into the hallway, but she moved in front of him and wrapped her arms around him, preventing him from going any further. There were tears streaming down her face, but she was not sobbing. She had swallowed her sadness for Sam, but her eyes refused to cooperate.

"I'm so, so, sorry Sam," Alice said into his chest, "We'll take care of it. Just go downstairs and I'll get Chris and Ronnie."

Sam thought about her offer and hugged her tighter for it, but shook his head. "No," he replied, "I gotta take care of it. It's my mom." Alice let him go and followed behind him as he passed through the threshold and into the bedroom.

The fetid odor had dissipated somewhat, but it did little to make the room any more inviting. The frail silhouette of Mrs. Williams looked deflated under the sheets and outlined in putrid hues of yellow and green from where she had begun to decay. Sam stood at the foot of the bed, taking all of it in and not knowing what to do.

"At least," Sam began, "I guess at least it looks like she just went to sleep and didn't wake up. Doesn't look like she suffered." Alice agreed, but it did nothing to make the horrible reality any more tolerable.

"What do you want to do?" Alice asked softly, "We could get the backhoe and bury her."

Sam considered what would be best. "I think we should leave her here. Mom always loved this house and wouldn't want to be anywhere else. Besides I'm not sure we can move her..." Sam gagged, "I don't think we should."

Alice was confused, "So what should we do?"

Sam was already moving towards the door, but paused at the dresser by the doorway and grabbed a few objects, but Alice could not see what. Over his shoulder Sam said, "I'm gonna talk to Mike, but I think we should burn it down. Just burn the friggin' house." And with no more to say, Sam slowly slunk down the stairs. Alice noticed that Sam made a point of avoiding the first step. He could not bear to hear the noise that had once comforted his mother and spoke of safety, not when she was laying a few yards away dead. Alice skipped the first step too and quickly followed Sam down the stairs.

The tears in Sam and Mike's eyes glistened brightly in the massive blaze that engulfed their childhood home. There were so many things to be said, so much that needed to be acknowledged, but no words available to do so. No one spoke, but Mike stood with his arm around his brother's shoulders. Alice had moved to the other side and had lightly taken Sam's free hand in hers.

After the flames had eaten away at most of the home, Hector had moved in with the backhoe and collapsed the walls onto themselves and into the foundation. The rubble still smoked as the last of the supplies were loaded into the vans and the convoy turned funeral procession, silently rolled further through the lifeless tomb that had once been a town.

● ● ●

"How the hell are we going to get through that?" Chris said completely flabbergasted into the CB receiver. The group had stopped on a small rise a few blocks from the Municipal Complex and climbed onto the roofs of their vehicles to survey the situation before proceeding.

The entire parking lot was swarmed with Shamblers. It appeared to writh and dance like a stormy ocean. The zombies had packed themselves in so tightly that the asphalt was no longer visible in some spots. It was now obvious to everyone why they had not encountered more zombies while they were going through the neighborhoods. Everyone must have fled here only to get sick and die and come back to infect their loved ones and neighbors.

"There's a small opening on the back side of the parking lot," Hector replied, "I'm pretty sure we can push through with the backhoe and get to the side entrance to the library that's over there."

Mike grabbed the receiver in his van, "What happens if all those Shamblers close in after you've pushed through? We'll be trapped." All the radios fell silent for a few moments. Then Ronnie's voice crackled through.

"I think we could use some of the extra gas to solve that problem," Ronnie stated.

After a few minutes of rummaging through a nearby home's recycling bins, Ronnie returned with four empty wine bottles. He filled them three-fourths of the way with diesel fuel from one of the gas cans in the back of the van, and stuffed some rags into the top from a shirt he shredded. With a few simple steps, Ronnie had created four large, deadly Molotov Cocktails.

"We throw these at one end, enter through the other and hopefully by the time we're ready to go, the fire will have burned down enough that we can escape. It'll cause a pretty good explosion and burn really hot, so whatever is there should be gone by the time we're ready to go," Ronnie said detailing his plan.

"Seriously, Ron, where the hell did you learn to make bombs, let alone know how they exploded?" Joey asked.

Ronnie shrugged, "Anarchist Cookbook. It's pretty interesting, but kind of dangerous stuff."

"The what?" Mike asked, "Where would you even find something like that?" But even as he said it, Mike and everyone else knew the answer.

"Internet," everyone said in unison.

After a few dry laughs, the group began to consider the plan. "What if it doesn't do that and we're still stuck?" Amelia asked, "Then we have to deal with fire and Shamblers." Everyone agreed, but for lack of a better plan, they decided to go ahead with Ronnie's.

Hector handed his lighter to Mike, who sat in the front bucket of the backhoe. "You sure about this?" Hector asked.

"Sure?" Mike replied, "Hell no. But what else are we gonna do?" The plan was for Hector to raise Mike high above the swarms of Shamblers where he could pitch the bombs into them and hopefully start a fire that would clear their escape route. The major flaw in the plan was that with Mike raised high above in the bucket, there was nothing left for Hector to plow through with, and that meant a sea of moldy, rotted teeth washing against the vehicles.

The backhoe rolled slowly towards the main entrance to the Muncipial parking lot. The loud rumble of the engine drew even more Shamblers towards that end of the lot, and Hector could not help but gag as the fetid air washed through the steel grate surrounding him and assaulted his senses. Ronnie and Chris, each driving the other vans, used the distraction of the backhoe to swing the vans around the back of the library and hide them behind the retaining fence surrounding the dumpsters.

A few Shamblers slowly loped towards the vans, but everyone quickly caved their skulls and moved towards the entrance of the library. Meanwhile, Mike surveyed the situation unfolding a mere ten feet below him.

"Shit," Mike muttered, "I guess here goes." He sparked the lighter and the flame immediately leapt onto the shredded rag stuffed into the heavy wine bottle. Mike checked his footing to make sure the other three bottles were not under his foot, drew the bottle back and lobbed it in a high arc towards the center of the mob of Shamblers that surged towards the backhoe.

The next few moments played out in slow motion. Mike watched wide-eyed as the bottle bounced off the chest of a Shambler, who dumbly looked down just as the bomb struck the ground and exploded in a loud *whoosh*. A large cloud of fire washed over the feet and legs of the surrounding Shamblers and hungrily consumed tattered clothes and putrefied flesh.

"Throw another!" Hector yelled from the operator's cage. Mike briefly looked back, nodded, sparked another, and threw it to the left of the previous one. An equally violent explosion tore through the nearest zombies and flung errant body parts through the air in morbid celebration. The other Shamblers showed no regard for the fire and contined forward through the sea of flames. Mike watched in horror as flaming corpses moaned and continued towards the backhoe, until enough muscle and tendon had been seared from their bones and they collapsed to the ground, only to be crushed under the horrid march of their cohorts. The burning of flesh and fat filled the air with a smell disgustingly similar to sizzling bacon, and try as he might, Mike could not help from keeping his stomach from rumbling and mouth from watering.

"Get in there!" Chris commanded as he brought his heavily booted foot down onto the skull of the Shambler splayed on the ground before him. The contents of its skull spilled across the asphalt like candy from a grotesque piñata. Amelia and Ronnie quickly used a cat's paw from one of the vans to force open one of the double doors as Sam, Joey and Alice made sure no Shamblers were silently dragging themselves around the sides of the fence.

"We're in!" Amelia announced, and everyone rushed through and into the dim hallway. The door was quickly barricaded with some of the refuse that littered the hall. It would not do much to keep any of the zombies out, but everyone hoped that if they could not see anything inside that they would just pass by. Besides, no one was planning on staying inside for too long.

"Let's get to the rec room, that'd be where they would set up any emergency stations," Ronnie offered and took off down the hall. As he passed the heavily shadowed rooms no one stopped to check them. The doors were closed and whatever was in there could stay put as far as they were concerned. Any living person would come at the sound of help and any dead ones would hopefully be too stupid to open the door.

Skidding to a halt outside of the rec room, the group pressed themselves against the wall. Ronnie and Sam peered through the door. There was no one inside. The entire room was destroyed and the floors were shellacked with a thick coat of blood. Footprints and smears preserved in the blood, told the story of the chaos that had ensued with in.

"I don't see anyone," Sam whispered, "Let's get in and out quick. Grab any medical or military supplies you come across. Be careful with any weapons you find, ok?" Everyone nodded and slipped into the room.

The only sound audible within the large room was the sucking of each step pulled from the tacky floor, and the occasional gasp as one person or another came across a horror scene worse than expected.

"Hey," Chris whispered loudly, "Over here. Look at these tracks." Everyone came over, arms laden with supplies and looked to where Chris pointed. Even in the dim light, they could see that his face had paled and small beads of nervous sweat percolated from his brow.

A set of footprints trailed across the floor, which was nothing out of the ordinary in the repulsive room that everyone currently stood in, but what disturbed Chris the most was the presence of a pair of handprints planted a few feet in front of each pair. Something had moved through here on all fours, something that looked like it had an unsettlingly similar posture to what had chased Chris and Ronnie through the Commons days earlier.

"Do you think there could be another one of those things?" Alice asked as she nervously checked around the room.

"Stalker," Ronnie added.

"Jeez, Ron," Amelia hissed, "Why bother naming these nasty things. They're monsters plain and simple."

"Because naming something makes it less scary," Ronnie offered and everyone knew he was right, "Besides, calling it a 'thing' doesn't make tactical sense. We need to know which kind and how many if anyone sees them so that we can respond appropriately."

"Fine," Amelia sighed, "Could it really be another *Stalker* then?"

Looking down at the tracks Sam replied, "If we saw one, we gotta assume that there could be another. Let's just be happy we don't see any more tracks." Everyone agreed and cautiously went back to scouring the room in search of valuable supplies. Thus far, they had procured a mixed bag of medical supplies, two defibrillators, some food and water and a .45 Glock with a half full clip; Ronnie thought it looked police issue. Strangely, there were no military supplies. Green canvas bags, few crates, and mangled remains wearing tattered strips of camouflage littered the room, so it definitely looked like the military had been here, but if that were true, where had the supplies gone?

"You don't think those crazy people we saw the other night took them do you?" Alice asked Sam as they opened a cooler only to find spoiled, useless bags of blood for transfusion.

"No, I don't think so," Sam assured her, "If they had been here, they probably would have burnt this building down too. That seems to be their M.O. The thing that worries me more is that I haven't seen a radio anywhere."

Alice thought for a second, "If the military supplies are missing too, then maybe some of the soldiers survived and took the radio. Maybe it's a good thing we can't find it in here, because then that means it's somewhere else. Right?"

Sam was about to answer when a loud explosion from outside shook the building. The drop paneling in the ceiling rattled and settled at strange angles. A light snow of dust wafted down from the ceiling and quickly coated the sticky floors.

"That came from the front," Chris shouted across the room, "Hector and Mike are out there. Grab what you can. Let's go." Long before Chris had even taken the breath required to form his words Sam was halfway down the hall.

● ● ●

"Throw the last one towards the right," Hector yelled above the rumble of the backhoe's engine and the crackling of seared, rotten flesh and rendered fat. Mike looked towards where Hector pointed and noticed a large group of Shamblers moving towards them, but something was wrong. The groups they had encountered so far had simply shuffled along, bouncing off of one and another, but something was surging from the center of this mob. Shamblers were being thrust forward and trampled, and there forcing its way through the throng Mike saw it, a Stalker.

The creature leapt and thrashed at the massive number of bodies that surrounded it, trying to gain some footing to propel itself forward. The wind wiping across Mike's back and shoulders told him everything he needed to know. The Stalker could smell his scent, even above the fires, fetid flesh and diesel smoke. With each putrefied wave, the Stalker pushed its way further through the crowd and closer to Mike and Hector.

"Shit, shit, shit," Mike said, voice rising with each curse. His thumb slipped on the wheel of the lighter again and again, but finally, after what felt like an eternity of acrid sparks and burned thumbs, a flame leapt hungrily forward and consumed the rag of the last gas bomb. Mike took a deep breath, drew his arm back and hurled the heavy bottle towards the Stalker.

The creature's eyeless sockets gave no warning of the impending danger that traveled towards it through the air in oblong circles of flame, but the Stalker still sensed Mike nearby and quickly drew back on its haunches and leapt into the air. The bomb narrowly missed the Stalker and bounced off of a nearby Shambler's arm and under a parked car. Mike was unsure of where to look, towards the possible explosion in the parking lot, or at the rotted missile that unbelievably was careening blindly right for him.

Seeing the Stalker leap for Mike in the bucket, Hector hurriedly moved to the controls to swing Mike away from harm, but the Shambler caught under the large tires and the mechanical clumsiness of the machine would not allow for such evasive maneuvers. Instead the backhoe lurched sideways and jerked angrily back towards its starting position, serving only to throw Mike off balance as the Stalker slammed into the side of the steel bucket.

Arms flailing in tight circles, Mike fought to keep his balance, but the Stalker had found purchase on the side of the bucket and caused the entire thing to shake violently. The greedy sucking of air through the Stalkers exposed nasal cavity could be heard above the chaos erupting around Mike, and the vacant ocular cavities ringed in dried, frayed bits of skin were fixed in his direction. Catching his balance, Mike made a quick move for one of the large yellow arms holding the bucket, but the Stalker leapt from the side of the bucket and blocked his path. It released a feral snarl and ground its cracked, jagged teeth. Mike was trapped.

Hector was panicked; he had no way to help Mike and was going to be forced to watch the boy get torn apart by a monster. He could not get out of the cage because the backhoe was swarmed with Shamblers and could not drop the bucket or shake it for fear of dropping Mike, but he had to do something. There was no way Hector was going to sit on the sidelines and do nothing. Spinning in the control seat to face the back controls, Hector unfurled the scorpion-like tail on the back of the backhoe and began to swing the smaller, sharper bucket in wide semi-circles, cutting a swath through the horde of Shamblers that surged around him. He only hoped that he could clear enough space and had enough time to spin the backhoe and drop Mike to the ground, where he might have a fighting chance to escape from the Stalker.

The Stalker dragged its pointed, fingers across the edges of the rusted bucket. The exposed tips of bone screeched loudly and left faint streaks of white. Mike thought it looked like it was sharpening its claws, but did not want to imagine for what. The Stalker slowly moved around the edges of large bucket, growling and swiping at the air. It might not have been able to see him, but it definitely knew he was there and it seemed to be toying with him like a cat with a mouse. It would make its move whenever it tired of this game, and when it did there would be nothing Mike could do; he was going to die up here or down there, the only choice he had, was whether it would be death from one set of teeth or many. Mike just hoped that wherever Sam was he would not see what was about to happen. The Stalker suddenly reared back, emitted a howl and leapt. From somewhere below, Mike heard a violent explosion and the backhoe shook ferociously.

● ● ●

Rushing out of the library, everyone haphazardly threw the scavenged supplies into the back of the vans and piled in. Sam threw the van in reverse and whipped it in a wide arc around the side of the dumpsters. Alice clung to armrests and quietly prayed that Sam would not crash into anything and more importantly, that Hector and Mike were ok. Chris, Amelia and Ronnie followed close behind in the second van. The loaded pistol was tucked into Chris's waistband.

As the vans rounded the corner of the Municipal Complex, a second explosion erupted from the parking lot launching a small mushroom cloud high into the dimming evening sky.

"There!" Alice yelled and pointed towards the backhoe. Hector was slumped over at the controls and Mike was nowhere to be seen, but perched on the edge of the bucket was a Stalker. It howled and swung its peeled fingers at something in the bucket.

"Mike's gotta be in there," Sam muttered, "If it's still trying, then he's gotta be alive still. Put your seatbelt on." Sam prepared to ram the backhoe in the hopes the Stalker would be thrown. Alice closed her eyes and prepared for the impact. Joey, who was getting tossed around in the back paled when he heard Sam's words.

"Uh, dude?" Joey said, "I don't have a seat, let alone a seat belt."

As Sam pushed the pedal down further and sped past the exploding parked cars, a loud *crack* rang out, audible above all the other noises. The Stalker reared back as if punched and a large piece of its shoulder appeared to be missing. Thick black jelly leaked from the massive wound, but the creature appeared to either not feel the pain or perhaps not care. Alice's eyes shot open. "What was that?" She asked, scanning the scene for the source of the sound. A second *crack* split the air and Sam's foot eased off the gas pedal as he saw the Stalker slump forward and collapse heavily into the bucket.

Kicking out, Mike struck the Stalker's hands and tried to knock it from its perch above him. He knew he was about to die a very painful and violent death. His only hope was that the Stalker would do enough damage that he would be unable to come back as one of those pitiful Shamblers. Suddenly a loud blast cut through the air and Mike heard a high-pitched whistle wiz past his head. A fist-sized chuck of flesh tore itself from the Stalker's shoulder and was flung backwards in grotesque pinwheel fashion. The Stalker appeared unphased, and swung its pointed fingers tearing through the thick denim of Mike's jeans. Before he could react, Mike heard a second whistle whine past him and the Stalker's head fractured and split, like a dropped egg. Thick ooze wept from the cracks and for a few seconds, the skinless face even seemed to contract into a look of confusion. The Stalker collapsed forward into the bucket and ceased to move.

"Get that thing moving kid!" A voice commanded and Mike whipped his head around to find whomever it had come from. 'Hurry the hell up and get that freaking thing over here!" Someone stood from where he had been perched high on the roof and waved to Mike.

Looking down into the control cage, Mike could see Hector slumped over. He was moving, but not much. The blast from the exploding cars must have knocked him unconscious.

"Hector! Hector!" Mike screamed, "Wake the hell up!" The man groaned loudly and rubbed the side of his head, but slowly he spun in the chair and his hands landed heavily upon the controls. Hector waved weakly, acknowledging Mike and shifted the backhoe into gear.

"He's ok! He's ok!" Amelia yelled through the radio, "Look Sam, they're ok!"

Sam let out a breath he was not even aware he had been holding in, and brought the van to a slow crawl behind the backhoe as it shuddered to life and lurched forward. He was still unsure of what had just happened, but did not care if it meant that his brother was ok. Alice reached across the van and squeezed Sam's hand. He looked over at her moist eyes and nodded. She smiled back and squeezed his hand one more time.

The backhoe slowly rumbled through the throngs of cold hands and vacant eyes that hungrily grabbed for the meal just out of reach. "Looks like there's a few soldiers on the roof," Hector reported through the radio to everyone else. "I'm gonna raise the bucket up for them and then we're out of here." Behind the vans, the tightly packed, parked cars continued to violently explode. Each burst rippled through the asphalt and vibrated up the vans' tires sending a strange electrical sensation coursing through the occupants' feet and legs.

"Get that thing a little closer kid," the solider yelled as Mike rolled closer. He had dumped the wrecked body of the Stalker out of the bucket and it was quickly lost in the seemingly endless parade of heavy feet that swirled below. The bucket slowly raised up to almost meet the edge of the roof. Fortunately, the Municipal Complex had been built out and not up over the years, so at its highest peak it only reached twenty feet.

The solider grabbed Mike's hand and helped him climb up onto the roof.

"Hey kid," the soldier welcomed Mike as he pulled him onto the roof. The man was not large, but seemed to possess an extraordinary strength and easily hefted Mike over the ledge. Mike hoped to find an entire army hiding up there, had hoped that maybe there would be some salvation or sense of order waiting upon the roof. What he found was a crude tent made out of a tattered blue tarp with two soldiers huddled underneath and an orderly arranged pile of supplies, but other than that, the three men appeared to be on their own.

"Where's everyone else?" Mike asked and could not help but let disappointment leak through with each syllable.

The soldier smirked, "We are everyone else. The rest of our unit and all of the civilians are either out stumbling around the parking lot or dead. Things went from bad to worse in a blink. We couldn't even call in a sit-rep before our CO was taking a bite out of some old lady."

"Shit," Mike swore, "I mean I'm sorry, look, it's just that..."

"No worries kid," the soldier smiled as he leaned on the barrel of a massive black powder coated rifle with a squat clip, "I would have been hoping to find help too, but as it turned out, you rescued us. Just sad that it couldn't have been the other way around."

In a world overrun with disappointments, Mike just chalked this up as one more and moved on. Allowing yourself to become depressed or hopeless was the quickest way to end up dead, so you had to suck it up and move on.

"I'm Mike," he stuck out his hand, "That's Hector down there in the backhoe and there's a few more people back at the school. We've been holding out in the gym for a few days now. Kinda lost track of time. And thanks." Mike motioned towards the large rifle.

"No problem. I wanted to shoot that piece of shit for days, but couldn't get a clear shot with the crowd. Not worth the bullets with the dead heads, but with those nasty fucks, it's definitely money well spent," the soldier paused, "I'm Bruno and that's Crawford and Watts over there. You said you were holed up at the school? Is it safe there?"

Mike shrugged, "Bout as safe as anywhere else. We cleared the main building and there's a solid fence around the grounds, so we're in pretty good shape. We heard your transmission and thought there might be help here or at least supplies, so we came over."

Bruno snorted loudly, "Yeah, that stupid thing. Watts wouldn't stop blubbering unless we kept it transmitting. Me and Crawford wanted to bug the hell out, but then the crowds got too thick. And then the other night we thought some people were coming to assist, but those shits just led more dead heads here and tried to set the building on fire."

Mike nodded, "We've seen them too. Bought forty, fifty people with torches right?"

"More like twice that man," Bruno replied, "Fortunately the sprinkler system still worked and put out the damn fire, but then they just left us up here. Should have shot a few of the bastards."

Suddenly realizing that the longer they stayed up here, the harder it was going to be to get out, Mike said, "Let's get your stuff and get out of here. We'll be better off back at the school." Bruno nodded.

"Alright, ladies on your feet," Bruno barked and Crawford snapped to his feet with an automatic rifle held at ready. Mike noticed that it took Watts a lot longer to get up and that he appeared to be favoring his left leg.

"He ok?" Mike asked pointing towards Watts.

"Just his period. Right Watts?" Crawford joked.

"You can suck a fart from my ass Craw," Watts muttered, "Twisted my damn ankle that's all and Dr. Bruno over there won't give me any more drugs."

Mike held his hands up, "Look man, as long as it's not a bite I don't care *if it is* your period. Just don't get any blood in the bucket." Turning to Bruno, Mike asked, "You really a doctor?"

"Field medic, but yeah I guess I'm kind of a doctor," Bruno replied.

"That's good to know," Mike nodded, "First bit of good news in a while."

The three soldiers began laughing as they loaded their supplies into the bucket. Mike helped Watts over the edge and into the bucket as the other two soldiers grabbed him under his arms. Once all four were securely inside, Mike gave Hector a thumbs up and the backhoe lurched back to life.

Heavy hands wrapped in loose, fetid skin banged upon the outside of the vans, leaving long greasy streaks and bits of rotted flesh behind. Any Shamblers that came too close to the backhoe ended up under the oversized tires and chunks of gore were clearly visible between the treads.

"Which way we going?" Chris rattled through the CB.

Hector looked around from his position high above the swarms of empty eyes and rotted hungry mouths. "Gonna head back towards the parking lot. The explosions cleared a pretty good path." Shifting the backhoe into its highest gear, Hector drove over the curb in the parking lot and through the small scrubby pines that had been scorched by a nearby burning car. Mike and the soldiers bounced around uncomfortably in the bucket, but held tight. The two vans easily followed and rolled into position behind Hector. A good number of Shamblers, some still smoking, scorched beyond recognition, and some in their rotted mint condition, ambled along behind the vehicles, but lost interest once the distance between them grew.

● ● ●

The three soldiers settled into the routine relatively easy and were quickly accepted into the group. There had been some worry that they might try to take control and lord over the school as their own little kingdom, but Bruno dismissed the idea.

"You've done better than us so far, and we have no interest in messing that up," he explained, "You all saved our asses, so as far as we're concerned, we're here to return the favor. Besides, with the way things have been going, I'm not so sure adults should be calling the shots. It's too risky, never know who's gonna get sick and make a bad call or die."

Crawford nodded, "He's right. The old way of doing things isn't gonna work anymore. The shelf life on anyone over twenty is way too unpredictable for them to be put in a position of power. Just look at what happened when our CO flipped. A room full of adults couldn't handle losing direction. You kids gotta get used to being in charge because then you'll be ready when you don't have a choice and have to be. It's the only way you got a chance."

"So what are you saying? That kids should be making all the calls?" Joey asked skeptically, "You gonna make Erick President?"

"I'd be a good President," Erick pouted.

"Of course you would sweetie," Elsie comforted him.

"So what did happen at the Municipal Building?" Ms. Kozlov asked trying to get the discussion back on track.

The three soldiers exchanged troubled looks and it appeared that none of them wanted to speak, but then Watts shook his head and began.

"Alright," he sighed heavily, "Look uh, why don't you take Erick and Emily outta here?" Elsie nodded and hurried the children into the kitchen to help her prepare dinner.

Watts continued, "We were mobilized as soon as the first cases of whatever this is began. The cities were largely under the control of the anti-terror units and National Guard, so any towns near military bases were the next logical place to lock down."

"We weren't even supposed to be there," Bruno added, "But when Europe started going to shit our deployment to Afghanistan got waylaid and we were put on standby at the base."

"Actually thought we caught a break," Crawford snorted sarcastically.

"Anyway," Watts said, "We get told by the base's CO that we're buggin' out to provide emergency aid for your town, and since Bruno's got med training, our unit was running point."

Bruno continued, "I got told that there was an outbreak of some sort, possibly a virus. Maybe some variation of a prion disease, like Mad Cow, but possibly manmade and released on purpose."

"This was a terrorist plot?" Mike asked skeptically, "The government thinks they have the sophistication to pull something like this off?"

Shaking his head Bruno responded, "They did at first. They think everything is at first, but that's not what it was. We all knew it wasn't. If it was a terrorist plot, it would make sense to see outbreaks in London, New York and western cities like that, but this is everywhere. There were reports from all over the Middle East and Africa, which makes no sense for terrorism. Why unleash this in your own backyard? If anything, putting it everywhere but your area would make it seem like you were holy and chosen. Besides, this virus, if that's what it is, is far too unstable to have been created in a lab, it's mutating too quickly, and there's no way they could have kept this stable enough in a lab to create the amounts needed to pull something like this off."

"That's why we're seeing differences in how the bodies are responding. Most seem to be Shamblers, but every once in a while, it seems like there's some variation and we see something nastier like the Stalkers. There's probably other things out there too," Alice interjected, "Probably even worse."

"Girl's good," Bruno added, "You studying to be a doctor?"

Alice shrugged, "I'm not studying anything anymore, especially not to be a doctor."

"Yeah, well we're gonna need to change that," Bruno said, "Cuz we need as many people with medical knowledge as possible. We're all safer that way."

Crawford picked up the story, "So we get to the Municipal Building and start setting up a relief post in the Community

Center, and as soon as we did, a flood of civilians starts pouring in. It was too hard to screen and quarantine anyone cuz the minute you saw one, another five showed up."

"We started getting people organized, just barely," Watts added, "But then our CO starts sweating like crazy, grabs his chest and drops dead. Right there on the floor, drops dead. And as if that weren't enough to cause panic, as soon as we get over to him he gets back up and attacks some old lady. We put him down, but it was too late. Everyone panicked and started running. We couldn't even see where the infected were until it was too late. We tried to get as many people out as we could, but there were more outside. By the time we got to the roof, we were the only ones left."

"That's why you kids gotta be ready to be in charge," Crawford finished, "Anyone who you're used to looking to for guidance could be gone in a hot minute. And waiting around for another adult to step in isn't gonna do anything except get you ate."

After some discussion, everyone came to see the point that Bruno was trying to make. The children could not rely upon adults as they had in the past. They needed to become more self-sufficient because they never knew when one of the adults might become sick. If they left adults making all the decisions, then there would be chaos if that person died, let alone tried to eat one of them. Bruno was right.

"Think of it like this," Watts added, "We're here for advice and to help out however we can, but you guys need to be ready to make the decisions."

Bruno nodded, "That being said, I think we gotta talk about the elephant in the room." Everyone screwed their faces in confusion but he continued. "We've all seen those whack-a-dos roaming the streets and it's only a matter of time before they run out of other things to burn and come here. We gotta be ready to defend ourselves not only from zombies, but other people too."

With that simple conversation Mike, Sam, Chris, Ronnie, Alice, Amelia and Joey found themselves in the command positions for their group. None vied for top spot, rather they decided to proceed as a council and put things to a vote, and the first vote that passed unanimously was that Bruno was right and they needed to prepare for battle.

● ● ●

The machine gun jumped and leapt wildly in Sam's hands cutting a jagged line in the dirt in front of his target. No cans were hit; no bullets went to their intended targets. He switched the safety on as he had been instructed to do and let the M-16 go slack at his side. A loud *ping* resounded from both sides and Sam watched in dismay as the others in his group dropped their targets.

The soldiers had emptied their supply cases and they contained mostly MRE's, weapons and bullets. There were some loose medical supplies that Bruno had added to the stockpile Alice had already compiled. Bruno was impressed with Alice's knowledge and had begun tutoring her in the ways of field medicine.

The group had been practicing and drilling for days now and Sam was not getting any more accurate with the guns. Even Erick had dropped a few of the cans when Watts had steadied the .45 in his hands and helped him hold it up, but not Sam. He simply could not seem to hold the gun straight, the minute his finger squeezed the trigger his shots went wild.

A dry laugh from behind him caused Sam to turn around. "You don't like guns do you kid?" Bruno asked, "I didn't either at first. What are you thinking about when you're shooting?"

"I dunno," Sam replied, "I'm trying so hard to focus on the first shot that I screw up all the others. Once the gun starts jumping in my hands I can't focus anymore."

'That's what I thought," Bruno said taking his rifle from his back, "This here is a SR-25 Ranger sniper rifle. Give it a try."

The look of confusion could not be hidden on Sam's face, "How's that gonna be any better?"

Handing the sleek black rifle over to Sam, Bruno said, "You mess up the shots with the M-16 cuz you think too much, the opposite is true with this. You gotta think about every shot, I mean every aspect of it, even the wind direction and the shots are much slower. There's no spray and pray with one of these, you better mean each shot you release cuz you only have ten in each mag."

Sam looked down at the rifle. It did not look that much different from the M-16 he had just handed over to Bruno, but it was much lighter and felt a little more comfortable in his hands. He flipped up the scope and looked down the field towards the cans. They seemed incredibly close and danced slightly with each breath he drew in. Bruno put his hand on the stock and drew it down.

"Flip out the bi-pod and lay down, it'll stop the dancing," he said and Sam followed his directions, "Now sight up on your target and slow your breathing. When you're ready to shoot, keep your eye open, exhale slowly and squeeze the trigger."

Sam prepared himself and did as he was instructed. The sound from the rifle resonated one time, but far louder than the stifled chopping of the M-16s. The can was still sitting atop the bench upon which Crawford had set it.

"Damn it," Sam gritted, "It went wide."

"Relax Sam," Bruno grinned, "Sight it again and control your breathing. This time, squeeze the trigger, don't jerk it or close your eye. You know what to expect."

Following the directions again, Sam set up his shot and the center of the can collapsed in on itself and tipped forward off its perch.

"I hit it!" Sam said astonished at his own feat, "I actually hit it."

'You're a good shot kid," Bruno congratulated, "I had seen you squeeze off a few rounds when no one was looking and you nailed 'em. You kinda reminded me of myself when I first got to boot. I sucked on the range when they were yelling at me, but could center every shot when no one was around. The Range Master caught on to that and recommended me for the sniper school. He said I needed time to plan my shots. I figured you might be the same way." He patted Sam on the shoulder. "Keep practicing," he said as he tossed Sam two more magazines.

"Don't you need your gun back?" Sam asked, secretly hoping Bruno did not.

"Nah, I got another in one of the crates. That one is yours kid," Bruno paused, "Just be careful."

Sam spent the rest of the afternoon meticulously lining up his shots and picking off his targets. By the time it became too dark to shoot, Sam was centering every shot on his targets. As dusk finally drew an end to Sam's range time, he carefully switched the rifle's safety on and wondered if Bruno had a night scope.

● ● ●

The serpent wound its way through another neighborhood, flashing its individual scales of flame as each member of the mob bobbed in step with the others, as they marched through the streets. The past few nights had seen the line moving closer and closer to the school grounds, burning everything in their path. Whoever these people were, they seemed intent on destroying as much of the town as possible.

"I've got eyes on forty to fifty unfriendlies," Bruno reported as he squinted through his night scope. Sam lay next to him on the roof and tried to view the same through his. Since his time on the range with Bruno, Sam had been spending as much time with him as possible, trying to learn everything he could about being a Ranger sniper.

The two had taken watch together and were growing more and more concerned from what they saw. This group, whoever they were, appeared to be growing in size and violence. The previous night, Chris and Watts had reported seeing them burn through one of the strip malls and two developments; the range of destruction was expanding in an ever-widening circle, one that would ultimately include the school.

The group had considered at first that maybe these people were simply trying to get rid of places where large amounts of Shamblers were holed up, but that theory was proven wrong as Sam and Bruno watched five of the members break off from the group and tackle a Shambler. They appeared to be trying to capture it, not kill it. As the five men wrestled with the zombie, it twisted its head around at an ugly angle and buried its teeth deep into an arm, even through the scope Sam and Bruno could see the Shambler tear a wet chunk from the man's arm and begin absent-mindedly chewing. But perhaps the most disconcerting aspect of the entire scene was the fact that the man did not appear upset or concerned, quite the opposite. He raised his arm high over head and allowed the blood to stream thickly down his arm. A cheer rose from the ranks of people and they seemed to be congratulating the bitten man.

"Are they celebrating?" Sam asked in disbelief.

A greasy knot twisted itself in Bruno's stomach. His tour in Afghanistan had shown him what fanaticism looked like and the mindless danger it could unleash. This was not good.

"Yeah kid," Bruno replied, "It sure looks that way."

The mob of people descended upon the Shambler and hog-tied it. Someone tied its mouth shut with a few rings of cord and they carried it off with them. The bitten man marched proudly at the front of the crowd as they cheered and lit more fires.

● ● ●

"Lemme go," Erick demanded as Elsie held his arm, "I wanna go help!" Over the past days he had become enamored with the soldiers and often trailed behind them as they went about their daily routines.

"Sweetie," Elsie said softly, "This isn't training. They aren't going out there to shoot at cans or run exercises. This could be dangerous."

"I don't care!" Erick pouted, "I'm brave enough."

Ms. Kozlov emerged from the weight room where she had been shouting at the elder students to "push" and "one more damn it". The soldiers had smartly enlisted her to assist with getting the students into a fitness and training routine that involved daily practice with both guns and weights. The other students, who had previously been numbed from the violence, had found solace in the structure and were coming out of their shells, but Crawford warned against taking any of them outside the school grounds.

"They're shell shocked," he explained, "Seeing what's out there would push them right over the edge. Keep 'em busy, but keep 'em safe." Everyone agreed.

Ms. Kozlov approached Erick and picked him. "We know you are strong and very brave too," she said, "Everyone knows that, but this is different Erick."

"Sorry little man, but she's right," Crawford added, "We're going outside the fence to see what those wackos are up to and it's not safe."

"Nothing is safe anymore!" Erick replied and everyone was stunned at the young child's insight.

The hard expression on Ms. Kozlov's face softened, "We need you here Erick. If the soldiers are gone then we need you here to protect us."

"That's right," Emily added from beside Elsie, "You gotta stay with me Erick."

Erick appeared to be considering the explanation offered and Crawford tried to cement the idea for the young boy. "Erick," he began, "You're gonna stay behind with Watts and keep the place safe. That's the most important job of all; to make sure we got a safe place to come back to. That's why we left it to you, boss."

The fight left the boy and Erick relaxed somewhat in Ms. Kozlov's steel trap of a hug. "Ok," he consented, "But I get a gun."

"Dunno bout that one buddy," Crawford said, "Lemme talk to the others."

The idea of arming such a small child was one that no one liked, especially Ms. Kozlov and Elsie, but after some careful discussion, the council voted in favor of the idea; Alice and Sam had objected at first, but ultimately consented to the idea. These were different times; harsher, more violent times and they had to admit that Erick had a point. He had been on the range just as much as anyone else and had internalized all of the safety lessons that the soldiers had drilled into everyone's heads.

"So it's agreed," Mike reported back to everyone, "But nothing crazy, ok? We're not giving Erick a RPG or SAW, no matter how good the little man can argue. It's gotta be something he can handle."

"I got something," Watt's said and reached down towards his right ankle, "Besides with the sprain and bandages, this thing is hurting like a bitch." He held out a small .22 caliber pistol. "Just be careful," he warned, "I'm not exactly a fan of this idea either." Erick's eyes lit up as he reached for the small pistol. He immediately checked the safety and dropped the clip out to inspect the gun, just as he had been instructed to do.

"What are you doing with a lady gun?" Crawford quipped.

Before Watts could answer, Erick replied indignantly, "It's not a lady you butthead. It's made for someone my size." And everyone did have to admit, that the small gun seemed to be made to fit into Erick's hand.

"That's right," Watts replied, "It ain't no lady gun. It's easy to hide. I kept it as backup in case Johnny Jihad ever took me prisoner. I'd damn sure try and scramble a few brains before I let them assholes behead me on Al-Jazir."

The clip clicked back into place and Erick sighted down the short barrel at an empty corner of the gym. "Thanks Watts," he said proudly, "I promise I'll be careful."

Watts smiled, "You better little man cuz the first hint I get that you're screwing around with that I'm taking it, no discussion. Ok?"

"Ok," Erick agreed, "I won't mess around. I promise."

As the two walked out the side doors of the gym to go and do a perimeter check, Watts chuckled, "I guess I'm glad I got someone with a gun watching my back...even if he's only eight." He reached over to mess Erick's hair, but the boy ducked it.

"I'm ten," he said firmly, "Double digits means I'm a big kid now."

A sad look flashed in Watts' eyes, but he forced a smile, "Yeah little man, I guess that does."

The van silently rolled through the street with Chris at the wheel. Crawford rode shotgun and scanned the street for any signs of hostiles. The only reason he had been allowed to take the passenger seat was because Ronnie had stayed behind to help Hector try and get the old generator in the school's basement functioning.

"Slow it up," Crawford said and leaned out the passenger window. A lone Shambler stumbled out into the street and groaned. As it caught onto the sound of the van's engine, it stiffly raised its arms and headed towards it. "You get one in the dome my friend," Crawford mumbled against the stock of his M-16, but Bruno reached over from behind and tapped his shoulder.

"Not worth it Craw," Bruno said, "You fire a round from that and who knows how many other dead heads show up. Do this one old school."

Dropping his rifle Crawford shrugged, "Ok, time to get medieval I guess." He slipped out of the car and let out a low whistle. The Shambler immediately began shuffling towards him. Crawford reached behind his back and withdrew a small black cylinder, no longer than six inches. As the Shambler hungrily reached out for him, Crawford sidestepped and whipped his hand in a tight arc. The small cylinder expanded from its center and reached its full length of a little over a foot. The small steel ball on the end of the baton crushed the skull of the zombie as it collided with its temple. The Shambler dropped to the ground and Crawford hit it two more times for good measure, then cleaned the baton and collapsed it.

As he got back into the car, Chris could not help but ask, "What was that thing? That was so cool."

"It's called an Asp," Crawford smiled, "We carried them to subdue hostiles during night raids. It's a nasty little shit, I'll give you that, but very effective." Chris nodded and shifted the van back into drive.

Behind the two pilots' chairs, Sam, Amelia and Bruno squatted on a few battered plastic milk crates that slid uncomfortably with every turn, no matter how carefully Chris took it. Alice and Mike had been positioned on the roof of the school with a surveillance scope and radio to stay in contact and provide intel.

"Looks clear," Mike confirmed through the radio that sat on Crawford's lap, "You're coming up on where we saw the fires burning last night, but there's no signs of any movement."

"Roger that," Crawford replied and turned to Chris, "Find a spot where we can park the van and we'll hoof it. We'll cover more ground faster that way."

The singed remains of a two-car garage still smoked lightly as Chris pulled the van inside. There were no vehicles left inside and one of the walls was almost completely gone, but the garage had otherwise stood its ground against the previous night's fire. The group slipped out of the van and quietly closed the doors.

Scrawled across the side of a seemingly intentionally not burned white house were the wide sweeping red words, "*No man shall enter the temple until the seven angels and seven plagues are fulfilled.*" Everyone stopped and stared at the letters trying to figure out what to say and no one wanting to ask the question they already knew the answer to.

"It's blood isn't?" Sam asked.

Crawford approached and touched his fingers to the letters. When he withdrew them, they were coated in a slick of blood. "Yeah, looks like it," he reported back, "But what the hell does it mean?"

"It's from the bible," Amelia clarified, "A quote from the Book of Revelation, but someone screwed it up. It has to do with the apocalypse."

"And you know this because?" Chris asked.

"I was a youth minister for my church," Amelia replied, "I used to help out with the bible study classes."

"Great," Crawford said sarcastically, "You're telling me that whatever these wing nuts with the torches are doing, they're doing it cuz of the bible and the apocalypse."

"Makes sense," Bruno said thoughtfully, "They keep going back the same way every night and the kids said that the only thing that's up there is some born again church."

The group carefully moved through the streets. Each set of eyes and gun barrel diligently swept the quadrant it had been assigned, but there were no signs of people or zombies. The entire development was destroyed. Homes stood as little more than charred skeletons of their previous pre-fab grandeur. The butts of old torches littered the edges of the streets and were scattered across the overgrown lawns like a giant child having found a box of matches and haphazardly played.

"Eyes on more writing," Crawford whispered from his point position, "Stay frosty, it looks like there might be some zombie activity up ahead."

*"The spirit of the Lord will be poured onto his people and knowledge will increase,"* emblazoned the side of the pool house located in the center of the development, flies swarmed around the clotted letters and the jumbled pile below them. Everyone turned and looked at Amelia with cocked eyebrows.

"More apocalyptic bible stuff," she answered, "I think from Acts and Daniel, but I'm not sure. I don't know how it ties into any of this, unless these people think this is the End of Days or something."

"Isn't there something in the bible about the dead coming back during the apocalypse?" Bruno asked, "Maybe these nut jobs are convinced that's what's going on?"

Amelia looked concerned, "Yeah, there's some mention of that, but I was always taught that the verse was about people going to heaven, not freaking zombies."

"Well, psychos screwing up religion for their own purposes ain't nothing new," Crawford spat, "Hell, I seen plenty of that before there were any zombies walking around."

*"There's movement on the outer edge of the development,"* Mike's voice rattled through the radio, *"Looks like a couple of Shamblers, just be careful. Over."*

The group slowly approached the pool house to further inspect the pile located below the inscription.

"Maybe this is what they've been doing with the Shamblers they were catching," Sam posed.

"I don't think so," Bruno said as he nudged the pile and a head rolled free, not one with molted diseased skin and milky eyes, but one that had recently been pink, vibrant and alive. Stacked like a tipped pile of firewood were the remains of at least four people, none of whom appeared to have been killed twice. These had all been survivors.

"What the hell man?" Crawford asked no one in particular, "Why would they do this to humans and wrangle the damn zombies? That doesn't make any fuckin' sense."

"Who knows Craw," Bruno said, "We couldn't figure out how Johnny Jihad could rationalize religion and using women and children as bombs, so how the hell we gonna make heads or tails outta this mess."

"It doesn't matter," Sam said coldly and everyone turned in surprise, "Their reasons I mean, they don't matter. These were our neighbors and family. Whatever the reason for doing this was, it doesn't matter. These assholes are a threat and I say if one walks in front of your gun, shoot him."

Bruno and Crawford exchanged concerned looks. "Hey kid," Crawford said, "I get it, trust me I do, but don't let your emotions get the better of you. We gotta stay clear headed to deal with whatever this is."

"Agreed," Bruno added, "But Sam's got a point. It doesn't look like any peaceful coexistence or friendships are gonna be found with these people and that means we gotta be ready to do whatever it takes to protect the group." Everyone agreed.

*"Guys you got a large group of Shamblers headed your way and you're losing light fast. I say you wrap it up and head back,"* Mike suggested.

Sam spied the first Shambler, but did not have a clear shot. They were still halfway around the block, but they were closing in quickly. Without thinking, Sam jogged towards the mob of zombies and dropped to the ground.

"Get back to the van," Sam said through the side of his mouth as he pressed his face against the stock of his SR-25 rifle. He quickly brought the crosshairs to bear on the lead Shambler. A morbid black flower sprung from the middle of the Shambler's head and it heavily dropped to the street. The others simply moved around it, as if it were nothing more than a pothole. Sam looked back over his shoulder and saw that no one was moving. "Why the hell are you still here. I'll slow them down. Move!" The others started to walk back towards the van, but stopped, not wanting to leave Sam alone.

"I'm on it," Bruno said and jogged over to grab Sam by the belt. He yanked him up from the ground causing his next shot to go wide. "Let's go Sam, there's gonna be plenty of time for this later."

Turning to face Bruno with tears in his eyes and a feral twisting line across his face, Sam snarled, "You screwed my shot!"

"Blame me all you want in the van," Bruno replied and pushed Sam towards the vehicle.

The group quickly made their way back to the van and piled in. As Chris pulled the van out of the destroyed garage, the group of Shamblers rounded the corner, but strangely, did not head towards the van.

"What the hell are they doing?" Amelia asked.

"Heading towards the pool house," Crawford answered from the front seat and everyone watched in horror as the zombies tore apart the tattered remains of the people who had been so callously piled there.

"It was a sacrifice," Sam said, "Those assholes left the damn Shamblers an offering." He turned and faced Bruno and with venom in every word said, "I was trying to stop them from getting there. Those people at least deserved that."

"I know kid. They do," Bruno said, "But we gotta focus on the living." Chris pressed the gas pedal harder into the floor and tried to fight the urge to vomit.

● ● ●

"There's lights on in the gym!" Amelia said astonished, "Hector and Ronnie must have gotten the generator running." Everyone stared towards where she pointed. The sun had seemingly just disappeared from the sky and they were suddenly enshrouded in darkness. Chris switched on the headlights as they approached the locked gates to the school grounds. Watts and Erick were waiting to let them in.

"You got any juice left in that walkie?" Bruno asked Crawford.

"Think so," Crawford responded and suddenly caught on. "Kill the lights ASAP. Mike if you can hear me turn the friggin' lights off now!" He said in rapid succession. Chris and Amelia exchanged confused looks.

"It'll give away our position," Sam explained, "We can't let those people know where we are."

"Exactly," Bruno agreed, "We gotta stay off their radar. And those lights are a huge 'please burn me' sign. I just hope they haven't seen them already."

The gates swung open and Erick jumped up onto the running board and pressed his face against the driver's side window. He blew hard against the glass, expanding his cheeks to an unbelievable width. His nose flattened and rose up like a pig's. Chris pretended to smack Erick's face through the window and then rolled it down.

"Oh man," Chris joked, "I was hoping your face would stay like that Erick. It was an improvement."

Erick was obviously too excited to respond to Chris's light-hearted insult. "I got one. I did. Watts tell them how I got one!" Erick said excitedly.

Watts had locked the gate and climbed up onto the running board to hold Erick in place as the van slowly rolled back towards the gym. "Little man's telling the truth," Watts said, "He dropped a Shambler from twenty feet. One-shot center of the dome. Got the rotten bastard while we were walking the fence. I couldn't believe it either, but the little guy is tough as nails." Everyone congratulated Erick for a job well done, but no one wanted to admit that celebrating a ten-year-old shooting someone in the head, alive or dead, was a disturbing reality check. Erick should have been getting the same accolades for good grades or Student of the Month, but that world had died with most of the people in it. The one that greeted them at the gate was born in blood and cut with teeth; this was no world for a child. This new world was wonderful at reminding everyone just how sadistic and brutal it truly was at the moments when they least needed it.

The lights in the gym were off long before the van had driven around to the back. Everyone met them at the door, a concerned look shared by all of them.

"What's the problem?" Mike asked Bruno.

"We've seen what those people are up to out there and trust me, the last thing we want is for them to know that we're here," Bruno paused, "But it's your call guys."

Sam stepped forward, "There's no lights, it's too dangerous. Any votes otherwise?" No one raised their hand. "Ok, good. We gotta start being more careful. These people are not going to offer any help and if they get close to here, we're gonna have to give them a pretty strong reason to leave."

The look of celebration had faded from Watts' face and the cold determination of a seasoned soldier had returned. "We got a SAW in one of the crates. I say we build a bunker behind the gates and station it there. That'll be a pretty strong 'don't fuck with us'."

"Sounds good," Bruno agreed, "I also think we oughta think about fortifying the doors to the gym and creating a fall back position further back in the school, just in case they break through."

"Ok, can you guys handle getting that stuff started?" Mike asked, "We'll get everyone else together in the gym and fill them in on the situation." The three soldiers nodded and went off to accomplish their respective errands. Erick trailed behind Watts.

"Whoa there boss," Watts said holding up a hand, "You gotta head back ok?"

A look of utter dejection crossed Erick's face, "But I can help." Watts hesitated, unsure of what to say. A ten year old had no business building a machine gun bunker, but then again, he was just as safe there as he was anywhere else and he really did not need to hear whatever awful things Sam and Chris had to report.

"Come on," Amelia said putting her arm around Erick, who grabbed her hand tightly interlocking their fingers, "I'll go and help Watts too." The three of them set off towards the Transportation Building to collect some of the massive road salt barrels from the garage. They would make a good substitute in place of sandbags.

"You got this man?" Chris asked Sam with a strange look of urgency in his eyes. Sam understood, "Yeah, no worries. Get going before she's too far ahead and Erick starts putting the moves on her." Mike and Sam both started laughing. Soon Chris was as well.

"I wish a ten year old trying to make moves on the girl I like was my only problem," Chris laughed and jogged to catch up with Amelia.

Everyone else had begun to move back into the gym, but Alice remained outside. She had a look on her face somewhere between angry and worried. "What was that out there?" She asked, her voice was trembling.

"What'd you mean?" Sam said, "That religious crap? We'll talk about it inside."

"No you asshole!" Alice almost shouted as she pushed Sam, "I'm talking about you running towards the Shamblers and Bruno having to drag you back towards the van. Are you trying to get yourself eaten? Is that what you want? To be the big bad hero only to get crapped out by some mindless zombie?" Tears were beginning to stream from Alice's eyes and Sam began to fully realize what he had been doing.

"No, no," he stammered, "It's just that those people had, jeez Alice."

"I saw the whole thing Sam. I know what was there," Alice said, "I watched through the scope. You think I want to watch you get torn apart because you're trying to prove that some higher moral code still exists in this world? Cuz it doesn't Sam, none of that does anymore. The only thing that is real anymore is what we have behind this fence. Out there. Out there it's no man's land; there are no rules or morals."

Sam blushed at Alice's words, ashamed that he had let his pointless sense of morality overcome his common sense and put everyone at risk. "You're right," he said softly, "I just couldn't stand the thought that anyone had died for such a stupid reason."

"My point exactly," Alice said and pressed herself against Sam's chest. She tightly wrapped her arms around him and squeezed. "I can't lose you Sam, especially not for something like that. You're what's been keeping me going. I can't lose that."

Sam could hardly believe what he was hearing. He and Alice had become close since the outbreak, but he had mistakenly thought it was simply friendship on her part. His heart knotted itself and leapt into his throat. Swallowing hard Sam said, "You won't. I'm sorry Alice. I promise that you won't." Before he could say anything else, Alice pressed her lips firmly against Sam's and kissed him deeply.

● ● ●

"Stop squirming," Alice commanded as Watts tried to pull his leg away from her, "You're such a little girl." He tried to pull his leg away again, but Alice locked her hands around his good ankle and squeezed. "Next time it's the other one girly man."

Watts cast an accusatory look at Bruno, "I see you've been training her in the arts of heartless medical care?"

"Just told her that when you're in the field you gotta get take control and get things done," Bruno chuckled.

"Did you give her the 'what do you do when a drowning person is trying to tip your boat' question?" Watts asked Bruno.

"Yeah, that's a classic training scenario, but you should have heard her response."

"Punching the person wasn't a brutal enough response for Dr. Frankenstein here?"

Alice lightly squeezed Watts' sprained ankle and he yowled. "No, I just thought it would be far more effective to hit the person with an oar. That's all."

"My god," Watts said sarcastically, "I think you've found your replacement Bruno."

"She catches on quick," Bruno said inspecting the job Alice had done re-wrapping Watts' ankle. "Good job Alice. Watts get back to walking the fence."

"Did anyone think that maybe assigning the guy with the screwed up ankle the job of walking the perimeter was a bad idea?" Watts asked sourly.

Alice laughed, "That's why we have Erick out there to keep an eye on you." Watts shook his head and slowly walked back out to where Erick waited in a gas powered golf cart that Hector and Ronnie had found for them in one of the maintenance garages.

"Alright, so now that Polly Pissy Pants is back on the job, let's get back to our previous conversation," Bruno suggested. He and Alice had spent the better part of the morning discussing what he knew about the virus and zombies, which was not much. The rest of the time was spent debunking whatever theory one had offered.

There was what Bruno already knew; that the virus appeared to be a mutated prion disease, so the neurodegenerative characteristics of these diseases could possibly explain the aggression shown by the infected. Some prion diseases, like Kuru, caused large-scale muscular degeneration, which could explain why the victims were rotting. And like the Kuru disease this appeared to be targeting certain ages within the population, while unexplainably leaving others untouched. It did not appear to be man-made and most importantly, the government really had no idea what the hell was going on.

Then, there was what Alice and Bruno had theorized about it; that it spread through bites, so the infection probably centralized itself in the salivary glands, instead of the brain. The incubation period was very short, which was unusual for a prion disease and the virus appeared to be mutating at an alarming rate. So pretty much everything they thought they knew could be completely worthless in a matter of a few epimutations of the virus.

"If it mutates that fast, is it even going to be possible to create a vaccine or antidote?" Alice asked.

Bruno shook his head, "I don't think so. These kinds of viruses usually burn themselves out; disappear for a while and then just pop up somewhere else. Besides, I'm not sure that there's any facilities left to even try and create one."

"I didn't think so," Alice said, "So what does that mean for us?" But she already knew the answer.

"It means survival," Bruno replied, "That's the most we can hope for right now. There's not gonna be a huge rescue or return to the world we used to know. My only hope is that we can hold it together long enough for you kids to have a shot at making something of what's left. I guess kind of what my generation should have been doing with the world before it totally went to shit." An acidic laugh escaped Bruno's lips.

"Well, let's get back to my training, so we can better our odds," Alice said. The two spent the rest of the day continuing Alice's medical training. Bruno was pleased at the rate with which she caught on and was sure that he would have a competent medic soon enough. Alice introspectively laughed with bitter irony at the present situation; her father would have been proud of his daughter becoming a doctor, that had always been his dream, but she bet he never imagined it would be like this.

● ● ●

The doorway leading into the administrative offices hung open like a gapping maw waiting to consume whoever was stupid enough to pass through it next. Granted, everyone was fairly certain that the offices were empty, but no one was volunteering to enter the darkened block of offices. The smell alone was enough to deter any sane person, but sanity was largely over rated these days.

"Alright," Mike said unhappily, "I'll go. Give me the lamp." Even though there was still a bright late autumn sun high in the sky, they were not going to open the blinds. The council had voted on new security measures and they included not opening the shades on any windows that could make someone visible. The soldiers were convinced that whoever was out there must know that the school was inhabited, but the last thing they wanted to do was leave the windows wide open so their movements and routines could be tracked.

Hector handed Mike the large battery powered lantern that they had recently scavenged on a trip to one of the local big box stores. These trips had become an almost daily ritual because, as Amelia had pointed out, if they did not get the stuff out of there now, it would be little more than ashes soon enough.

The blood that stained the cheap, industrial carpet had darkened to the point that it looked more like a cartoonish hole in the floor instead of a dried pool where someone had painfully bled to death. Mike carefully worked his way around the stains, even though he knew that they were just as much part of the floor now as anything else. The scattered remains of victims still lay strewn about the room, but they had become somewhat less disturbing as the days had passed, becoming dried and leathery, slowly mummifying rings of bite marks as if to preserve themselves in testament of the horror that had unfolded within these walls.

"Looks safe," Mike called back, "Come on." Hector, Crawford, Joey and Amelia slowly mimicked Mike's path through the door and into the center of the offices. Flashlights illuminated the room and cast distorted shadows. Nothing moved, there were no growls or moans and slowly everyone began to relax.

"We gotta put people on body detail ASAP," Crawford said, "But we should talk to Alice and Bruno first. Probably not a good idea to be touching any of this shit without gloves, even if they think it's passed through bites."

"I'll get on that," Hector said, "I can dig out part of the soccer field with the backhoe. Once we get this stuff in there, we can burn it. I'll talk to Alice and Bruno, but I'm pretty sure that should do the job."

"Sounds good," Amelia said, "Let's get this spot checked out and then me and Joey will help you out with that."

"We will?" Joey asked, a look of disgust on his face.

"Appreciate it," Hector said.

Prior to Bruno's suggestion, the group had had no reason to inspect the office beyond making sure there were no zombies swaying silently in the shadows within.

"Why's he think this is a good spot anyway?" Mike asked Crawford, "How's this a better fallback position than anywhere else?"

"It's centralized," Crawford said, "Not too many windows and most of the hallways branch out from this area, which means no matter where someone is in the building, they can fall back to this spot." The explanation was easily accepted and the group set about clearing out the cheap particleboard furniture. "Keep anything heavy, like filing cabinets. We'll use that shit for barricades by the windows." The indiscriminately placed body parts were left where they were until the ok was given to touch them.

"Check this out," Hector called from the desk near the principal's office. The desk was spattered with thick globs of blood, much like the others in the room, but what had caught Hector's attention was the smashed TV that lay scattered across the top. "Looks kind of strange don't you think?"

The other three had wandered over to see what had caught Hector's attention and were equally perplexed by what they found.

"Who knows man," Joey said, "Could've been broken in the attack. Maybe someone fell on it?"

Crawford leaned in to examine it closer. "Bring the lantern closer," he said waving Mike over to his right, "I'm not a hundred percent on this, but it looks like there's bits of skin here." As Mike illuminated the desk with the amber light, they could see that Crawford was right. Small, but thick ribbons of flesh clung to the jagged edges of shattered plastic.

"Look around the edge," Amelia pointed, "Move that junk over." Crawford swept the electronic and plastic scraps out of the way and a large fist print was easily identifiable underneath it. "Jeez, it looks like someone punched it, but look at the size of the freaking hand."

"Bout the size of my head," Hector added, "You think that's possible?"

"Maybe it was someone's head," Crawford added, "Not that that makes me feel any better. Whatever did this was strong as hell. It broke through the TV and right into the desk. Damn."

Nothing else offered any explanations within the office, so the group went back to clearing out the unwanted furniture. Eventually, the main office was cleared and they began entering the offices and continuing the cleaning. Hector and Amelia were shuffling around the vice-principal's office and piling random material outside the door to be taken outside by Mike. Crawford continued around the room checking the other offices, his rifle at ready, safety off.

The door to the principal's office was closed, but not shut. A small crack ran on the left edge of the door and the smell that wafted out caused Crawford to gag and hold his hand to his mouth. "Shit guys," he retched, "Found where that smell was coming from. Mike, on my six." Mike trotted over and withdrew a Glock pistol, recovered from a dead police officer, from his waistband.

"Alright man," Mike said, and tapped Crawford on the shoulder. The group had been practicing breaching drills and Mike, accustom to memorizing football plays, had quickly learned and even improved upon the steps taught to him. Crawford pushed his foot out and nudged the door open with his booted toe. It swung open easily, but bumped upon an unseen obstacle within the office. Having no windows, it was too dark to see what the door had caught, but there appeared to be no movement within. Crawford withdrew a long plastic tube, cracked it and shook it. A sickly green glow quickly leaked through the stick and Crawford tossed it into the office.

"Nice and easy," Crawford said and stepped slowly into the room. He swept his M-16 back and forth as he moved further into the office. Mike moved his pistol in the same fashion, but opposite direction as Crawford, ensuring that no spots were left uncovered. "Looks empty. Let's see what the hell the door hit." The two moved back through the office towards the door. A large pile was collapsed partly behind the door. "Looks like a body."

Mike moved closer to inspect and could not make sense out of what he was looking at. "It looks like skin," he reported, "But I don't see anything else." Crawford moved closer and spread the pile out across the floor with his foot. A large sheath of dried skin partially unfurled across the floor. The tattered remains of a cheap business suit were lying tangled around the legs of the skin suit.

"It's like a complete person," Crawford muttered, "Like someone just peeled a fuckin' person. Man every time I think shit can't get any grosser."

"Yeah man," Mike agreed, "But what the hell happened to who used to be in there?"

They quickly finished clearing out the offices and returned to the gym to get Alice and Bruno. Some sort of medical explanation was needed here; no one had any idea how to make sense out of a peeled pile of skin.

Alice and Bruno carefully grabbed corners of the skin with gloved hands and spread it across the floor. Errant patches of hair were still visible where the head would have been, but the rest of the skin was laced with long jagged tears, as if it had split and small puddles of a pink, viscous jelly oozed from the folds. The edges of the skin had begun to dry and harden, causing some of it to crack as it stretched.

"This is disgusting," Alice said, "It almost looks like someone molted like an insect. I don't even want to think about it."

Bruno walked back, climbed up onto the desk and looked down at the wrinkled peel of personhood. "Agreed. Ranks really high on the puke scale," Bruno said, "But what the hell happened to the person inside. We would see signs of them being eaten and no Shambler or Stalker has done anything like this. At least not yet." He looked around the room, hoping for some sort of answer. "Shit." He had found an explanation.

Standing on the ground it was easy to miss, but from his high vantage point, Bruno could see a wide set of footprints trailing out of the office. Each foot was three times the size of a full-grown man's and the heel was easily the size of a dinner plate. Whatever had been in here was massive. The tracks appeared to be outlined and dried in the same putrid liquid that leaked from between the folds of discarded skin. "I think whatever was in here walked out," Bruno said pointing to the tracks.

Alice had come to stand next to Bruno on the desk and could not believe what she was looking at. "Do you think it's still here?" She asked concerned, "I mean could it still be around the school?"

"I don't think so," Bruno said, "Whatever was in here was friggin' huge. Where the hell would it hide? But we better do a sweep in the outer buildings to be safe."

Alice had climbed down from the desk and was rummaging through the frayed, soiled remains of the business suit. She found an overstuffed, brown leather wallet in the trouser pocket and carefully flicked it open. Her principal's hammy, bloated face angrily peered through the small plastic window that kept his driver's license in place.

● ● ●

Watch had been relatively uneventful. Thankfully, there had been no fires or torches. Sam watched as a few groups of Shamblers wandered around the abandoned neighborhoods. There seemed to be no reason to their motions, rather they simply bounced off one another, never showing any real sense of intelligence.

Sighting one through the scope on his rifle, Sam practiced his breathing, but did not shoot. There was no point in giving away his position or wasting a bullet. The lessons Bruno had been teaching him on the range had become Sam's new religion. He began and ended every day with one ritual or another, all intended to make him a better, more deadly shot. The Shambler he had sighted was pushed out of the way by another zombie and it stumbled away into the darkness.

Sam lifted his head from the stock of the gun and sat back on the roof. He switched the safety near the trigger and laid the gun across his lap. He stared out into the darkness and tried to imagine that things were different, changed back to how they used to be, but it was too dark. Strange, Sam thought, that it could be too dark to imagine all the ugliness gone and the town returned to normal. He had never noticed that his town was never completely dark, no matter the time of night. There were always lights that cast a sickly yellowy-pink hue into the night sky, light pollution, Sam remembered his dad telling him when he asked what it was. At first, it had angered Sam that the new pharmaceutical plants moved into his town and dirtied his night sky, but now he would have given anything to see it again. Something scuffed the gravel behind him and Sam turned to see Chris coming across the roof.

"How the hell do you get them up?" Sam asked motioning towards Gozer and Zule, Chris's pitbulls.

"They can climb ladders. Never really had to teach them," Chris replied, "They just used to follow me up into my tree house. Hard part is getting them down."

"Was just about to ask about that," Sam smirked as he reached down to scratch Gozer behind the ear. He seemed to appreciate Sam's attention and pressed himself into Sam's legs, almost knocking him over.

"I gotta make trips and carry them back down. Looks like you got a friend there," Chris laughed. Since he had brought the dogs back to the gym, they had stayed faithfully beside him, even sleeping on either side of him. Gozer made periodic rounds to the other group members, demanding to be petted, but Zule refused to go further than a few steps from Chris. She often stood between him and others, as if unsure of whether or not to trust them, but she never did so with Amelia. Zule seemed to know Chris's feelings instinctively, and allowed Amelia a certain degree of trust not afforded to others.

Chris came and sat on the edge of a ventilation unit next to Sam. He leaned his M-16 against the sheet metal and sighed deeply. "You holding up ok man?" He asked, "Need anything? You been up here for a while."

"No thanks. Not unless you can rewind time," Sam said bitterly and then tried to hide it, "I'm good, just tired I guess." Chris nodded and tossed him an energy drink. Sam looked at it strangely, opened it and drank about half the can.

"I never could figure out why they sold that shit in schools either," Chris said, "But Hector popped one of the vending machines open and we figured you might want one."

"Thanks," Sam said and took another drink, "This crap tastes like battery acid, but it's the best damn thing I've had in days." The two sat for a few moments in silence. Gozer trotted around the roof, finding random puddles and lapping them up. Zule had curled herself around Chris's feet, but did not appear to be truly relaxed.

"So you and Alice huh?" Chris said with a wicked grin on his face.

"And you and Amelia?" Sam replied arching his eyebrows for effect.

"What the hell are you talking about?" Chris scoffed, "Nobody's seen *us* sneaking kisses outside the gym."

"Yeah, well Mike's got a big freakin' mouth," Sam said, "Anyway I've seen everything I need to know about you and Amelia right there." He pointed to Zule, who raised her head as if to question Sam's accusation. "My grandfather used to say that if you found a girl that your dog liked, then you better marry her," Sam paused, "Never could figure out why he said that when I didn't have a dog." Both boys erupted into laughter.

Gozer stopped drinking out of a puddle and raised his head, ears standing up. Zule had sprung up from where she lay coiled at Chris's feet and a low growl was rumbling from deep within her chest. Sam and Chris immediately began scanning the area for any signs of danger, but none presented itself. Zule's growl deepened and she curled her lips back in a humorless grin.

"Something's up," Chris said, but Sam had already dropped onto the blanket he had folded near the edge of the roof and was scanning the darkness with his scope.

A single torch was lit just on the outside of the fence surrounding the school grounds. As Sam sighted the carrier of the torch, a deafening blast resounded from somewhere followed by three more.

"What the hell was that?" Chris said.

"It sounded like a trumpet," Sam said, "Like four notes from a trumpet."

● ● ●

"What the hell was that?" Watts muttered as he slowly awoke from where he slept in the gym. Everyone else was flicking on flashlights and looking around, confused as to where the strange sound had emanated. Chris flew into the middle of the gym followed close behind by Gozer and Zule.

"Wake up!" he shouted, "Everyone up. Watts get on the radio to Bruno down at the bunker and see what the hell is going on. One of those religious fruit loops is outside the fence and the others are blowing friggin' horns from somewhere." Watts grabbed his radio and began getting reports from Bruno. He was seeing the same things that Chris had reported, but nothing more.

"Chris this is bad," whispered Amelia, who had come up beside him.

"Yeah, I know," Chris said without looking, "Who knows what the hell those idiots are up to."

"I do," Amelia said solemnly and Chris turned to face her. Confusion was written into every wrinkle that creased his brow. "It's more religious stuff Chris. This is more Book of Revelation apocalypse crap. The four angels blew their horns to bring about a time of darkness. It was when things got really, really bad during the apocalypse."

"Is anything ever good during it?" Chris asked.

"Well no," Amelia replied, "But this is bad going to worse. This was when people really started dying in large numbers. I'm worried those assholes are sounding it as a battle cry. Chris I think it means they're coming here!"

Chris turned to Ronnie, Joey and Mike, "You guys grab your weapons and haul ass in the van down to Bruno. Park it sideways across the gate." They nodded and took off running. Moments later the screech of tires could be heard. "Watts stay in here just in case."

"Me too!" Erick said firmly, "I'm staying with Watts."

"Ok, ok," Chris said rapidly, "Alice on the roof with Sam. Radio in the minute you see anything. Amelia and Crawford, we're taking the other van and checking the perimeter. Elsie and Ms. Kozlov get everyone else into the locker room and lock the door. Hector, get the generator running. I don't think it matters anymore and get as many outside lights on as you can. Then get down there to help the others at the gate." Everyone nodded and ran to their assigned duty. Within moments, lights began clicking on outside. The sodium lamps cast a strange orange hue that painted the night in sepia tones.

"Nothing new to report," Sam called in over the radio, "Bruno you got eyes on anything?"

"One torch near the far end of the fence," Bruno reported, "But it's not really moving. We'll know more in a second." Bruno nodded and Mike and Hector quietly slipped into the shadows and began working their way towards the carrier of the torch. "Ronnie, grab that other ammo box and have the belt ready to feed," Bruno said, "I hope we don't need it, but sure as hell wanna make sure we have it if we do." Ronnie turned and grabbed the heavy, green metal box. He flicked one of the side handles and withdrew a long belt of ammunition. Joey stacked and restacked the boxes, his nerves unable to allow him to stand still.

As Mike and Hector drew closer to the torch, they could see that the person was pressed up against the fence. They appeared to be reaching through the bars.

"What is that dumb ass doing," Mike said, but Hector simply held his finger to his lips and pointed towards the person. They kept moving along the fence, but did not appear to be trying to get through. Mike and Hector watched them for a few more minutes before deciding to move closer. Hector slowly approached the person, as Mike lay hidden in the shadows covering his movements.

Raising his rifle to his shoulder, Hector loudly commanded the person to get down on the ground, but they did not respond. He moved closer and shouted, "On the ground now! I'm not asking again!" The person turned in Hector's direction and let loose a low, angry growl.

"Shambler," Hector called over his shoulder, "Call it in." Mike reported back to everyone, but told them to keep their guard up. Hector slowly moved closer and then noticed that the zombie appeared to dragging something behind it. He also noticed that it did not appear to be holding the torch, rather it looked like someone had savagely driven the sharpened end of the torch into the neck muscle of the Shambler, causing its head to twist at an unnatural angle.

'What the hell is going on?" Mike asked as he came up beside Hector.

"Dunno," Hector said, "Looks like someone stuck a damn torch in that thing like candles in a birthday cake. It's dragging something behind it too."

Mike peered through the bars of the fence as the zombie tried in vain to grab him and moaned in frustration. "It's got a chain wrapped around its waist. It's like weighted down or something." He passed along this information to everyone else. No other activity had occurred.

"Mike," Sam called in from the roof, "There doesn't appear to be anyone else out there. I say you drop that thing and we'll check it out in the morning."

"Agreed," Chris responded over the radio, "Amelia thinks this is a message instead of an attack. Drop the dead head and we'll clean it up in the morning."

Mike clicked the safety off and shifted the lever to single shot on his M-16 and split the zombie's head with a round. The Shambler still reached out for a few more seconds and then its milky eyes rolled back in its sockets and it collapsed onto the pavement. Shining a flashlight through the fence, Mike looked down at the zombie and the chain wrapped around its waist.

"You think this can really wait till morning?" Hector asked, "Something is really wrong here. I mean more than just the day to day wrong."

"I don't think anyone is sleeping tonight anyway," Mike replied, "But let's just wait it out until first light. I don't want anyone taking any stupid risks." Calling back over the radio Mike reported that the zombie had been dispatched, but suggested that everyone stay on post for the rest of the night anyway. "Let's kill the lights and then get back to walking the fence." Hector nodded. Soon the school grounds were again cloaked in darkness, but as Mike had predicted, no one slept.

"Amelia seems to think this is all some religious crap," Chris muttered as he and Ronnie made their way towards the Shambler Mike had shot on the previous night. They had drawn clean up duty, while most of the group tried to rest. Sam and Alice had refused to change shifts and stayed on the roof providing cover for Chris and Ronnie.

"Could be," Ronnie answered, "A lot of bad things have been done throughout history in the name of religion. It makes sense that people would turn to it now. Their fear is making them irrational and dangerous."

"Yeah, maybe," Chris said, "But those people had to be screwed up long before any of this shit happened. This is some hardcore crazy."

Nodding, Ronnie replied, "Most people are crazy. They just hide it really well."

"Gee, thanks Ron," Chris said sarcastically, "Can always count on you for a reassuring word." The two boys fell silent as they approached the body of the zombie.

*"Don't see anything out there. No movement,"* Sam called over the radio, *"Keep your eyes open."*

Setting down the can of gasoline he was carrying, Ronnie approached the Shambler. Chris stood a few feet back with his gun pointed at the body. It did not move. It was dead for good this time.

"Where do you think this chain goes?" Ronnie asked as he began to follow it. The chain extended a good twenty feet and had wound itself around a wrecked car, preventing the boys from seeing where it ended. "Let's follow it."

"Is that really a good idea?" Chris asked, but Ronnie was already moving towards the burned out car. Chris jogged to catch up with Ronnie. Soon they were rounding the car.

The chain did not extend beyond the car and had become tangled around the rusted, scorched rims that had partially sunk into the pavement. A large green canvas bag was attached to the end of the chain and seemed to be what had prevented the Shambler from walking any further. "It was weighted down," Chris observed, "Maybe so it couldn't walk away?"

"That doesn't make sense," Ronnie replied, "They had to have known that it would walk towards the school the minute it heard any movement. I think they wanted it to get closer to the gate, but it got stuck. We were supposed to see whatever is in that bag. Amelia was right, this was a message or maybe more like a delivery."

"Delivery?" Chris scoffed, "What the hell could they possibly be delivering to us?" Ronnie withdrew a utility knife and cut the bag free. Its contents spilled onto the pavement and the boys fought the urge to vomit.

"Are those heads?" Chris gagged, but he could see that they clearly were heads and worse than that, they were not the heads of Shamblers. Much like the offering they had found near the pool house, these were from people who had been alive. But what was the message they were supposed to convey? The vacant stare of the four heads seemed as confused and terrified as Chris felt at that moment.

"There's a note," Ronnie said through his shirt, which he had pulled up to shield his nose. Attached to the inside flap of the bag was a folded letter written upon thick, yellowed paper. Small blotches darkened the paper where blood had soaked in from the heads. Ronnie snatched the letter and back peddled quickly away from the fetid smell and blank stares. He unfolded it and read it:

*The grace of the Lord was visited upon these four souls. These angels were chosen and made vessels for His divine knowledge and delivered unto to you by one of His holy messengers. You have been made known to the Lord, and His angels have sounded their holy trumpets to announce His coming. Make ready for His salvation. Make ready to receive the Lord's knowledge, as it will be visited upon the people of Earth in this, the End of Days.*

"Holy shit," Chris gasped after hearing Ronnie read the message, "They think the zombies are holy? This is bad, Ron. Really, really bad. We gotta get back to the school and tell everyone cuz I don't think this was a one- time 'welcome to the neighborhood' kind of message." They quickly moved the heads back into the bag using their feet and placed it near the body of the Shambler. Ronnie doused it in gasoline and Chris threw a lit book of matches towards it. The fumes lit before the matches had even touched the ground and the flames consumed all they touched. As Chris looked back at the funeral pyre, he could not shake the feeling that there would be a lot more of these in the coming days, a lot more flames and a lot more death.

● ● ●

The council gathered in the gym to listen to Chris and Ronnie report what they had found. Amelia found herself in the uncomfortable position of resident biblical expert, and drew on the limited knowledge she had to try and make sense of the terrifying ramblings contained within the note.

"There's supposed to be seven angels and seven trumpets," Amelia said, "That was what brought about the different stages of the apocalypse. The first four were kind of minor compared to what came next."

"Minor?" Joey asked, "Is anything minor in the apocalypse?"

"Well, yeah," Amelia replied, "We're talking about starting with locusts and ending with poison water, bloody oceans and total darkness. So yeah, that stuff was kind of minor in the beginning, but the first four trumpets were supposed to be what announced the Four Horsemen."

"You mean like Death? The pale horse and all that stuff?" Sam asked.

"That and Conquest, Famine and War," Amelia shuddered, "I'd say it definitely looks like those four are around here."

The discussion continued as Erick walked into the room. He stood near the group for a moment, swaying back and forth before they saw him there. He looked as if he were trying to say something, but the words in his mouth were forced down by the vomit that spewed forth and leaked down his chin and the front of his shirt. Before anyone could react, Erick collapsed to the floor.

"What the hell happened?" Chris demanded as he picked Erick up and moved him to one of the mats used for bedding. "Alice do something! Get Bruno!" But Bruno had already seen from across the gym and was running in a full out sprint. Erick's eyes were rolling in their sockets and he began to convulse violently. A random onslaught of words spilled from Erick's mouth in an incomprehensible stream. Watts, who had been sleeping nearby, awoke from the commotion and rushed to Erick. Emily could be heard crying somewhere in the gym and Elsie and Ms. Kozlov were trying in vain to console her.

"What's going on?" Watts demanded, fear causing his words to crack and rise.

Bruno and Alice were trying to remain calm and tend to Erick, but could not figure out what to do next. Suddenly, Ms. Kozlov had joined the group.

"He was fine today. Nothing wrong at all," she said, trying to help.

"Where was he before any of this happened?" Alice asked, "What was he doing?"

Ms. Kozlov thought for a moment and then answered, "He was in the training room with me and the other students. He was just sitting there watching me work with the other children."

A loud scream sounded from the weight room and more students began to drop to the floor and convulse, though none as violently as Erick. Moments earlier, the other students had been going through their daily training routine and seemed completely healthy and the next they were vomiting and hallucinating.

"Nobody drink or eat anything," Bruno commanded and then he turned to Ms. Kozlov. "Did you open anything new in there? Any food or water?"

"No, no food," Ms. Kozlov said, "But we did put a new water bottle on the cooler. Erick had been drinking from it!"

Bruno and Alice exchanged worried looks. "Shit," Bruno murmured, "Where did we get that one from?"

"That came from one of the raids on a strip mall," Amelia answered, "We found a bunch of Poland Springs jugs in one of the office supply stores." Chris, whose eyes were wide and panicked, nodded in agreement and tried to comfort Erick as he moaned weakly, stopped shaking and went limp.

'That was near where those religious nuts were, right?" Alice asked, "It was near one of the developments they had burned down."

Picking up on Alice's line of reasoning Bruno continued, "And if they were near there, why would they leave a supply of clean water behind? Because it's not clean! Damn it! They must have found some way to put something in there to poison it!"

"Ok, ok," Alice said trying to remain calm, "We don't know what they put in there, but it seems to cause convulsions, vomiting and hallucinations. That means it could be some kind of drug right?"

"I guess so," Bruno said, "But a large dose of either of those would be hard to get and whatever it was, it had to be in liquid form. They probably injected it through the safety seal with a syringe, so that rules out a lot of narcotics that could have these effects. Shit, shit! I don't friggin' know!" Bruno was beginning to panic.

No one noticed that Watts had gotten up from the group and gone into the weight room. Ms. Kozlov, who had returned there, was busy trying to keep the children from banging their heads on the heavy equipment and did not see Watts pick up a paper cone and fill it from the cooler.

Sniffing the water, Watts could not detect anything. He stared angrily into the small paper cone demanding an answer and getting none. "Fuck it," he muttered and took a small drink from the cup. His face screwed as the liquid hit his tongue; there was a slight bitterness to the water, something you would not have noticed if you had been taking large gulps, but it was something oddly familiar to Watts. His vision began to blur on the edges and he shook his head, trying to clear his thoughts and remember why this seemed familiar.

A thought popped into Watts' mind randomly. "France!" he yelled, "Bruno remember France!"

"What the hell are you talking about?" Bruno said angrily and then he noticed the cup in Watts' hand, "Did you drink the water? You idiot!"

"Remember when we had leave in France," Watts slurred before he slumped onto this butt. His eyes were swimming in their sockets, unable to focus on anything.

"France?" Bruno said confused, "What the hell does this have to do with us taking leave in France?"

"What did you do there?" Alice asked firmly, "What happened while you were on leave?"

Bruno thought and tried to remember, "I don't know. Nothing really. We spent two days drunk off our asses on illegal bottles absinthe, so things are kind of blurry. Wait!"

But Alice had already connected the dots, "Absinthe! Isn't that illegal because it makes you hallucinate?"

"Yeah and makes you really sick if you have too much," Bruno replied, "But how would they get that in there?"

'What's in there that makes you trip out?" Chris demanded.

"I'm not sure," Bruno replied, "But I think it's wormwood or something like that."

Amelia's eyes suddenly lit up, "Wormwood? That's what it is! That's what it is!" Everyone looked confused. "The third trumpet blew when the Wormwood Star fell to Earth and poisoned the Earth's water. It's gotta be what they put in there! Those assholes!"

Bruno relaxed a little, "That makes sense. If that's what it is, then everyone's going to be sick for a while, but they'll be ok. They need to just get it out of their systems. Keep an eye on Erick. He's small and that shit is going to hit him harder, but as long as we keep him hydrated, I think he should be ok."

"Alright," Mike said, "Sam and Ronnie with me. We gotta dump any water we got from anywhere near those assholes. From now on, we boil all drinking water and only scavenge bottles with a hard cap. They shouldn't have been able to puncture those without us knowing." The three left the group to dump the contaminated water. Alice and Bruno began moving around the gym to assist with the other students, while Chris and Amelia held Erick in their laps. He seemed to be getting better, but was still ghostly pale and mumbling incoherently. Amelia put her head on Chris's shoulder and could feel the anger radiating off of him.

"He's gonna be ok," Amelia said softly, but her words were riddled with doubt.

"He'd better be," Chris said with a deathly chill on every word, "Cuz the assholes that did this aren't."

● ● ●

Erick had yet to regain consciousness. It had been less than two days, but the minutes stretched to feel like years. While everyone took turns tending to him, Chris and Watts refused to leave his side and were constantly checking his breathing, which remained strong. Emily was never far away, but Ms. Kozlov and Elsie were doing their best to try and comfort her and keep her busy.

"I found an old anthology on plants in one of the biology classes," Alice said, when Sam asked what book she had been reading for well over an hour. She and Bruno had been exhausting every source they had in an attempt to bring Erick back around, but without serious medical equipment there was little they could do besides hope he would pull through.

"Does it say anything that might help?" Sam asked, knowing that Alice must have read the book multiple times, but hoping that she found something new.

Alice looked defeated, "Nothing good. We can't know how much he ingested, but there's really no treatment for wormwood poisoning. We're treating the effects, but the longer he's in the coma the better the chance that he'll suffer some level of brain damage."

Small, cold beads of greasy sweat broke out along the back of Sam's neck and trickled down his back. "Wha...what can we do? There's gotta be something. Isn't there some medicine or something?"

"I don't know Sam," Alice said and she seemed to sink in on herself, "I'm not a real doctor. I don't know what to do. Shit! I wish I did, but I never learned about this stuff at any of those bullshit meetings my dad used to make me go to." Tears began to run down Alice's cheeks, but she refused to allow herself to cry fully. Sam did not know what to say. They had faced death every day since the dead had risen, but somehow the thought of such a small child dying, especially because of the actions of other human beings, was more than anyone could comprehend. The thought of Erick dying seemed to overload everyone's minds and they entered their own versions of semi-comas. Sam looked up from where he had buried his face in Alice's hair and saw Chris sitting next to Erick's small body. He could see Erick's chest rising and falling with each breath. Chris held his hand lightly on the small child's stomach, checking each breath. The posture and actions of Chris's body spoke of the intense emotions and concern that coursed through him. He had been overtaken by a deep desire to protect Erick, they all had, Erick and Emily were everyone's child or sibling, but Chris seemed to feel this responsibility at a level deeper than the others. Perhaps it was because no one had ever taken care of him, or because Erick and Emily were alone, much as he had been for most of his childhood. Whatever the reason, Sam could see a rage smoldering within Chris that threatened to consume him if Erick did not get better. It was terrifying to consider Erick dying, but perhaps even more so to think about what Chris might do if the small child did not wake up soon or worse yet, at all.

● ● ●

The following days were a blur of preparation and double-checking. Every aspect of the group's daily life had to be examined to see where there were any weaknesses or openings for the church members to attack again. The wormwood poisoning had been problematic, but not deadly and everyone except for Erick had recovered completely. Erick still lay prone, breathing slowly, on a pile of gym mats with his head propped up by a makeshift pillow that Chris had constructed out of some towels.

No one wanted to give the church members an opportunity to progress in their attacks, but that left two dangerous and contentious questions that hung over the group members like a toxic fog. How could they prevent another attack, and perhaps more importantly, should they strike first? These questions were beginning to divide the group and any infighting was an invitation for death.

Chris and Watts were strongly arguing for action. They wanted revenge for what happened to Erick and even though Sam and others tried to convince them that an emotional response was a dangerous one, they knew they were losing. As each day passed, Chris and Watts would have a few more people in their circle as they discussed the need to attack Zion before they attacked them.

"They're coming back," Chris said forcefully, "You know they are and it's only going to get worse. We're lucky that no one died from the wormwood...yet. What's going to be enough to get you off your ass?"

"I'm not saying that I disagree with you," Sam said, "But if they're going to come back anyway, then why not prepare for them and fight on our own turf?" Sam knew that trying to talk them out of violence was going to be near impossible, but he hoped that he could at least delay it or control where it occurred. "We don't know what the hell they have up there at the church. Attacking them could be exactly what they wanted. How's it going to do anyone any good if you get caught or killed?"

Chris had to admit that there was a certain amount of sense to what Sam was saying, but his anger had kicked his survival skills into high gear and he was ready to fight. No one was aware of when the change had over taken the group, but at some point, they all seemed to have made the silent, unconscious decision that the only law that mattered any longer was kill or be killed.

"Look, man," Crawford said as he approached the argument ensuing between council members, "I know we all decided that you kids need to be in control and making decisions, and that's fine, but I'm not going to sit by and watch you get yourselves killed, and I'm sure as hell not going to help." Everyone turned to face him and stopped yelling at one another. "You do whatever you think is right, but I'm going to at least say my part. When we were in Afghanistan, I saw plenty of my friends have far worse shit happen to them than a coma or poisoning. You better believe, that me, Watts and Bruno wanted to chase those bastards back into the mountains and flatten their villages."

"See!" Chris said emphatically.

Crawford shook his head, "But if we did that, if we allowed that insanity to overtake our ability to reason, we would have died too. The best thing we can do is try and help Erick get better and plan for those bastards. Believe me, they come near this place again and I'll be the first one to put a hole through them, but running headlong into their territory is just plain stupid. They're crazy, I'll give you that, but they're organized, so we gotta assume that they have some level of defense."

Chris was about to argue, but had lost some of his steam. Getting himself killed or captured was not going to help Erick. There would be time for some equalizing of scores, but it was not now. "Fine," Chris acquiesced, "But if he dies..." Chris's words trailed off. He was unable to complete his thought, unable to consider that that may actually occur. Chris had not realized that up until this point, he had been blindly believing that Erick would get better, but Crawford's words had proven that wrong. People you loved, you counted on, your friends and your family can and will die. You spend most of your life selfishly anticipating and hoping that time will be kind enough to allow your death to precede theirs, and spare you the pain of facing each new day without them, but those plans so often painfully fall through and you are left with nothing more than faded memories, and a cancerous gash in your heart that festers and grows with each passing moment. One that tears a little further with each revisited memory, until eventually, the very things that should remind you of better times and give you solace do nothing more than add to your tortuous existence, and prolong your suffering, unless you found some way to deal with it or at least make sense of it. Chris realized all of these facts long ago and knew that life cared little for what he wanted, let alone needed, and that this could very well just be another of those situations.

● ● ●

"He's not going to die!" Amelia shouted at Chris, "Stop saying that!"

Tears welled in Chris's eyes, "It's been days Amelia and he's still not awake. He's just too little for his body to handle that crap they put in there."

"Shut up! Shut up!" her words were choked, "He's strong damn it!"

Chris was about to reply and realized that Emily had silently come up beside them. "Do you really think that?" Emily asked, her emotions causing her voice to catch and hiccup in her throat, "You need to believe like Amelia does Chris!" Emily was beginning to lose it.

"I do," Chris lied, "I want to sweetheart. I'm trying."

The tears suddenly stopped and a look of defiance set Emily's features in stone, "He's strong. He saved me from the monsters and you're stupid if you think anything else. You're stupid!" Chris tried to explain, but the small girl refused to listen and ran back across the gym where she buried herself in the arms of Elsie.

Amelia shook her head, a look of anger igniting her eyes. "Are you happy now?" She hissed, "Is that what you wanted?"

"Of course not," Chris said weakly, "It's just that…I mean, how can you keep hoping? How do you hold onto that, when everything has just gone completely to shit?"

"Because that's all we have left," Amelia said, "Besides one another. You can't lose that Chris." Not knowing what to say, Chris dumbly shook his head.

"What if I never had it?" He said.

"Then you better friggin' find it," Amelia said angrily, "How can you not? Look at everything we've done, everything we've survived, and you're telling me you can't find some small splinter of hope? Damn it Chris, I love you for your strength, but being emotionally dead isn't going to make you any stronger. What you're feeling now, not the bad shit, but what you're feeling now you need to use that. You owe Erick that much."

"Did you just say you loved me?" Chris asked bewildered.

Amelia blushed, "I guess I did...and I guess I do."

"I...I...love you too," Chris stammered, having never told anyone that other than his dogs.

"Ummm, sorry," Ronnie said, "I, um, thought you might want to take a break and get some food or get washed up." Both Chris and Amelia looked thankful for the interruption punctuating the awkward conversation.

"Thanks Ron," Amelia said, "I think we could use a little rest." She gently led Chris across the gym to where a few of the others were quietly eating a stew that Elsie had prepared for them. Ronnie noticed that they held hands the entire way.

"How's little man doing?" Bruno asked as he came up beside Ronnie.

Ronnie shrugged, "Seems about the same, I guess." Bruno knelt down next to Erick and began going through one of his many daily physical exams. He withdrew a small penlight and shone it into Erick's eyes.

"Shit!" Bruno yelled, "His pupil constricted! Look! Look!" The sound of bowls clattering on the hardwood floor, followed by the pounding of feet resounded throughout the gym. A large semi-circle formed around Erick and Bruno. "His eyes are responding to light! He's responding to light!"

"What the does that mean?" Chris demanded.

"It means that his coma is no longer that deep and that he's probably coming out of it," Alice said excited, "Bruno pinch his hand." The soldier did as he was asked and everyone gasped as Erick's hand pulled away from the source of pain. "If his auto responses are still working, there's a really good chance that he's going to be ok!"

Everyone shared an uneasy smile, but erupted into raucous cheers as Erick's eyes weakly fluttered open. "Why are you yelling?" He said softly, "Stop. My head hurts." He continued to complain weakly, but everyone cheerfully listened. It was the best thing that they had heard in a long time.

Bruno pulled Alice aside from the others as they excitedly crowded around Erick. "We got a problem," he said, "I'm worried that Erick might have some swelling in his brain. He's complaining a lot about his head and he's got a slight tremor. I'm not sure. Could be nothing, but if he does and we don't do something, he'll die."

"What do we need to do?" Alice whispered.

"We need to get him steroids to reduce the swelling and take the pressure off his brain, but we don't have that kind of medicine here."

"Then we'll get it," Alice said firmly.

● ● ●

The plan was simple, drive to the hospital because all of the pharmacies had been burnt down. Get the steroids for Erick, come back and everyone is happy again. The plan seemed relatively simple, which immediately let everyone know it had the potential of becoming a massive cluster fuck.

"I'm going," Chris said, "It's not up for debate."

"Me too," Watts added, but he was soon buried under reasons for him not to go.

"How are you going to run if you need to?" Joey asked.

"Ankle's better," Watts said flatly, "Alice gave me the thumbs up yesterday."

"I said you could walk around without the wrap," Alice said defensively, "I didn't say anything about running through a zombie filled hospital."

"Well, whatever," Watts said, "I'm going."

Eventually it was agreed that one van would go carrying Chris, Watts and Sam. Hector would lead the way in his backhoe with Bruno in the bucket, his rifle ready in case any Stalkers turned up. Alice and Amelia demanded to go, but narrowly lost the vote.

'You're being sexist!" Alice protested.

A look of befuddlement on his face, Sam countered, "No, no it's not that at all. If we have Bruno with us, you need to stay here to take care of Erick. That's all." She knew he was right, but did not want to let him go back out into the world beyond the fence without her.

"Please be careful," Alice whispered to Sam as she wrapped her arms around him, "No hero games ok?" Sam nodded and squeezed her tighter.

Amelia and Chris were having a similar argument, although one much louder and strewn with curse words.

"Misogynistic prick?" Chris said, "I'm not even sure what half of that means, but I'm not being the last part of what you just said."

Amelia seethed, "You think I can't hold my own huh? That I'm some pansy ass, hot house flower?" She followed her statement with a powerful blow to Chris's arm.

"Jeez, chill the hell out," he said rubbing his arm, "I want you to stay here to help Crawford, Joey and Mike. Please, I know better than to think you're some little princess."

"What's that supposed to mean?" Amelia hissed, "You calling me butch? Now I'm a dyke, is that it?" Finally, realizing that rational arguments were not going to work, Chris grabbed Amelia and kissed her. "You think your shitty chapped lips are gonna shut me up?"

"No," Chris said, a smile curling the corners of his mouth, "But I find you insanely irresistible when you shout the word 'dyke'. Also, I was wondering if there was any truth to that, ya know? We could like work out a three way or something. That'd really give a guy something to come home for."

"Shut up," Amelia said, but all the fight was out of her, "Just be careful. We all want Erick better, but also want you alive. No stupid mistakes, ok?"

On the other side of the gym, Hector was talking to Emily. Since watching her neighborhood burn down from the roof, she had placed Hector into a pseudo-father role and was having a difficult time letting him leave, especially because Erick was unable to give her strength and comfort.

"Please!" she sobbed, "Promise!"

"I do and I will," Hector said, "I promise I'll come back sweetheart. I will." Tears were beginning to gather in the corner of his eyes. He would never admit to the others that Emily and Erick reminded him of his young niece and nephew in Lima, both of which he was fairly certain were now dead, but he had no means of finding out.

As Sam made his way towards the doors, Amelia grabbed his arm and slipped a scrap of paper into his hand. "Shopping list," she explained, "Lady stuff."

Quickly looking at the paper, not really understanding it, but knowing better than to ask, Sam nodded. "Um, yeah ok, but why not ask Chris?"

"He's too uncomfortable with that stuff," Amelia said quickly, "He gets all grossed out and stuff." Sam shrugged and slipped the paper into his pocket. Amelia appeared to breathe a sigh of relief, but for the life of him, Sam had no idea why.

After the goodbyes had been said, they loaded into their respective vehicles and rolled slowly towards the gate. Bruno settled awkwardly into the shaky bucket of the backhoe and tried to stay as comfortable as possible. Crawford and Mike gave them a wave as the convoy rolled through the gate near the machine gun bunker. Watts followed closely behind in the van with Chris in the passenger seat. Sam was doing his best to find a comfortable position, but Gozer and Zule kept wrestling to sit in his lap. Eventually, Sam gave in and lay down. Both dogs clambered on top of him and began savagely licking his face.

Aside from a few Shamblers along the side the road, which at this point were becoming as commonplace and mundane as a McDonalds, the ride towards the hospital was uneventful. Hector plowed through the wrecked, burnt out cars, forcing them over to the side of the road, while Bruno carefully scanned the horizon from above. What he did not want to admit, was that he was more worried about sighting a human than a Shambler or Stalker. If the lunatics from Zion had poisoned the water, what would they have done to the hospital? They seemed determined not only to see the apocalypse, but also to help it along.

"Looks good," Hector rattled through the radio as they approached the hospital parking lot.

"Ok," Watts responded, "But, and I'm not saying this to be a dick, but didn't you think there would be more zombies here? I mean shouldn't this place be even more swamped by the dead heads than the Municipal Complex?"

"Point taken," Bruno said into his handheld as he climbed down to walk point, "Back the van up to the emergency entrance and park it facing the road. Hector, you do the same. I want to make sure we can bug out fast if we need to."

The backhoe pushed an ambulance with a crumpled side panel out of the way, so the vehicles could be positioned according to plan. Sam and Chris jumped out of the van and used a pry bar to pull open the automatic doors. Gozer and Zule were the first through the doors and immediately began circling the room; everyone could not help but notice that the wiry tuft of hair between each dog's powerful shoulders stood completely up. Carefully, they made their way into the shadowy emergency room waiting area. Crumpled piles of abandoned coats strewn across chairs cast strange silhouettes, all of which looked ready to leap forward at any moment to tear a glistening chunk of flesh from someone.

"We move through quick and quiet," Bruno said, "We're not here for anything other than the medication. So let's find the pharmacy and get the hell out of here. Good?" Everyone nodded and fell into line behind Bruno as he walked point. "Anyone know where the pharmacy is?"

"Saw a directory back there," Hector said with a note of hesitation, "It's downstairs, by the morgue."

● ● ●

Each step in the empty hallway resounded louder than anyone was comfortable with, but there seemed to be no way to place a foot down that was not a dinner bell ringing for whatever Shamblers hid hungrily in the shadows. Fortunately, no footfalls echoed off the hard tiled floors aside from those of the living that painstakingly picked their way past overturned gurneys, wheelchairs and various other medical equipment that lay in disarray. The only members of the group that had figured how to move silently were Gozer and Zule, but the instinctual skill set from which they drew, had long since been bred out of their human companions.

"It should be up here," Hector whispered as he pointed around the next corner.

"Ok," Bruno said, "Me, Watts and Chris go in and grab the steroids Erick needs and whatever other drugs we can carry. Sam and Hector watch the halls." Everyone nodded.

The three men moved slowly towards the mesh wire windows that adorned the front of the drug dispensary. The door leading in was slightly ajar; the leathery remains of a genderless corpse in stained, green scrubs blocking it from closing.

Sam and Hector moved a little further down the hall and uncomfortably took their post next to the morgue. Sam pressed his face against the small porthole window that centered on the two swinging doors. It was dark inside, no windows, but the little amount of ambient light that trickled through from the hallway allowed Sam to discern clumped groupings of varied shadows in the room. None were moving and no noise could be heard from within.

"Nothing moving," Sam said quietly, but kept one eye trained on the doors. Hector pushed his back against the opposite wall and looked down the darken hallway in the opposite direction of Sam. All that could be heard where the shaking of pill bottles as the others scavenged the pharmacy.

"Hurry up ladies," Watts said checking his wind-up watch. The small indigo tick marks let him know the time and it was getting late. "Gonna be dark soon. We don't want to be driving back when those torch toting fucks come down the hill." Chris and Bruno did not answer, but their pace picked up. There were numerous pill bottles, most of which looked the same in the dim light cast from their flashlights.

"Here's the stuff we came for," Bruno said, shaking a small white bottle with an orange safety top. "Screw the other stuff. Let's get moving." He began to move towards the door, but stopped when he saw that Gozer and Zule had frozen near the door with their ears pricked up. Zule's lips curled back in a silent snarl. The three men looked at the two dogs growing more concerned with each second.

Clicking his tongue, Chris moved through the door, followed close behind by his dogs. He nodded to Sam and Hector, but before any progress could be made towards the doors the tinny rumble of a horn blared, audible even in the lower reaches of the hospital.

● ● ●

"You think they'll be ok don't you?" Amelia asked Alice as they walked the perimeter of the fence. The others had been gone for almost half the day and Alice could no longer just sit in the gym. Erick was hanging on, but she could not expect that to last very long; his headaches were increasing in magnitude, the small child could hardly keep his eyes open and had spent most of the day whining weakly and trying not to vomit. Fortunately, Ms. Kozlov and Joey had relieved Alice for a while and she had offered to join Amelia on her rounds.

"They'll be ok," Alice replied, but Amelia noticed she did not look her in the eyes, "It's kind of getting dark though, but I'm sure they will."

"Yeah," Amelia said without conviction.

"So can I ask you something?" Alice said gently, "I mean you can totally tell me to shut up or something, but I just wanted to know…"

"Just ask," Amelia cut in with a dry laugh, "Whatever it is."

Alice appeared uncomfortable, but she continued. "Ok, um, I just wanted to know what was on that note you gave Sam. I mean, was it like, um, I mean do you guys have something…" Alice could not finish the sentence. While there had been no public declarations, and certainly no marriages, she could not stomach the idea of Sam being with someone else. He was hers and if something was going on, she wanted to know.

An enormous laugh erupted from Amelia's lips and a smile crept across her face. She turned to face Alice and grabbed her by the shoulders. Looking straight into her eyes she said, "There is nothing between me and Sam I can promise you that." Then she laughed again.

"What's that supposed to mean?" Alice replied indignantly, "Like's he's not good enough or something?"

"No, no," Amelia said holding her hands up, "Sam's great. A little too sensitive for me, but he's great."

"Sensitive?" Alice said with a mix of confusion and defensiveness painting her words.

Amelia laughed again, "I'm not calling him a wuss, Alice. He's just not my type, that's all."

"Well, then what was the note?" Alice asked, beginning to relax, but feeling somewhat embarrassed over her reaction.

"Things I needed Sam to get me from the hospital. You know, like vitamins and stuff," Amelia said dismissively.

The words seemed to light a connection in Alice's mind. "Vitamins?" She asked, "Anything else, like maybe folic acid?" Amelia appeared to be at a loss for words. "Does he know?" Alice said gently, "Does Chris know that you're pregnant?"

Tears began to well in Amelia's eyes. "No," she chocked, "I'm not even sure, but I think I am...Please don't say anything. Please." Her cheeks glistened in the afternoon sun as the tears streamed over her then.

"I won't say anything," Alice promised, "But you've got to tell him. He'd want to know." Amelia nodded and buried Alice in a bear hug.

On the other side of the school grounds, Mike and Crawford lay back against the barrels packed into a tight semi-circle in front of the SAW machine gun mount. "They've been gone for a while," Mike said in response to Crawford's unspoken question. Crawford nodded and checked the ammo belt feeding the large gun. The nervous energy in the gun nest had been bubbling throughout the day and was reaching a boiling point.

*"Mike,"* it was Ronnie on the roof, *"We got movement. Not sure who it is, but it looks human."*

"Ok, Ron," Mike replied, "Let us know if you see anything else." Before Mike could relay the information to Crawford, the man had already pulled back the heavy handle on the side of the SAW and chambered the first bullet on the ammo belt.

"Something's wrong," Crawford said sourly and almost on cue, a loud horn blasted one long, rusty drawn out note that lasted for longer than it seemed possible for human lungs to sustain.

"Ron?" Mike said nervously into the radio.

*"Heard it too,"* Ronnie replied, *"It's hard to tell, but I think there's a group moving towards the school. Looks pretty big."*

The torches could be seen igniting a few at a time in the distance, but soon an entire lake of fire danced towards the school.

*"Guys,"* Amelia called through the radio, *"We got torches in the back woods. Looks like a lot of people."* Alice and Amelia had ducked behind one of the shadowed corners afforded by the school's construction, and watched as amber tongues of fire leapt into the air and punctuated the darkness under the trees like the eyes of a large feral cat. Shadowy outlines of human forms could be seen swaying in the pools of darkness below the trees. Something between a prayer and song was faintly audible above the sounds of the day. The words were lost, but the message was clearly not one of comfort or praise. "We need to get back to the gym," Alice said, "Make sure everyone is ok." Amelia nodded and the two girls faded back into the shadows.

Near the front gate, Mike watched as the group of people spread their ranks and began circling the school grounds. They stood just beyond the fence. "There's gotta be close to a hundred," Mike gasped.

"That's fine," Crawford sneered, "We got thirty times that many bullets."

● ● ●

The shuffling of feet outside of the hospital emergency room could be heard all the way down the hall. The blaring of the trumpet had alerted everyone to the fact that they were no longer alone, but having heard the horn, they assumed it was more of the Zion Church members, so they were shocked when they rounded the corner and came face to face with a writhing pack of Shamblers held at bay by the large panes of glass that adorned the front of the hospital emergency room.

"That glass isn't gonna hold long," Hector said, observing the pressure cracks that were already stretching their thin fingers across the glass. "How the hell did so many of the Shamblers get here so quick? The parking lot was empty before." On the other side of the parking lot, barely visible above all of the rotted heads, they could see a few humans near the massive employee parking tower that filled the back of the lot. The people were running quickly from ramp to ramp, pulling up the large metal security doors that typically were held in place by electronic locks, but were now easily pried open with the power off. As the gates came up, more Shamblers stumbled down the ramp to join the already massive herd.

"That's why we didn't see any!" Sam spat angrily, "They were keeping them in the damn garage? What the hell?"

"It's an ambush," Bruno said, "They must have known at some point we would need to come here and trapped all of the dead heads in the garage until they were ready to release them." A shot rang out from one of the upper levels of the garage and pinged loudly off of the concrete outside.

"What the hell are they doing?" Chris asked, but a second shot ricocheted loudly off of the glass and caused it to crack even further. "Shit, they're trying to break the glass!" Everyone started stepping slowly back down the hall, not wanting to move too quickly and excite the Shamblers.

The zombies were milling about outside, bumping into one another and making little progress towards getting inside, but the third shot hit dead center on one of the panels and it collapsed inward. The Shamblers began tripping over the low sill and pouring into the emergency room. They showed no regard for their fallen cohorts and simply stumbled over them or stepped down on their backs, pushing them down further onto the jagged glass teeth that protruded from where the window had once stood.

"Run for the front!" Bruno yelled as he and Watts fired a volley of bullets into the first huddled mass of zombies that ambled towards them. The others fell back behind the two soldiers and headed for the doors. As they approached the front, they were relieved to see that no Shamblers were waiting there, but as Sam got to the doors he saw five men, all holding bottles with long flaming rags stuffed into them, heading for the doors.

"Come on," Sam said angrily and sighted the foremost member of the group. His first reaction was to put a bullet through the center of the man's head as Bruno had taught him, but he heard Bruno shouting from behind him.

"Shoot the bottle!" The soldier yelled as he took up a firing position next to Sam and squeezed off a shot. Sam followed suit and watched horrified as two of the bottles burst and engulfed the men carrying them. Their screams were muffled by the roaring of the fire, but they continued towards the doors. Sam's next shot went wide and hit a third man in the bicep. The man tried to bring the bottle back to throw it, but the large caliber bullet had shredded his muscle and tendons. With nothing to do but hold the bottle, the man broke into a sprint and flung himself at the doors.

A wave of fire washed across the front doors and engulfed the man. Sam was sure he was smiling as he pressed his burning body against the glass. With the flames blocking their view, Sam and Bruno could not sight the remaining two men.

"Save your bullets," Bruno commanded to everyone and quelled the urge to unleash a volley of wild fire through the front windows. 'We're gonna need them." The next two firebombs sailed through the air and broke on the sidewalk near the front doors. Flames engulfed the front entrance of the hospital, making it impossible to get out.

"There were ambulances out there," Chris said, "We gotta move now!" The first of the cars exploded, sending small shards of molten glass sailing through the air. If not for the receptionist desk, they would have all died a death of a million small cuts, but even so, they still scrambled to pick the scalding splinters of glass from the tops of their heads.

"Back downstairs," Watts cried out, as he headed for the staircase, "We can figure something out when we get down there!" The others sprinted from behind the desk as another ambulance exploded behind them. Zule and Gozer flanked the door and took up defensive stances as the first Shambler rounded the corner. Watts moved as fast as his ankle would allow, but the others quickly caught up to him and helped him through the doors.

Chris was the last one moving through the door, refusing to go without his dogs. "Gozer! Zule! Come!" he commanded, and the dogs trotted down the stairs after him. The door clattered loudly as it banged shut, but they all knew it was only a matter of time before enough Shamblers pressed against the bar to release the door inward and stumble down the stairs after them.

"Get back to the pharmacy," Sam shouted down the hall. It seemed like a logical place to make a stand, being that it had a reinforced door and wire mesh over the windows.

"Split up," Watts shouted, "You guys in the pharmacy. Wait for them to pass and then hit them from the back. Me, Chris and Hector will lead them down the hall and then duck into the morgue. That way we catch them in the middle." As Sam was heading into the pharmacy, Chris grabbed his arm.

"Take Gozer and Zule for me," he asked, "They'll be safer in there." Sam was about to argue but could see the concern in Chris's eyes. What they were about to do required a clear head. He could not worry about his dogs while leading a pack of zombies down the hall. Sam nodded.

"I'll take care of them," he promised, "They'll be safe." Chris quickly reached down and scratched each dog behind the ears and then pushed them into the room with Sam and Bruno. The dogs immediately rushed the door and tried to follow Chris, but he pulled the door closed and remained in the hall. Gozer whined weakly and paced by the door, while Zule stood on her back legs and frantically tried to work the doorknob. Not being able to protect Chris was driving the dogs insane; even they seemed to comprehend the danger that was slowly stumbling down the hall.

The three men in the hallway took up position with Watts slightly ahead of Chris and Hector. "As soon as they get past the pharmacy start shooting," Watts said, "No wild fire. Go for head shots, but keep backing towards the morgue."

"Does anyone else find this plan ironic?" Chris asked, "I mean that we're hiding from a bunch of dead people in a morgue?" He let out a dry laugh that carried with it no humor.

"Irony is your mother calling you a son of a bitch," Hector said bitterly, "This just sucks."

A group of about forty Shamblers had massed at the bottom of the stairs and more could be heard moaning hungrily from within the stairwell.

"Here goes," Watts said and fired off a shot that exploded the head of the lead zombie. The others immediately responded to the sound and quickened their pace down the hall. The three men slowly walked backwards while trying to carefully aim their shots. A few zombies fell and were quickly trampled under the feet of their advancing comrades, but there seemed to be an endless supply of them.

Sam and Bruno ducked down behind the counter when they heard the first shot go off. Numerous shadows walked in a halting gait past the window. The groans of the undead grew louder and louder causing Sam's skin to crawl. He was dying to know what numbers his friends were facing, but knew that he needed to wait. He and Bruno were going to flank the zombies from the side and back, thereby splitting the attention of the horde and hopefully confusing them, but having a plan did not make waiting any easier. Bruno seemed to pick up on Sam's energy.

"Soon," he whispered, "When their shooting stops, we step out and open fire. Draw them back this way." Sam nodded.

"Go!" Watts yelled, as he kicked open the door to the morgue. The swinging doors were not going to hold very long and they could only hope that their plan would work. Hector and Chris slipped past Watts while they squeezed off their last shots, dropping another of the horde. Watts ducked in and put his back against the door; Hector already had his against the other.

As soon as the shooting stopped, Sam and Bruno peeked out from under the counter. There were a few Shamblers outside the window, easy targets at this range. They quietly stood up and began popping off close range shots through the glass. The zombie's heads seemed to explode and coated the windows in a thick, viscous layer of fetid gray matter. The window was becoming hard to see through from the blinding level of gore that was smeared across, but this also provided Sam and Bruno with a blind from the other zombies.

"I'm going for the door," Sam said and moved towards it.

"On three," Bruno said, "Then I'll draw their attention this way and you clean up." Sam nodded and Bruno signaled a three count with his fingers. On three, Sam stepped into the hallway and placed a handful of carefully aimed shots into the heads of the Shamblers outside the window. More were coming down the hall, but Bruno joined Sam in the doorway and began firing down the hall.

"Out," Sam said and ducked back inside to reload. Bruno chambered and fired off his last round and then slammed the door closed. Zule and Gozer, who were still pacing angrily inside, snarled at the window as more zombies began to beat their dead hands on the bloody glass.

"We're up," Chris said and pushed open the doors to the morgue. Hector and Watts followed close behind and fired a volley down the hall. They switched the M-16s to three round bursts and began peppering the horde with bullets. Zombies crumpled and fell as they advanced down the hall. After completing this sequence a few more times, a pile of ruined Shamblers chocked the middle of the hallway.

"Looks clear," Watts called and stepped into the hallway. A shot rang out and the bullet tore a chunk from Watts' shoulder. "Damn it," he screamed, "What are you doing?" But it was not Sam or Bruno firing.

"It's not us," Bruno yelled as bullets peppered the glass above his head.

"What the hell is going on?" Sam said through gritted teeth as he pulled Gozer and Zule under the counter.

"It's gotta be those assholes from Zion," Bruno shouted as he blind fired three shots over the counter, which were answered with a shotgun blast that scattered glass and shook the wire mesh.

Down the hall, Chris pulled Watts back into the morgue. The shot to his shoulder was not a mortal wound, but it was definitely causing him a great deal of pain. "Jeez," Watts wheezed, "I never thought I'd miss the damn dead heads." Chris ripped his shirt and tried his best to stop the bleeding while Hector leaned out into the hallway and squeezed off a few rounds.

"There's a bunch of them down there," Hector said, "Looks like they got hunting rifles and shotguns."

The group of Zion Church parishioners returned fire and moved closer to the shattered pharmacy windows. As Bruno leaned over the counter to fire off a few rounds, he saw a man advancing with another firebomb in hand. He tried to get a bead on the bottle, but the cover fire being laid kept him pinned. A wild shot from Bruno's rifle whizzed pass the man, but did not slow his stride. He raised the bottle high over head and the last thing Bruno saw before flames exploded through the mesh and across the ceiling, was the man's wide, grinning face. The flames blew backwards and engulfed the man, who did not so much as scream, rather he continued to smile as the flesh melted from his bone.

"Stay low! Move now! Move! Move!" Bruno screamed as he pushed Sam towards the large steel refrigerator in the back of the pharmacy. He threw the doors open and hastily pulled the racks and contents out. Tossing Sam a large orange pill bottle, Bruno pushed him into one side of the refrigerator and piled Zule and Gozer into the other.

"Wait!" Sam yelled, "Where are you gonna go?" But Bruno was already closing the doors. He crouched low and moved back towards the front. The flames had kept the Zion Church members from seeing inside, so Bruno hoped that they would not think to look for Sam in the back. He lay prone on the floor, away from the window and sighted the door.

Slamming his body against the door, Sam tried to release himself from the steel box he was currently trapped in, but could not shake it hard enough to release the latch on the outside. The sound of the front door collapsing inward was overshadowed by the pounding of feet and a rapid volley of fire that Sam recognized as Bruno's SR-25.

Inside the morgue, Chris and Hector heard the explosion from the firebomb and watched as the flames lit up the darkened porthole windows on the doors. Chris leaned out the door and tried to see what was going on.

"They're in the pharmacy!" He shouted as he fired into the crowd of men, "Shit! We gotta do something!" But his few shots were answered with a spray of buckshot that tore a huge chuck of wood from the doorframe near his head. As Chris dropped low and pulled his head back into the room, he caught a glimpse of a ragged flame, pin wheeling through the air towards the morgue.

"Get dow..." was all Chris could say before the doors exploded inward and tossed him across the room knocking him unconscious. Hector pulled himself off the floor. The ringing in his ears kept him from hearing the footsteps pounding down the hallway towards the morgue, but he knew that they would be there soon.

"Get up!" Hector yelled at Chris as he pulled Watts across the room. The man moaned as Hector put pressure on his wound, but seemed otherwise fine. "You aren't gonna like this, but it might just save your life." Hector reached up and pulled the handle adorning the front of one of the numerous square metal doors that lined the room. He slid out the body tray, which was thankfully empty, and hoisted Watts onto it. Before the soldier could protest, Hector slid the tray back inside and slammed the door closed.

The ringing in Hector's ears subsided just enough for him to hear the yelling of the approaching men. "Shit," Hector muttered as he realized that he would not have time to get Chris and himself into one of the drawers as well. Flipping over a stainless steel gurney, Hector pulled Chris behind and knelt down and checked his magazine. He racked both his rifle and Chris's, which he leaned against the gurney for when his was empty. If they were going to kill them, Hector was determined to at least make it difficult. As the first man came through the smoldering doorframe, Hector gritted his teeth and squeezed the trigger.

● ● ●

Crawford flipped open the top of the SAW machine gun and slapped in another belt of ammo from the box Mike had opened. The people outside the gate seemed unaffected by the chatter of the large gun and the glistening chunks it tore from their ranks. They continued to mass outside the fence and lob flaming gas bombs over, which smashed on the pavement and sent waves of fire washing across.

"These assholes don't seem to be getting the message!" Mike yelled over the rattling of the SAW. Crawford did not respond and kept moving the gun in a slow arc, cutting through the attackers, but for every one he saw fall, two seemed to take their place. He and Mike were quickly becoming stranded on an island in a sea of fire and molten asphalt.

As the belt of ammo choked its way through the machine gun and out the other side, Crawford yelled over his shoulder, "Get on the radio and figure out what is going on!"

"Ronnie? Joey," Mike yelled into the radio over the noise, "Can you see what the hell is going on from up there?"

Lying flat on the roof, Ronnie was firing shots off into the back of the crowd, hoping to slow them down, but his shots were having little effect. Joey was watching the crowd through a scope; his guts churned more and more the longer he watched. "Mike," Joey replied, "They're everywhere. The school grounds are completely surrounded, but they don't appear to be climbing over the fence. It's almost like they are waiting for something."

Mike relayed the information to Crawford, who muttered some obscenity and continued spraying large amounts of bullets into the crowd. The mob did not appear to be heavily armed, but they had a seemingly endless supply of Molotov Cocktails that they were lobbing continuously towards the machine gun bunker. The mass of people near the front gate began to thin and Mike saw a large set of headlights bearing down on them.

"Crawford!" Mike screamed, pointing at the approaching truck, "The gate!" Crawford spun the SAW on its tripod to face the gate, but even as the bullets from the gun tore into the engine block of the large moving truck, it crashed through. The gates were thrown wide open and the mob flooded in through the opening.

"Fall back!" Crawford screamed, as he picked up the large machine gun and cradled it in his arms. Mike fired off a rapid volley of cover fire as the two ran at break neck speed for the doors of the gym. "Ronnie and Joey lay some rounds to cover us," Crawford shouted into the radio, which was quickly answered with the chatter of two machine guns from the roof.

Alice had been listening to the exchange over the radio and opened the doors to let Mike and Crawford in. Amelia and Ms. Kozlov leaned out the other door and sprayed the perusing crowd with cover fire. Many of the Zion members fell as the bullets struck them, but they were swiftly covering ground and catching up to Mike and Crawford.

Inside the gym, Elsie had taken Erick, Emily and the other remaining students into the men's locker room and tipped a stack of lockers in front of the door. "It's going to be ok children," she lied, "We just have to stay safe until this is over." The children noticed that Elsie held a shaking pistol in her hand, something she had never relied upon before.

Mike and Crawford reached the open doors of the gym and tumbled inside. The large SAW machine gun clattered across the floor as Alice and Ms. Kozlov slammed the doors shut and wrapped a chain around them. Picking himself up off the floor, Crawford grabbed the SAW and pushed it into Mike's arms. "Get this to the fall back position. Amelia, you go too. Take the others with you." Mike nodded and sprinted towards the locker room. Amelia hesitated, but fell into stride behind him.

Banging loudly on the door, Mike shouted, "Elsie fall back to the offices. Get everyone moving." Inside he could hear the shuffling of feet as everyone moved towards the back door and through the halls. He quickly cast a glance over his shoulder to see Crawford, Alice and Ms. Kozlov climbing high into the stacked bleachers. They had prepared for this, but having a worst-case scenario plan did not make facing one any easier. Mike sprinted to catch up with Elsie and the others.

"They're gonna be in soon," Ronnie reported over the radio, "We're shooting the ones near the doors, but we're running low on ammo."

Grabbing his radio Crawford commanded, "You two fall back to the offices with Mike and resupply there. We'll buy you guys some time." Ronnie sprayed the last of his rounds into the crowd and sprinted towards the ladder. Joey was close behind. Within minutes, the two boys were beside Mike helping to mount the SAW.

High above the gym floor Crawford, Ms. Kozlov and Alice went over the plan. "When they get in," Crawford said uneasily, "Stay low until there's a decent number of them. Then, Alice you throw that smoke grenade. As soon as that pops, Ms. Kozlov follow it up with that incendiary one. Then just shoot." The two women nodded. Holding the heavy grenades in their hands was disconcerting, but that was the plan. Using a grenade on a group of Shamblers seemed like a waste, so the council had decided to save them for this kind of situation.

The chain on the doors rattled loudly and shook as the Zion members battered their bodies against it. The doors could not take much more abuse. They were going to get in soon.

"This isn't right," Mike said as he began to barricade the door, "We gotta go back and help them. Screw the plan!" Ronnie was about to protest, but Amelia cut him off.

"Mike's right," she seethed, "I'm not letting these assholes wreck our place so easily." Elsie looked concerned as other students were beginning to agree. They had previously been stupefied by the horrific events in the early days, but the daily training and routine had brought many of them back. More than that, it had strengthened them and given them purpose. A small number of the other students moved to the back office, which had been designated as the ammo dump and armed themselves. They were done hiding.

"Alright," Mike said, "Ronnie and Joey, you gotta stay here, just in case. There has to be at least one of the council members left to ensure that Elsie and the smaller kids are ok. Barricade the door and shoot anything that's not us."

"Man fuck that," Joey retorted, "I'm coming with you."

Ronnie looked nervous, "Are you sure about this Mike?"

Something malevolent burned in Mike's eyes, "We've worked too hard, come too far for it to get ruined now. We want to keep this, then we need to fight for it." Mike, Amelia and five other students turned to head down the hall.

"Wait!" Ronnie shouted from inside the office, "Take the SAW with you. It won't do much for us in such a tight space, but it'll be good in the gym." Mike nodded and picked up the large machine gun. He then led his army silently down the hall towards the gym, towards war.

● ● ●

The dogs' howling was intolerable, trapped in such a confined space, but Sam could not get them settled down. In between moments of ear-splitting barks there was silence, which both troubled and comforted Sam. No sound meant the Zion members were gone, but it also meant that Bruno was not out there either, or worse yet, he was, but could not make any noise.

Sam thought about trying to shoot through the door to break the handle, but he worried that Bruno might be injured on the other side and unable to move out of the way; he could not risk shooting his friend, but he had to get out of the steel box in which he was presently trapped. Slamming his body into the door, Sam noticed that it gave a tiny bit, not enough to get a finger through, but surely wide enough to slip the edge of a blade out. Fumbling through his pockets, Sam found the small lock blade knife that his father had promised to give him when he graduated. It had been Sam's grandfather's knife and he always liked the yellow bone handle with the embellished silver acorn adorning the center. His father had always told him that a man should always have a knife, just because he will never know when he might need it. Sam had never really found a use for it, but kept it in the small key pocket of his jeans since he had grabbed the knife, and a few other objects, off of his parents' dresser before burning the house down.

Lately, he had been keeping it there because it reminded him of his parents and their love for their family. It had become a totem that Sam kept with him for protection, and it maintained a tie with his family that the world had been working so diligently to sever and destroy.

The blade clicked open, no longer than the palm of Sam's hand, but he had to believe that it would be long enough to reach the latch. He pressed his weight against the heavy, insulated door and forced the small space to open. Without looking, Sam slipped the blade into the small crack and began to move it back and forth, but could not find the spring holding the latch in place.

Frustrated, Sam collapsed to the floor and buried his face in his knees. How could he have come this far, survived this long, only to starve to death, trapped in a giant refrigerator? As much as he fought them, tears began to well up in his eyes. There was no one left to let him out. He was going to die.

A large black nose pressed itself into the side of Sam's head and nudged him. Looking up brought Sam face to face with Gozer's blocky head. The dog pushed him back against the door and stared at him with huge, honey colored eyes. The dog's eyes conveyed so much to Sam, spoke volumes of emotion and told a story that was entwined deep within its DNA. This was a creature that did not know how to give up, did not know how to accept failure. It was bred to survive and somehow wanted Sam to know that he had been too. That regardless of how much his instincts had been whitewashed by civilization, there was still an uncultivated caveman secreted away within him, waiting to get out, waiting to rage against the torrents of fate and, in spite of everything, survive. There were no words, but the message was clear to Sam that he was not allowed to give up. He reached down and nuzzled Gozer's large flat head. "Thanks," Sam said and got up from the floor.

Sam slammed his shoulder angrily into the door and shook it in its frame. The small crack between the door and rubber gasket widened a little more, just enough for Sam to peek through and see the spring that held the latch in place.

The tip of the blade nicked the spring, but could not move

it. Sam's hand trembled as he tried to hold the knife steady. Finally, in a fit of desperation, he blindly thrust the blade forward, while putting his weight behind it. A light click echoed within the refrigeration unit and Sam tumbled into the destroyed pharmacy.

Looking around, eyes wide and gasping, Sam saw that the interior of the pharmacy was empty. The smell of burning plastic hung heavily in the air from all of the melted pill bottles, and most of the shelves were heavily coated in grime and ash. Piled outside the door were the bodies of Shamblers and Zion members, but Sam did not see the faded fatigues of Bruno and Watts, or the heavy boots of Hector or Chris. He allowed himself to breathe a minor breath of relief at not having found the bodies of his friends, but that left only three other possible explanations. One, that they left without him, unlikely, or that they were now dead and Shamblers, but they should be somewhere nearby if that were the case, or most likely of all, that they had been captured and were now prisoners of the church. The thought of what those zealots could possibly be doing to his captured friends sent an icy bolt of electricity coursing through Sam's bones.

Gozer and Zule bounded out close behind Sam and made the turn to head for the morgue. They seemed to sense that Chris had been there and were desperate to find him and make sure he was safe. Sam followed close behind with his rifle raised and fanning back and forth down the hallway. The doors leading into the morgue were choked with bullet-ridden corpses and stuck partially open. Sam quickly checked them over and made sure none were his friends. Gozer and Zule showed no regard for the fallen enemy, and simply leapt over them and into the room beyond. They circled the room and began searching for Chris. He was not there.

A wet cough rattled from somewhere in the back of the morgue and Sam immediately snapped to attention, and whipped his rifle around to face the noise. He took slow side steps towards the noise, flanked on either side by the two large dogs. The noise echoed again, but this time was followed by a groan and a long string of Spanglish curse words.

"Hector?" Sam said softly and then repeated a little louder.

"Over here," Hector strained to reply from behind the overturned gurney. Sam rushed to his side and knelt down to inspect his friend. The darkness and gloom made it difficult to determine the extent of Hector's injuries; all the bruises and shadows seemed to melt together into a veil of pain that enshrouded his face. Hector had been beaten savagely, but Sam could not find any bullet or stab wounds.

"Where you shot?" Sam asked frantically, still checking his friend.

"No," Hector wheezed, "At least I don't think so. I mean everything kind of hurts." He let out a pained chuckle. "They worked me over pretty good until I passed out, but before I did, they said I need to tell everyone that the Lord's judgment was at hand, and that Chris and Bruno would be the first to experience his knowledge."

Sam shuddered as he thought about what that statement might mean. "We gotta get you back to the school and then figure out what we're going to do." Hector nodded and painfully got up from the floor. He almost collapsed, but Sam caught him. "You can't put weight on your leg?"

Hector grimaced and tried to support himself, but his leg gave out again. "I think it's broken," he gritted, "I can't really tell what is or isn't." Sam threw Hector's arm over his shoulder and began slowly limping towards the door. He turned and called for Gozer and Zule, but the dogs refused to follow. They were busily scratching at one of the body drawers and whining loudly. "Shit!" Hector yelled, "Watts! I thought they got him!" Sam carefully lowered Hector to the floor and sprinted to where the two dogs were scratching. He grabbed the shiny steel handle and threw open the door.

"Eat shit!" Someone screamed as a pistol shot whizzed past Sam's cheek. He could still hear the whine of the bullet in his ear.

"Whoa! Whoa!" Sam yelled, "Watts! It's me! It's Sam!"

From somewhere in the darkness of the body drawer, Watts replied sheepishly, "Oh shit! I'm sorry man. I thought it was those assholes coming to get me."

Sam let out a loud sigh of relief and grabbed the handle on the end of the sliding tray. "Come on, we gotta get Hector back to the school." Watts slid off the tray. His shoulder was bleeding from where he had been shot, but he otherwise appeared ok. The two men helped Hector out of the morgue and back upstairs. Gozer and Zule trailed close behind. By the time they had reached the burned out emergency room lobby, Hector and Sam had filled Watts in on what happened.

"Fuckers!" Watts spat, "We gotta go get Chris and Bruno back."

"I know," Sam said, "But the three of us are in no shape to do it. We have to regroup at the school and make a plan." The three men passed through the shattered windows and into the parking lot. 'There's no Shamblers," Sam said cautiously, "What gives?"

"They must have taken them," Hector said, "If those nuts think the zombies are holy, then they must have taken them back with them."

The van had been completely destroyed; having been fired bombed. The burned out husk rested on four melted tires and was still lightly smoking. "Shit man," Watts said angrily, "How the hell are we getting back?"

"We still got the backhoe," Hector said, motioning to where he had left it parked. The bulky machine stood with a few scorch marks surrounding it. "They must have tried to wreck it, but gave up." Reaching into his pocket, Hector withdrew the key fob and passed it to Watts. "You gotta drive. I'm too messed up."

"Can't be any harder than an Abrams," Watts smirked, "Got really drunk and stole one of those one time." He climbed up into the driver's cage and fumbled with the controls. The machine grumbled to life after a few minutes and lurched forward. Watts lowered the bucket down. "Lay Hector in there," he shouted to Sam, "Then get your ass and your rifle up top!" Sam nodded and carefully helped Hector into the front bucket, which Watts then raised up. Gozer and Zule leapt into the bucket and flanked Hector while keeping an uneasy watch. Grabbing the back ladder, Sam clambered onto the high roof and lay down. He began scanning the distance with his scope, sure that they would be attacked at any moment. What he saw in the distance filled him with panic and his hands began to tremble as he tried to hold the rifle steady. A thin cloud of acrid black smoke twirled in the breeze as it leaked out of the gym.

"The school's on fire!" Sam yelled over the rumble of the diesel engine.

● ● ●

The chain on the doors rattled loudly one more time before the handles groaned and ripped from where they were screwed into the doors. A flood of Zionists poured through the doors. Alice's eyes widened when she saw the overwhelming numbers they were up against. Crawford appeared unshakened and counted down from three with his fingers. When he hit one, Alice lobbed the heavy smoke grenade from where she was laying between two bleacher seats.

The green canister spun in tight circles as it traveled towards the gym floor. It hissed loudly and trailed a thin stream of purple smoke behind. As the marker clattered loudly to the floor, a few of the Zionists turned to see what was going on and were quickly engulfed in the fog that burst force. They rushed to get away from the smoke, but it was quickly filling the gym with equal amounts of smoke and confusion.

The smoke popped right as Mike and Joey got to the large metal double doors leading into the gym. It had taken them longer to get there because Mike wanted to go around the school and come through the back of the gym. The purplish, strangely sweet smelling gas wound through the cracks in the gasket that lined the doorframe. Joey's nose scrunched up as he breathed in some of the fog.

"Smells like crap, but I don't think it's tear gas," Joey replied rubbing his nose. The other students were antsy, amped on adrenaline and finally having something to vent their weeks of caged anger upon.

"It's not tear gas," Mike said smacking Joey on the back of the head, "It's marking smoke, that's why it's colored. We were keeping it to use as cover."

"Musta missed that part of the meeting," Joey shrugged and slipped through the doors. The small army followed behind Joey and waited for the signal to open fire.

Mrs. Koslov sat up from where she lay hidden and pitched the oblong incendiary grenade high into the air. It seemed to hang, suspended for a few moments and then dropped rapidly towards the floor. Seconds later, before it touched the floor, the small bomb detonated and unleashed a wave of fire over the heads of the Zion Church Members. The 800 grams of thermate contained within the grenade ignited at close to 4000 degrees Fahrenheit and greedily consumed the flesh, bone and gristle of the unfortunate people below. The weapon, usually used for destroying weapon caches, had little problem burning through organic material. Where a small drop of the flaming thermate touched the top of someone's head, it simply continued to burn straight through skull and brain with a wet hiss. The screams of agony and reek of chemically charred flesh filled the gym. Alice and Ms. Kozlov were fortunately spared the spectacle thanks to the acrid smoke. Crawford had seen worse long before any zombies had risen.

"Now!" Mike screamed, and his M-16 angrily burped round after round into the smoke. "Joey! Get on the radio and let Crawford know we're here!" Joey nodded and relayed the information. Two of the other students flanked Mike and spread the legs on the large SAW machine gun. The gun leapt wildly back and forth, while it dug jagged furrows into the polished wood of the basketball court. The loud crack of a hunting rifle echoed from out of the smoke and a large caliber bullet dug itself into the floorboards a few inches shy of Amelia's foot. "Break left!" Mike shouted to Amelia and Joey. They nodded and sprinted towards the other side of the gym with three other students close behind.

"We're up!" Crawford bellowed and leaned over the edge of the bleachers with his gun. Alice and Ms. Kozlov followed suit and soon the three were raining down rounds on the Zionists below.

Bullets flew in all directions from the smoke, but the attacking church members were armed with civilian grade weapons, and had no way of competing with the high rate of fire chewing them apart from three different directions. A spray of buckshot belched from the purple smoke and peppered Amelia's arm.

"Damn," she screamed and grabbed her arm. Joey rushed to Amelia and ripped the tattered sleeve from her shirt, as the other students formed a line in front of them and emptied their guns into the smoke. A handful of bb-sized holes dotted Amelia's arm and wept blood, but they were nothing fatal.

"Looks like it was just birdshot," Joey said uneasily, "Alice can pick them out later." Amelia grimaced, looked at her arm and angrily hefted herself up from the floor. She unleashed an untamed scream and emptied her entire magazine into the smoke.

"Hold your fire! Hold your fire!" Crawford shouted from high above the gym. The smoke was beginning to dissipate and he could see that most of the Zionists were little more than bullet-riddled corpses. A few groaned loudly and stammered prayers, but none of them seemed to be in any position to fight. "Get the SAW outside and make sure those bastards are leaving!" Mike and the others jogged towards the door with the cumbersome gun.

"They're gone!" Mike shouted as he leaned out the ruined gym doors. "Looks like they retreated!" A few of the students let loose a victory cheer and shouted threats to any Zionists within earshot.

"Amelia, secure the intruders," Crawford commanded as he began to climb down from the bleachers. The thermate still smoldered in a few spots, fueled by both skin and wood. The smoke lazily wafted out the open doors and curled into the darkening evening sky. "Alice, medical attention to any of our people. Then see if any of these assholes can be stabilized long enough for us to have a conversation." Alice rushed to Amelia, but the girl waved her off.

"I'm fine," she said, "Keep one of these bastards alive. We need some information." Alice nodded grimly and began picking her way through the mangled corpses haphazardly strewn about the gym.

Ms. Kozlov began spraying the fire in the gym with an extinguisher, but Crawford shook his head. "Don't bother with this. The thermate needs to just burn itself out. Get a few of those things outside and see if you can't deal with some of the mess from the fire bombs." Joey and the other students followed Ms. Kozlov to get more extinguishers and headed outside. Mike and the others escorted them towards the fires and made sure no threats were near.

"Mike," Joey said, "You guys should secure the gate. Block it off however you can. It's getting dark and Shamblers might be attracted to all the noise." Mike and the others soon had the ruined truck and some other debris blocking the entrance to the school. The SAW was mounted back in its bunker, manned by two students. Mike stood guard from atop the hood of the moving van.

Back inside the gym, Alice was finishing bandaging up a few of the Zionists. She had done the best she could, but between the burns and bullets, she did not think any of them would survive. "I did the best I could," she said weakly to one of the mangled attackers. Crawford gently moved her aside and withdrew a long, wicked looking combat knife.

"As long as they can still talk you did just fine," he sneered and traced the razor edged tip of the blade across the man's forehead. "Now, I have a few simple questions I'd like answered."

● ● ●

Traveling back to the school took longer than expected and the darkness was quickly closing in, blanketing Montville in menacing shadows. Watts did not seem to notice or care and pushed the backhoe further towards mechanical failure. The cumbersome machine groaned and protested, but rolled steadily forward.

With each bump, a long string of Spanish curse words erupted from within the raised front bucket, but Sam took these as a good sign. As long as Hector was cursing and awake, he must be feeling a little better. Gozer and Zule stood like stone sentries on either side of the large rusted bucket. Bad things had happened and even worse ones were coming and the two animals seemed to sense it, so did Sam.

A greasy, cold rain had begun to fall as they neared the destroyed gates of the school. The fires were gone, but still smoldered with errant wisps of smoke twisting and dancing into the air.

"Hold up!" Mike yelled from where he lay atop a ruined moving van. He looked tired, worn thin and threadbare, but he forced a smile when he saw Sam bouncing around on top of the backhoe. "You're gonna have to leave that there or push this piece of shit out the way with it." Mike paused and a dark shadow settled on his face. "Where's the van? Where's Chris and Bruno?"

"Keep it together," Sam said sternly as he climbed down the small ladder on the back of the machine, "Others are watching. Panic isn't going to make anything any better. Let's just get Hector inside."

Mike nodded. Something had changed in his little brother. The innocence that had once made Sam seem timid and unsure, had been burned away, smelted into steel. The person who stood in front of Mike was a man, this was an adult. Whatever had happened outside of the school's gates had forged Sam into something new.

The bucket jolted to life and lowered slowly towards the ground. Zule and Gozer leapt out and stood slightly behind Sam. "You two," Sam commanded the students in the machine gun nest, "Get Hector inside and to Alice." They nodded and Sam threw one of them the large pill bottle tucked into his sweatshirt's front pouch. "Make sure she gets these too and gives them to Erick." The students carefully helped Hector out of the bucket and supported him between them. They slowly started moving towards the school.

"What the hell happened?" Mike questioned, panic rising in his voice.

Sam turned to face his brother, the steel in his eyes waivered for a moment, but were forced to harden again. "Probably the same shit that happened here. Those fucking Zionists attacked us at the hospital. They took Chris and Bruno.

Said something to Hector about them being messengers or some religious crap."

"They attacked here too. They got as far as the gym, but most were cut down. The incendiary grenade started a small fire in there, but it's out now. Amelia's a little banged up, but otherwise we're ok," Mike reported.

Watts had climbed over the small step on the tail of the moving van and caught the end of Mike's recounting of the events. "I'm sure she's not gonna be any happier when we tell her Chris got taken."

"We gotta wait," Sam said, "We have to have a plan to rescue him and Bruno or she's gonna go off the rails."

"That's a good idea," Watts said grimly, "Hope you can make one in about thirty seconds cuz here she comes." Amelia, Joey, Ronnie and Crawford were running towards the front gate. Even from where they stood, the three men could see Amelia's cheeks were wet and her lips curled back into an expression somewhere between pure unadulterated rage, and a broken heart. She must have been keeping watch from the roof. She already knew enough.

● ● ●

A smiling, poorly painted sun grinned stupidly down at Chris. The bright, blue carpet underneath his feet had long since been stained and soiled by things he had rather not think about. He hurt everywhere, and had a few minor burns on his face and arms from where the Molotov had exploded in the morgue, but he could still stand, could still move, so that meant he could still fight.

From somewhere in the dark of the room, Chris heard a low moan and froze in his steps. The moan repeated itself and Chris whipped his head around the room trying to find the source. Would these psychos be crazy enough to lock him in a room with a frigging Shambler? Probably.

A small, horseshoe shaped table bumped against the back of Chris's knee as he tried to back pedal to the wall. Flipping the table over, Chris ripped off one of the metal legs and gripped it tightly. The groan grew louder and a shadowy figure tried to lift itself from the floor. Figuring it was better to attack than be attacked, Chris rushed the shadow and lifted the metal table leg high over his head.

Seconds before he brought the makeshift cudgel smashing down on the head of the zombie, Chris heard it mutter a stifled "shit" and cough wetly. "Bruno?" Chris asked, as the table leg fell from his hands. The soldier rolled over and looked at Chris through swollen eyes.

"Hey kid," he coughed, and then looked to where the table leg lay, "Glad you didn't brain me, but wouldn't have blamed you." He tried to smile, but he winced as the muscle contractions put pressure on his blackened cheeks. "What the hell happened and where the hell are we?"

Remembering the events at the hospital sent a shiver through Chris's battered body. "Not really sure," Chris admitted, "I got knocked out by an explosion and kinda remember getting carried in here, but not much else. You?"

Bruno was quiet for a moment. "I shoved Sam and your dogs into a big fridge that was in the back of the pharmacy. I was hoping that they would be safe and no one would look for them in there." Bruno sighed deeply. "After I got them in there, those whack jobs kicked the door in. I dropped a few before they beat me unconscious, but there were just too many. I don't know if it worked, but Erick needed those meds."

"You probably saved Sam," Chris paused, "And my dogs. Thanks man." Bruno nodded, but said nothing.

Chris looked around the dark room. "This is gonna sound really stupid, but I think we're in a kindergarten classroom."

Pushing himself painfully up from the floor, Bruno observed the room through the small slits that were his eyes. "Is that the Raisin Bran sun on the wall over there?"

"Yeah, some shit like that," Chris replied, "There's all kinds of shitty, kiddy stuff on the walls." The two slowly made their way around the room and found that Chris's initial observation had been correct. They were in some kind of classroom. The walls were covered in bright, sickly sweet cheery murals, but they were obscured under a layer of filth. It could have been dirt or mud, but even in the dim light, they could tell it was blood mixed with other things too disgusting to name.

"What the hell?" Bruno mumbled as he picked up what looked like a coloring book with Jesus on the cover. The Savior was smiling and had open arms in an expression of welcome and acceptance, but the pages were stuck together with gore and bits of offal. "I think this is a CCD workbook," Bruno said through split lips as the book dropped from his hands to the befouled floor.

"I was worried about that," Chris muttered. The doorknob rattled loudly and both swung around to face the door. Voices seemed to be chanting or praying outside. "Grab that table leg and I'll get another." Bruno nodded and the two prepared for a fight.

• • •

The snarl on Amelia's face silenced the discussion and everyone turned to look at her. Sam really wished Alice was there with him, providing her quiet support; she seemed to spread a certain degree of peace, even in the most angst-ridden situations and he really could have used that right now. But Alice was busy; she had to attend to the injured and to Erick. The steroids seemed to be working, even after only a few hours, which made Sam silently ask questions he could never force past his lips. Did Erick even need the medication? Could he have recovered without it? Would Chris and Bruno still be here if they had not gone to the hospital? But Sam knew this was a pointless line of thinking. There was no way anyone was going to do anything besides run headlong into that hospital. Spending valuable time playing the "what if" game and trying to rewrite the past, was going to do nothing but waste time.

"We go now," Amelia spat, "Kick in the fucking doors and start killing until we get them back! There's a fucking plan for you Sam!" She glared at him and Sam knew that Amelia somehow blamed him for what had happened, even though Chris had made his own decisions. Maybe she wanted to blame Chris, but could not do that until she knew he was ok.

Sam held his hands up defensively, "Yeah, that's one way we could do this, but that's probably exactly what they're expecting us to do. They think this is just a school full of kids and that we're going to do something stupid and impulsive. If we want to stand any chance of success, then we gotta surprise them."

Her teeth clicked a few times as Amelia considered arguing and angrily slammed her mouth closed. She knew Sam was right. "Alright," she said venomously, "What do we do?"

The debate continued a while longer and every time a plan began to solidify, the same detail derailed it, they needed some tactical advantage to offset the numbers they would be facing; surprise alone was not going to be enough.

"We've got better weapons," Mike offered, "And I think a few of the grenades are left."

"They know about that stuff already," Crawford said, "We need something they don't know about that will tip the scales and throw them off. Something to fuck up their plan."

"Did you guys leave anything behind at the Muncipal Complex?" Mike asked, "Anything we could use?"

Watts shook his head, "Nah, the only reason we even had the ordinance that we did was because we were deploying for Afghanistan and didn't have time to unload the trucks. We're lucky we had that shit, I guess."

"Well what they hell are we gonna do then?" Amelia demanded.

Up until this point, Joey and Ronnie had been listening silently to the debate, never offering or shooting down an idea. But a sudden jolt of electricity seemed to dance through Joey as he began to nervously bounce slightly.

"Hey, hey," Joey said raising and waving his hand, "I think I got an idea."

"Jeez Joey," Sam said, "We're not in class. What the hell is it?"

"My uncle Steve said something a while ago," he said excitedly, "You know the one that's a cop?"

"And..." Sam said anxiously.

"Well a few weeks ago he was running the drunk checks at the circle where the highway dumps out near town, and he pulled this guy over, like a real hillbilly. The dude was drunk as all hell."

"So your idea involves a drunk inbred guy?" Crawford asked, "Not following."

"No," Joey said quickly, "It involves what the guy had in his van. My uncle said the guy was on his way down south towards like Kentucky, or something for some big gun thing called Cob Creek or something." "You mean Knob Creek?" Watts asked and Joey nodded enthusiastically. "That's some serious gun nut shit down there, totally lax gun laws. What'd he have?"

"I'm not sure, but my uncle said it was some serious shit," Joey replied, "A whole van full of it."

Crawford and Watts looked at each other and finally shrugged. "If that guy was going down there, we at least got a chance that he had some pretty heavy stuff. Might be our best chance. Where'd they take his stuff?"

"My uncle said that they couldn't unload it or touch it until Homeland Security came, cuz this dude was on some kind of watch list," Joey paused, "So I think it's locked up in the back of the impound lot."

"Shit," Sam sighed, "Sounds like we're going back to the Municipal Building."

● ● ●

The door leading into the grimy former CCD classroom swung open slowly, and a mass of people could be seen just beyond the reaches of the weak light that trickled in through the small rectangular windows set high on the walls. Chris and Bruno hesitated, but refused to lower the table legs that they held high overhead. A smaller shadow detached itself from the mass and slowly walked into the room. A small girl, no older than fourteen or fifteen, stood before the two surprised captives with a radiant smile across her face. Her silken, golden hair was pulled back into a loose braid with a blue velvet ribbon cinching it together tightly at the bottom.

"Don't be scared," she said gently, "We're here to help you."

"What the hell are you talking about you fruit loop?" Chris said and he could see the girl blush from his coarse words.

The small girl seemed to compose herself and continued in

what was obviously a well- rehearsed or frequently used speech. "You have been living out in the wilds. In the corrupted, immoral world, but a world that God has not forgotten. You are bathed in sin, but we're here to help you wash away the impurities and set your souls free."

"Listen," Chris said, "That sounds great and all, but whatever your fucked up zombie cult is selling, I'm not buying. You need to get the fuck out of my way before something bad happens to you little girl."

The girl's young features seemed to harden, but she forced the smile back on her face. Her eyes bore into Chris as she glared at him from across the room. "Zombies?" She said slowly, "Is that what you really think they are? That only shows how impure and crooked your soul has become. These are the messengers of God, risen to herald his return. They are angels."

"Yeah, well your *angels* have been out there eating people," Chris retorted, "I suppose that's part of God's plan, huh?"

The girl spread her arms wide and replied coyly, "They are consuming sin, consuming this rotten, broken world and bringing it back to God. We are not here to question his plan or methods. But I can understand why a heretic like yourself would be scared, but don't worry, you'll understand it perfectly soon enough." The venom in the little girl's words stole the breath from Chris's lungs and he fell silent.

"That's much better," a voice said from the mass of people beyond the door. "The Lord's plan can only be understood with a closed mouth and an open heart." A man moved through the crowd and stood beside the girl. He smiled down at her and patted her on the head. "Straight from the mouth of babes, oh yes. I see that you gentlemen have had the pleasure of meeting my lovely daughter, Judith." He gently messed the girl's hair.

"Stop it Daddy," Judith said playfully, "I don't want my hair to get mussed."

"Now Judith," her father said with feigned reproach, "You know vanity is a sin."

Judith laughed, "And you know cleanliness is next to Godliness and you've got dirty hands from working at The

Church."

"Such an imp," the man said to Bruno and Chris, "With enough faith and biblical knowledge to give her old man a run for his money. But where are my manners? I haven't even introduced myself to our guests. I am the Reverend Abel Stone, and you have been lucky enough to have been rescued by members of my congregation, The Pillar of Zion."

"Rescued?" Chris scoffed no longer able to hold his tongue, "Is that what you call what you did at the hospital?"

"Well," Abel said somewhat sheepishly, "I can understand your confusion, but as Judith had told you previously, you will understand soon enough. The Lord has plans for you my friends, plans for all of us." The crowd behind Able responded with a round of feverish "Amens".

Having seen blind religious faith and the mindless danger it bore, Bruno whispered to Chris, "You can't argue with crazy, so save your strength kid. I think we're gonna need it." Chris stayed quiet.

● ● ●

Erick was slowly getting better as Amelia rapidly got worse. The longer they waited, the more frantic she became. Alice worried about the stress effecting Amelia's pregnancy, but she could not get her to calm down. It had been hard enough for Alice to get Amelia to sit still long enough for her to pick out the buckshot pellets from her arm, let alone have a discussion about carrying a baby.

The makeshift hospital that they had created in one of the classrooms felt like it was filling up pretty fast, and the walls were beginning to close in on Alice. She had been basically living in the infirmary for the past few days and the lack of sleep and food was beginning to take its toll, but there was no one else to administer the care that everyone needed, and that pressure alone was enough to make Alice want to break.

A few of the students, who had fought in the counterattack, were battered and bruised, but they would recover. Hector lay against one of the walls atop a pile of the tumbling mats that Ms. Kozlov had dragged in for him. He was awake and seemed like he would recover, but Alice was certain he had at least a few broken ribs and a fractured leg. A collapsed lung seemed unlikely because Hector seemed to be breathing somewhat normally, but he had been beaten savagely and Alice only hoped that there was no internal bleeding, because there was nothing she would be able to do.

"You doing ok?" Sam asked from where he leaned on the doorframe, "Want a drink or food or anything?"

"How bout a veggie burger with cheese and some onion rings? Maybe an ice cold Coke?" Alice smirked.

Sam smiled, "I got lukewarm bottled water and something that Elsie made that kind of looks like bean soup." He held out the bottle and small white foam bowl. Alice crossed the room and gently kissed Sam on the cheek as she took the food. "What was that for?"

"Oh," Alice said pretending to be offended, "Didn't realize I needed a reason to kiss you. Won't do it again."

"Don't do anything crazy," Sam joked, "You can do that anytime you want. I was just, I don't know surprised."

Looking Sam directly in the eyes Alice said, "The world is falling apart and everything looks terrible, except you. You remind me there's a reason to keep trying. I guess I was saying 'thanks', that's all." Sam blushed.

"We're going at first light. Me, Crawford, Amelia, Mike and Joey." Sam said shattering the moment, but not knowing how to tell Alice that he had volunteered to go back to the Municipal Complex.

"Amelia's going?" Alice said with a note of panic.

"She volunteered," Sam replied, "Wouldn't listen, but she'll be ok. She's just shook up over Chris."

"You have to promise me that you'll make sure she's ok," Alice said firmly, "Promise me Sam."

A look of confusion crossed Sam's face. "Yeah, ok. I promise," He said unsure of why, "I mean we're all gonna watch out for each other. I'm not gonna lose anyone else." Alice could see the tempered rage flare in Sam's eyes. He had not said so, but she could sense that he felt responsible for what happened to Chris and Bruno. She knew that Sam had developed a sense of responsibility extended to every member of the group, and that even though no one asked or expected him to do that, something in Sam made him feel that way.

"It's more than that," Alice said, "You can't tell her that you know, but I think I have to tell you. I mean, you need to know."

Completely confused Sam replied, "Alice I haven't the slightest idea what you're talking about. What could be...oh shit!" Enough brain cells had rattled together that Sam was able to piece together what was going on. "The vitamins? She's pregnant isn't she?" Alice nodded, relieved that she no longer solely owned the secret. "Oh, wow. Holy shit! Does Chris know?"

"No," Alice said shushing Sam, "She's not sure, but she thinks she is and he doesn't know."

A weight greater than the one he had carried before settled on Sam's shoulders, and Alice immediately regretted telling him about Amelia, but he needed to know. "We have to get him back," Sam said flatly.

"Sam," Alice said, "What if he's not coming back?"

"That's not an option," Sam said, "We gotta get him back. No more wasting time. We'll leave right from the Municipal Complex. Everyone is coming back!"

"Please be careful and promise me," Alice said as her voice cracked, "Promise me you'll come back to me. I love you Sam."

"I love you too Alice, and I promise. I promise I'll come back," Sam choked and then kissed Alice hard on the lips and strode purposefully out of the room. There was so much that Sam wanted to say, that he knew he should say, but both time and words were short. Before she could stop herself, Alice found her body trembling and tears running silently down her cheeks.

● ● ●

The church loomed in front of Chris and Bruno as they were being frog marched towards the heavy, wooden doors. The front of the building jutted out to a high point, almost as if the bow of a large boat had been used as a blueprint for the structure. It dawned on the two of them that perhaps this had been intentional; maybe Able had constructed the church to look like an arc to further reinforce his apocalyptic diatribe and control his congregation? But the church had been here long before the dead had risen, so Able must have been planning for and preaching The End of Days well before the first zombie had sunken its rotted teeth into a hunk of warm flesh. The outbreak of this virus or whatever it was had simply been a convenient and convincing bit of happenstance that suited Able's purpose.

The realization that The Pillar of Zion Church had been preparing for the end of the world even before the zombies had shown up, sent acidic knots roiling through Bruno's stomach, because that meant that this situation was even worse than he had thought. Initially, he had hoped that these people were simply scared, albeit violent and stupid, but never the less scared and just trying to make sense out of a senseless situation. If that were the case, there still existed a chance that he and Chris could appeal to reason, maybe talk some sense into them and get them to see that there was another explanation and another option, but he realized now that was impossible. These people were hoping for the world to end. They prayed for it with every fiber of their being and welcomed it with open arms. This was something they had been anxiously waiting for and had soaked their brains in enough bastardized religious folktales, that they were willing to do anything for their vision, for Able's vision.

"My church," Able said proudly from where he stood on the heavy stone steps leading into the building, "Beautiful isn't it? I know pride is a sin, but surely you'd agree that the Lord himself would be proud of such a handsome house of worship?"

Chris and Bruno had been woken early in the morning, fed something that looked like cold oatmeal, but tasted like shit and then had their hands bound behind their backs. They had marched through the muddy paths that snaked through the church grounds and saw firsthand the refugee camp that Able had constructed here. A few bunkhouses dotted the grounds, but these had quickly been filled and numerous people huddled under makeshift tents and tarps or around large fires. Their faces were all blank, eyes all empty, these people were broken; whether it was by the violence of the zombies or the words of Able, these people had surrendered to his interpretation of the world. Bruno had seen something similar to this in the eyes of the insurgents, you had to feel that way to strap a bomb to yourself or your little girl, only to blow it up in a market full of innocent women and children, but he had seen hesitation and fear in the enemies' eyes over there, which meant there was still hope of a rational resolution, some small splinter of lucid humanity still alive buried inside. Here, there was none, no fear, no hesitation, and just blind submission; that scared Bruno far more than anything he had seen since the world fell to shit. The zombies were something instinctual and based in the scientific world, a virus or sickness that would burn itself out, but the idea of a working brain behind a commitment to seeing the end of the world, well that was a monster of an entirely different caliber.

Bruno shouldered the man next to him to make a small bubble of space for himself amid the crowd of congregation members. "You designed it to look like an arc?" Bruno shouted to Able, who smiled at the question.

"I see that you're a man of religious knowledge Mr. Bruno," Able said through a crocodilian grin, "Perhaps there's still hope for you yet my friend, but to answer your question, yes it's an arc. Built to resemble that of Noah, a holiest of holy men, chosen by the Lord to be saved from the floods that purified a diseased, dying world. And like that most knowledgeable and blessed Noah, I saw a flood coming, saw that this world was drowning in its own filth and degradation. So we built an arc, so to speak of, because if we could see that the flood was coming, then obviously the Lord had chosen us to be saved from it and we needed to make ready, just as Noah had."

"So where are the animals?" Chris sneered, "Shouldn't you be loading them in by twos or some shit?"

"Those who haven't been touched by the Lord's knowledge always hide behind cynicism," Able replied calmly, "You'd be wise to heed these lessons my son. To repent from your sinful ways before you face His most just judgment."

"What the hell are you talking about?" Chris spat and immediately regretted his choice of words.

"Hell?" Able replied coolly, "Is exactly what I'm talking about." With that he turned and threw open the doors leading into the church. The smell of rank decay and purification rolled down the stairs in humid fetid waves, and caused Chris and Bruno to retch violently. The church parishioners held their stomachs, evidently having grown accustomed to the repulsive smell and pushed closer to the open doors. Able held the sliver of a smile and motioned with his arms, as if welcoming them into his home.

Inside the church, dim rays of sunlight slanted through the high stained glass windows and dappled the floors in radiant pools of rainbow, but that was where all awe and splendor ceased. Cutting through the light were swirling masses of fat black flies that noisily buzzed from one indiscernible pile of meat to the next that lay strewn about the church. Pews were pushed into haphazard piles along the walls, but a few had been moved into a semi-circle in the center of the chamber. The pulpit and alter remained at the front of the room, but were visibly dirty and stained with dark flecks that could only be blood. Judith skipped happily around the pews humming the chorus from "When the Saints Come Marching In." When she saw her father, she skidding to a stop and smiled broadly.

"Hi daddy," she beamed, "Are they ready for church?"

Able smiled back and turned to look at Chris and Bruno. "I believe so honey." He turned to the parishioners that held the ropes leading to Chris and Bruno. "Move them to the pews if you would be so kind." The church members began to hum some hymn, but neither Chris nor Bruno could identify it.

The smell of death increased with each step closer that they reluctantly took, but Chris and Bruno, struggle as they did, could not get free. As their feet were knocked out from under them, they were continuously dragged forward until they were eventually forced into pews facing a large, ragged pit that had been chewed into the middle of the church floor. It had originally been a one-story building, but had recently received the renovation of a gapping forty-foot wide hole with steeply sloping sides that led into a darkened cavern. Rank tendrils of rot reached up from the darkness and even Abel's eyes could be seen watering. His voice held its usual timber in spite of vomit-inspiring smells that hung heavy in the air.

"I'm sure that fear has gripped you my friends, that you may be wondering why we would have something like this in our beautiful church," Able crooned, "But understand, that looking into the eyes of the Lord is a frightful thing."

"Eyes of the Lord?" Bruno asked figuring that keeping Able talking was their best chance at staying alive longer.

"Yes," Able replied smoothly, "One would think that the eyes of God would be imbued with blinding light, but we have learned, oh yes, we have learned." The dingy collection of church members raised their arms and nodded at Able's words. "But as any truly saved, truly enlightened person would tell you my friends, you must stare into darkness, must truly walk through the shadows before you are embraced in the warmth and grace of the Lord's light." Able nodded to Judith and the girl skipped over to where an orange industrial extension cord lay on the floor. She grabbed the cord and twirled it, smiling the entire time. A rough electrical outlet had been patched into the wall and hung slightly crooked with the thick white wires running to a questionable looking electrical panel.

Neon lights clicked and fluttered from somewhere within the pit and the shuffling of numerous feet echoed from down below. A chorus of dull moans resounded as the lights flickered to full blast. Chris and Bruno craned their necks and peered down into the expansive cavern yawning at their feet. With the sickly-yellowed light bathing the insides of the pit, they could see that it stretched back much further than they had thought and that it appeared to have crooked passages stretching out into other unseen rooms. A few pairs of clouded, milky eyes turned upwards and gazed towards the warm faces returning the stares.

"What the fuck?" Chris almost shouted, "You have a fuckin' pit full of zombies." Bruno shook his head, he had anticipated something of this caliber of crazy, but even this was beyond his expectations.

"Zombie?" Able said with false confusion, "Such a nasty and untrue word. These are messengers, purveyors of the Lord's wisdom and knowledge. It is true that their flesh has died and rotted, but that is simply weakness falling away." He paused for a moment and with a philosophic gleam in his eye continued, "I believe there was a saying about the flesh being weak, but the soul willing, right? Well, I would argue my young friend that these blessed souls are the physical embodiment of that sentiment. The physical world is what polluted and weakened their bodies, but now with those concerns sloughing off, it leaves behind a clear mind and pure soul."

Cold beads of sweat began to form on Chris's forehead. "Able those aren't people anymore. They aren't holy, they're dead! They're fucking dead and eating people. That's not God's plan! How could that be?"

Judith had skipped across the room and stood behind Bruno. She playfully toyed with his hair. "Daddy, isn't it funny that the nonbeliever thinks he can lecture you on God's plan?" Bruno angrily shook his head, but Judith continued anyway.

"So true my blessed child," Able said and then turned to Chris, "Do not think yourself so insightful my ignorant young friend. Your eyes are blinded by the materialism and sins of your life." Able paused and inhaled deeply. He continued with an icy edge to his words, "But once your eyes change my friend, oh yes, once they are clouded with the knowledge of the Lord and not the impurities of this world, you will see things much clearer." The congregation began singing and swaying as Able moved towards the pulpit. Judith began once again skipping around the edge of the pit, each lap stirring more and more commotion from below. Able raised his arms high over his head and everyone fell silent. "Lower these fortunate young men into the welcoming arms of the Lord's wisdom and let us rejoice in their salvation."

● ● ●

"Well it ain't getting any easier," Watts said sourly, "So just shoot the fucking thing and let's get on with it." Sam nodded and centered the Stalker in his scope. The creature had been pacing back and forth behind the Municipal Complex since they had arrived. Amelia and Watts were raring and ready to go, but their energy was making Sam and Joey nervous. They were not thinking and were acting impulsively, which was exponentially increasing the chance of making a mistake, most likely a fatal one.

"Hold up," Sam said lifting his head from the stock of his rifle, "I drop that thing and the sound is gonna draw every Shambler within earshot. What then?"

"Sam's right," Joey added, "One Stalker's a problem, an entire horde of Shamblers is gonna make this impossible. We don't have time to screw around. We gotta meet up with Crawford, Mike and Ronnie in less than two hours."

Watts exhaled loudly and surveyed the back parking lot running in front of the high gate leading into the impound lot. "Ok," he said, "Ok. Look, we gotta do this quick and clean. Joey, you've got an idea what the van looks like, so you and me are going over the gate."

"What about the friggin' Stalker?" Amelia hissed, "The longer you three are standing around playing circle jerk, the longer we're taking to save Chris." She paused and then quickly added, "And Bruno."

Quickly sensing that he needed to take some control, Sam offered, "I'll drop that thing and as soon as I do, Amelia get the van rolling towards the gate. Watts and Joey, you're on the roof and over the gate as soon as you're close enough, then find that van and get it moving."

"Where's that leave you?" Joey asked hesitantly, "You're just going to stay out here when all the Shamblers start limping around from the front? That's insane, you'll be totally on your own."

Sam had not really thought about that aspect of his plan and had to admit that he seriously did not like it, but there was no time to come up with a different one. This plan was no doubt a shitty one, but it was the only one they had.

"Point taken," Sam replied dismissively, "Now get your ass

on top of the van and make sure Watts doesn't fall off and roll his other ankle."

Watts smirked, "Yeah, he'll do that and you make sure not to miss that shot. Alright Deadeye Dick?" Sam nodded, but could not come up with a sufficiently sarcastic response.

Everyone turned to go back to the van, but Joey stopped and jogged back over to where Sam was preparing for the shot. "Be careful," he said, "Make the shot and then, I don't know, climb a fucking tree or something ok?"

"Man, you gotta focus on what you've got to get done," Sam replied, "I fuck up the shot, I'll get off another one. You don't find that van full of weapons, then we're all fucked."

Joey smirked, "Yeah, I know. No pressure, right?"

As soon as Sam heard Amelia start up the engine to the van, his focus became zeroed in on the Stalker. He had to get a head shot and drop that thing. The Shamblers would not be able to get over the fence, but that thing could do it easily and would tear Joey and Watts apart before they could find the van. Sam really wished that Bruno was here to take the shot, someone who had been properly trained to shoot, but he quickly buried that line of thinking in the dark recesses of his brain and focused on his breathing. In his head, he could hear Bruno's voice telling him to control his breathing, squeeze the trigger, don't pull. Take his time and plan the shot.

The Stalker stopped its frantic pacing and seemed to stare directly into Sam's scope. The empty ocular sockets betrayed nothing, but the thin, leathery layer of muscles tightly wrapped around the creature's face where sun bleached patches of skull did not glisten, seemed to contract and snarl at Sam. He let out half of a slow breath, remembered not to squeeze his eye closed and gently pulled the trigger.

The rifle barked loudly and pushed itself backwards into Sam's arm, but he was used to the recoil and let the energy disperse through the rest of his body, instead of trying to stop it. The gun quickly came back to its firing position and Sam checked his target. The Stalker was done, lying in a tangled pile with a large hole through the center of its forehead. It was a clean kill; Sam could not help but being proud of the shot.

Pressing the pedal to the floor, Amelia accelerated the van down the small rise towards the gate. "He got it! He got it!" She shouted, more in celebration than in a relay of news to the two on top of the van. On top, Joey and Watts tightened their grips on the low side rails. They knew there was no way Amelia was going to ease to a slow stop; they only hoped that she would not slam on the breaks at the last minute and send them careening into the gate.

The body of the dead Stalker crumpled under the tires as Amelia skidded to a stop in front of the high chain link gate. The strips of green plastic woven through the fence made it impossible to see what was on the other side, but Joey and Watts leapt off the roof of the van and grabbed the top of the gate. Thankfully, there was nothing waiting on the other side. They quickly swung their guns around on the nylon straps and swept them back and forth across the impound lot.

"Let's go," Joey said, "It should be in the back." Watts nodded and the two started moving towards the rear bays.

Outside of the impound lot, Amelia was quickly becoming surrounded, but Sam could do little from where he watched. He was able to drop a few of the Shamblers as they ambled towards the van. Through the scope, Sam could see that the rotted flesh on many of the zombies was blackened and charred, most likely from the group's previous visit and Ronnie's firebombs, but burned or not, they still came faster than he could reload and eventually he could no longer risk shots for fear of hitting the van or Amelia.

Over the dull groans of the horde of Shamblers, a low, angry sound rattled across the parking lot. Slowly, the sea of zombies opened in a ragged channel to make space for a large, putrid mass that lumbered towards the van. It's large bald head greasily glistened in the sun. Neither Sam nor Amelia could tell what this thing was, but as it collided with the side of the van, it caused the vehicle to rock violently onto two wheels.

"Sam, a little help here," Amelia said frantically into her radio. He did not bother to respond and sighted the top of the massive, blubbery creature and squeezed off a shot that tore a chunk from the top the monster's skull, but it continued to bash its massive, hammy fists against the van leaving basketball-sized dents behind with each blow.

"Sam, Sam!" Amelia shouted into the radio, "I can't get any space to reverse the van!"

"Amelia," Sam yelled into the radio, "I'm coming." Before he could think, Sam was on his feet and sprinting towards the van.

● ● ●

"You smell like shit," Mike said, holding his nose as he walked into the auto shop. Ronnie had been in there for most of the day and Mike needed to get him ready to move. They needed to meet up with Sam and the others in a little less than two hours, and Mike hoped that Ronnie had something running because otherwise, they had a long walk ahead of them.

"I don't smell like shit," Ronnie said flatly, "The shit smells like shit." He turned back to the large workbench he had been hunched over before Mike interrupted him. The fading light trickling through the high, grimy windows provided enough illumination for Mike to see what looked like a loose pile of batteries, a ball of red wire, and some large soup cans arranged in tight rows on the table.

"Ron, what the hell are you talking about?" Mike said, trying to hide the fact that he was pissed to see Ronnie fooling around with junk instead of getting a car mobile, "What the hell are you doing man? We need to get a car working and meet up with everyone else. We don't have time for you to go fuckin' around with a science fair project."

Without turning around Ronnie mumbled, "Got that truck working over an hour ago and that little Toyota from the parking lot too." He reached over and scooped a large amount of something from a bag leaning against his stool. Mike noticed several identical, but empty bags littering the floor around Ronnie's bench.

"Ron, we gotta get moving man," Mike said, his voice betraying his words, "Why didn't you tell me the cars were working? We could have been out of here an hour ago?" Ronnie shrugged and kept working. "Man," Mike sighed, "What the hell are you doing anyway and what are you talking about the shit?"

Pointing to the bag Ronnie replied, "That's fertilizer. Found it out back in the Buildings and Grounds garage."

"So filling industrial sized soup cans with shit is going to help us how?" Mike asked motioning towards the workbench.

"It's fertilizer, not shit," Ronnie said, "Mixed with diesel fuel I siphoned off one of the trucks." Ronnie could see the gears grinding in Mike's brain. "I layered it with some broken glass, nails and bolts."

"You made pipe bombs?" Mike asked, "What the hell are you going to do with a bunch of pipe bombs McVey? This isn't Bagdad Ron, they're not gonna let you drive a truck full of bombs up to their front door."

Pointing over to one of the darkened corners of the shop, Ronnie motioned towards a shadowy contraption that looked like it used to be an Ellison weight machine; it still had four or five, forty- five pound plates loaded on each side of the slide bar, but it looked like Ronnie had cut out the back supports and added a long piece of metal in the middle.

"What the heck is that?" Mike asked going over to inspect, "Is this a catapult or something?"

"Trebuchet," Ronnie corrected, "French designed catapult that works off counter weights. I was going to use one of the engine lifts to load it into the back of the pickup truck and use it to lob these things over the fence. We made a smaller one in the physics club and it could shoot a golf ball about two hundred feet. With the increased size and weights, this one should easily be able to shoot a hundred yards or more. Should be a good first attack. It'll cause a lot of chaos, maybe start a few fires and we can use that confusion to get in there and rescue Chris and Bruno."

Mike thought about Ronnie's plan. "That actually might work," he had to admit, "I mean it's totally crazy, launching exploding cans of cow shit out of a weight rack turned French catapult, but I guess crazy's selling pretty well these days."

"Help me load this, well, this shit I guess, into the truck

with the catapult. We'll pick Crawford up at the machine gun nest," Ronnie said as he got up from the table. "Grab those glass jars too." Mike picked up the jars filled with some kind of yellowy brown jelly.

"Should I even ask what the hell this is or do I not want to know?" Mike asked looking at the jar.

"What do you mean?" Ronnie asked.

"Well you have cans full of shit so I was worried these are jars full of pee," Mike laughed.

Fighting the urge to lie and say 'yes,' Ronnie replied, "No, those are just something special I thought of from all of the stuff Amelia has been talking about. I was thinking we might be able to use their religious convictions against them."

"The gospel according to Ronnie, has jars of piss in it huh?" Mike grinned and picked up one of the large, heavy cans from the workbench. "Should I even ask Ron?" He said as he looked at the batteries and wires attached to the can.

Ronnie raised his eyebrows comically high. "Internet," they both said in unison and hurried to load the remaining cans and catapult.

● ● ●

Chris and Bruno had hung for what felt like hours over the pit in the floor of the Pillar of Zion Church. Judith had gone out onto the grounds and was ushering more and more congregation members into the chamber to join in the singing, and swaying while Able droned on and on about some apocalyptic verse or another. Neither of them could tell what Able was talking about anymore, because the throbbing pain in their joints and muscles had become unbearable and was causing a deafening ringing to resound in their ears. Chris and Bruno had their arms and wrists lashed to heavy pieces of timber. A thick cord of rope ran from the center of the wood and bound their ankles together forcing them into a crude rendition of a crucifixion. They were sure that this had undoubtedly been done on purpose.

Suddenly Able held his hands out flat and the entire congregation stopped signing and fell silent. "The time has come to ask the sinners to repent," Able said strongly, "Time to see if they are willing to accept the Lord into their hearts." He turned and looked towards where Chris and Bruno dangled in the air, spinning in slow circles.

Chris looked up, his head swimming from the pain, "Go fuck yourself preacher, cuz you and I both know it doesn't fuckin' matter what we say. You're still gonna do whatever horrible fucking thing you got planned, so stop torturing us with your shitty sermons and get on with it, cuz as soon as you're done, I'm gonna fuckin' kill you."

"Empty threats from an empty soul," Able chided, "Your anger would be better directed at yourself and your sins. Turn that rage inward young man and seek redemption. Even in his final living moments upon this Earth, the Son of God found it in his divine heart to bestow forgiveness upon a dying sinner. Just as I am offering you now."

A dry laugh came from Bruno. "What is this some Calvary re-enactment Able? We supposed to be the murders crucified next to Jesus? Isn't comparing yourself to the Son of God blasphemous?"

"One would think that a man with such knowledge of the Good Book would know that the one sinner who asked for Jesus' forgiveness, was cleansed of his sins and would be intelligent enough to do the like," Able paused, "That man had sinned his entire life, but sought forgiveness, truly opened his heart and was welcomed into the house of the Lord. It may be too late for our hard headed young friend, but perhaps not for you."

"I like how you left out the part that he still died," Bruno scoffed, "I'm not looking for the kind of forgiveness you're selling."

Able looked hurt for a moment, but quickly recovered his composure. "It is true that he still died a physical death, but he was at least spared a spiritual one. We all must shed our mortal coils. What matters is what we did with our flesh and bone while our spirit inhabited it, and sadly for you two, I can see that your sins are going to drag you down to the fires of Hell. I can only hope that in your final moments, while facing the Lord's most righteous and just judgment, that you too will find the spiritual fortitude to repent for your sins and seek the warm embrace of his cleansing forgiveness." Raising his arms high over his head, Able continued, but with a far more dramatic tone. "It is time my children to save these men's souls. They will either become messengers of the Lord's knowledge, or food that fuels the fires of their most holy message!" The entire congregation resounded with a harmonious 'Amen' and began swaying once again.

"Is it time Daddy? Is it time?" Judith said joyously, as she skipped towards a large mechanical winch connected to two car batteries.

Able's eyes gleamed with intensity and conviction. "Oh yes, my blessed child. It is time. Time indeed." He motioned towards Judith and she pressed the button on the control cable connected to the winch. It groaned to life and slowly began lowering Chris and Bruno into the pit and the hungry outstretched arms that awaited them.

● ● ●

The only sound from within the impound lot was the crunching of gravel underneath the feet of Joey and Watts. On the other side of the gate, they could hear numerous dull moans of numerous Shamblers and the metallic groan of metal being crumpled. Amelia shouted for Sam over the radio and the loud crack of Sam's rifle resounded throughout the complex. They had started back towards the gate, but before they could climb it, Amelia's voice rattled through the radio threatening to shoot them if they came over the fence before finding the van. So even though every fiber demanded that they ignore Amelia's threats and go back over the fence, they went deeper into the impound lot.

"Let's get this done quick," Watts said and picked up his pace. There did not appear to be anything on this side of the gate so they picked up their pace and before long, they were sprinting towards the back of the lot where Joey thought the van might be.

A large, semi-circular aluminum hanger that was open on

both ends filled the back end of the lot. A handful of vehicles were parked underneath, but peeking out from the shadows in the back was a large, maroon panel van. The windows were heavily tinted, so they could see nothing from the side, but Watts pushed his face against the windshield and peered inside. His breath fogged the glass, but he anxiously wiped it away with his sleeve.

"There's some stuff in there," Watts said, "But it's under some blankets. I can't believe that they would leave this shit in the van. Why wouldn't it be locked up in one of the evidence rooms?"

Joey shrugged his shoulders as he walked around the van. "My uncle said the ATF had told them not to touch anything. I think the guy was on the Homeland Watch List or some shit, so the Feds told everyone to go hands off until they could pick it up. His loss our gain I guess?" Joey tried the side handle and it did not budge, but he never really expected a van full of illegal weapons to just be sitting open, even one locked inside the gates of a police impound lot. "How are we going to get in? I really don't want to go wander around the police station looking for a set of keys."

Looking around, Watts spied a length of pipe, probably used for propping open hoods or doors, but also perfect for smashing a window. Watts hesitated for a second and looked towards Joey.

"What?" Joey asked, "Just smash the damn window and let's get going. I don't think the cops are gonna care."

"It's not that smart ass," Watts said, "I'm just trying to think what's the best way to do this. I don't want to be driving around with an open window."

"Just smash the side window," Joey offered, "It's higher up than the others, so it'll be hard for the zombies to get at as long as we're moving."

"Yeah," Watts replied, "As long as we're moving." He turned the pipe and thrust it into the small tinted rectangular window. The glass cracked, but was held in place by the cheap, purple film that covered the window. Slipping his hand through the hole, Watts pushed his arm inside. His sleeve caught on the glass, but he pushed harder and managed to fit up to his elbow through the space. He felt around for a few seconds until he was able to locate the handle and open the door from the inside. After some cursing and an angry tug, Watts freed his arm and threw open the door.

A large bundle lay wrapped in moving blankets and a few smaller ones were tucked off to the side. Something unidentifiable was mounted onto a piece of thick plywood and wrapped tightly in a blue plastic tarp.

"You gotta be fuckin' kidding me!" Watts exclaimed as he peered under the tarp. "Man it's no wonder this guy was on the Watch List."

"What the hell is it?" Joey asked looking inside the van anxiously.

Moving a thick, black cable and following it to a car battery, Watts looked back at Joey with wide eyes; he was obviously excited. "This is a fucking mini gun. I don't know where this nut job got one. These are usually mounted in helicopters. I mean shit, this'll rip through a few thousand rounds a minute. Check that box over there to see if there's any ammo."

Joey climbed inside the van and began rummaging through the numerous boxes of ammo underneath the quilted moving blankets. The more he searched, the more weapons he found. It seemed that each layer held another trove of illegal automatic weaponry and ammunition. Finally, Joey found a box laden with a heavy black belt. Through the small spaces, Joey could see the bullets tightly packed within. "Is this is it?" Joey asked, holding up the belt and watched Watts' eyes grow even larger.

Watt's nodded and grinned, "We can deal some serious hurt on those assholes with this baby. What else is there?"

"Looks like some AK-47s and Uzis," Joey said and then saw the quizzical look on Watts' face, "Videogames man. Anyway there's this monster too." Joey held up the barrel of a long vicious looking rifle. "What the hell is this thing anyway?"

"That's an SASR," Watts said, "Fifty cal sniper rifle used for shooting trucks and blowing up ordinance. It's got a range of over a mile."

"Trucks?" Joey said, "Not people?"

"We're told not to target humans with these cuz the people who write the rules get nervous when heads start blowing up, even if it's attached to a bunch of Johnny Jihads. The bullets in this thing will take a head clean off the shoulders," Watts paused, "Though that's not to say it doesn't get used for that. Sam will be interested in that thing. What color are the rounds in the box next to it?"

Joey looked closer at the bullets. "It looks like white and green I think, but it's hard to tell in the dark. Why does that matter?

An evil smile spread across Watts' face, "White with a green tip? That's an Mk 211 round. It's a multipurpose round with incendiary, armor piecing and explosive uses all rolled into one lovely little bullet."

Watts hunched low and moved forward through the van, being careful not to step on any of the weapons. He checked the visor, but found nothing. "Didn't think it'd be that easy anyway," he said withdrawing a stainless steel Leatherman Tool from its holster on his belt. Flicking his wrist, Watts withdrew the pliers and reached under the steering column. The plastic fell away and he pulled out a nest of multicolored wires. Carefully selecting a red one and a yellow one, he stripped their rubber coating with the small blade on the back of the tool. Scraping the exposed copper ends and pumping the gas, Watts jumped the van to life after a few moments of mechanical coughing and shuddering.

Plopping into the passenger seat, Joey looked strangely over at Watts. "That's a nifty trick. They teach you that one in basic?"

"No, they taught me that one in juvie," Watts replied, "Why the hell you think I enlisted? It got my delinquent ass outta going to jail. Who'd have thought that I'd actually end up liking it?" He pressed the gas pedal slowly and rolled out of the hanger towards the gate. As they slowed, Joey opened the passenger door to jump out, but a loud screech stopped him in his tracks.

"What the hell was that?" Watts shouted, "Get on the radio

and find out!"

"Amelia? Sam?" Joey yelled into the radio, "What's going on out there?" But before a response could be given, Watts and Joey watched as the gate bulged inward and Amelia's van, barrel rolled into the impound lot. Following close behind was a small army of Shamblers and something larger and angrier than anything they had previously encountered. It's massive bulky frame lumbered through the gates as it released a deafening howl from its large toothy mouth. Before Watts or Joey had a chance to react, the massive creature rushed their van. A loud crack resounded and a greasy spray of clotted black liquid exploded from the creature's neck and splattered across their windshield.

● ● ●

A loud bang shook the roof of the pickup truck as Crawford climbed into the bed and squatted against the weight rack turned catapult. Mike nodded briefly through the rear windows and rolled the truck through the recently repaired gates. Ronnie followed close behind in the small sedan weighed down by a truck full of makeshift explosives. Mike had refused to drive the car claiming it smelled like shit, but Ronnie suspected it probably had more to do with the fact that he was concerned about what would happen to the homemade shit bombs if he stopped short or hit a bump. Knowing that the bombs were inert unless they received an electrical charge, Ronnie felt no qualms over driving the Toyota, other than the fact that the CD player was broken and the tires were bald, but he figured none of that really mattered; they would not be keeping it long.

Besides, Ronnie had wanted to drive the small sedan anyway; it was where Gozer and Zule had chosen to ride and he liked the dogs. Zule looked over at Ronnie from where she sat in the passenger seat and seemed as anxious to get going as anyone else. Gozer dozed in the back seat dreaming of chasing something and periodically let out a muffled bark. Ronnie had always found animals easier to understand than humans, there were no hidden meanings or motives to their actions; it was purely instinctual and Ronnie respected and understood that. People always seemed to operate based off some ulterior motive he could not quite discern, and this caused him endless amounts of frustration, but he had to admit that strangely enough, since the dead had risen, he had never felt closer to the living.

Alice, Ms. Kovloz and Elsie had come down to the machine gun nest to see the group off. There had been some brief debate regarding whether or not they would accompany them, but Mike, Crawford and Ronnie had refused. While the extra guns would definitely have been welcomed, the other students were still too fresh to be left on their own, and Alice still had to stay behind to tend to Erick and Hector. Mike looked briefly towards Alice as he drove out and her eyes said it all, even though she spoke no words; she felt remorseful and cowardly that she could not come, terrified for what might happen to her friends and her heart teetered on the edge of shattering for fear of what might happen to Sam. Mike nodded to Alice as he drove out and made a silent promise that he would bring everyone back or die trying, especially Sam.

After the Zionists had attacked and wrecked the gate, the Shamblers had begun gathering around the school. The group was used to small groups of two or three zombies stumbling around outside the fence, but the overwhelming noise of the battle had attracted at least twenty times the usual number, and there had not really been time to deal with them yet. All time and energy had been devoted towards planning on how to rescue Chris and Bruno, so as the truck rumbled through the gate it was immediately swarmed by cold hands, dead eyes and hungry mouths. Before they were overwhelmed by the zombies, Crawford yelled at the top of his lungs, "Light em up!" and a volley of bullets spat from the SAW, which had been moved to the edge of the fence. Alice and the others followed with a blast of fire from their own weapons, dropping numerous Shamblers to the ground. When a pause came in the fire, the truck rolled out over a carpet of fetid bullet chewed body parts that rapidly turned to a foul smelling paste under the heavy tires. Crawford stayed in the middle of the bed and picked off any Shamblers that came too close.

Mike pushed the truck further into the zombies and Ronnie stayed close behind, but whatever little space the vehicles made was quickly filled in by the writhing mass of rotted bodies. With the vehicles getting further and further away from the fence, it was too risky for any of the others to provide cover fire, but the horde had been thinned enough for Mike to push a path slowly through to the street. As the two vehicles reached some open ground and accelerated, the zombies quickly fell behind. Crawford palmed his radio and said, "We're clear. Get rid of the rest of them." The rapid staccato of automatic gunfire punctuated the noises of the day, but stopped as suddenly as it had started.

"All clear," Alice reported, "Good luck." With no more to be said, the two vehicles and their occupants drove in silence to rendezvous with the others.

● ● ●

The winch was painfully slow in its lowering of Chris and Bruno from where they hung suspended among the high rafters of the Pillar of Zion Church. They were both sure that this was not an unintentional detail; Able seemed to have created an entire world for himself and his followers, in which zombies seemed not only normal, but welcomed, and that the apocalypse was something to be greeted with a smiling face and warm heart. As far as The Pillar of Zion Church was concerned, they were not murdering the two men who dangled before them spinning in slow circles, rather they were saving them, sending them to salvation.

Knowing that they were well beyond the point of reasoning, Bruno's mind quickly tried to form a plan that did not end with being torn apart or becoming a zombie, but all paths seemed to lead to the same place, death, a painfully toothy one. As one plan after another was rejected, the winch caught and the cables suspending Bruno and Chris bounced and pulled. The pain was excruciating, the jerking movements putting the full stress of their weights on the already wrenched and pulled joints, but it also shook a thought loose in Bruno's mind and he began swinging his feet and knees with the motion of the cables, and soon his momentum had him moving in a small, but growing circle.

"Chris," Bruno yelled, his voice hoarse and cracking. He looked and saw Chris nod, he understood what the plan was or at least that there was some sort of plan, and he too began moving with the motion of the cables.

Able looked upset, his salvation ceremony had been interrupted by mechanical failure. He rushed to where Judith stood next to the groaning and smoking machine. "I think it's broken daddy," she said timidly, "We never tried two salvations at once. Maybe we broke it?" Able seethed and silently cursed his own vanity. He had allowed his ego to get the better of him and now he was losing face in front of his congregation. All of his power and clout was rooted in his ability to convey a sense of control and mastery over the world; if that started to wane, then so too would his hold over them. Some serious flagellation and flayed skin would be required later to cleanse Able of his vanity and sin. He never would admit that he looked forward to the chance to flagellate himself, relishing the pain and hating the urges it always stirred within him. He tried, oh Lord yes, Able tried, but the cleansing of one sin always lead to the committing of another. But if the Lord truly thought that it was wrong why would he make Judith so closely resemble the visage of her dear departed mother. A mother who had been taken into the Lord's arms in the beginning of The End of Days, a mother who currently resided in Able's zombie pit. Besides, it was love, not lust Able always rationalized to himself, and Judith never protested, at least not anymore.

The arc of the cables began to widen more and more as Bruno and Chris shifted their weight back and forth. Congregational members were beginning to shift their gazes between Able's angry kicking of the winch and strange twisting of the two men bound and suspended before them. Judith kept her joyous, celebratory façade up throughout the entire bizarre scenario and was happily skipping around Able and the jammed machine.

"Surely," Able spat through gritted teeth, "The Lord has decided to give these heathens a few more moments to seek his divine forgiveness." He stopped his tantrum and began to compose himself, smoothing out the front of his crumpled, but immaculately white button up shirt. With his usual timbre he continued, "We should thank the Lord that he would visit a final act of kindness, even upon those most unworthy. Truly, the Lord God is great! For think my children, if the Lord saw fit to offer a small act of favor to these nonbelievers, then what wondrous gifts must await those who keep sacred his holy covenant?" The church members shattered psyches and minds were easily swayed and soon they too were offering praise and celebration for the gifts that awaited them.

The room was beginning to meld into a mass of swirling sounds and colors as the speed of Chris and Bruno increased. They were now rapidly cutting back and forth across the width of the pit. The Shamblers waiting below were being worked into a frenzy by the rapid motion and promise of a meal. They were massing in the center of the cavern and slavering hungrily. Bruno only hoped that his plan would work. Chris had no idea what was going on, but figured following Bruno's plan, no matter how crazy, was better than just accepting death.

Following a few raucous rounds of "Amens" and "Hallelujahs," Able gently motioned with his hands for everyone to quiet down and gather around the pit in the center of the church. Judith had come to stand beside him and he gently mussed her hair. "Daddy," Judith cooed, "You're so silly getting angry at a machine. You know the mechanisms of man are fallible, but those of the Lord never break down."

"So true my child," Able replied calmly, "I had momentarily lost sight of the Lord's plan. I should have never questioned for the Lord works in mysterious ways."

Judith nodded, "Very true Daddy." A wicked smile spread across her face and curled the corners of her mouth. "And Daddy," she said coldly, "Instead of kicking the winch, you should have just pulled the release bar in the back." She pointed towards the handle that would release the spool of cable.

"You are truly a blessing my child," Able said proudly, "So imbued with the good sense of the Lord." He turned to his congregation, which had seated themselves in the pews surrounding the pit. The two nonbelievers still spun circularly through the air, but all that would soon cease. "My friends," Able said proudly, "The time has come to deliver these men into the loving embrace of the Lord." Everyone began to cheer and Able slowly reached back and pulled the release handle. The spool lurched forward and began to spin rapidly; the whiz of the unrolling wire could be heard even above the fevered prayers of the congregation.

The path of Bruno and Chris was cut suddenly short by the release of cable. As Bruno had hoped, Able did not think to time the release and had pulled the lever as the two swung outward away from the hole. Bruno knew there was no way that he and Chris were going to avoid getting tossed into the pit; there was no way that Able was going to allow them to escape, but he had to at least try. What he had hoped for was that when the wire was finally released, he and Chris would be on the further point of their arcs and the sudden slack of cable would drop them to the floor and maybe break the timber to which they were tied. After that, Bruno figured he would make it up as he went along.

Realizing that his "converts" were going to land on the floor and not in the pit, Able leapt for the winch, but Judith was already standing next it. "Don't worry Daddy," she said with a reptilian glimmer in her eyes, "I'll make sure they get delivered to Jesus." She grabbed the handle and pulled it, putting all of her weight into the pull and causing the spool to lurch and grind loudly, a few errant sparks jumped wildly into the air. The cable bounced and flexed, and then broke with a loud metallic snap sending the two human pendulums careening for the edges of the room, towards the center, and directly into the gaping maw of the pit.

As the tremble of the wire vibrated through its length, time seemed to slow down. Chris heard the snap, felt the wire suddenly go slack and then things started to go blank, but he forced himself to try and concentrate on anything; he knew he needed to focus if he was going to survive. He felt his body moving through the air and knew he was heading towards the pit and an almost certain death, but strangely these things did not pervade his consciousness and thoughts. Rather, he had one singular thought that kept repeating in his mind, Amelia. He silently thanked God or fate, or whatever for giving him this small reprieve, this tiny splinter of kindness before an agonizing death at the hands and mouths of the Shamblers below. Amelia was all he could think about. She loved him, she had said so and stupidly Chris had never fully told her how deeply he felt in return, but there had never been the right moment or time. There had always been another crisis or errand that needed to be dealt with just to make it to the next day, but somehow Chris felt that Amelia knew his feelings. That some unspoken message had been passed in their few moments alone and as he screwed his eyes tightly closed, her smile was the last thing he thought of before a tremor of excruciating pain tore through his body and he blacked out.

● ● ●

The Buildings and Grounds van spun on its roof as the massive creature bashed its hammy fists against the battered metallic skin of the vehicle. Watts and Joey sat temporarily paralyzed, unsure of what do. They had grown somewhat accustomed to the Shamblers, even the Stalkers fit somewhere into the new structure of the world that had been forged since the dead had risen, but this thing that angrily raged before them made no sense. Its large, bulbous, hairless head and numerous folds of skin glistened with some kind of oily excretion, and even though the massive size and overwhelming bulk of the creature seemed to indicate that it should be slow, it moved with ferocity and speed. Even more concerning was that it had clearly already been hit by a handful of bullets and it showed no signs of fatigue or fatality; even the shot to its neck that had spattered their windshield with a spray of greasy, clotted, black, blood seemed to have no effect.

A group of Shamblers moved clumsily across the wrecked

gate and ambled towards the van. Amelia could clearly be seen hanging upside down in the driver's seat, kept in place by her seatbelt. She did not appear to be moving.

"That shot should have killed it," Watts said blankly, still in shock, "That would have killed any of the zombies we've had to deal with." Joey just nodded.

*"Hope you found something good in that fuckin' van,"* a voice rattled through their radios. Sam followed the small horde of Shamblers through the gate. He walked in a slow, sideways gait with his rifle raised and carefully aiming each shot at the back of the zombies' heads. A carpet of dead Shamblers was unfurling in front of Sam. He had already buried three shots into the massive beast that was trying to get at Amelia, but it showed no reaction, so Sam shifted his attention to the Shamblers and began swiftly thinning their ranks. A few zombies turned to stumble towards Sam, but he calmly slapped another clip into his weapon and split their heads like rotted melons. Joey and Watts watched in awe as Sam moved calmly through the chaos. His face was set in stone, a mask of pure purpose and resolve without an ounce of self-preservation or concern.

Shaking his head, Watts snapped into action. "Load that fucking SASR up with the Mk 211's. Now!" Joey leapt from the passenger seat and began fumbling with the rifle and massive fifty caliber bullets. His hands refused to stop shaking and he kept dropping the rounds as he fumbled with the large weapon and tried to figure out how to arm it. Watts opened the door and climbed onto the roof of the van. Switching his M-16 to full auto, he sighted the creature's greasy, bald, skull and squeezed the trigger. Bullets erupted from his rifle and tore into the monster, but the massive folds of flesh and fat that surrounded its head seemed to absorb most of the damage. It momentarily stopped assaulting Amelia's van and turned to snarl at Watts, as if promising that it would deal with him soon enough. Stamping down on the roof, Watts screamed, "Hurry the hell up Joey! Get that gun out here!"

Sliding the last bullet, Joey racked a round into the chamber and climbed out of the van. In his rush, he had forgotten to check before jumping out and ran directly into the chest of what had once been a man. The Shambler slowly reached out for Joey and moaned hungrily. Joey tried to push away from the zombie, but the strap of the M-16 slung across his back had become tangled in the exposed ribs of the Shambler, forcing Joey into a disgusting embrace with the creature. He swung away trying to flee from the zombie's yellow, jagged teeth, but the slim, desiccated corpse simply moved with Joey in a morbidly comic pirouette. Panic was beginning to overwhelm Joey and he beat his fists against the zombie, succeeding in only painting himself in a rancid slick of gore and sloughed grayed skin.

Seeing his friend engaged in a literal dance between life and death, Sam sprinted across the impound lot, shouldering any Shamblers out of his way, but catching the attention of the monster that was battering Amelia's van. It turned and began following close behind Sam, grunting and snarling loudly with each step. There was no way he could risk a shot with the zombie so close to Joey, but as he came close, Sam raised the stock of his rifle and brought the butt crashing into the exposed and sun bleached temple of the Shambler. There was a dull crack and then both Joey and his dance partner tumbled to the ground. Joey quickly threw the husk of a former person off himself and scrambled to his feet.

"Thank you, thank you," Joey panted, but Sam just grabbed his shoulder and began running. The loud thud of large, bare feet could be heard pounding across the lot towards them. Watts spun from where he stood on top of the van and pumped a full clip into the creature, but it did little to slow it down.

"Hey you fat fuck!" Watts screamed as he reloaded, "Over here you ugly bastard!" He began firing again, but the monster paid him no mind and pursued Sam and Joey around the back of the van. Watts tried to place a shot into the back of the beast's knee, in the hope that he could gimp it, but the bullet seemed to disappear into the monsters bloated flesh. "Joey!" Watts screamed as the two boys sprinted towards the back of the impound lot, "Use the SASR!"

Sam heard Watts yelling about something, but had no idea

what he was talking about. What Sam did know, was that he and Joey were quickly running out of ground and that soon, they would be up against the fence and then the beast would have them.

Looking briefly over his shoulder, Joey seemed to nod in agreement with whatever it was Watts had just yelled. Without looking, he thrust the SASR sideways where it banged against Sam's arm. "You're a better shot," Joey choked, completely out of breath, "I'll draw it." Before Sam could argue, Joey had made a half turn and was running headlong towards the monster.

Even the creature seemed confused by Joey's sudden change of direction and faltered in its steps. At close range, Joey popped off a quick shot into the monster's left eye, which exploded in a torrent of black goo tinged with stringy bits of red. The humongous abomination reared its head back and unleashed a blood curdling howl that seemed to shake the entire impound lot. Defying its massive size, the Ogre turned on its distended feet and began to pursue Joey, who was running full speed back towards the gate. Watts saw Joey coming, but was busy protecting an unconscious Amelia from the throngs of undead that were trying to smash through the overturned van's windows.

Sam skidded to a stop in the gravel and dropped to one knee. He had no idea what kind of rifle Joey had thrust into his hands, but he figured it had to be something powerful from the size of the barrel, and the fact that it had been inside the gun nut's impounded van. Flipping open the large scope, Sam sighted the back of the monster's glistening, bulbous head. Looking at the creature in such detail made bile rise in Sam's throat and his stomach churn. Its head looked like an overly swollen pimple, ready to burst and wrapped in bluish vines of broken veins. But Sam did not have time to reflect upon the disgusting nature of this creature, he needed to put a bullet in its head before it tore Joey apart. Centering the scope, Sam squeezed the trigger and was thrown onto his butt by the unexpected kick of the weapon.

Joey spun to try and cut back towards Sam in the hope of giving him a better shot, and also not wanting to run into the writhing sea of corpses that swarmed all over Amelia's van. As he turned to lead the Ogre around towards the other side of the lot, Joey's eyes widened in surprise as the monster's swollen head exploded in a small burst of flame and a sizzling spray of slick fleshy confetti. Its massive bulk stumbled a few more steps, running purely on electrical muscle impulse, and then collapsed in a leaking pile of skin and rotted meat.

"Get the fuck up here!" Watts yelled from the top of the van. Joey stared for a few more stunned seconds at the ruined, swollen body of the Ogre. He could not shake the idea from his head that, in spite of its disgusting visage, the Ogre had looked somewhat familiar; kind of like Mr. Carson, the old principal, but he shook the strange moment of recollection from his mind and turned towards Watts. The loud crack of another shot ripped through the air and snapped Joey into action. As he sprinted towards the van, he saw the remains of a Shambler spiraling through the air. It must have been almost on him. He had let his guard down and for the second time today, one had almost got him. Also, for the second time today, Sam had saved his ass and he would have to be sure to thank him again when they got the chance.

The second shot from the large rifle had not caught Sam with such surprise this time, but it had still kicked like a pissed off mule. Joey had been dumbstruck and was staring blankly at the Ogre's headless corpse completely blind to the female Shambler limping up on his left. The few tangle strands of poorly dyed, red hair fluttered in the wind and danced lightly around her head, as Sam centered it in his scope and squeezed the trigger. The round exploded in her head and sent her fetid remains cart wheeling through the air away from Joey. Sam reached the back bumper of the van as Joey was clambering over the hood. Soon they both stood beside Watts on the roof. A few Shamblers had been attracted by the boys' sudden motion and swarmed the van. Watts quickly moved around the perimeter of the roof and fired off a round into the top of each zombie's skull.

The remaining Shamblers still surged around Amelia's wrecked van that lay on its back like a dead turtle. "We gotta get her outta there," Sam said, sure that everyone already knew that, but unsure of what else to say.

"Me and Joey'll clean up the rest. That monster you got there will punch a hole through the van, so no shooting it," Watts said, "We'll clear the path and you get her out."

"Ok," Sam said, "Ready?" Joey and Watts began dropping the zombies with carefully aimed shots. As soon as the first bullet had been fired, Sam was off the roof of the van and moving towards Amelia. He could see her faintly moving inside, which he hoped was a good sign. The knowledge that she was pregnant did little to calm Sam's nerves as he cut around one zombie and kicked the next one in the knee buckling it to the ground. As soon as it hit the ground, a bullet whizzed through the air and buried itself in the Shambler's face.

The windows had somehow stayed intact as the van tumbled through the gate into the impound lot and was battered by the Ogre. If they had given way, Amelia would have been trapped upside down and been peeled like gyro meat by the Shamblers, but now the windows were keeping Sam from getting to her and the doors had been crumpled to the point that the hinges refused to work.

Striking the driver's side window with the butt end of his rifle, Sam shattered the glass in a handful of irregular diamonds that cascaded across the roof. Amelia groaned loudly and her eyes fluttered. Sam leaned in and tried to release the seatbelt, but Amelia's weight was holding it in place. Shots resonated throughout the lot as Watts and Joey covered Sam, but he knew he still needed to move fast. There were always more Shamblers and with the amount of noise they had been making, Sam was sure that every zombie within a mile was slowly making its way towards the Municipal Complex.

"Amelia, come on," Sam said urgently, "You gotta wake up." He shook her shoulder and she groaned loudly, her eyes slowly opening. "Come on," Sam urged her, "I need you to wake up." Amelia's eyes stayed open, although the right one was purple and swollen.

"Sam?" Amelia said weakly, "What the hell?"

"Time for that later," Sam said quickly, "You ready to go?" Amelia nodded and Sam swept the chunks of safety glass away from under her. "Ok, let's go." The seatbelt refused to give, staying securely in the buckle.

"What's wrong? Why won't it give?" Amelia asked, panic causing her voice to rise. Sam looked around quickly and could see that more Shamblers were stumbling over the gate into the lot.

"Hurry up!" Watts yelled from across the lot, "We don't have much ammo left!"

"Shit, shit, shit," Sam muttered as he panicked and pulled at the buckle. Something heavy smacked against his leg from within his pocket and caught his attention. "The knife!" Sam almost shouted as he rapidly drove his hand into his jeans pocket to fish out the lock blade knife. He had never understood why he felt compelled to carry it with him, but now was more thankful for it than any other bit of wisdom his father and grandfather had ever given him. Flicking open the small blade, Sam easily cut through the webbing of the seat belt and freed Amelia. She tumbled to the floor, but recovered and scrambled through the shattered window.

"You ok?" Sam said as he helped her up from the ground. Small rubies of blood and glass glistened on her skin. It was almost as if Amelia had returned full circle to the day that Chris saved her in the school parking lot, but that thought quickly vanished from Sam's mind when Amelia pushed him off.

"Let's go. We gotta get moving," Amelia said firmly as she moved around the front of the wrecked van. Sam moved to follow her, but a scream erupted from her throat that froze Sam in his tracks. Amelia angrily stomped down again and again while she unleashed a feral snarl.

"What happened?" Sam shouted, now his turn to panic. But he could see the ring of teeth puncturing the side of Amelia's leg and soaking her jeans in blood. "Oh shit," Sam said sadly, "You were bit?"

Amelia looked back at him with wet eyes, "Please Sam, we just gotta go save Chris. It was just half a body. It wasn't moving. I thought it was dead. It couldn't have infected me right?" He did not know how respond. "Please don't Sam. I didn't see it. I'm fine. Really, I know I am." Her eyes fell on the rifle that hung heavily at Sam's side.

"No," Sam said quickly, his hand jumping from the gun as if it had been burned, "Amelia, I'd never. I mean I won't." His head was swimming; he had not even realized that his gripped had involuntarily tightened on his weapon upon seeing the bite wound on Amelia's leg. Had they really come this far to lose Amelia? Had they battled a monster for her to be killed by the upper half of a Shambler?

Amelia's chest was beginning to heave and silent tears were streaming down her cheeks. "Sam," she croaked, emotions cracking her words, "I'm pregnant. I can't be one of those things. I can't. I just can't." The zombie that must have been bisected by the tumbling van had somehow managed to crawl the upper half of its body out from under the van and surprise Amelia. It now lay motionless at her feet, its skull collapsed in on itself along a jagged line. Amelia's shoes were caked in thick decayed bits of jellied gray matter and globules of chunky blood.

Ripping the sleeve off of his shirt, Sam knelt down and bound Amelia's wound. The bite was not as bad as Sam had previously thought; Amelia's jeans had stopped most of the teeth, but still a few had punctured the skin. "I know," he said, unsure of his own words, "I know you are. We don't know how any of this shit works. You look fine. You'll be fine. You have to be." Sam stood up and pushed Amelia towards the van. "You cut your leg crawling out of the van, ok?" Sam whispered to Amelia, "That's what we'll tell them until we figure out what's going on." Amelia sniffed loudly and drew her sleeve across her nose.

"Ok," she said weakly, "Ok Sam. Thank you."

As Amelia and Sam climbed into the back of the van, Watts and Joey dropped into the front seats. "Everything ok?" Watts asked as he scraped the wires on the van's steering column.

"Yeah," Sam answered, "Just cut her leg crawling out."

● ● ●

The small hill overlooking The Pillar of Zion Church compound gave Ronnie, Crawford and Mike an unobstructed view of the grounds. The loud hum of gas generators could be heard even from the distance at which the group sat. Between the few lights and numerous fires, they could see that the church had become something of a refugee camp filled with mud, refuse and numerous ragged looking people. As they watched, it was hard to tell if the people within the camp were Shamblers or living, or both, but occasionally a fevered bible verse or hymn would be carried by the gentle night breeze, revealing the fact that at least some of the people below were still living, at least in the physical sense.

"Where are they?" Mike asked, as Crawford scanned the area with a pair of night vision binoculars. Sam and the others should have been in position close to thirty minutes ago, but there had been no signal, no radio contact and now Mike was beginning to worry. "What we do?" He asked, turning to Ronnie and Crawford.

Dropping the binoculars into the open cab of the pickup truck where Zule and Gozer impatiently waited, Crawford replied, "We keep going with the plan. They probably just got held up. They'll be here. Ron, you ready?"

Ronnie nodded and began checking his medieval weapon for the third time since they had arrived. He wanted to be absolutely sure that it would fire. Knowing that the Zionists vastly outnumbered them meant that they needed surprise on their side, as well as luck and superior weaponry, which was supposed to have arrived already with Sam and the others. "I'll wait till I see you get into position," Ronnie said to Mike, "And then we'll start the apocalypse."

Their end of the plan involved two parts. First, Mike needed to drive up in the old Toyota sedan and park outside the gate. The church members had no way of knowing he was from the school and Mike's hope was that he could convince them he was simply a lost soul looking for salvation. Once he was inside, Ronnie would begin raining destruction down from above, giving Mike the opportunity to detonate the bombs in the trunk of the sedan and disappear into the confusion. He would then meet up with the others as they cut a hole in the fence and slipped in through the back.

In theory, the plan seemed sensible and completely plausible, but as Mike slowed the Toyota to a stop, he began to become overwhelmed by every reason as to why it would fail. Maybe he would get out of the car and the Zionists would just shoot him? Maybe they would know it was a trap? Maybe Ronnie's catapult would not work and Mike would be stuck inside the compound? All of these possibilities and more weighed down upon Mike as he took a deep breath and opened the car door.

"Hello?" Mike called as cheerily as he could muster, "Hello? Anyone?" The gates slowly opened and massive sodium floodlights blinded Mike in a sudden burst of luminance. Holding his hand in front of his eyes Mike continued, "I've been traveling and thank God I saw your lights. Please, is there anyone I can talk to?" He had left his gun in the pickup truck with Ronnie and Crawford, but wished that he had found some way to bring it.

"Come forward," a voice called from behind the floodlights, "Keep your hands out at your sides!" Mike followed the directions and walked towards the gates. A shadowy group of people waited for him there. They were holding what appeared to be hunting rifles and shotguns.

"I'm so glad I found you," Mike smiled and then added, "God must truly be looking out for me today." As he got closer, he could see that most of the people at the gate looked terrified and underfed, but they all seemed to have the same empty eyes and broken smiles.

"Welcome," a man said stepping forwards. He wore an orange hunting jacket that had become more brown than orange from the wide inky stains that crept across it. Mike could not help but think that the stains had originally been red.

"I've been driving for days," Mike lied, "And there was no one, but I saw signs for a church and knew that God's hand was pointing the way." While they were drafting their plan, Amelia had coached Mike in various evangelical phrases that he should drop to gain the Zionists trust.

"Must be," the man beamed, "The Lord has a hand in everything. Please young man, bring your supplies in and warm yourself by one of our fires. We always have room for another servant of God."

"Praise him," Mike said in response and the others echoed his words, as he was clapped on the back and welcomed into the compound. After retrieving his backpack, Mike left the battered Toyota sedan parked next to the front gate.

● ● ●

The van chugged up the hill, struggling to make it to the top. Since leaving the Municipal Complex, Sam and the others had ridden in relative silence, the only audible noises made were from the motions of loading and checking the numerous weapons stashed within the van. Watts pushed the van further up the hill, using as much gas as curse words to urge the failing vehicle forward.

Amelia kept casting a worried glance to her bandaged ankle. It itched a little, but no more than any other cut she had ever suffered. It did not smell like death and she did not feel like she was dying, perhaps a little sweaty with an upset stomach, but that could easily be attributed to nerves. She hoped.

"You're going to be fine," Sam whispered as he leaned past Amelia to grab more Mk 211 bullets for his new rifle. "So is the baby." Sam prayed to everything that he knew of and hoped against all odds that he was right. With everything that had happened to his group, he knew that they could not suffer a loss of this magnitude; it would tear them apart, but it was more than that. Amelia being pregnant was a sign of hope, a glimmer of optimism. It meant that while everything in the entire world had fallen apart and broken down, that some things still mattered. That love and the conception of new life still counted for something beyond setting the table with another meal for the Shamblers. Amelia forced a weak smile and nodded.

"We're here," Watts said as he slowed the van to a stop. As she stepped out of the sliding door of the van, Amelia was immediately beset by the affections of Gozer and Zule. The dogs seemed to instinctively know she was worried and were doing their best to comfort her. Amelia buried her face in their large boxy faces and allowed herself to be slobbered by dog kisses. Sam scratched both of the large pitbulls as he slipped past, but they hardly took notice.

"Where's Mike?" Sam asked somewhat confused.

"He already went in," Crawford said, "We thought you were already in position."

"Shit!" Sam spat, "What the hell was he thinking?"

"He was thinking that the sooner he got in there, the better our chances of finding Bruno and Chris alive," Ronnie said matter-of-factly.

Sam took a deep breath and tired not to panic, "Ok, so that means we gotta get moving. Everyone load up with some of the new stuff in the van. Ronnie you're up here, the rest of us need to get moving."

"I need someone to help me with the catapult," Ronnie said motioning to the massive machine, "I can't move the counterweights on my own."

"Amelia, you stay," Sam began, but she cut him off.

"No," Amelia said strongly, "I'm not staying up here. I'm going down there."

Shaking his head emphatically, Sam retouted, "Look, we all want to get down there and cause some hurt and find our friends, but I think it's better if you stay up here." Anger seethed from Amelia and she firmly grabbed Sam's arm to drag him away from the others.

"You know damn well that I can't fuckin' stay up here," Amelia hissed.

Trying to comfort her, Sam replied, "I promise I'll find Chris. I'll bring him back. Besides, you're pregnant. We can't risk that."

Amelia seemed to deflate and her shoulders sagged as tears filled her eyes. "Sam, it's not about that. I know the baby is important. How could I not be thinking about that? Besides, I know that all of you will find Chris and that if he's," she choked, "If he's alive I know you'll bring him back."

"Well, then what is it?" Sam asked confused.

"I was bit," Amelia said, "You can't leave me up here with Ronnie. What if I...what if I change and hurt him?" She could not bring herself to say anymore on the subject, but Sam understood. Only he and Amelia knew that she had been bitten and possibly been infected, and whether or not either one wanted to admit it, the possibility that she could change and become a flesh hunger, undead monster was very real. And if she did change she could quite possibly make her first meal from one of their friends.

"Ok," Sam sighed, "But you're staying with me so I can make sure that *both* of you are safe."

"Fine," Amelia sighed, "But if anything changes, *anything*, you have to promise me that you'll take care of it. Baby or not, Sam you have to make sure I don't hurt anyone." Amelia's eyes were ice cold, but compelled Sam to agree.

Sighing heavily and feeling the magnitude and weight of what Amelia was asking, Sam hesitated. Finally, knowing that he may very well have to follow through his end of the agreement, Sam acquiesced, "Yeah. Fine."

The two walked solemnly back to the group. Joey was going to stay with Ronnie and help load the catapult. Everyone else was in the van. Once Ronnie had done his part, everyone else needed to be ready to move on the Zionists. They had three people on the inside of the compound and Sam was determined to bring them all out.

● ● ●

The body of Chris collided full force with one of the heavy wooden pews and went limp. The impact of the collision appeared to have knocked him unconscious and most likely broke a few ribs, but it also delivered him safely onto the floor of the church instead of sending him to the "mercy" of the countless sets of teeth that gnashed hungrily below him. At least for the moment, Chris had achieved a level of relative safety compared with what awaited him below the church.

As Bruno tumbled through the air, he watched the huge wooden bench that Chris had crashed into tilt forward and hang for a few seconds on the splintered edge of the pit. Had the Zionists stayed still and not panicked, it might not have continued forward, but as they shifted their weights and clambered over one another in a failed attempt to get to safety, the pew pitched forward and tumbled into the zombie pit, taking a handful of congregants with it. A hungry moan resounded throughout the large church and then was followed by the wet gut wrenching sound of flesh being peeled from the bone. Strangely, none of the Zionists screamed as the zombies consumed them.

The fevered prayers increased in their ferocity as Able and his followers rejoiced at the recently "raptured" members of their church. With their attention diverted to the pit or eyes raised in praise, none of the Zionists paid much attention to Bruno and Chris, assuming they would quickly be joining the "saved". Bruno had a different idea. As he swung towards the line of pews that surrounded the pit, he pushed his feet out in front and bent his knees to brace for impact.

Colliding with the pew sent painful reverberations jolting through Bruno's legs. He felt his guts dance and was pretty sure that he broke his legs, but somehow he managed to push them out and tip the heavy pew forward. Fortunately, Able and his followers liked to watch as close to the action as they could, so the pews were already tettering on the edge of the pit. One end of the pew swung outward and dangled over the void. Bruno collapsed to the floor and struggled against the ropes that bound his arms to the hunk of crude lumber. The fall had loosened the cords, but Bruno still struggled to free himself.

The loud groan of wood scrapping against wood caught Bruno's attention and made him strain to look up. The pew he kicked had skidded forward and was seesawing dangerously at the mouth of the zombie pit. A lone Zionist sat complacently on the end of the pew closest to Bruno and smiled blankly. The man seemed content to see if gravity or God would decide whether or not he was delivered into the cold hands of the undead.

Bruno could hear heavy footfalls rushing towards him and knew that the congregation members would be on him soon if he could not free himself, but he figured at least he and Chris had not made it easy. They had taken a good number of these cultish assholes with them, which had to count for something. As he struggled to look behind him, he felt himself jerk forward and slide a few feet across the polished wooden floor.

'What the fuck?" Bruno murmured as he snapped his attention back towards the pit. His eyes widened as he watched the man on the pew yank a few feet of the wire still attached to the timber bound to his arms. The man smiled coyly as he wound another length of the metal wire around his arms and pulled Bruno closer. Bruno skid a few more inches and heard the congregants come to a stop behind him.

The man in the teetering pew seemed to light up and come alive. "Rejoice!" he shouted, "For I shall deliver the heretic into the arms of our Lord!" A wave of accolades and religious phrases of encouragement swept past Bruno from behind. Able's voice boomed above all the others.

"The Lord gives us all divine opportunities to do his work brother!" Able shouted and then knelt down beside Bruno. A smile creased his face and looked down to where Bruno struggled. "There's no need to fight anymore," Able said softly, "Soon you will be washed in the love and knowledge of God and the need to fight shall disappear. Struggle no more my child."

Bruno gritted his teeth. "I'll be waiting for you in fuckin' Hell." Able simply shook his head slowly and rose to his feet.

"Deliver him my brother," Able said to the man in the pew.

"Praise Him!" The man shouted and slid across the pew to the end that hung over the pit. The pew lurched forward and dragged Bruno with it. A few jagged splinters leapt up from the floorboards and chewed into his back, but these were the least of his concerns. The rate at which Bruno moved increased drastically as the man and pew tumbled into the gapping maw of the pit. Soon the floor disappeared from beneath Bruno. To the equally disturbing chorus of hymns from above and moans from below, he felt himself tumbling through empty space.

The inside of The Pillar of Zion compound looked like something out of a third world photo spread in National Geographic. There were haggard dirty people skulking through the mud with their heads hung and wrapped in tattered clothes. Mike wondered how these people had lost so much so quickly, but the farther he went into the camp the more it became apparent.

Moving in between the masses of hollow people were smaller, more determined looking groups, who where obviously better dressed, better fed and better armed. They must be guards and enforcers Mike thought. More than once, he came across one of the enforcers yelling about "God's law," and taking food or supplies away from a terrified, starved person, yet no one protested or fought back. It seemed that everyone was willing to trade rational thought and basic supplies for the protection of compound and crude army. They were even willing to go along with, possibly even believe, a dangerous religious interpretation of the zombies and how the world now worked. Mike smiled, nodded and carefully picked his way through the camp. Even though he was free to walk where he chose, Mike had the uneasy feeling that at least one of the guards were never far behind. He was a new face in the camp and he was being watched.

The fires cast inky shadows over everything in the camp, but Mike could tell that Chris and Bruno were not among them. He carefully checked each vapid face huddled next to the fire and moved on. They must be held somewhere else, maybe in one of the buildings. He needed to move quickly. The bombs in the Toyota were going to blow any minute and Mike needed to make sure that he had some idea where he was moving so that the distraction would not be wasted.

Moving in the pools of darkness that languidly shifted around the foundations of the crude buildings, allowed Mike to catch quick glimpses through the windows. Most of the buildings appeared to be the barracks for guards with little more than a camp stove and high racks of bunk beds. The shanty cabins were hardly luxurious, but they were far better than anything that the other people had. Mike had no idea who was running this camp, but it was obvious that some form of caste system had emerged. As Mike moved along the outer wall of the cabin, he heard the loud whine of the screen door opening and banging shut. Mike froze and pressed his back against the wall.

"Come on," a voice commanded, "I want to get over there before that asshole Kelly is completely eaten." The two men laughed and rushed towards a strange, almost ship-like building in the center of the camp.

Mike peered out from behind the building. Had they been talking about *Chris Kelly*? It seemed terribly unlikely that they could have meant anyone else. Even in the darkness, Mike could see that the two people who had been speaking were wearing grimy Montville varsity jackets. These two must have known Chris before the world went to shit. Sticking to the shadows, Mike followed the two, hoping they would lead him to Chris.

The two varsity boys bounded excitedly up the stairs and into the strange building. Mike stopped a few yards shy of the steps and slipped into a nearby group warming themselves by the fire and expectantly watching something meaty and greasy turn on a crude spit over the fire. Whatever it was, they were waiting to eat, it was nothing that Mike had ever seen and sure as hell was not going to stick around to sample. When he felt it was safe, Mike broke away from the group and began walking towards the building.

As soon as Mike's right foot hit the first step a scream echoed from within the strange boat shaped building. He could hear people running from all directions, some storming out of the building and others running towards it. Just as the first person emerged from the front of what Mike thought must be the church, a loud explosion erupted from near the front gate.

A large ball of fire leapt into the sky above the charred and twisted remains of the small sedan. Mike could not help but smile. Whatever the hell Ronnie had filled those cans with had worked. The people within the camp seemed to split into two groups; one rushing towards the fire raging near the front gate, and a smaller one circling around the church.

"What's going on?" A frightened voice asked. Mike shrugged and tried to look equally bewildered, but he was soon forgotten as the people emerging from within the church began to report. Mike could only hear snippets of the story over all the shouting voices, but what little he did hear sent icy shivers dancing down his spine. Zombies were trying to break loose in the church and it had something to do with the two "nonbelievers" that had been brought in. Using the confusion, Mike slowly worked his way up the stairs and slipped into the church.

• • •

"In the words of the illustrious Lil Wayne, it's time to make it rain on dem' hoes," Joey said as he held his hands in his best gangsta pose. Ronnie looked at him confused and went back to checking his catapult. Joey continued, "What'd you think happened to him anyway?"

"Who?" Ronnie asked without looking.

"Lil Wayne," Joey replied, "You know, the rapper. I mean, what do you think happened to all the celebrities? Are they just hiding away in panic rooms waiting for this to pass or what?"

Ronnie looked up from where he was loading a large soup can and a small glass jar that was filled with a yellow tinged gel into the catapult. "Dead," he said flatly, "Celebrities were probably some of the first to go because they rely on other people to do everything for them. Privilege and money made them helpless. The cast of Jersey Shore and the Real Housewives were probably eaten by their personal assistants and now they're zombies too. Who cares?"

"Well, in all fairness," Joey smirked, "The Real Housewives were all zombies and monsters long before the first Shambler ever showed up." Ronnie missed the joke, but Joey continued. "I dunno man, I guess I'm just asking if you think things will ever go back to how they used to be?"

Leaping down from the bed of the pickup truck, Ronnie looked Joey in the face. "Why would you want to go back to that? We shouldn't be striving to return to a time where we were so fat and lazy. Everyone was so empty and bored with life, yet all they wanted to watch was reality TV. No one even knew why they were living, but spent all their time watching actors pretend to do it. If every reality star is dead, I say good riddance."

"No, no," Joey replied, "I'm not saying that I'm lamenting the world's loss of Snookie or anything like that. I'm just saying, I guess, do you think we'll ever get back to a point where we have time that doesn't have to be used for fighting or surviving? Ya' know, like will we ever get back to a point where we're guaranteed more than a day?"

"We never were," Ronnie shrugged, "You could have just as easily been hit by a car before any of this happened. There were probably twice as many cars speeding on the road as there are zombies trying to eat you. You shouldn't waste time focusing on things you can't control."

"Gee," Joey sneered, "Thanks for making me feel better."

Ronnie held his hands out at his sides. "Was the world ever really that great before any of this? We were killing ourselves with poverty, war and genocide faster than the Shamblers could ever eat us. I guess I look at this as a second chance. At least now, we have a reason to fight and a chance to make things different, if not better. With the zombies around none of the old stuff matters anymore. All social and economical barriers have broken down and now we're left with one choice, work together or die. That's the most primal, but purest aspect of society."

"You are one seriously screwed up individual," Joey laughed, "But I dunno, maybe you're right? Maybe we'll find some way to come out of this even better?"

"Or we'll fuck it up," Ronnie replied, "Our species likes to do that a lot." Joey laughed and helped with the final preparations on the catapult.

"So what's in these jars anyway?" Joey asked, "I know the cans are pipe bombs, but what the hell are these?"

"A mix of Vaseline, dish soap and gas," Ronnie said as if he were reading a cookie recipe.

Joey motioned with his hand for Ronnie to continue, "And that makes…"

"Oh," Ronnie continued, "It makes a crude version of napalm." Joey's eyes widened. "Basically, it makes liquid fire or at least I hope it will."

"Um, ok?" Joey replied, "I guess that's a good thing?"

Ronnie nodded. "Amelia came up with the idea. There's something in the Bible about a rain of fire during the apocalypse. She figured we could use that to confuse the Zionists. Hopefully, between Mike's bomb and ours, we'll confuse them and it'll give us an edge."

A loud explosion echoed from within the Zionists' compound and sent a ball of fire curling into the night sky. Ronnie rushed to the catapult and pulled the long rope that held the release pin in place. The heavy weights on the sides of the machine silently fell and whipped around the long metal arm that was welded to the center bar. Joey watched in amazement as Ronnie's catapult hurled his makeshift bomb spiraling into the night. Just as Joey could no longer see the metallic glimmer of the jar's lid pinwheeling through the darkness, it burst into flames and sent large greasy globs of fire raining down over the camp.

"Holy shit!" Joey shouted, "It actually worked! What's next?"

Ronnie let an uncharacteristic smile curl the edges of his mouth as he grabbed another firebomb. "Load it again and then we, how'd you put it? Make it rain?"

● ● ●

Knowing you are going to die is one thing; accepting it is another. There were many moments in Bruno's life where he felt certain that he was going to die. Everyday he woke up in Afghanistan, Bruno accepted the reality that he was more likely to get killed than he was to be in the mess tent for dinner, but never was he ready to die. He steeled his mind against the possibility and forged an ironclad determination to give odds and fate the middle finger on a daily basis. He had never questioned his multiple deployments to a country full of people who viewed him as evil. Not even when his third tour of duty resulted in a painful divorce from his wife, did he resent the military or the promise he made to serve. Some small piece of him, one that he always tried to quiet, often questioned how his life would have been different if he had listened to his ex-wife and not re-upped. Where would he be? Possibly a father and still married? He had always known on some level that a white picket fence and two point five kids were never in the cards for him, rather he was the guy that ensured that every other American got that luxury and that quiet acceptance had always given him strength to keep pushing forward, even when Death's fetid breath loomed coldly on his shoulder.

Never in his life had Bruno been more thankful for that mindset than he was as he freefell into the darkness below the church. He knew that there was pretty much no chance he was going to survive, and that even if he did live through the fall, all that waited for him was a painful death at the teeth of the Shamblers in the pit. But Bruno had never been a betting man. He hated to gamble and leave things to chance. Complaining about odds and luck always seemed like a cop out to him; something weak people used as an excuse to stop trying. So even with the odds stacked immeasurably against him, Bruno was determined not to die in Able's damned zombie pit. All of these thoughts and more coursed through Bruno's mind. He knew the fall was little more than ten or twelve feet, but it seemed to take forever. Space seemed to stretch before him and prolong his inevitable impact. Maybe this was the time where his life was supposed to flash before his eyes? Was this where he should be making his peace and reflecting on how he had lived?

"Fuck that," Bruno muttered and spun his body so that his feet where facing downward. In the gloom below, he could faintly make out the outline of one of the pews that had tumbled into the pit. It appeared to have landed at an angle, being propped up by another pew and the splintered edge of a support rafter. It was definitely going to hurt like hell, but if he angled himself just right, Bruno figured he would be able to hit the incline and break his fall. He only hoped that the pew would remain in position, giving him a possible escape route.

The heavy polished wood collided with Bruno's body and

released a loud slap that echoed off the packed dirt walls of the pit. Bruno gritted his teeth and fought through the urge to pass out as he slid downward. The impact had also shaken the cords that bound his wrists and he was able to slip one hand out. He was thankful that none of the Zionists seemed capable of tying a decent knot. As his feet touched the grimy floor of the cavern, Bruno came into a combative stance with the heavy cut of timber raised behind him like a baseball bat.

A tripod construction lamp swung upside down to and fro from where it hung by its electrical cord. The lamp was still hooked into the gas generator and cast a sickly-yellowed neon light around the cavern. Bruno was grateful for the small amount of light it provided, but wished it would stop swinging and creating an almost strobe like effect in the pit. He struggled to stay in or near the light, but every step made him feel like he was walking directly into a snapping set of undead jaws.

From somewhere in the darkness, a dull moan rattled out of a dead throat. It seemed like most of the Shamblers where preoccupied with devouring the Zionists that had tumbled into the pit. Bruno took this small reprieve to move himself back towards the slanted pew. He knew he needed to move fast, because every body that distracted the Shamblers soon meant another zombie in the pit. Soon enough, the meal would be over and Bruno would be next on the menu. A gristly snap resounded from the other side of the cavern and Bruno whipped his head around to come eye to milky eye with an undead Zionist. Half of the zombie's face had been chewed and jagged ends of gnawed bone poked through the cheek. The lower face of the Shambler's mouth had been eaten, giving it the unsettling look of a permanent smile. The zombie lunged forward and grasped for Bruno with clawed hands and gnashing teeth. He quickly dodged the zombie, but could feel the air brush his cheek, as the rotted set of teeth snapped close, no less than a few centimeters from his face.

"Time to go," Bruno told himself and reared back the thick length of wood he was carrying. The zombie had recovered from its initial attack and clumsily threw itself towards Bruno, completely unaware of the danger that the wood posed.

The timber connected with the side of the zombie's head and vibrations danced through Bruno's arm like an electrical shock. The Shambler's head had spun almost one hundred eighty degrees and hung strangely from where it attached to the zombie's neck and shoulders. Bruno wasted no time and brought the board high overhead in a wide arc and connected with the side of the Shambler's neck. The rotted flesh gave far less resistance than the thick bone of the zombie's skull and split on either side of Bruno's blow. Thick black ooze bubbled up from either side of the board where the putrefied skin had cracked and peeled away. The Shambler groaned loudly and took one more dragging step forward before its head rotated backwards and swung violently under the force of its own weight. The desiccated flesh crackled and resisted the momentum of the monster's heavy skull arcing backwards, but eventually, gravity won out and its head tumbled haphazardly to the floor. The zombie collapsed to the muddy ground and ceased to move.

Heavy footsteps scrapped the dirt behind him and Bruno spun around just in time see a pair of pale hands grabbing hungrily for him. He dodged sideways, but still felt the broken, cracked fingernails scrap against his neck and peel a thin layer of skin away. He hoped that whatever sickness was causing the dead to reanimate could only be transmitted through saliva. The small scrape on his neck was not a major injury, perhaps it would leave a light scar, but surely nothing life threatening. The blood that welled up from the cut was an entirely different story.

Bruno could feel the warmth of the blood as it trickled errantly down his neck and into the collar of his shirt. Suddenly, the entire cavern was filled with a deafening chorus of groans. Whatever faculties and cognizance the zombies lacked, Bruno was sure of one thing; they still had their olfactory senses and right now, they could smell his blood. He needed to move fast before a feeding frenzy erupted.

Even through the tinted windows, Sam could see flames light up the night sky. Whatever it was that Ronnie had made seemed to be working because massive clouds of fire streaked across the blackness and then fell to the earth in a dazzling display of pyrotechnics. From where the van was parked in a tightly packed copse of trees, no one could see what was actually happening inside the Pillar of Zion compound, but between Mike's car bomb and Ronnie's rain of fire, the camp undoubtedly was in a state of utter chaos.

"Check your ammo," Crawford said, "As soon as Ronnie and Joey are here we're moving. The confusion won't last long so we gotta make the most of it." Watts, Amelia and Sam checked their weapons again, even though they had done so repeatedly since the van had stopped moving. The small cache of automatic weapons had been divided up between everyone, but Sam had chosen to keep the large SASR rifle and the SR-25 that Bruno had given him. He also stashed a heavy Glock pistol in his waistband, just in case. Amelia nervously petted Gozer and Zule, but had already racked and stashed an uzi to accompany her M-16. She had not spoken since her argument with Sam; no one felt brave enough to try and get her started. "I see the truck coming," Crawford said, "Get ready."

The truck rolled to a stop beside the van and Ronnie rolled down the window. "The roofs are burning on a bunch of the buildings," he proudly reported, "And we could see people scattering all over the place, but it looked like a large group was taking up position near the front gate."

"You got any more of those shit bombs left?" Crawford asked and Ronnie nodded. "Roll a little further up the road and send one right through the front gate. After that blows we'll unload on those assholes." He turned to the back, "Sam and Amelia you guys use that time to slip in. The four of us will keep them busy. You find Mike and the others and then get the fuck outta there. Understood?" Sam and Amelia nodded, but said nothing.

Moments later, Sam heard the loud bang of metal falling on metal followed by a few seconds of silence and then a deafening explosion. Crawford floored the van in reverse and sped past where Ronnie and Joey had parked the truck. "Out the side," Crawford yelled, as he crested the small rise before the compound's main gate. Sam and Amelia threw open the side door and leapt from the moving vehicle. They spilled out across the dirt and gravel. A tangle of undergrowth and vines wrapped around their legs and brought them to a skidding stop. The pickup truck sped past them as they pulled themselves free and disappeared into the shadowy woods. Gozer and Zule leapt from the open van door and stealthily followed behind.

As soon as Sam and Amelia had jumped out, Crawford floored the van over the small hill. The van skidded to a halt and was enshrouded in a massive cloud of dust. Ronnie pulled the pickup truck just behind the van. He and Joey slipped out the side doors and pressed themselves against the grill of the van. Crawford offered them an uneasy smile from the driver's seat.

After the explosion, an eerie silence settled over the camp. Everyone in and around the van seemed to be holding their breath, waiting for something to happen, but they had no idea what. Joey carefully peeked his head out from around the van. Through the flames he could see what looked like a few mangled bodies splayed out on the ground. He took a tentative step from behind the van, but as soon as he placed his foot fully on the ground, thunderous gunshots banged from somewhere near the gates. A handful of pellets peppered the van's side, mere inches from Joey's head. Had Joey been a few steps forward or had the gun fired been anything other than a shotgun loaded with buckshot, he would be dead.

"Get behind the fuckin' van!" Watts yelled from inside the van. Ronnie leaned out from the other side and fired off a quick burst to draw the Zionists' attention as Joey scrambled back around the van. Crawford motioned through the windshield for the boys to stay put and duck down.

"They wanna shoot at the kids huh?" Crawford said acerbically to Watts who nodded and moved towards the back of the van. What neither soldier needed to say was that they had seen enough wars involving children and the idea of these lunatics shooting at the kids they had grown so close to, viewing them almost as family, enraged them; these children were theirs to protect. Over in the Middle East, they never could tell which child actually carried their schoolbooks and which one had an IED hidden between the covers. They never blamed the kids, always knew that some twisted adult had forced them into carrying the explosive, but that never made it any easier to draw a bead on a child and see their expression as you decided whether they lived or died. Furthermore, it never made it any easier to tell your friend's wife or parents that their boy is dead because you could not make the tough decision and pull the trigger. Regardless of the friends and limbs that were lost to these attacks, neither Watts nor Crawford could stomach the idea of violence committed through or against children.

As more shots pinged off the van, Watts pulled the tarp that covered the large mini gun and hooked the cables to the car battery mounted beside it. He only hoped that the whack-a-do that made this thing, knew what he was doing. Crawford dragged a heavy box of ammo over and handed the belt to Watts.

Crawford grabbed an AK-47 and racked the first round as a golf ball sized hole chunked through the roof of the van. The Zionists were firing some high caliber bullets from deer rifles. They would need to be careful, but once Watts opened up with the mini gun, the Zionists would not be able to do a thing. Pushing the rear doors open, Crawford sprayed a wide arc of bullets back and forth across the fence line. "Ready?" He screamed over the sound of his weapon.

"Let's give these assholes the apocalypse they've been waitin' for," Watts smiled and pressed the button that started the barrels spinning

● ● ●

The inside of the building looked like it had once been a church, but much of its religious façade had been stripped away. There were still pews stacked against the walls, some born-again styled paintings and a pulpit, but the center of the room was empty. A few pews appeared to have been moved into a semi-circle in the middle of the large room and the loud hum of a gas generator resonated throughout the room. If not for the five or six construction lights positioned around the room, Mike would not have been able to see much of anything.

Most people seemed to have run out of the building when the car exploded by the front gate, but Mike could hear movement somewhere further into the main room. He wished that he had found some excuse to have brought a weapon with him, but knew there was no way the Zionists were letting him through the gate with a loaded M-16. A large brass candleholder was tucked away in a corner and caught Mike's eye as he moved past. It stood about four feet tall and was heavy, but it was far from being an M-16. Mike figured it was better than nothing, and the weight of the candleholder could do some serious damage if he swung it hard enough.

A scream echoed from somewhere in the center of the room, catching Mike off guard and almost causing him to drop the candleholder. It was definitely the scream of a living person, but just underneath it, Mike was fairly certain he could hear the dull moan of the undead. He wanted to rush forward and help whoever had let loose such a cry, but he forced himself to go slowly. There really was no way of knowing what was in here and who or what could be hiding in the inky shadows.

Moving slowly with the heavy ornamental candleholder held like a baseball bat, Mike crept across the room. The further he moved into the room, the louder each subsequent scream became, but they did not sound like cries of pain, more like ones released in battle. Nearing the few pews arranged in the middle of the room, Mike realized there was a massive opening in the floor. Some kind of pit had been dug and the pews arranged like stadium seats to view whatever events took place below. Mike could not help but wonder why someone would build such a thing, let alone in the middle of a church, but then he reminded himself that this was the same congregation that had been worshiping zombies and burning down neighborhoods. The thought of what they might be doing with this set up made Mike queasy.

A second scream echoed from below and Mike saw someone dart across the center of the pit. "Hey!" Mike screamed, "Up here!" There was a loud, hollow sound and then the ruined body of a Shambler spilled into the dim circle of light in the middle of the cavern. Suddenly, Mike knew exactly what this pit had been made for and felt dizzy thinking that one or both of his friends might be down there. He frantically searched the room for a ladder, a length of rope, anything that would allow him to help whoever was down in the pit. A frayed piece of thin metal cable, no longer than ten feet or so, lay tangled on the floor, some smaller ropes were nearby, but they appeared to have been cut and were far too short to be of any use. Grabbing the cable, Mike wrapped it around his arm and then his hand, ensuring a strong grip.

"Rotten motherfucker!" A familiar voice yelled from inside the pit. Another Shambler fell backwards into the center of the pit. It appeared to have been hit in the mouth and its lower jaw hung by only a few strings of rotted flesh. The zombie showed no apparent knowledge of its current condition and rose back to its feet and stumbled forward with its arms outstretched and dried, blackened tongue lashing the air as it tried to moan, but succeeded in only a sickening gurgle. Bruno rushed forward to finish the zombie off and swung his splintered piece of timber as hard as he could. He had already finished off more zombies than he could count, but knew that there were others still busy eating, who would soon be coming after him.

When Bruno had first tumbled into the pit a few of the more capable, less decayed Shamblers began to slowly claw their way up the haphazardly piled pews and sent the Zionist fleeing, only to comically tumble back into the pit moments later. After bashing the skulls of those Shamblers, Bruno had tried to follow their example and scramble up the tilted pew in the hopes that he would be able to jump and grab the edge of the floor, but the ground inside the pit, slick and muddy, mixed with human waste, bodily fluids and spilled blood, had coated his boots. He had made it a few frantic feet forward before his legs slipped out from under him and he tumbled back into the pit. With no other option, he had stood his ground and fought. His muscles burned as he forced himself to raise the heavy piece of wood again and again to put down another undead parishioner. He was unsure if he would be able to lift the board another time. It only weighed a few pounds, but felt as if had been made of forged steel, not timber. As the splintered piece of lumber connected with one more Shambler's face, it fell heavily from his hands and lay at his feet. It was completely caked in gore and had yellowed, chipped teeth embedded up and down the edges like some kind of crude medieval mace. It had stood up well to the abuse Bruno put it through, but looking at it there on the ground, he knew it would not survive another hit.

"Bruno!" Mike screamed as he threw the other end of the cable into the pit. "Grab on!" Unsure if he was hallucinating or not, Bruno looked around to see who had called his name. Maybe he had become so exhausted that the moans of the Shamblers sounded like speech, or maybe Death was calling him by name? "What the fuck are you waiting for?" Mike shouted.

Using his last bit of energy, Bruno forced his head to tilt upwards and saw a shadowy figure silhouetted against the neons that lit the upper room. "Who?" He began to say, but then figured it did not matter. The chance of escape called upon some last reserve of energy and Bruno forced his legs to move forward and up the pew one more time. The frayed bit of cable dangled tantalizingly before him, gently scraping on the end of the uplifted pew.

Cold, dead hands clawed at Bruno's pant legs as he pushed himself further up the slippery polished wood ramp. His entire body hurt and wanted to give up, but Mike urged him forward. With one last burst of strength, Bruno leapt forward and grabbed the cable. He wrapped it around his arm and clung on with what little strength remained in his body.

"Hold on!" Mike screamed. He had moved the cable as close to Bruno as he could by laying down flat on the floor, but that meant it was going to be near impossible to stand again and there was no way Bruno had the strength left to climb.

Mike needed to think of something. The cable jerked and became taut. Mike forced himself to roll backward and wrap the cable around his body. He felt the weight of Bruno and the cable digging into the flesh through layers of cloth, but he continued to roll and wind the cable tighter and tighter. The pain began to reach a crescendo and Mike felt like he was either going to pass out, or be torn in half. Black spots were beginning to swim through Mike's vision, but it was hard to tell them apart from the shadows that swarmed all around him. Slowly the blackness and shades crept in to pinhole his vision. The shadows suddenly shot forward and Mike passed out.

The edge of the broken floor was not more than a few inches from his reach, but Bruno doubted he had the energy left to grab for it. The cable stopped moving. Bruno was about to call out, but the unexpected lurch of the line caused the words to catch in his throat. With his free arm, Bruno reached up for the floor, but his fingers only graced the splintered tips, which broke away and gently drifted into the bottom of the pit; the same place he was sure he was going unless he moved fast. With the cable wrapped around his arm, he could not use both hands, but somehow, against all odds and physical constraints, Bruno managed to bring his free hand up and over to grab the cable and pull. Even as he struggled to pull himself just a tiny bit further, he could feel the cable slowly slipping and making it incrementally harder to succeed.

As his hand graced the fractured oak boards of the floor, Bruno clamped down with a vice-like grip that caused jagged splinters to pierce the toughened skin of his hand, but this pain was easily ignored. After the days that he had endured, a few slivers in the palm of his hand were a vacation and the fact that they meant he had reached the floor made them an almost welcome hurt.

He knew that Able had to be somewhere, that the Zionists had to be nearby, but Bruno could not muster the strength to give a shit. He collapsed onto the floor and lay on his back staring at the high ceiling from which he and Chris had previously been hung. Chris! The soldier inside of Bruno demanded that he get up immediately and find Chris. This was no time to lie around feeling sorry for yourself, a voice commanded from deep within Bruno's head. Pulling a few of the longer splinters from his hand, Bruno rolled over and forced himself first to his knees and finally to his shaking feet.

"Chris!" Bruno shouted, "Chris!" But no answer came. From somewhere nearby, a dull groan rattled out of someone or something that Bruno hoped was not or used to be Chris. Urging himself forward, Bruno stumbled towards the sound. What he was going to do when he found it was anyone's guess. He barely had the strength to walk, let alone kill another Shambler, but right now, he was only dealing with one problem at a time.

A darkened mass lay on the floor wrapped in tight rounds of cable. It shifted and groaned loudly. "Mike? What the hell?" Bruno said unsure of his own words.

Large black globs still swam across Mike's vision as if he were swimming in some murky lava lamp, but through the blobs, he could see the muddied, blood flecked face of a mad man, a mad man he thought he recognized.

"Bruno. What's up man?" Mike said between hacking coughs he was sure were speckled with blood. "That was you down there?"

Pulling the cable away from Mike's body, Bruno helped him sit against one of the large support columns that were evenly spaced around the room. "Yeah, you got me out buddy," Bruno said as cheerily as he could muster, "Don't know how the hell you did it, but you did."

Mike let out a pained cough and tried to stand, but his legs gave out and he collapsed to the floor. "Shit," Mike said dejectedly, "Just gimme a sec."

"No," Bruno replied, barely hiding the concern in his voice, "You stay here. I'm going to go find Chris. You didn't see him when you came in?" Mike shook his head slowly in response to the question. "Ok, ok," Bruno continued trying to think, "Where'd you come in?"

"The front," Mike coughed, "Bunch of people rushing out, but I didn't see Chris."

"That means there must be a back exit. That fucker Able

must have taken him," Bruno said grinding his teeth.

"Able?" Mike asked.

"Later," Bruno responded, "For now, we gotta hide you somewhere safe. I'll come back and get you once I find Chris."

"Great rescuer I turned out to be huh?" Mike laughed, but soon began hacking.

"You did fine kid," Bruno said, "Better than most of the soldiers I've ever served with." With that, Bruno knelt down and helped Mike from the floor and propped him up behind a pile of pews. "Stay quiet. Stay down." Mike gave a sarcastic salute and Bruno smirked. Then he turned and took off running towards the back of the church.

● ● ●

Moving through the woods at night was far from easy. Amelia and Sam moved as fast as they could without being careless, but still tripped over the occasional root or log. They never asked if the other was ok, instead just helped them up and kept moving. It was understood that their window of opportunity was slim and there was no way they were going to waste it nursing a twisted ankle or sprain.

A pile of stone had been dumped a few feet away from the main gate, most likely having been moved during the original construction. Sam motioned for Amelia to stop and then pointed to the rocks. She nodded and counted down from three with her fingers. They both ran headlong towards the boulders and slammed their backs against the barrier. Gunshots rang out in both directions, but the rapid chatter of Ronnie and the others' automatic weaponry quickly drowned out the sporadic rifle rounds and shotgun blasts of the Zionists. A group of shadows rushed past the boulders and ran towards the direction of the van. Moments later, a loud *whirl* was heard, followed the release of so many rounds of ammunition that it was impossible to tell the spacing between each shot.

Sam and Amelia peered out from behind their hiding place and in the fading light of the fire set by Mike's explosion, they could see a pile of what looked like chewed beef. "What was that?" Amelia whispered.

"The sound?" Sam said, "I think it's the gun Watts had in the back of the van. And the meat? Probably used to be people." He found the sight repulsive, but could not avert his eyes.

"Disgusting," Amelia said, "Let's move." With the gate guards left as little more than disjointed clumps of chopped beef, Sam and Amelia met with no resistance passing through the gate and into the compound. Gozer and Zule trailed a few feet behind, but took off running as soon as they were through the gate.

"Wait! Sit! Heel!" Amelia shouted, but the two dogs kept running deeper into the compound.

"They know how to take care of themselves," Sam consoled, "They'll be fine. I'm sure we'll find them or they'll find us."

"Yeah," Amelia said without any belief in her own words or Sam's.

The entire camp was in a state of utter chaos. Ronnie's firebombs had rained down upon the roofs of many buildings and set them afire. Thick black smoke curled into the air from where the tar paper and shingles burned and painted the bedlam in strange iridescent colors. Periodic bursts of gunfire could be heard outside the fence, but there was none within. Perhaps the most disconcerting detail of the entire situation was that once they were through the gates, Sam and Amelia had not encountered any resistance, not one angry Bible thumper could be found. Sam and Amelia kept their weapons trained in front of them and swept them back and forth, as they moved along the muddy, rutted path.

The twisting dirt path wound its way through the compound, past more burning buildings and a periodic body. Sam hesitated near one of the muddy corpses. After a few steps, Amelia noticed and jogged back to where he stood. "What's wrong? We don't have time for sightseeing," she chided, but immediately regretted it when she saw what Sam was looking at.

"It's a kid," Sam said flatly. His eyes appeared glassy in the dim light of the fires. "Do you think we did this?"

"It wasn't us," Amelia said firmly, "We didn't make this situation they did. Whatever happens is their fault."

"I guess so," Sam replied, but his words were devoid of any conviction, "Let's go." They set off further into the camp, but came to a grinding halt as the trail converged with three others creating a crude town square.

In the middle of the paths was a small patch of scrubby grass with a large bonfire burning in the center. The fire flicked huge tongues of flame into the air and roared ferociously as it consumed itself. Strewn around the conflagration in small groups were what appeared to bodies. "What the fuck?" Amelia said as she took a step forward. The barrel of her gun waivered in front of her and finally hung limp at her side. "Sam?" she said weakly. He stepped in front of her to examine the closest group.

"It looks like a family. A mom, dad and three kids," Sam said, "What do you think happened here?"

"Those cups," Amelia pointed at the ground, "There's more solo cups around here than a frat party. They must have drunk something."

Sam looked around and saw that she was right. There was a cup within reach of each corpse. "Is this some kind of Jones Town thing?" Sam asked, "A mass suicide? But why are the kids dead too if this is about becoming a frigging zombie. There haven't been any children that got infected. Would they really kill their own kids?"

"Maybe," Amelia replied as she looked at the purple face of a little girl no older than four or five years, "Probably, if they really believed that world was ending and didn't want them to suffer or something. They could have drunk some poison, or...or... zombie blood or something. Fuck if I know."

"Maybe," Sam said hesitantly, "But that doesn't really make sense does it? I mean in like Biblical terms. I'm no scholar, but I'm pretty sure mass suicide is frowned upon."

Amelia nodded, "Yeah, that's true." She hesitated, "Unless, well, unless they didn't really think of it as death."

"What do you mean?" Sam asked growing concerned.

"These people were basically worshiping the zombies right? They obviously thought that the Shamblers were holy," Amelia said looking around the area, "What if they were just speeding up becoming one? I mean what if this was also a tactical move instead of a purely religious one?"

Sam paled, "You mean you think they did this to intentionally try and make an army of Shamblers? Could they really have seen this as a defensive move? That's crazy. It might not even work. It's just totally fucking crazy." As he finished his words, a small twitch of movement grabbed his attention out of the corner of his eye. Soon at least half of the bodies around the small square released a dull groan and struggled to rise from the muddied ground.

"Which is why it makes perfect sense," Amelia said timidly as she stared wide-eyed.

● ● ●

It hurt to breathe. It hurt to move. Hell, it even hurt to think, but Bruno forced all of these thoughts and feelings down. He had been trained to ignore his body, disregard physical messages that got in the way of the mission. He could go days without sleep or food. Spent days in the mountains of Afghanistan with little more than his rifle and a canteen and never complained. That was the job of a soldier and that was all he could allow himself to focus upon as he limped through the main room of The Pillar of Zion Church. The three steps leading up to the altar felt like a thousand, but he would have time for pain later. Right now, the only thing that mattered was finding Chris and to do that, he needed to figure out where Able had taken him.

Outside of the church, Bruno could hear gunfire and could see the erratic glow of an uncontrolled fire dancing behind the stained glass windows. The others must have started their attack. Bruno only hoped that he would be able to link up with them and get a weapon. He was more than willing to kill Able with his bare hands, but did not relish the idea of any more hand-to-hand combat with Shamblers.

His boots echoed loudly as Bruno moved across the polished marble altar. A loud groan rose up behind him and Bruno spun to face the zombie who made it, but there was nothing there. The groan resonated again and this time he realized it was echoing out of the pit. The other bodies down there must have reanimated and added new vocals and volume to the undead chorus below. Even though he knew the zombies were trapped in the pit, the noise still unsettled Bruno.

A cheap wooden door, located behind the altar, led to a back room that must have served as Able's office. Various religious posters cluttered the wall and books with dog-eared pages and massive amounts of highlighting lay open in haphazard piles near a cheap metal desk. Bruno quickly surveyed the room, but there was no evidence of Able or Chris. As he moved towards the rear door, he noticed a pile of strewn papers and books. It was scattered and trampled across the floor by at least two different sets of large footprints that were evident on the papers. It had to have been Chris and Able, and if Chris was on his feet then there had to be a good chance that he was still ok. Granted, Mike said the Zionists had scattered after the explosion, but with the level of control that Able maintained, there was no way they would intrude into his sanctum; Able's ego would have never allowed the parishioners to enter where he wrote his sermons. The tracks pointed towards the rear door that led out into the compound. Able must have taken Chris outside.

As Bruno moved down the steps, he could feel his body beginning to relax and respond a little more normally. His training had taught him to break through those physical walls when he hit them. Human beings were far tougher than they gave themselves credit for and could be pushed well beyond what they thought were their physical limits. Pain was a mindset, one that could be changed.

Bruno picked up the tracks again once he had moved a little further away from the church. Rings of frantic, erratic footprints where everywhere, but most were pointing towards the center of the camp. After carefully looking, Bruno found only two that seemed to be heading towards the back fields. He picked up his pace and before long was running.

The long grass whipped at Bruno's legs as he pushed himself to run faster and faster. The trail left behind by who he hoped was Able and Chris, became easier to follow once her got further away from the church. The grass was snapped and pushed down, all pointing in the same direction and with far too much distance between the strides to be a Shambler. Something glistened in the moonlight on one of the stalks. It shown like wet tar, sticky, thick and black. Blood. "Shit," Bruno hissed between breaths and then broke into a full sprint. He needed to move fast.

As the grass gave way, Bruno skidded to a halt in a large clearing. There was a forest of posts staked into the ground. Each one was of a decent sized tree, but completely stripped of all branches and foliage. "What the fuck?" Bruno muttered, but then heard the tell- tale moan of a Shambler. He spun in every direction, looking for the monster and finally having no other way to look, glanced up. The Shambler struggled against the nails and ropes that held it to a crossbar. Even from its position three feet above Bruno, it gnashed its cracked teeth and struggled to take a bite out of Bruno. The zombie seemed completely unaware of the fact that it was crudely crucified and had no way of fulfilling its insatiable hunger.

"My god," Bruno gasped as he backed away and his eyes better adjusted to the darkness. Dark shillouettes writhed and struggled on almost every post. Some held desiccated cropses that showed no signs of struggle, but most were occupied by a set of milky eyes and clacking teeth. Able had planted an entire forest of crucified zombies, but for what reason, Bruno could only guess.

"You were close my friend," a voice said with silken tones, "But it's *my God* we serve here." The words were followed with a small spade swung at full force aimed directly at the base of Bruno's neck.

● ● ●

The noises outside the church had started to die down. Sporadic gunfire reported periodically throughout the camp and the fires appeared to still be burning brightly outside and casting an eerie reddish glow over everything inside the church. Mike forced himself up to a sitting position, which sent fiery splinters shooting through his chest. He gasped and forced a breath. That had to be somewhat of a good sign, he figured, if he had collapsed a lung there was no way he could take a full draw of air, but the pain was intense nonetheless. Rolling the cable around his body had seemed like a logical move at the time, but the tension and force of Bruno's body struggling on the other end must have cracked a few ribs, if not broken them completely. But Mike would gladly trade a few ribs and days of pain if it meant that Bruno was alive. Now he was left huddled behind a stack of pews waiting for Bruno to return, hopefully with Chris.

Light footfalls echoed softly in the room. Mike held his breath and listened to the movement. It was far too elegant and soft to be a Shambler and did not sound heavy enough to be an adult. As quietly as possible, Mike shifted his body and lay down on the floor to look out from under one of the pews.

A small pair of highly polished Mary Jane shoes with bright silver buckles stopped in front of the pew, and turned back and forth, as if trying to decide which way to go. "Mister?" A voice cooed softly, "Please come out from behind there. I need your help mister. Please help me." Mike could hear the tears in each word and figured there was no point in pretending that he was not back there, because obviously this child knew. Besides it was only a child. She was alone and probably terrified. "Oh please mister," the girl sobbed, "There's monsters attacking everyone. I don't know what to do. Please…" The girl collapsed to the floor and from where he lay Mike could see her holding her head in her hands, sobbing.

"Hey," Mike called as he shifted uncomfortably, "Back here. Come here." He watched as the girl lept up from the floor and ran towards his hiding place. She squeezed behind the pews that Bruno had moved to hide Mike. A lightly colored floral print dress fluttered lightly from her sides. It was immaculately clean, as were her shoes, which Mike found strange. How could someone move around the camp on all the rutted, muddy trails and still stay this clean. But somehow this girl, of probably no more than fourteen, stood before him looking as if she were ready to go to Sunday mass.

"Oh thank you mister," she said with the over done exuberance of youth, "You don't know how much better you're making me feel. It looks like the whole world is falling apart out there."

Mike struggled to his feet and leaned his weight on the wall. "Yeah," Mike coughed, "It sure seems that way these days. My name's Mike. What's yours?"

The girl feigned shyness for a few moments, but then blurted out, "My name is Judith and I can't find my Daddy."

"Your father is here?" Mike asked suspiciously, "He's a member of this church?"

A small giggle escaped from Judith's lips. "No Mike," she said shaking her head theatrically, "My Daddy's not a member of this church."

Mike was unsure of how to proceed or say next. The girl seemed somewhat unbalanced, but who knows what horrors she had seen while she was with the Zionists? There was no way to know what these lunatics were doing with the people they found scared and hiding in the neighborhoods they burned down. Maybe Judith and her father had been captured? Maybe he was one of the moaning hungry monsters in that damned pit?

"Alright," Mike said slowly, "We're gonna get outta here. My friends will help us find your father once we meet up with them." He took a step forward, but the pain caused Mike to double over. Judith jumped forward and caught him before he fell to the floor.

"You don't look so good," she said full of concern, "But I guess you probably know that, huh?" She giggled and helped Mike put his arm around her shoulder. "You just lean right there and I'll help you." Judith and Mike struggled past the heavy stack of pews and back out into the main room of the church. The dull groans of the undead could still be heard coming out of the pit, but they were far less emphatic now that Bruno was out.

"Was your father captured too?" Mike asked, "My friends

were. That's why I came here to save them from these monsters." He could feel Judith's body go rigid and then forcibly relax as he spoke. He figured the mention of her father had been unsettling.

Judith stopped and readjusted Mike's arm. She grabbed his wrist and pulled it tightly down towards her waist. Her other hand had moved behind her back and silently withdrew something tucked away in the blue ribbon circling her petite waist. "You know Mike," she said, her voice cooling considerably from its previous tone, "My Daddy always says that a smart man not only asks questions, but asks the right questions."

"What are you talking about Judith?" Mike asked as he tried to pull away from her, but she yanked his arm forcibly and suddenly an explosion of pain blossomed Mike's lower back. Judith stepped away and let Mike collapse to the floor. A small dagger, no longer than three or four inches, dangled before his face as Judith giggled joyfully.

"You asked me if my Daddy was a member of my church and I said 'no'. Now I know the Lord doesn't like liars, but that's not really a lie now is it?" Judith said. Her entire demeanor had shifted in a matter of seconds. The façade of a scared child had quickly melted to reveal the cold, bottomless eyes of a killer. Something predatory stood in front of Mike, something hiding in the guise of a small girl, but far more dangerous. "No," Judith continued, "I guess that's not really a lie because you see my Daddy is not a member of this church. *My Daddy is this church.* He built it with his hands and gathered God's children to make ready for the End of Days and now you and your dirty, unworthy cohorts have come and wrecked it all!" She slashed Mike's back again, but had yet to deliver a cut that would be life threatening.

Mike tried to talk, but Judith lashed out and kicked him forcefully in the face. She walked around to the front of Mike and knelt down and took his chin in her small hands. "Mike, I could never expect you to understand. My Daddy thinks everyone has a chance for redemption. That even the twisted sinful souls of people like you and your friends could be saved, maybe even transformed into a messenger." She stopped and laughed, but it was entirely devoid of humor. "But me, well I know better. My Daddy's a good loving man, but he has misunderstood the Lord's plan. Salvation is not for everyone. Some people aren't worth saving. They are simply fuel for the conflagration that will consume the wickedness of this world."

"What the fuck are you talking about?" Mike spat.

"Fuel, Mike, to feed God's holy march forward," Judith said coldly, "Or perhaps its more appropriate to say food instead of fuel. Yes, I believe it is. Some people, people like you Mike, aren't worth saving. No, the only thing you are here for is to feed His messengers." Mike struggled to move away from Judith, but she quickly circled around him and stomped on his legs repeatedly. Moving around to the front, Judith tightly grasped Mike's wrists and dragged him forward. "Yes," Judith crowed, "Yes I believe the Lord simply views you and your kind as stocks for the larder." She dragged Mike forcefully across the floor, each step increasing the volume of the moans resonating from below and Mike's propinquity to death.

● ● ●

A tepid, wax-white hand clamped around Sam's ankle as he stumbled backwards away from the raging bonfire in the middle of the camp. Amelia turned to run and a recently reanimated obese woman clad in a mud stained denium sack dress grabbed at her jeans legs with thick, sausage like fingers and moaned hungrily. Despite the woman's short, fat digits, she grabbed a fistful of Amelia's pants in an iron grip and refused to let go. Her stumpy swollen legs, wreathed in bruises and broken veins, writhed in the mud as if she were trying to swim in a pool with no water. Fortunately, the considerable size of the woman's gut kept her legs from moving her considerable girth forward. Amelia fiercely shook her leg, but the woman 's grasp was unflappable. Sam and Amelia had encountered plenty of Shamblers since the dead had risen, but none so fresh and agile. These zombies had not begun to putrefy or suffer any stiffening from rigor mortis. The tendons and muscles were still warm and supple, still able to move and flex close to normal.

"Let go!" Amelia screamed, as she stomped down on the fat woman's arm. The excess skin and fat bulged like a water balloon being squeezed, but the fingers remained locked in place. A loud shot split the air and the back half of the obese woman's skull fragmented and disappeared. The fingers slowly opened as the round, bloated hand heavily fell away from where it gripped Amelia's jeans.

The barrel of the Sam's SR-25 rifle was still smoking as he rammed the stock backwards into the face of the Shambler that had grabbed him. Amelia watched as the zombie pitched backwards and a spray of shattered teeth sailed through the air. Sam never even flinched or looked behind him. Throughout the entire exchange, Sam had not even spoken; Amelia was not even sure that he blinked. It was almost as if he had turned off the part of him that knew to be afraid, the rationale part that knew they were surrounded by death and impossible odds. The Sam that had only moments ago stood beside Amelia was gone; what remained was something different, something dangerous. Everyone had seen it slowly building in Sam. Had seen cracks in the cheery demeanor he kept up for everyone else. Alice had worried and asked Amelia about it days before they left to rescue Chris and Bruno, but Amelia had assured Alice it was simply stress from everything that happened at the hospital, but even then, Amelia had known she was lying. Sometimes a person is pushed too far, endures too much, and something simply breaks or turns off and she worried that was what she was watching finally happen in Sam right before her eyes. The glimmer of life, that spark of joy that he refused to extinguish seemed to waiver and flicker weakly in his eyes, getting smaller with each shot he fired. Amelia's guts twisted in her stomach as she thought about what might be left of Sam once this was over. She only hoped that some fragment of the old Sam was still in there and could be tenderly nursed back to life; not by her of course, Amelia knew the most she could hope for was to tell Alice to do so before someone had to put a bullet in her head to keep her from hurting their friends. Sam strode slowly, but forcefully towards Amelia while firing careful shots into the Shamblers that sloshed towards them through the muck and rain.

All the grime, death and horror that surrounded them, was painted in a wash of blacks, reds and oranges from the massive fire that raged in the middle of the compound, and as Amelia and Sam turned to run from it all, she could not help but think that this is what Hell must look like, that maybe this really was Hell. But before these thoughts could overwhelm her, Sam grabbed her arm and pulled her forward. Every few steps he would stop and fire another round, dead center in the head of another Shambler, but for every zombie that Sam dropped, two more seemed to be clumsily pulling themselves up from the ground.

"This is a fucking waste of ammo," Sam sneered, "Run for that building." Amelia turned to see which one he was motioning towards. It was a large wooden building with a bowed front and high point, which extended forward giving it the appearance of a boat. From its central location and size, Amelia figured it had to be the church and looked like it would have solid doors. Besides that, it was one of the only structures not burning, so it was really their only viable option. "Go," Sam said forcefully and the two broke into a full out sprint.

They crashed through the main doors and slammed them shut. The doors appeared to be solid wood and would definitely hold, until enough zombies pushed on them to rip the hinges out of the frame, but they could deal with that problem when it happened. Amelia gasped for air as she collapsed against the door and noticed Sam looking down at her. "You're ok? Right?" Sam asked coldly, as he barred the doors. His gun was down, but not exactly at rest.

"Yeah," Amelia wheezed, "I'm fine." But the undertones of Sam's question made her soul shiver.

● ● ●

Chris really did not remember much after crashing into the pew. His entire body was racked with pain, but someone was forcing him to walk, dragging him forward. Chris's feet gave out and he collapsed heavily onto the floor, but it was mud, not the polished hardwood of the church's floor. Someone had moved him outside. Slowly Chris came to realize that there was a cold rain falling steadily to the ground. He focused on the coolness of the water and let it provide what little support it could. With great effort, he forced himself to raise his head and look up. In an instant Chris's heart shattered and littered his soul with hopelessness.

"It's not time to sit down my young friend," Able said with a smile that held no happiness, "Oh, no there will be no rest for the wicked." Chris tried to leap forward and tackle Able's legs, but the man easily sidestepped the attack. A heavy kick knocked Chris onto his back and the edges of the world started to close in on him.

Not long after Chris awoke to feel the coarse caresses of wild grass on his bare skin, he was being dragged through a field. Able had lashed his feet together with rope from somewhere. He had the other end of the rope over his shoulder and plodded steadily along through the grass. Somewhere in the distance, Chris could hear what he thought were gunshots, but he could not be sure that the noises were not from within his own head, which throbbed and felt ready to split. Chris weakly struggled, but Able ignored him and continued to march forward whistling a cheery hymn.

After awhile, Chris really could not tell how long, Able came to a stop and dropped the rope attached to Chris's feet. They were still in some sort of overgrown field with no distinguishing characteristics besides the rough, waist high grass. Walking over to Chris, Able knelt down and smiled that same crocodilian smile, "Well, my young friend it seems that the good Lord has decided to give you a second chance to repent for your sins. Should consider yourself lucky my boy, yes, lucky indeed. Most men are never given a second chance to be welcomed into the Lord's good graces."

Chris had no idea what the hell Able was talking about, but knew it was not good. He wanted to break free, to fight, to scream, to do something, anything, but his body refused to comply. The rain had stopped falling so heavily and Chris could now definitely hear the sounds of a vicious battle being waged.

Carried wetly on the breeze was the distinct scent of wood burning. A half smile curled Chris's lips and he let his head fall back into the grass.

"I sure do hope that smile is one of divine acceptance," Able said threateningly.

"No," Chris said weakly, "No, I'm smiling because I can smell your world burning. It's over you fuckin' nut. My friends are gonna kill you."

"I guess some people just can't be saved," Able said shaking his head, "Some horses will have their heads held under the water and still not drink, but that doesn't really change much for you. You see, the Lord will judge us all, whether we want him to or not. The only choice we ever really have is whether or not we repent for our heathen ways and face judgment with a clean soul or not."

"I'm sorry. So sorry," Chris said and watched Able's eyes light up.

A true smile washed over Able's face, "See now, not so hard was it? All you need to do now is tell the Lord what it is you're sorry for and you will be forgiven. Simply confess to your imperfections and transgressions and be forgiven."

"I'm sorry," Chris continued, "So very sorry that I won't be there to see my friends put a bullet through your fucking head. I'm sorry that I won't be able to piss on your corpse as the last bit of life drains out of it. Think He'll forgive me for that?"

Able said nothing. His smile seemed to crack and splinter, and slowly fall away from his face in jagged pieces. He reared back his foot and kicked Chris in the ribs sending an overwhelming amount of pain ripping through his body. Chris involuntarily curled into fetal position and began coughing violently, but forced himself to laugh. Able became further enraged and continued kicking Chris, sending gleaming gems of blood arcing from Chris's mouth and spattering the grass.

Stepping back, Able took a deep breath and composed himself. He fumbled to tuck his white button up shirt back into his dress pants. "Mustn't let ourselves get sidetracked," he said, but whether he was speaking to himself or Chris was unclear. "No, there's a plan for this child. God's plan, indeed." Able bent down and picked up the thick rope to continue dragging Chris deeper into the field. After what felt like miles to Chris, but was in reality no more than a dozen yards, Able came to a clearing. It looked like it had once been a small forest or grove of some sort, but many of the trees had been cleared. A few still appeared to be standing, but their branches had been removed. In his weakened, abused state, Chris could not muster the strength to truly take in the magnitude and horror of where Able had brought him.

Dragging Chris over to the side of the clearing, Able placed him next to what seemed to be a large pile of crudely cut logs. "You see," Able began, "In the beginning we were unsure of the best manner in which to cleanse sins, so we turned to the Good Book and read of many different approaches. We tried extended baptisms, but holding the messengers underwater proved both difficult and ineffective. I tried feeding them the holy sacrament, but these children of God had transcended the need and that was when we began to realize that they were not the ones who needed to be cleansed of sin. They had no sins. It was us who needed to have our souls washed, but with the times being so extreme, the old ways were no longer effective. Maybe they never were?" Able paused and pulled a long log from the pile. It appeared to be about ten feet long, but had been notched out about two feet from one end and had a crude step hammered in a few feet below that. "So anyway," Able grunted as he moved the log, "We began to think about what God would want. How would he want us to cleanse ourselves of sin and it came to me. Why try and use anything other than what He had chosen for his own son? But not everyone was comfortable with that, at first, so myself and some of the others collected sinners and cleansed them here to prove to the others that it would resurrect them as messengers of the Lord."

Chris rolled over onto his side and tried to see what Able was doing. The man was hunched over a second log he had collected, but this one was smaller. Able appeared to be struggling to fit them together. "What the fuck are you rambling on about?" Chris coughed. Looking up from his work,

Able smiled and set down a heavy framing hammer.

"You haven't figured it out?" Able smiled as he walked over to where Chris lay. "Sometimes I forget how ignorant the unwashed masses truly are. I was speaking of crucifixion of course. That was how the Son of God cleansed the world of sin once, so why wouldn't it work again? And as soon as I can retrieve my spade, you too shall be purified." Able turned and slowly walked back the direction they had previously come to search for his shovel in the long grass.

The wind shifted and the somewhat pleasant smell of burning wood was rapidly replaced by the distinct smell of rot and decay. Chris's eyes watered as the scent became overwhelming and seemed to fill the entire clearing. There was a lull in the chaotic chatter of automatic gunfire and that was when Chris first heard the distinct moan of the undead. Rolling over, Chris looked up and almost screamed in disgust. Lashed high above him was a crucified human, or at least what had been a human and come back as a Shambler. Next to it, hung the dried, leathery corpse whose gender could no longer be determined, but as the clouds moved and the moon shone a little brighter, Chris could see the stained tattered remains of a Montville High School varsity jacket. He was sure it was monogrammed with the name "Tim," and while he had most definitely never liked the kid, Chris never would have wished this fate upon him. His body involuntarily shuddered as Chris realized that he would not be the first young person Able had tried to convert.

The zombie struggled against the thick, coarse ropes binding its wrists and ankles, causing it to cut into its flesh, tearing ragged fetid chunks that formed a revolting perimeter around its perch. It groaned angrily and glared at Chris. As he attempted to fight the terror screaming inside his head, Chris gazed about the field and in the pale moonlight could see numerous other shadowy figures silhouetted against the night sky struggling to be free, and moaning hungrily.

● ● ●

A large group began amassing near the main gate and

moving towards the van. Watts cut a quick sideways glance at Crawford, who lay prone next to him on the floor of the van. After unloading the AK-47, his M-16 had finally fallen silent after sending what seemed like an endless volley of bullets towards the Zionists. Most had been chewed apart by the mini-gun and had fallen into wet piles of former people. Some had run. The handful of people who had survived huddled behind a few wrecked cars and debris that had been used for barriers, but tucking their heads to avoid bullets left them blind to the fact that many of their friends, who had just been shot, were lumbering towards them. The screams were horrific, but no one could find an ounce of empathy for the Zionists, as they were torn apart by their former friends and family. There was a certain sense of poetic justice in watching these people being feasted upon by the undead.

That had been close to an hour ago. The few Shamblers that had reanimated were quickly and easily put down after they had eaten their comrades. Things had fallen deathly silent following the banquet. No more Zionists came to defend the gate, even though everyone was sure there were plenty more inside the compound. After the painful stretch of silence, a few people appeared to be stumbling towards the gate. Then a few more, and soon there was a massive shadowy mob ambling towards the gate. There seemed to be an endless stream of bodies emanating from the center of the camp.

"Don't give me that fuckin' look," Crawford snapped at Watts, "Everytime you give me that look it means bad shit is going to happen."

"What are you talking about?" Watts said, but never took his eyes off the growing group of people.

"Man," Crawford groaned, "Last time you gave me that look was in Kandahar right before that kid rolled a grenade into the mess tent. Bad shit always happens when you give me that look!"

The mass of people had become so thick that it was impossible to tell distinct forms apart, rather they seemed to have merged into one massive cloud. They stumbled through the gate, passing the burning wreckage of Mike's blown up

Toyota sedan. Their faces were almost as pale and grey as their eyes.

"That's all fucking Shamblers!" Crawford went on, "See I fucking told you Watts! Anytime you make that god damn face!" He grabbed his radio and pressed the call button. "Ronnie? Joey? The group coming our way is nothing but zombies. Check your ammo and fire high."

"Hold on a sec," Ronnie's voice called back.

"What the fuck do you mean 'hold on a sec' Ron?" Crawford yelled into the radio. Seconds later, a loud bang sounded from behind the van followed by a loud whoop from Joey and Ronnie. A large *boom* resounded soon after blowing a ragged hole in the middle of the horde. Zombies, both part and whole, tumbled through the air and landed in wet chunks.

"Ok," Ronnie's voice crackled through the radio, "That was the last one."

Watts started cackling hysterically as he began spinning the multiple barrels on his mini gun. Laughing was something Watts always seemed to do when he was under pressure and something that had always made Crawford uncomfortable. A heavy burst of ammo rattled from the numerous barrels and began ripping apart the Shamblers. The zombies continued tripping through the gate and directly into the spray of bullets. Crawford, Ronnie and Joey continued firing from their positions and cutting down more of the undead.

"Not much left in the box," Watts shouted over the sound of his gun, "We got more coming. Gotta think of something soon." The mini gun stopped spinning and fell silent. However, no sooner had Crawford picked up the radio than the pickup truck careened past the two soldiers in the van, fishtailing and throwing a massive spray of dirt and gravel.

"What the hell are you two doing?" Crawford yelled into the radio, "Get the fuck back here now!"

"Hold on a sec," Ronnie responded, disturbingly calm. The truck crashed into the lead Shambler and was swallowed up by the writhing sea of bodies. The two soldiers could see bodies being tossed and jostled as the truck dove deeper into the mob.

Inside the cab of the truck, Joey stared wide-eyed as

Ronnie accelerated into the massive group of zombies. Bodies tumbled over and under the hood of the speeding vehicle. One slammed heavily into the windshield and banged its motled fist against the glass leaving behind greasy streaks.

"Get it off! Get it off!" Joey screeched. Being that close to the hungry mouth of a Shambler was more than he could handle. Ronnie turned on the windshield wipers, which began slapping the zombie in the face and further smearing the greasy marks it had made. "If that's your idea of a joke Ron, it's really not funny. Seriously not funny!"

The zombie angrily swiped at the wipers and bared its teeth. Ronnie seized the moment and slammed on the brakes sending the Shambler sailing off the hood of the truck and into several of its comrades. Before Joey could speak, Ronnie had floored the gas pedal and the truck heavily bumped over the bodies.

As the truck broke through the last of the zombies, it screeched to a halt just inside the compound. "What are we gonna do now?" Joey yelled, "We can't run them all down. The truck won't hold up."

"Here," Ronnie said handing his backpack to Joey, "Open your window and dump these jars as we drive through."

"Open my window?" Joey screeched, "Are you fuckin' serious? No way!"

"If you have a better idea then I'd love to hear it," Ronnie replied.

Joey sighed heavily and turned his window handle a few cranks. Inside the backpack, Joey found three more jars of the oily, yellow mixture that Ronnie had used to make firebombs. He unscrewed the first lid.

"Ok," Joey said sadly, "Can't believe I'm fucking saying this, but let's go." Ronnie rolled the truck back into the swarming mass of undead monsters. Hands immediately began filling the space between Joey's open window and the top of the doorframe. Joey instinctively rolled away from the grasping hands and began kicking at them.

"Sit up," Ronnie commanded, "Stop kicking them and dump the jars on their arms."

"Oh man," Joey whined and kicked out one last time to make some space. He splashed the greasy mixture out the window, getting as much inside the truck as out. He followed with the second and third jar. "All done. Go!" Ronnie waited a few more minutes, as the zombies became more and more agitated. "What the hell are you waiting for?" Then Joey could see how Ronnie's mind worked. The longer they sat there, the more the zombies grasped for the truck and inadvertently smeared the mixture all over one another. Ronnie waited for a few more seconds to be sure and then the truck shot forward into the swell of Shamblers. The bodies tumbled and fell under the tires of the heavy pickup, but Ronnie refused to slow down until the truck shot past the van and back to its previous position. The front of the truck was covered in deep dents and a thick, jellied layer of viscous gore.

"Open the glove box," Ronnie demanded. Joey clicked the two sides of the lock and the drawer yawned open. Ronnie's hand shot over and grabbed a long thin bag before he leapt out of the car and began running towards the horde of zombies.

"Kid!" Watts shouted, "Ron, what are you doing? Stop!" Crawford and Watts were out of the truck chasing after Ronnie. Suddenly Ronnie skidded to a stop in the mud and unzipped the bag. He pulled out a long, faded cardboard tube and popped the white plastic cap off the end.

A sudden burst of acrid smoke filled the air followed by a blinding red light. Ronnie hurled the road flare into the crowd of zombies and then followed it with the two remaining in the bag. At first, nothing happened and the zombies continued to close the distance between themselves and the van, but slowly a small dancing flame began passing from one Shambler to another. The flaming zombies became disoriented and banged into those nearby, setting them ablaze. Within a matter of seconds, the entire mass of bodies was one writhing sea of flame. They continued for a few more steps and Ronnie began to worry that they might have to fight an entire horde of flaming zombies. Then the first few collapsed to the ground followed by more. Watts and Crawford fired into the crowd and dropped even more of the undead.

"How the hell is the fire passing so fast?" Crawford asked in amazement.

"It's raining," Ronnie replied. When he saw the confused look on the faces of his friends he added, "I mixed dish soap into the gas and Vaseline, so water makes it run and the fire spread. It's basically a kitchen sink version Greek Fire."

"Fucking amazing," Watts gasped as the unsettlingly, appealing scent of cooked meat filled the air. "How'd you know it would work?"

Ronnie opened his mouth to answer, but Joey came running up besides them and shouted, "Fuckin' amazing Ron! Dude, you can find anything on the Internet!"

● ● ●

Hands hammered the thick wooden doors of the church, oblivious to the smears of blood and ribbons of tattered flesh they left behind with each blow. The doors had been built to be solid; massive planks banded together with wide strips of brass and large ornate bolts. Sam figured that the Zionists had probably expected some sort of confrontation, probably with the ATF or FBI, definitely not zombies, but they were obviously planning on falling back to the church and had built the doors to take a massive amount of abuse.

Outside, Sam had felt himself losing it as he watched all the Zionists begin to come back as Shamblers. He had felt something wither and snap within himself as he looked at all the still corpses of the children. They had been given poison by their parents, the very people who were supposed to protect them and instead had sent them to oblivion. Their short lives had been snuffed out for what? The empty promise of something better? The chance to come back as a mindless monster? Was this what religion was? Was this God's plan?

Sam remembered taking a long, deep breath and the next thing he knew, he was pushing Amelia through the doors of the church. His hands stunk of cordite and his rifle was still warm, so he knew he had been shooting, but could not really remember at what. Amelia was keeping her distance from him, so he figured whatever had happened out there had terrified her. The possibility that he had blacked out terrified Sam as well, but whatever had occurred outside of the church had to be done. It had saved their lives. Sam's guilt was easily assuaged by the knowledge that they had survived.

"Hey Amelia," Sam said softly, "Are you ok?" She refused to look at him and mumbled something into her knees, where she had buried her face. "Amelia?" he tried again, "Hey?" Sam reached out and gently touched her shoulder. Amelia flinched and pushed back against the door.

Lifting her eyes to meet his, Sam could see that Amelia had been crying, but her lips were pulled back in a feral expression of anger. "What the fuck was that?" she seethed.

"Amelia, I..." Sam hesitated, "I'm not really sure what happened. If I did anything, I'm sorry. Really."

"If you did anything?" Amelia sneered, "Like think about shooting me?"

Sam could vaguely remember asking her if she was ok, but did not think he had meant it as a veiled threat. Regardless of his intentions, it was clear that Amelia had interpreted Sam's question as more of a threat than genuine concern.

"No, Amelia," Sam almost cried, "I wasn't gonna do that! I swear it! I wouldn't, I couldn't!" For some reason this response seemed to anger Amelia even more and she leapt off the floor slamming Sam into the doors.

"Well you fuckin' promised Sam!" She spat through gritted teeth, "So find your balls and do it." The rage seemed to suddenly wash out of Amelia and she sat down heavily on the floor. "Just get it over with," she said weakly and hung her head.

"No!" Sam shouted, "I'm not doing a damn thing until I don't have a choice! We're all getting out of here!"

"Then what was that about out there, Sam?" Amelia sniffled, "I saw it in your eyes. You were gone. Completely gone. My god do you even remember smashing that Shambler's face in with your gun?"

Sam shook his head. "I don't," he said timidly, "I was just so worried about you and the baby and then I was thinking about never seeing Mike or Alice again and I don't know I blacked out. I just wanted to make sure you were ok. I swear! That's all I wanted!" Tears began to stream down Sam's cheeks and Amelia began to realize that bloodlust was not what had gripped Sam, but rather an insane desire to protect his friends. Strangely enough, the scenes of depraved violence she had witnessed him commit were motivated, oddly enough, from a place of love. It was not that Sam had broken or snapped; instead he had reached a point where he ignored his own safety and was single-mindedly focused on ensuring the safety of everyone he cared about.

"I thought you were gone," Amelia said, "That you had gone nuts and were enjoying it."

"I can't stand the fact that I need to carry a gun," Sam sobbed, "Or that one of my best friends made me promise to shoot her if she becomes a fuckin' monster! I hate that this is the world I have to live in, but what choice do we have!" Amelia picked herself up from the floor and drew Sam into a bear hug. They held each other and cried, but the sound of a soft scraping from inside the church interrupted the reconciliation and snapped both of them back into the world they lived in; one of monsters and death. There would be time for tenderness later, but not now. Amelia nodded and checked her gun. Sam was already moving through the door with his weapon trained in the direction of the noise.

A small girl was struggling with something in the middle of the church, but Sam and Amelia could not see what, due to the large polished wood pews that blocked their view. Sam switched to his SASR and shouldered the smaller SR-25. With the larger scope, Sam was able to zoom in and get a better view of what the girl was doing. The small girl stood up from what she was doing and began laughing. She was saying something to whoever was on the floor in front of her and it looked like she was holding some sort of knife or dagger in her hand. It was dark, but the distinct sheen of blood glistened on the edge of blade. As Sam watched, a foot dropped heavily to the floor and echoed a dull thud throughout the church. He immediately recognized the sneaker.

Within a matter of seconds, Sam was on his feet and

moving towards the girl. Amelia was confused, but followed. "What is it Sam?" She whispered, but was not sure she really wanted an answer. Sam briefly turned his head and Amelia could see the same look of indomitable resolution and purpose that had previously scared her.

"Mike," was all Sam said and brought the large SASR rifle up to ready. Amelia was not sure what Sam meant, but if it had anything to do with Mike then she was on board, even if that meant attacking a child. If recent times had taught Amelia anything, it was that people were capable of acts of great wickedness, as well as kindness, regardless of their age; it was simply a facet of the human condition. If this girl posed any threat to Mike or any of her friends, Amelia would put a bullet through her head without blinking.

"Put it down!" Sam shouted as he came within twenty feet of the girl. She stood up from where she was pushing something across the floor. "I'm not asking again," Sam said matter-of-factly from where his face was pressed against the stock of his rifle. His finger twitched on the trigger, anxious to pull it.

The girl turned to face Sam and Amelia; a wicked smile was stretched across her young face. "I'm not sure who you are my friend," Judith said calmly, "But your turn for judgment will come soon enough. The Lord always has time to judge the wicked." Of that, Judith was sure, but first she needed to deal with the sinner who lay at her feet. She had carved enough lines into his back that the messengers below had become aware of the presence of blood and began to gather in the center of the pit. Their moans increased as Judith flicked the blade sending droplets of blood raining down upon them.

Amelia had circled around to the side and pointed her M-16 at the girl's head. "I don't know what the hell you're talking about, but if you don't listen to my friend right now, I'll drop you where you stand," Amelia cautioned the girl, but she showed no response or fear of the threat.

"Sam," a voice called weakly from behind the pews. Sam immediately recognized the voice and squeezed the trigger, but the girl was already moving. She ducked sideways and sprinted towards the back of the church. Amelia and Sam's shots went wide.

"Help, Mike," Sam yelled as he took off after the girl. Amelia moved to where Mike lay and her gasp was audible even to Sam. The girl had mounted the stairs on the altar and briefly turned back towards Sam.

"The Lord is far from done with you and me!" Judith screamed, but Sam had already pulled the trigger. The large round belched from the SASR and split the air within the church like a thunderclap, but the shot went wide and struck one of the marble columns flanking the sides of the altar.

Judith had hardly finished her words when the rounded edge of the pillar near her face exploded. A mix of jagged shards of marble and incendiary bullet fragments burst inches from her eye, cutting a ragged starburst into her flesh. Judith involuntarily pulled away from the explosion, but the searing fragments had already torn across the left side of her face, digging tattered gouges athwart her cheeks. Blood began to cascade down her face and neck. As she wrinkled her face in anguish, the blood seeped into her eye, burning and blurring her vision. Judith released a scream that was rooted in rage as much as it was in pain. She seethed with anger and the desire to inflict divine judgment upon these heathens, but she could see that the one who had fired was preparing to shoot again and she did not want to test her luck twice.

"Sam!" Amelia shouted, "Help!" Sam turned to run back to where Amelia tended to Mike, and Judith seized the small opening to slip through the back door located behind the altar leaving a trail of blood. Sam turned back quickly, but the girl had already disappeared. "SAM!" Amelia screamed, "NOW!"

Leaping over the pew, Sam saw why Amelia had been screaming. She held Mike by the ankles and was struggling to keep him from being pulled into a massive pit below the church floor. A group of Shamblers had clawed their way up a pew that had fallen in and grabbed hold of Mike's backpack straps. Fortunately, they had not gotten high enough up to bite him. That girl must have been trying to push him in there when Sam and Amelia interrupted her.

"Shoot the fuckin' zombies!" Amelia yelled, as she pulled Mike back a few inches. The zombies growled and pulled back, but Sam shot the lead one through the head and it tumbled downwards knocking the others back into the pit. Amelia pulled one last time and yanked Mike back from the edge.

"There's blood," Amelia said, panting for breath, "Was he bit? Was he bit?" The two of them quickly checked Mike over, but could find no evidence of him having been bitten by a Shambler. All that they could find were numerous superficial cuts, that while they would hurt, were not life threatening. Mike groaned and rolled over to face his brother and Amelia.

"Thanks little bro," he coughed and then passed out. Sam and Amelia worked fast, wrapping his wounds with ribbons of cloth cut from their clothes.

"You gotta get him back out to the van," Sam said and Amelia's eye's widened.

"What?" she almost shouted, "We're not splitting up. You promised me Sam, don't you fucking think I forgot. You aren't leaving me alone with anyone!"

Sam's shoulders sagged. Amelia was right. "Ok," Sam said as he checked Mike's bag. He found the radio hidden in the bottom. "Watts? Crawford?" Sam said into the receiver, "We got Mike." The others offered a series of shouts and congratulatory words, but Sam cut them off. "Don't get too happy just yet. We're trapped in the church surrounded by Shamblers. You're gonna have to get us out."

● ● ●

Bruno heard the footsteps before he heard Able's words, and by the time Able had brought the spade up to strike, Bruno was throwing himself into a forward roll. The blade of the small shovel nicked the back Bruno's neck as he tumbled forward in an awkward somersault. The trickle of blood down his back was concerning, but there was hardly time to consider any injury that was not mortal. He had anticipated coming out of the roll on his feet, ready to fight, but slipped on the wet grass and smashed his head against something hard and unforgiving. Looking up, Bruno saw the rotted feet of the

Shambler tied to the post he had collided with. The zombie was frantic to get free of its captivity and thrashed wildly against the ropes binding its rancid flesh. The blood winding down Bruno's neck and back was driving the animated corpse above him into a frenzy, and it threatened to rip off its own limbs for the chance of a meal. Bruno's head throbbed from the abuse his body had recently suffered and his vision began to get a watery edge to it. He knew he had at the very least, suffered a concussion, but fought to remain conscious as Able rushed towards him, screaming wildly.

Able growled furiously as his attack sliced through the empty space where the soldier had just moments before stood. He did not have time to waste on this one. He wanted to finish him off quickly and get back to the more glorious act of crucifying the other one. Truly, God would see fit to grant him the strength to dispatch this heathen quickly, so he could return to his holy task. The boy would learn to respect God's laws, from what Able had seen before, the boy would have plenty of time to consider a change of heart and seek absolution before death took him. Most of the other offerings had lasted at least three or four days before they transitioned, either having been found worthy and returning as messengers or they were denied entry to God's kingdom and left to rot in the sun.

Raising the shovel high over head, Able rushed towards Bruno to deliver a deadly strike to his head. But Bruno had been trained and every lesson he had learned in boot or in the field rattled through his head, as this psychopath rushed towards him swinging a spade like a medieval battle-axe. The attack was obvious and telegraphed, but Bruno's body would not respond like the well-trained machine he expected it to be. Instead, he sloppily rolled sideways as the spade cut across in a wide arc and connected with his shoulder.

Able saw the soldier moving and tried to correct his attack mid-swing, but in doing so, turned the head of the spade so that the broad, flat back connected with the soldier's arm. It was far from a deathblow, but it sent the man tumbling sideways and left him sprawled on the ground. Now it could end.

Bruno looked up and through the haze that clouded his head and vision he could see Able standing astride his body smiling. The sharpened point of the shovel rested just below Bruno's Adam's apple.

"I had hopes for you," Able grinned, "You showed such knowledge of the Word of God. I thought how could a man of such wisdom not be smart enough to repent? But I guess knowing the Word and living it are two different things." Bruno struggled to push the blade of the shovel away, but Able pushed his foot down upon his neck, forcing his head sideways and grinding it into the wet grass and dirt. Bruno struggled weakly, but his body did not seem able to muster any further strength. "I'm going to take your head," Able continued, "Then feed your body to the messengers just so that I can be sure there is no chance of you receiving any divine absolution. You will not be coming back, of that you can be sure my friend."

Somewhere in the gloom of the waning night, Bruno watched a shape loping carefully through the field. It paused and raised its head, as if listening to or scenting the cool night breeze and then continued forward silently. Could Able seriously be crazy enough to have brought a Stalker back to his compound? Or maybe it had simply been attracted by the sounds of fighting and smell of fresh blood? But as Bruno watched, hoping that Able would be torn apart by the creature, it stopped and sprinted off to disappear in the shadows of Able's sick forest.

"It's time," Able said resolutely, and raised the shovel high. Suddenly, Bruno felt the weight of Able's foot disappear, followed by the sound of the preacher falling heavily into the grass screaming. A howl of such feral ferocity shattered the night air, causing even the imprisoned Shamblers to momentarily silence their incessant moans of hunger. The watery sounds of flesh being torn and muscle shredded, filled the vast void of the night with a series of nauseating snaps and tears. Able's screams reached a wet crescendo that was cut short by the noise of what Bruno was sure could only have been Able's throat being torn out. The clamor of Able's body spastically flopping against the damp grass finally ceased, and the night once again fell silent. A series of growls followed. Then silence once more.

Scared to move, Bruno remained silent on the ground. If the Stalker had just killed Able, he was grateful, but in no rush to be the second course. He remembered that the Stalkers had no sense of sight, so his only hope was to remain silent and hope that the rancid smell of a forest of rotting corpses would disguise him from the creature's sense of smell. He pushed himself against the cool ground and squeezed his eyes shut, but even as he did so, he could hear the sound of steps lightly padding towards him through the grass.

A rough, hot tongue dragged itself across Bruno's face leaving behind wet trails that he was sure were tinged with Able's blood. He had to stifle the urge to scream; determined that his last noise in this world would not be a shriek akin to that of a twelve-year-old teenybopper. Something thick and heavy pushed itself against Bruno's head. Was the Stalker trying to see if he was alive and worth eating? Was it just playing with him?

After what felt like an eternity of waiting, Bruno decided he would open his eyes. If the Stalker was still there, well then it was going to kill him, but at least he was going to his grave with the knowledge that Able's crazy ass was dead too, and could not hurt his friends any further. Bruno forced his eyes open. There was nothing. No set of jagged teeth snapped closed on his face, no claws tore his flesh. Nothing.

Forcing himself up from the ground took every ounce of energy left in his wrecked body, but somehow Bruno managed to push himself up to a sitting position. He knew that Able's corpse lay somewhere off to his left, but was more concerned with figuring out where the Stalker had gone. A twig snapped loudly behind him and the blood froze in Bruno's veins.

Something was moving behind him and he knew there was no way he could possibly put up a fight, but he had to try. The man was exhausted and broken, but there was no way the solider could simply just accept defeat and death, not when people were still relying on him. Bruno screwed his eyes shut, let out a battle cry and flung himself in the direction of the movement. He would meet death's snapping jaws on his feet.

Moving forward, many thoughts ricocheted through Bruno's head; numerous regrets and second thoughts, opportunities blown and loves lost, but none of that would matter in a few seconds. Then he tripped, stumbled a few steps and fell flat on his ass. Something solid had collided with his legs. Almost embarrassed, Bruno looked up and found himself staring into a pair of large, moist honey colored eyes.

Zule sat in the grass, staring at Bruno with an air of indignant disregard. She had no idea why the human was acting so ridiculous. The bad man was dead and there was no time for screwing around; they needed to find their boy. He was near and she could smell him over the scent of all of the dead things. Gozer seized the opportunity of an open lap, and leapt towards Bruno to force himself on top of the man's legs. He was a good dog. He had made the bad thing go away and now he wanted attention and affection. As far as he was concerned, a good butt scratching had been earned. It was only fair.

Bruno could hardly believe what he was seeing. He hugged Gozer and then moved to stand up. The muscular pitbull protested for a few seconds, but then happily trotted over to where Zule sat impatiently. As soon as the dogs saw that Bruno was on his feet, they immediately began moving, stopping briefly to proudly show him the mangled corpse that had only minutes earlier been Able Stone. Only a few meaty strings of flesh attached one of his arms to his body, presumably the one that had held the shovel. The area below Able's chin was largely absent of flesh and tendons, leaving the exposed edges of his windpipe visible to Bruno. Gozer and Zule had torn the preacher apart, but the dogs were not stopping to celebrate the violence, they did not enjoy hurting other creatures, but they were good dogs and that meant protecting their people from danger; of that they were proud.

Zule's ears perked up and she took off running into the tall grass. Gozer grunted loudly and trotted after her. Bruno followed close behind.

● ● ●

A pile of wrecked bodies clogged the gate into The Pillar of Zion compound, preventing Joey and the others from driving into the camp. They did not have the time or desire to attempt moving any of the corpses and could not risk trying to drive over and getting the vehicles' axels tangled with meat and rags.

"So we're walking?" Joey asked, not really loving the idea, but knowing they were out of other options.

"Fucking looks that way," Watts said sourly, "Sam said the church is some large funky looking building in the middle of the compound."

"Yeah," Joey added, "That's surrounded by a ton of undead, religious nut jobs."

"We gotta figure a good number of them came this way when we started firing," Crawford said, "But we chewed through a lot of rounds back there. Check your mags." The four began checking their weapons. They still had a good amount of small rounds left for some of the handguns in the van, but the M-16s were low and the mini gun empty. They were going to have to face an entire horde of Shamblers with little more than side arms.

"Wait," Ronnie said, "I've got an idea. The Shamblers seem to be attracted to movement and sound right?"

Crawford nodded, "Yeah, that's why they were all coming this way. Why?"

Ronnie inhaled and let it out slowly, "Well, what if we give them something to chase and lead them away from the church. The Shamblers don't move fast, so they could easily be out distanced with just a brisk walk. We can lead them back here and catch them in crossfire between Sam and Amelia, and us. It should be pretty easy and effective." Everyone thought about what Ronnie had just suggested. It should work. Joey was the first to speak.

"When you said 'something,' you really meant someone," he said unhappily. Ronnie shrugged and nodded.

"Well, it makes sense," he replied, "And it should be relatively safe."

"I'll go," Crawford said, "Watts has a bum ankle."

"No," Joey said quietly, "I'll do it. I'm faster than the rest of you, besides the three of you are better shots. We don't have ammo to waste, so the shots gotta count."

Everyone hesitated. "You sure?" Crawford asked, doing little to mask his concern.

"Fuck no, I'm not sure," Joey said bitterly, "But what else are we gonna do? Just make sure Sam knows the plan and is ready to move as soon as he hears the signal."

"What's the signal going to be?" Watts asked

"Probably me screaming like a little girl and trailing a long steamy stream of piss from my pants," Joey laughed dryly, "I guess all those laps Ms. Kozlov made me run are finally gonna pay off."

● ● ●

The heavy *thud, thud, thud* against the church doors seemed to slow and eventually all that Sam, Amelia and Mike could hear was an occasional scratch or forlorn groan. Something was drawing the attention of the Shamblers, but they needed to wait until Joey gave them the signal to move. What that signal was, they had no idea. Watts had said something, but the battery of the radio was dying out, making communication spotty at best.

"I guess we just need to be ready to go whenever it seems clear," Sam said. Amelia nodded and pressed her ear against the door. "How are you doing?" Sam asked. Mike waited nearby, but Sam had not yet filled him in on Amelia and the wound that was tightly bound on her leg.

"I'm fine," Amelia replied resolutely, "Let's just get out of here so we can find Chris. This whole day has been nothing but a great big cluster fuck. We came here to rescue Chris and Bruno and now we're the ones that need to be saved. We haven't even found them!"

"I saw Bruno," Mike said weakly, "He was ok. Beat to shit, but still ok." Amelia and Sam had not had time to ask Mike if he had found anyone and had assumed Zionists had attacked him. "He was going to find Chris."

"You saw him?" Amelia croaked, "But not...?"

Mike shoot his head weakly, "No, I'm sorry Amelia he wasn't here, but Bruno seemed to think he had an idea where. He'll find Chris, Amelia, I know he will." She sniffled loudly and wiped her eyes with the sleeve of her shirt.

The noise outside the door had almost completely stopped. "You think we should go?" Sam asked hesitantly.

"Watts said that Joey was gonna give us a signal," Mike replied, "We should wait until we know for sure."

Sam worried about the plan that they had cooked up and worried even more that Joey seemed to be the lynch pin of the entire thing. He had put himself in harms way back at the impound lot by drawing the attention of the Ogre, and if they had not lucked out and found the SASR in the van it would have torn Joey apart.

It had been silent now for at least ten minutes. As they pressed their ears to the doors, Sam, Amelia and Mike could hear the noises of early morning beginning to break. It seemed ironic that the birds were singing and the sun most likely breaking the horizon painting the sky in brilliant hues. How could the sun ever really shine again in a world like this? It felt like the sun should be rancid and dying in the sky like everything else, but somehow, there it was beginning to creep through the ornate stained glass windows set high in the walls of the church.

"I think we should try and go," Amelia said peering through a small crack she had opened in the doors. Sam expected waxy, green fingers tipped in bone to fill the space, but nothing happened. Most of the Shamblers seemed to have gone somewhere else.

"You ready to move Mike?" Sam asked his brother concerned that he might not be able to move fast enough. There was no way that Sam had come this far to lose anyone now, especially when they were so close.

Mike struggled up from the floor, taking labored short breaths. "Yeah, man. I'm good to go," Mike gritted.

Sam handed Mike his SR-25 rifle. "It's still got eight rounds in it," Sam said, "And this clip, but it's still not a lot of ammo, so only shoot if you have to. Amelia and I will do most of the shooting, ok?" Mike nodded and checked the weapon. The long SASR held at ready, Sam stepped through the doors of the church. But nothing could have imagined what waited for him outside.

● ● ●

Zule ran back and forth between whatever lay ahead and Bruno. Everything hurt like hell, but he forced his body to respond, forced his legs to make each step. Gozer trotted a few feet behind Bruno and would periodically stop to scent the air and growl. Bruno hoped that the dog was only catching the rancid smell of Able's forest.

"Mother fucker," someone cursed loudly, hidden by the long grass. Bruno recognized the voice.

"Chris?" Bruno shouted as he moved a little faster towards where Zule barked impatiently. As he came through a tuft of grass, he saw Chris bound, laying on the ground next to a half-finished cross; he cursed loudly and kept struggling against the ropes that were tightly wrapped around his ankles and wrists. Bruno had known what Able intended to do with Chris, knew that Able was dead and would not have the chance, but seeing the boy laid out in the wet grass next to a cross, made Bruno want to go back and stomp on Able's mangled corpse.

Rolling over onto his back, Chris looked up at Bruno "You look like shit man," he said forcing a chuckle.

"Said the pot to the kettle," Bruno smirked as he began working on the knots and freed Chris. Gozer and Zule immediately rushed to Chris and enthusiastically leapt at his sides.

"Ok, ok," Chris laughed, giving in and sitting back down on the ground so the two large pitbulls could swarm over him and sufficiently cover him in dog spit and mud. "There's my buddies," Chris said softly and buried his face in the dogs wet fur.

Bruno reached down and scratched both dogs, but they were too busy with Chris to notice. "I'm breaking into a PetSmart on the way back to school," Bruno said, "And I'm feeding these two every fucking dog cookie I can find." Chris looked up and smiled, but was unsure why the soldier was showing such gratitude towards his two dogs. "They saved my ass," Bruno continued, "Able had me pinned, was gonna bury a fucking shovel in my neck and these two came out of nowhere." Chris's demeanor immediately changed to one of concern and he began checking both dogs for injuries, but found none. "They tore that piece of shit apart," Bruno said as he itched behind Gozer's ear.

"They always were smart," Chris said, "Just kinda wish I could have seen it."

"Yeah, well you still might," Bruno said with a look of disgust, "I lit out of there before seeing if he changed. We should get back there and take the fucker's head off just to be sure he doesn't come back as a Shambler."

"Fuck it," Chris said shaking his head, "It's time we got the hell out of here. Besides if that asshole has to wander around and rot on his feet, I say he's getting what he deserves."

Bruno looked over his shoulder, "Kinda makes sense, I guess." He helped Chris up from the sodden ground and the two slowly made their way back towards the center of the Zionists' camp.

As they approached the camp, Chris hesitated. "What's up?" Bruno asked, "You see something?" But the words for what Chris saw had escaped him and he simply motioned towards the center of the camp. The scene unfolding there was simply beyond words and soon Bruno was as equally as dumbstruck as Chris.

● ● ●

Life should have a soundtrack. Music should play at that crucial moment, when nerve faltered and resolve turned to jelly. It would be so much easier to be brave with a strong 80's power tune thumping in the background. Having that right song fade in at the right moment would make it so easy to talk to that cute girl or score the winning touchdown. Or in the case of Joey Potts, to run headlong into a horde of twenty to thirty flesh hungry Shamblers.

The thick, soupy mud squished and sucked at Joey's shoes as he forced his legs to move faster and faster. He was afraid that at any moment he would lose his footing, quite possibly as he got within biting range of the zombies, who were just beginning to notice the thin, crazy eyed boy who ran directly towards them humming the chorus from some unidentifiable song. If life was not going to give him a soundtrack, Joey was going to damn well give it to himself.

No other song came to Joey's mind as he kept moving forward, so as cliché as it felt, he fell back on a classic, Survivor's "Eye of the Tiger". The low rattle of the guitar notes reaching higher and higher echoed in Joey's lungs and throat. The first words of the verse began to wheeze out of his clenched teeth as Joey noticed the Shamblers turn slowly away from the church doors.

Heavy hands fell away from the wood and feet shuffled in gradual half steps until they had turned away from the church and back towards the bonfire that still raged in the middle of the camp. The few zombies that had been pushed down the steps by the shear mass of their own numbers were the first to begin ambling towards Joey, as he made his first lap around the fire. He slowed to a jog to make sure the Shamblers did not lose interest; to further it, Joey increased the volume of his singing. More and more of the zombies tripped down the stone steps. The groaning became louder and louder, adding a back track to Joey's theme song. "Great," Joey gritted, "The zombie remix."

The pace Joey set was just a little faster than the zombies could walk, but was one he could easily keep up without getting fatigued. Slowly, the song faded away from Joey's head, and the gruff voice of Ms. Kozlov became louder and louder repeating the mantra Joey had heard so many times during gym class. "Faster Joseph! Shut up and run!" her voice now encouraged, instead of chided.

The heat from the bonfire darted warm fingers through the chilly early morning air that gently warmed Joey's side with each passing lap, but did nothing to provide comfort because with each circuit, more and more zombies slowly fell in behind. By the seventh or eighth time around the fire, Joey was beginning to catch up with the fetid caboose that limped painfully along at the end of the rotted conga line that trailed hungrily behind him.

Out of the corner of his eye, Joey saw the doors of the church creep open a small crack. His friends emerged tentatively onto the steps outside the church, thankfully with weapons. Joey motioned for them to be silent. He needed to keep the attention of the Shamblers on him, even though he was slick with sweat, lungs burning and his heart threatening to burst through his ribcage at any moment.

The theme song slowly began to rise in Joey's head as he broke from his path and headed back towards the main gate. As he sprinted past the smoldering outer buildings, he could see the vague outlines of more shapes loping towards him, through the waning darkness and gloom. A group of Shamblers, smaller than the one trailing Joey, stumbled out of the shadows in front of him. Moans resonated and teeth gnashed on both sides. His eyes darted to the sides, trying to find another route back to the front gate. "Shit," Joey wheezed as he watched more zombies staggering through the shadows around him.

● ● ●

Judith tenderly ran her fingers across the ragged lines that streaked across her face and thought about her future, if there was one. The bleeding had subsided, but the cool early morning air stung and burned as it gently kissed her tattered cheek, but this physical pain was infinitesimal compared to the howling wound that seeped and festered within Judith's mind and heart.

Her world was ending, both literally and figuratively. Judith had believed the words of her father, had faithfully served him and for that matter, God. And this was how she was getting repaid? Everything was crumbling; her entire universe seemed to be teetering on the brink of destruction. But what was it her father had said? That the Lord tests us? That the moments when we feel the most alone and cannot find God anywhere, it is because he is carrying us or is behind, pushing us forward? It was something encouraging and insightful, but the words lacked all of those attributes, as Judith repeated them to herself. She needed her father's quiet confidence, his conviction and devotion. She had always drawn from his strength, but he had vanished when the heathens had attacked, surely to take care of God's work. But Judith could not help but question why he would not have taken her with him to do whatever it was he was doing.

The amazing thing about devotion, not just religious, but pure devotion, is that it finds a way to rationalize and justify its existence, no matter the circumstances or evidence to the contrary. A small splinter of doubt had twisted and festered in Judith's mind, but the blind devotion to her father burned in her heart, overwhelming all scenarios that could possibly be explained by anything other than his greatness and righteousness. Her father had left her because he knew she was strong, wanted her to be so, and knew that the Lord would provide that strength if she only believed. So she did, she blindly and whole heartedly trusted that the death, the fire, the pain, all of the insanity that raged around her was simply some part of a divine test, one that she was determined to pass with flying colors.

The early morning sun punched ragged holes through the clouds and slowly fought its way to its rightful place of prominence in the sky. As Judith stopped momentarily to ponder the sun and appreciate its euphemistic qualities, she felt her insides turn, felt something twist. It was not painful, no not even so much as a knot of hunger, but it refused to be ignored. Gently placing her hands on her stomach, Judith waited for the strange feelings to abate. Surely, it was some after effect of nerves or jitters, but nothing of any real concern she told herself. As soon as she found her father this simple case of butterflies would pass. Then she felt it, at first unsure, but by the second and third kick it was undeniable.

Judith's hands began to tremble as she held them over her stomach and felt the small life growing inside her turn and push. The womanly needs of her body were always something that her mother had assisted with and guided, but the lessons had been incomplete, cut short by her mother being called into the fold of the Lord's messengers. Judith would never question God's plan, but at that moment, she truly wished that her mother was still in her corporal form and able to help. But the dark voice of doubt within Judith raged at this thought, battered its angry form against the bars of her mind. If her mother was alive! If she were still here, then none of this would have happened! Her father never would have moved his daughter from the cradle, to an incestual wedding bed if her mother were still here! So what point was there in lamenting a situation that was never going to change?

The tears streaming down Judith's cheeks mingled with the open cuts, slightly stinging with their salt, and then turning a faint pink hue and continuing on their journey to splash silently to the ground. These feelings remained for a few moments longer, tearing at Judith's heart, but then she forced them to be silent. Caged the dark voice and locked the door. This was God's plan. This child was something holy. Eve had been of Adam, and they had created all of God's children upon the Earth, so would not the Lord seek to follow the same or similar plan once again? Judith was of Able, and the child they had created was holy. It was the new beginning of the Lord's people. A smile, still wet with tears, stretched across Judith's face and this time she lovingly caressed her stomach. This child was a gift. This child was holy.

Judith continued plodding through the high, wet grass, as thoughts of jubilation danced through her young mind. Surely, her father would rejoice when he found out about the coming of this child. Surely, he too would see the sign and promise that this child carried. It was not too much further now. Able had told Judith that if anything were ever to happen to their church that she should meet him in the forest of rebirth, because it was the most holy of places and surely the Lord would see to them finding one another in the place where they had converted so many.

The dew coating the tall grass soaked into Judith's dress causing the fabric to cling annoyingly to her legs. She angrily reached down and snatched at the sodden material as she continued to push through the grass. Finally, Judith emerged into the clearing and was comforted by the sounds of the converted. The smell of weakness rotting from bone and the groans of celebration reminded her that some things in this world were still right. That no matter what those horrible people burned, some of the work she and her father had accomplished remained. The messengers all were still tied in place, struggling against their ropes and praising the Lord. Judith walked beneath the rotted corpse, playfully tickling rancid or missing feet. The zombies moaned and snapped at her, but she just giggled and joyfully skipped to the next one. Her father had to be here somewhere, she was sure of it.

Through the dim, empurpled light of the morning, a shape slowly approached Judith with outstretched arms. It must be her father. It had to be! But he appeared to be limping. His head seemed to be hung in shame as he came towards her, painfully slow. Judith hesitated for a second, but then rushed forward to meet her father. He must have been injured by those horrible people and he needed her help.

"Daddy!" Judith shouted as she rushed forward. As she neared him, she knew something was wrong. Her father did not say anything, just swayed and slowly hobbled towards her. Some part of her knew what had happened, knew what she was looking at, but refused to accept it. She could not reconcile the idea of her father becoming a messenger, even when she knew it was a holy transition that should be met with joy and praise. "Oh, no Daddy," Judith said weakly, her voice cracking and strained.

Able's pace increased when he saw his daughter, but still was little more than a painfully slow shuffle. As he neared his daughter, she could see that slick bib of gore that streamed from the tattered remains of his neck and down the front of his shirt. Jagged ribbons of flesh flapped with each pained step, and his arm hung by little more than a few glistening shreds of muscle fiber. The arm swung like a heavy flesh pendulum every time her father hobbled a little closer. Judith had no idea what those evil people had done to her father, but it enraged her. Sending him to his holy transition was one thing, but desecrating his body was another. Rage roiled through Judith as she laid eyes upon the full wreckage that had only hours ago been her father. It settled in her gut and twisted itself into fiery knots around the baby. She refused to let it diminish or falter. She would keep the rage and allow it to mature and grow in her stomach along side the baby, determined that she would eventually bear the fruits of both into this world.

Her father struggled to lift his head, but without the required muscles failed, and it fell heavily against his chest with such force that Judith heard her father's teeth clack. He groaned mournfully, causing the ragged flaps of flesh around his windpipe to flutter and smack. Arm stiff and outstretched, Able reached out for his daughter as if to hug her. She hesitated, and then stepped forward into her father's open arm. One cold, clammy arm closed around Judith and brought her into her father's embrace. The other arm swung uselessly at his side and brushed against her leg a few times before it dropped heavily to the grass with a sickening snap. Able did not appear to notice and pulled his daughter closer.

"Daddy," Judith said sadly, "I know that you have been chosen, but I still will miss you." Her father slightly raised his head as if to say that the feelings were shared. Judith stared into his grayed, milky eyes; his fire was gone, what had terrified the congregation and electrified Judith so many times during a sermon, had been snuffed out, and what remained was little more than a slowly rotting shadow of the man she had once loved.

Pushing away from her father, Judith tried to turn and continue traveling farther away from the compound, but her father held tightly to her arm and forcefully pulled her back. For the briefest moment, she entertained the silly idea that he wanted another hug, but as his teeth sunk in the soft flesh between her thumb and index finger, she knew nothing could have been further from the truth.

● ● ●

Holding his finger against his lips to motion for everyone

to be silent, Sam slipped through the doors of the church and onto the half-circle stone stoop. He could not believe what he was looking at; Joey appeared to be leading a conga line of zombies around the fire. If it had not been so dangerous and terrifying, it would have been hilarious. Over the dull moans of the undead and crackle of the raging bonfire, Sam was certain he could hear Joey singing, terribly, but singing nonetheless.

"Is he singing?" Amelia whispered and Sam nodded.

"It sounds like the song from Rocky," Mike added.

"He always was a huge Stallone fan," Sam shrugged as he watched Joey motion briefly for them to be quiet, and then hung a left and begin leading his undead dance line towards the main gate. The three waited for more of the Shamblers to follow Joey and then tentatively stepped down off the stoop.

Each pebble, every dry leaf, felt like it released an echoing thunderclap as they moved away from the church and further into the camp's center. Amelia was sure that at any moment, the zombies would realize they were behind them and turn to attack, but Joey's loud singing and the motion of the other Shamblers seemed to be enough to keep all the monsters moving forward. While neither of the boys spoke, Amelia noticed that neither Mike nor Sam lowered his rifle, and she knew the same terrifying doubt was furiously tormenting them as well.

Following behind the horde of zombies seemed to take forever. The sheer number and slow gait of the monsters were making this rancid parade last forever. But when Mike looked behind, he saw that they had actually made it much farther than he thought and tried to remain focused on watching the Shamblers. He felt Amelia watching him and offered a nod and weak smile, which she returned. Something was wrong with Amelia, Mike had no idea what, but ever since she and Sam had blown through the doors of the church and rescued him, he had sensed some tension or secret weighing them down. There had not really been time to ask, even though that was never Mike's style, but he knew something was wrong and from the look on his brother and friend's faces, it had to be serious.

Suddenly, all forward progress stopped and the Shamblers

dumbly bumped into one another. Joey's singing had stopped too, leaving the vacuum to be filled with the hungry groans of the twenty or so zombies that had been led onto the narrow dirt road with the hopes of getting them near the gate. Amelia turned quickly to cast a worried glance at Sam, but he had no answers; nothing was visible above the heads of the undead Zionists. Maybe this was part of their plan? Were they supposed to wait here?

The zombies lurched forward trying to get closer to Joey, but succeeded in only tripping over each other. As five or six of the Shamblers tumbled to the ground, Sam caught a glimpse of Joey. He was frantically looking to either side and seemed to be on the verge of panic. The zombies slowly pulled themselves, caked with mud, from the ground and reclaimed their position in the horde. As the hole closed up, Sam was sure he saw more Shamblers limping towards Joey from behind the smoldering outer buildings. He was surrounded. This was not part of the plan.

Sam wanted to tell Mike and Amelia, tell them that Joey needed help, that he was surrounded, but with the horde coming to a stop, Sam knew even the slightest noise could draw their attention. He could not risk breaking silence and having the mob come after them, the ammo was too low and Mike was too beat up to fight. But Sam could not stand idly by as his best friend since kindergarten, was torn apart by the undead. He had to do something.

The mass of zombies had not moved forward and the longer they stood there; the more Mike and Amelia realized this was not part of the plan. Something had gone wrong. Fear and panic began to rise in Mike, gripping this throat and making it hard to breathe. His body was too battered to put up any sort of fight and there was no way he could run away fast enough. If the Shamblers turned, he was dead, his brother was dead, and Amelia was dead. A heavy hand softly smacked the back of Mike's head causing him to shake it and clear his thoughts.

Amelia's eyes were wide and serious as she stared at Mike and the message was clear. This was no time to lose it, no time to fall apart, so get your shit together. A hand anxiously tapped Amelia on the shoulder and she turned to see Sam staring at her. He pointed at her and then at Mike, and motioned for them to hide behind one of the buildings and stay quiet. Amelia was about to argue or at least angrily shake her head "no," but the look on Sam's face caused all the fight in her to wither and die. There was no way she was going to talk him out of whatever it was he was about to do.

A softer look crossed Sam's face and he reached over to give Mike's arm a hard squeeze. Tears were welling in his eyes; he was doing his best to say, "Goodbye, I love you," without using words. Mike forced a painful smile to crack his lips and nodded. "Love you too little bro," he whispered as Sam turned and headed behind one of the burning buildings.

● ● ●

"What the fuck is he doing?" Chris asked, amazed at the sight of Joey leading an entire horde of zombies through the camp.

"Damned if I know," Bruno replied. They had emerged from traipsing through the overgrown grass on the side of the camp, behind some burning buildings. They had intended to end up back at the church, reasoning that it would be the most logical place to try and link up with the others, but must have gone off course somewhere.

The massive crowd of zombies was just beginning to move down the central street, as they came out of the field and they watched in amazement as a singing Joey led the way like some kind of pied piper. He was doing a good job of keeping a safe distance between himself and the lead Shamblers, but as Joey neared what Bruno thought looked like bunkhouses, numerous zombies emerged from the shadows and smoldering houses cutting him off.

"Shit," Bruno hissed, "Joey's got his dumb ass surrounded." Gozer and Zule shook with the rumble of a low growl. "Chris, grab them. I don't want them rushing off into that mess."

"You sure?" Chris asked as he grabbed the dogs by their collars and forced them to sit.

Bruno shook his head and patted both dogs. "I promised those two some cookies and we're making good on that promise. You stay here."

"Man, what the hell are you going to do?" Chris asked incredulously, "You're beat to shit and have no weapons."

A dry chuckle escaped Bruno's lips, "A very good question." But he offered no answer and took off at a quick jog towards the tangled knot of zombies that was slowly closing in around Joey.

Bruno looked back as he made his way across the grass. Chris had knelt down on the edge of the field and was hidden away in the tall grass. At least, that was one less person he had to worry about, but somehow that did not relieve any of the stress that Bruno was presently feeling. What the hell had Joey been trying to do any way? The answer slowly emerged from the shadows cast by the eves of one of the bunkhouses.

"Bruno," Sam hissed and passed the soldier a .45 that he had kept tucked into the waist of his jeans. Sam was amazed to be looking at his friend in relatively decent condition.

"What the hell was Joey doing?" Bruno questioned, "Has he completely lost his fuckin' mind?"

"Long story," Sam whispered, "But he was getting us out of the church. Is Chris with you? How'd you get free?"

"He's back there with the dogs. He's ok, but there'll be time for that later," Bruno grinned and checked the pistol. "Let's go." The two slipped back into the shadows and moved quickly, but silently past the twisted remains of the burned structures.

A long, rectangular building that looked like it had been used as a mess hall smoldered in front of Sam and Bruno. Three of the building's walls had collapsed inward, but strangely, one wall remained standing and aside from the charred inner side, looked as if nothing had occurred at all. They quickly moved past the blackened bones of the old mess hall and into the relatively hidden vantage, provided by a dented, greasy green dumpster that had been placed against the one remaining wall.

"What's the plan?" Sam asked as Bruno knelt down behind him.

"Plan? I was hoping you had one. What were you going to do?" Bruno asked and immediately regretted sounding like a petulant child. "I mean, I hadn't really had time to think about it. Was just kinda making it up as I went."

A frown creased Sam's forehead, "Same. I guess we're sticking with that." He peered around the rusted corner of the dumpster and saw that Joey was rapidly running out of space. The Shamblers were not fast, but were relentless and every inch of space that Joey gave up was quickly filled by another set of gnashing teeth. "We gotta do something quick," Sam demanded, "He's running out of room."

"On three?" Bruno offered and Sam nodded. The soldier silently counted down with his fingers and the two sprang from behind the decrepit dumpster.

"Joey!" Sam howled, "This way!" He really did not remember much after he had screamed; things happened so rapidly, but strangely felt slow. Sam's brain whirled through all the things that were wrong with what he was doing and his arms and legs felt like they were moving through pudding. After stepping out from behind the dumpster, things seem to explode into a blur of tangled limbs and bullet casings that Sam found himself running straight into.

● ● ●

Not being able to go with his brother gnawed at Mike. He did not want him to face all of those monsters alone, but there was no way he could have gone and been anything other than a liability.

"I know," Amelia whispered reading the look on Mike's face. They had been crouched down behind one of the buildings for what had felt like hours. "I wish we could have helped, but there was no way he would let us." She leaned back exhausted, and stared down at the now filthy bandage that was tightly wrapped around her bite wound. It had begun to itch terribly and she worried that it might be the beginning stages of infection setting in. Without realizing it, Amelia pulled at the bandage, further fraying its edges.

"What happened?" Mike asked softly, "Is that why Sam

wanted you to stay behind?"

"Shut up!" Amelia hissed, finding it hard to control the volume of her voice, "He left me back here to watch your stupid ass. That's all!"

Moving closer, Mike put his arm around Amelia's shoulders. The anger he had just seen was not directed at him and he knew it. Only one kind of injury could cause Amelia to become angry and react so defensively. "How long ago did you get bit?" Mike asked and felt the rigidity wash out of Amelia's body.

She looked up at him from where she rested her head against his arm. Tears were welling in her eyes and her lip was beginning to tremble slightly. Mike could see Amelia forcing herself not to cry, refusing to allow herself to be weak.

"I guess a little less than a day ago," Amelia sniffled, "It happened at the Municipal Building. One of those fucking things was trapped under a car and got me as I walked past. I'm so damn dumb. I should have never been so careless." She drew her arm across her nose and looked down at her feet.

Mike hesitated for a moment. He was unsure of what to say in this situation, never having been in it before. "Well, that's a long time right?" Mike said, doubting his own words. "I mean, if you were gonna get sick don't you think it would have happened already? Ms. Woodland, the guidance counselor, changed after only a few hours. If you've gone this long, maybe you didn't really get bit."

"I don't know. Maybe," Amelia answered and gently pulled away the stained bandage Sam had wrapped around her leg. There was a clearly visible ring of teeth decorating the skin just above her ankle, and the punctures were undeniable. Small, crooked veins of yellow and black streaked away from the edges of the bite marks like some kind of morbid road map. Amelia's hands began to shake uncontrollably.

"It's ok," Mike said softly as he reached over to re-cover the wound. "I'm sure you're going to be ok. We'll figure something out."

"I don't fuckin' care about me Mike!" Amelia burst out and immediately regretted making so much noise. "It's not about me," she repeated softly, and her hands unconsciously cradled her stomach.

"Oh shit!" Mike gasped, "No, I mean...oh shit! Seriously?" Amelia nodded her head weakly. "Oh my god," Mike continued, "For how long?"

Amelia sighed loudly, "I dunno, I just figured it out a little while ago. Maybe a couple of weeks I guess."

Part of Mike wanted to scream at Amelia and shake her for being out here in the first place and not safely back at the school. But Mike knew she could not have stayed, not with Chris being out here. "Does Chris know?" Mike asked quietly, "Does anyone know? Shit, that's why Sam made you stay behind isn't?"

"Sam does," Amelia whispered, "He does and Alice too. She didn't even want me to go, but I had to. I had to. God, now who knows? What's going to happen to my baby? I'm so frigging stupid! I was just so worried about Chris."

"Oh, shit..." Mike said, his voice cracking and trailing off. Amelia just shook her head and began crying quietly. "We'll figure something out Amelia. We have to." Mike was going to continue trying to say something reassuring, but he was sidetracked by the thunderous clap of Sam's rifle followed by the *clack clack* of a semi-automatic pistol.

"Is that a second gun?" Amelia asked, looking up from where she had tucked her head into her knees.

Mike's eyes were wide and concern was causing his voice to shake, "Yeah, I heard that too. I just hope it wasn't in the hands of a fucking Zionist."

● ● ●

Moments before a spray of bullets erupted from behind a rusty dented dumpster and whizzed past his head, Joey stood pacing anxiously in the middle of the narrow muddy path. The realization that he was going to die, slowly dawned upon Joey as he saw all avenues of escape become choked by fetid corpses with empty, clouded eyes, and gaping, hungry mouths. It was definitely not going to be a glorious death, but he hoped that it would not be a pointless one, and that his friends had escaped safely from the church. As the ring of Shamblers slowly closed in around him, Joey tried to force a brave, inspiring, theme song to rise in his head, but all he could muster was a repetitious chant of, "Oh shit, oh shit, oh shit, oh shit..."

Now Joey was sprinting, hunched over, head down. Every ounce of common sense told him to stopping running directly into a hail of bullets, but given the other option, Joey's current one seemed the most logical. He had to trust that Sam and Bruno were good enough shots that he would not get nicked and fall back into the stiff arms of a Shambler.

A round whizzed past Joey's ear and he felt gore and jagged pieces of skull pepper his back. A zombie collapsed to the ground next to his feet. It was missing the upper left half of its head. A heavy, cold hand grabbed the back of Joey's shirt and yanked backwards. He started to fall, but something rushed past him and the Shambler's grip suddenly went slack.

"Keep moving!" Sam shouted as he pushed Joey forward. Bruno was waiting beside the dumpster laying down cover fire. Each shot was aimed and carefully picked.

"Nice to see you too," Bruno smirked as he looked at the blank expression residing on Joey's face. "Plenty of time to explain later kid. Just get your ass moving." Joey could hardly believe that he was looking at Bruno alive, let alone saving his ass, but he pushed down a million questions and just kept moving past the rank dumpster. As Joey got to the corner of the burned out building, he stopped, and turned to see Sam and Bruno walking backwards, keeping perfect pace with one another. Bruno's gun let out a light click and he cursed loudly.

"Keep going," Sam shouted over the chorus of groans. "Find Mike and Amelia. Just go!" Bruno and Joey hesitated, but had no choice. There was nothing they could do without any more ammo or weapons. Sam had the only gun with bullets left, so like it or not, he was standing point while the others dropped back. The SASR barked thunderously, as it tore chunks from the zombies and spun them wildly to the ground. Joey started to move, to run back towards Sam, but Bruno grabbed his arm and pulled him in the opposite direction.

319

"Go," Bruno said firmly, "Sam knows what he's doing. Just keep going." Joey hesitated and as Bruno dragged him away, he watched the Shamblers slamming into the dumpster and swarming to fill the small opening on the side. Sam was somewhere in the middle of all of it, but as he was finally pulled around the corner, Joey had no idea where.

● ● ●

The moisture and coolness of the grass was causing Chris to begin to shiver. Gozer and Zule pushed themselves against him, instinctively sensing his need and trying to meet it, but even with the warmth of the two large dogs, Chris could not stop himself from shaking. He hoped it was nerves; that maybe he had been on a massive adrenaline high, and was finally coming down, but the fear that he might be going into shock loomed darkly in the back of his head.

"Just my luck," Chris muttered, as he stared up at the sky, slowly changing from indigos and cobalt to the warmer hues of pinks and yellows. "Get through all this crazy shit," Chris continued, "To die in the fucking grass." He closed his eyes and exhaled loudly. When his eyes opened, Chris found himself face to face with Zule. Her warm eyes conveyed an unwavering sense of loyalty and love, but also the promise to tear his ass up if he did not get up and start moving. There was no time to lie around lamenting an unknown and uncontrollable future. Chris needed to live in the moment, like Gozer and Zule, concerning himself with only the here and now; only the things that were within his realm of control.

"Alright, alright," Chris said, pushing himself up from the ground. He was stiff and his body racked with pain, but Zule had been right. The more Chris moved, the better he felt. His muscles loosened and the pain ebbed, becoming more tolerable. He had plenty of fight left in him and Zule had sensed it.

Moving through the camp, Chris easily followed the trail Bruno had beaten into the mud with his steps. The groan of Shamblers could still be heard from somewhere on the other side of the ruined buildings that Chris moved past, but he did his best to block out the noise. As long as the zombies did not see him, he was relatively safe. Edging along the charred skeletal remains of what had once been a ramshackled, two-story cottage, Chris's heart jumped as a massive barrage of gunfire erupted from nearby.

The hollow thudding of feet pounding on the ground echoed off the sides of buildings that had escaped the fires. Chris had no way of knowing whether the people coming towards him were friendly or not, so he quickly forced himself under the blackened remains of the closest building. Fortunately, the structure had been built on raised cinderblock legs, leaving a perfect amount of space for him and the two dogs to scuttle under and get out of sight.

From his hiding place, Chris watched two sets of feet go past. While holding Gozer and Zule in place, Chris poked his head out and saw that it was Bruno and Joey.

"Hey! Wait!" Chris shouted as he wriggled out from under the building. "Bruno! Joey!" The two skidded to a halt.

"What the hell are you doing under there?" Bruno asked. "I left you in the field."

"Couldn't just sit there," Chris shrugged, "It felt wrong. I had to get moving." Bruno nodded, but said nothing.

"Well we gotta get moving now," Joey wheezed. "There's a huge crowd of Shamblers coming this way and I don't know how long Sam can hold them."

"Wait," Chris said angrily, "You left Sam back there by himself? What the fuck is wrong with you two?" Chris turned and started heading in the opposite direction.

"Chris, stop!" Bruno shouted, "He's gonna be ok. I'm sure he'll be here any minute. That was the plan. It was what Sam wanted us to do." Heat prickled the back of Bruno's neck as he formed the words; he had been wrong. It had seemed like the right decision at the time, but Sam was no soldier. He was not trained for this. He was just a kid and the look on Chris's face said it all. They had made a cowardly snap decision.

"I don't give a fuck what Sam wanted," Chris spat. "I'm going to get him."

"Dude wait!" Joey shouted and Chris spun to face him. "I'm

coming too. I've been doing dumb shit all day I can't see why I should stop now." Chris grinned.

"Me too," Bruno said, ashamed that he had even allowed the situation to occur. "But we're out of ammo."

"I don't need any," Chris said confidently and clicked his tongue for his dogs to follow. They barked once and then fell quickly into a trot beside their boy.

● ● ●

One more fast look over his shoulder confirmed for Sam that Bruno and Joey had gotten away. He was glad that they had listened to him and left, but the idea of facing down the horde in front of him alone was terrifying. Joey had been tired and had already done his part, and Bruno was beat to hell and out of ammo. If the two of them had stayed behind, they would have been overwhelmed and eaten; there was no way Sam could have let either of them stay behind.

The decrepit dumpster had been pushed over opposite of the one remaining wall, creating a narrow passageway, forcing the zombies into a crude single file line. They lurched towards Sam and tripped over one another, falling in all directions. Sam winced as he heard the dull echo of one Shambler's head smashing against the corner of the dumpster near him as it fell forward, but he found it difficult to feel any empathy for the creature and stomped heavily down on its head. It wriggled and groaned under Sam's booted heel, but by the third or fourth blow, had gone silent.

A pair of stiff hands grasped for Sam, but missed as he leapt backwards. A ragged tear followed behind as the zombie's fingers trailed down the front of Sam's shirt. Teeth gritted, Sam let out a loud grunt and angrily smashed the butt end of his rifle into the face of the Shambler. Teeth scattered as the zombie's lower jaw exploded and unhinged to hang crooked from a few strands of flesh. The zombie's tongue lulled in its mouth as it showed no reaction to Sam's attack and continued forward. Sam kicked his foot out and knocked the zombie backwards into the ones behind it, but they had become so tightly packed, that the monster simply rebounded off of its compatriots and was propelled back towards Sam.

"Shit," Sam spat and brought his SASR up to fire. He did not have many bullets left and was hoping to ration them, but the mob was already closing in and getting too thick. The round split the jawless Shambler's head like an m-80 stuffed melon, painting the walls with a slick, tie-dye swirl of cranial contents and greasy black smears of coagulated blood. The large caliber bullet continued through the head of the jawless zombie and continued through three more, tearing hunks of flesh and bone as it went.

The crowd of zombies surged forward and filled in every inch of empty space near Sam. The dumpster groaned in protest as the sheer mass of the bodies began to force it backwards in the mud. As more and more Shamblers pressed on it, the back wheels dug deeper and deeper into the ground. It was going to tip over and Sam would be overwhelmed if he did not do something soon.

Swinging the stock of the SASR, already caked with gore and blood, Sam knocked as many of the Shamblers back as he could. With a small pocket of space opened up, he was able to swing the rifle towards the group pressing forward and tipping the dumpster. Sam angled his shots and tried to make the massive round pass through as many of the zombies as possible. The burning fragments of the bullets spread out in all directions and tore into the crowd. Had they been alive, Sam's shots would have easily stopped the advancing enemies, but they felt no pain and showed no reaction, as ribbons of skin and hunks of muscle were angrily torn from their bodies. Sam had panicked and tried to do what seemingly made sense, but ultimately had been a waste of bullets; only headshots would make a difference. Sam lined up the closest Shambler and centered its head in the crosshairs. He took a deep breath, held half, and squeezed the trigger. Sam's heart shattered and tumbled into his gut as he heard the empty *click* of the gun.

● ● ●

Something flew in a haphazard arc from the zombie's mouth and Chris was sure it was teeth or maybe even a jaw.

Whatever it had been, Sam had just delivered a devastating blow to the nearest Shambler. Chris was suddenly relieved that he had never actually had the chance to get into that fight with Sam; the kid was skinny, but scrappy as hell and seemed completely capable of defending himself. The empty space around Sam was quickly closing in and as Chris screamed his name, Sam began firing into the crowd of zombies. Chris's voice was lost in the cacophony surrounding his friend.

Heavy bodies tumbled as Sam's bullets tore through them, but there always seemed to be another Shambler to take the place of the one that had previously fallen. The firing stopped abruptly and even though Chris was not close enough to hear the empty click of the rifle's chamber, he knew that Sam had run out of ammo. Sam began backpedaling away from the horde and the undead shuffled forward to fill any open space. He began to swing the stock of his rifle wildly, knocking the nearest zombies over, but doing little to stem the flow of bodies.

Chris was only a few hundred feet away, but it felt like miles. There was no way his battered body was going to allow him to get to Sam before the Shamblers did, and it seemed that all he had succeeded in doing was gaining a front row seat to watch his friend's flesh tore from the bone.

Gozer whimpered loudly, but stayed next to Chris. Zule shook with a deep growl and was nervously inching forward. They knew Sam was in trouble and wanted to help him. It seemed that they had adopted everyone in their group and Chris knew he had to let them go. They needed to do what good dogs did and protect their people no matter the cost or obvious danger.

Taking a deep breath, with tears glistening in his eyes, Chris pointed towards the writhing mass of zombies and gave the command, "Gozer! Zule! Get it!" And with those simple words, the two dogs took off in a blur of bulging muscle and the primal instinct to tear anything apart that threatened what you cared about. Chris struggled to keep pace, but was easily outrun by the athletic animals and watched wide-eyed as they launched themselves into the swarm of monsters. They were quickly swallowed up by the surging mass of dead bodies.

The empty click of the chamber had sent icy bolts of electricity shooting through Sam's body. And even though he still fought vicously, smashing the stock of the rifle into the face of any Shambler that came close enough, Sam knew it was all going to be over soon. The dumpster was tipping over and when it did, the zombies would swarm through the narrow alley and overwhelm him. His friends would be safe and have the chance to make something out of this shattered, shitty world and that counted for a lot, but Sam would not. He was going to die and the most he could hope for, was a quick death and to not come back as one of these mindless monsters.

*"Promise me you'll come back to me. I love you Sam."* Alice's tear stained words from only days earlier echoed through Sam's head. He had promised her that he would come back. She had said that she loved him and he had said it back. Sam had dreamed of Alice saying those words more times than he could remember, but never did he imagine it would be like this. But that did not matter. What mattered was that they had both said it and meant it. She loved him and he had promised her that he would return to her, and that mattered more than the odds Sam was facing down. He was not going to let himself die. He would say those words to Alice again. Would take the time to say them right and at a time when they could both enjoy the peace and comfort of each other.

A set of broken, yellowed teeth snapped loudly mere inches from Sam's hand. He reared back and brought the rifle stock down with more anger than he had ever felt before. The reverberations of the blow shook through Sam's hands and arms as he made contact with the Shambler's skull. A thin, ragged line of black blood trickled down the zombie's forehead and its milky eyes rolled back into its wrecked skull. Collapsing heavily backwards, it knocked down three more advancing zombies, but others rapidly stepped into the void.

Sam could feel panic beginning to grip him and worried that he might lose it at any second. The searing prickle of a nervous sweat stung his flesh and his body threatened to revolt. Arms burning and sore, Sam forced himself to ignore all physical limits and warnings and brought the heavy rifle up again and again. He fully intended to keep his promise to Alice, but as the dumpster groaned loudly and tipped over into the mud, Sam began to worry that he might not be able to.

The shear weight of the Shamblers slamming against the dumpster had driven the wheels deep into the mud, and as more and more of them piled against it, the hulking box of rusted steel finally gave in and slammed into the ground with a wet slap. The dumpster was still in the zombies' way, but was much shorter after having been tipped over, and the lead Shamblers were forced onto it. They swarmed across the chipped front of the dumpster like insescts, hunger driving them towards the only prospect of a meal.

They were going to surround him. The narrow alley that had once afforded Sam a certain degree of safety had betrayed him; the limited space quickly filled with the reanimated corpses of the Zionists and cut off his only avenue of escape. Sam was surrounded.

Clammy, torn hands grabbed for Sam, pulling at his hair and ripping his clothes. Each one that nicked his flesh and drew a small ruby bead of blood, inspired the others to become even more feverish in their attempts. Sam kicked out at the knees of the zombies with as much force as he could muster, but the ground was slick and muddy and sucked at his feet, throwing off his balance. Tumbling to the soupy ground, Sam watched in horror as the Shamblers slowly closed in on him and cut off his view of the early morning sky. He looked for any angle of escape, but all he found where more hands grabbing, more legs blocking his path and more mouths gaping with want and hunger.

A Shambler, that looked as if it had been a Sunday school teacher, complete with embroidered denium smock, loomed over Sam. The woman's face was shredded on one side from where one of Sam's rounds had exploded. The flesh of her cheek hung in tattered ribbons, and her left eye dangled from little more than a few red chords of nerve tissue, all of which swung casually to and fro as she leaned in to tear a chunk from

Sam's stomach. Writhing in the mud, Sam rolled away from the Sunday school teacher, but only succeeded in knocking into another zombie. The Sunday school teacher, having been knocked down by another Shambler, continued towards Sam through the mud on her hands and knees.

Kicking out with both legs, Sam knocked the Sunday school teacher's head back. No sooner had Sam drawn his legs back to strike again did he see a flash of orange sail past his face and collide with the body of the former Sunday school teacher. The Shambler growled angrily and snatched at Zule, but she easily avoided the zombie's clumsy, slow attacks. Weaving between the monster's legs, Zule ducked under the stained denim frock and clamped down with a vice like grip on the soft hank of flesh behind the zombie's knee. Hesitating for a second, the Sunday school teacher snarled at Zule, but then attempted to continue forward; hunger winning out over self-preservation.

The thick-knotted muscles in Zule's neck tensed and bulged, as she whipped her head back violently, tearing a stringy hunk of tendons and meat from behind the Shambler's leg. The Sunday school teacher looked backwards at the infuriated animal, comprehending nothing more than the fact that it had been momentarily stopped, and then tried to step forward on its ruined leg. The zombie collapsed gracelessly to the ground in a heap of blood- stained, light blue denim, and angry moans.

Rolling over, the Sunday school teacher reared back her clawed fingers to swipe at Zule, but before the creature even had the chance to shift its shoulder, Gozer shot forward and locked onto its arm. With one angry wrench of his neck, Gozer dislocated the zombie's arm and left the zombie flopping angrily in a puddle.

Both dogs turned and looked at Sam, their expressions softening, as if to let him know that they were there out of love for him, but seconds later, that ancient fire once again lit their honey colored eyes. The dogs moved in perfectly synchronized aggression; moving from one Shambler to the next, tearing out the backs of knees and snapping spinal columns with a vicious twist of the head.

As he sat in the mud, completely stunned, heavy hands grabbed Sam and pulled him up. Momentarily panicking, Sam swung around, ready to attack, but instead of the waxen emotionless face of a Shambler, saw that it was Chris that had pulled him from the ground.

"No time to sit around on your ass," Chris smirked, and then his face clouded with rage as he stomped down angrily on the head of a Shambler that pitifully grabbed at him from the ground. Gozer and Zule were making fast work of the horde, but some zombies still writhed through the muck like slugs, dragging behind them useless, heavy legs. Sam shook his head to clear it and joined Chris in finishing off the monsters. Even while smashing the butt end of the SASR down repeatedly on the heads of the gimped zombies, Sam could not help but marvel at how the two dogs worked in unison to dismantle the horde of Shamblers. The zombies stood no chance against Gozer and Zule, who moved with ease and speed. By the time a zombie had rattled together whatever braincells were left in their rotted brains and stiffly bent over to swipe at one of the dogs, it had already torn out the back of the creature's knee and was moving on to the next.

Bruno and Joey came tearing around the corner of the burned out mess hall. Both armed themselves with slightly charred lengths of timber and without a word, went to work beside Sam and Chris. By the time they were done, the mud underneath the Shamblers had been churned into a repugnant brownish soup of cranial matter, blood and slop. The four men stood panting in a hard packed circle of dirt, surrounded by the tangled remains of at least twenty zombies.

"Gozer! Zule! Come!" Chris bellowed and the two dogs emerged from behind one of the buildings. He immediately fell to his knees and began checking his dogs for injury, but it was hard to tell if the blood that streaked and caked their coats was theirs or that of the numerous zombies they had just dismantled.

"Here! Joey, help me." Bruno shouted as he dragged over a heavy barrel of rainwater that had stood next to the destroyed mess hall. It was singed, but still sloshed loudly as the soldier dragged it closer. Joey grabbed the other side of the barrel and the two men dumped the freezing, ash-tinged water over the backs of both dogs. Zule glared angrily at the two men, as if questioning if this was her reward for all the good work she had just done. Gozer happily unleashed a full body tremor that whipped water in all directions, soaking the four humans that surrounded him, perhaps attempting to even the score.

Sam and Chris dropped to their knees in the turbid puddle surrounding the two dogs and frantically checked them over. No one was willing to celebrate or relax until they knew that everyone was ok, including Gozer and Zule. Running their fingers carefully through the matted coats of both dogs, neither Chris nor Sam found anything greater than a few scratches. Amazingly, the two dogs seemed to have come out of the battle relatively unscathed.

"That was insane," Sam almost whispered as he checked Gozer. It was unclear if he was talking to the dog or the people. "Totally fucking insane," Sam continued and then wrapped his arms around Gozer's thick neck. The dog leaned heavily back into Sam, pressing his full weight into the boy and knocking him to the muddy ground. Sam laughed, something he was unsure that he would ever do again, as the muscular dog climbed into his lap and attempted to curl up.

"Always did think he was a lap dog," Chris chuckled, "I think he's a pocketbook dog trapped in a pitbull's body." Zule pressed herself against Chris and gazed at him adoringly. "You did good girl," Chris choked, tears welling. He reached down to pet Zule, but she leapt up planting her paws firmly on his chest and spilling Chris to the ground beside Sam. Viciously, Zule began licking Chris's face; she seemed as relieved as he was that everyone was safe.

Something caught the attention of Gozer and Zule, their ears suddenly perking up. With one curt bark, both dogs turned and trotted back the way they had come. All four men trailed behind them, going as fast as their fatigued and battered bodies would allow. As they rounded the corner of the destroyed mess hall, they found Mike and Amelia petting the dogs.

Chris found himself suddenly unable to move, unable to comprehend the fact that Amelia stood only a few feet from him. Suspended above the pit, Chris had accepted that he would never see Amelia again, never hold her or be able to tell her how he fully felt. And now that she stood in front of him, he had so much to say to Amelia, wanted to thank her for giving him something to fight for, giving him some small splinter of hope in an otherwise bleak world, but the most he could muster was a weak, "Amelia..." before she threw herself into his arms and erupted into a deluge of tears.

Amelia buried her face in Chris's shoulder, uncaring of how soiled or smelly his clothes were; she was just happy to see him again, to be able to wrap her arms around him again. Somewhere deep inside Amelia, a burble of oozy black reality turned into a torrent of crushing revelations. First and foremost, that she needed to tell Chris that she was pregnant, secondly, she had to tell him about being bitten, finally, and perhaps most depressing of all, that this might be the last time that she ever held Chris again. The soul tearing thought that at any moment she could change and he would have to kill her, and unavoidably, their baby, or Amelia would attack Chris and their friends.

Saddness and depression began to bleed through Amelia like a cancerous growth and her body shook uncontrollably. Her shoulders heaved and her words choked in her throat.

"It's ok," Chris said, misinterpreting the messages Amelia's emotions conveyed. "I'm ok. It's over now."

"Don't fucking condescend to me you douche," Amelia spat angrily, but the venom in her words quickly faded away. "It's not ok," she said weakly, "It's the furthest thing from ok." Amelia tried to say more, but was crying to hard and her words became impossible to understand.

Chris looked concerned, but had no idea what Amelia was talking about and looked to his friends for help. Joey and Bruno were equally as shocked and lost as Chris was, and could only offer weak smiles and confused looks. Mike and Sam on the other hand, knew exactly what Amelia was talking about. Chris looked pleadingly to the two brothers.

"What?" He said, growing more concerned by the minute. "Someone just tell me what the fuck is going on here!"

Sam stepped forward and put his hand gently on Amelia's back. "I'll tell him Amelia," Sam said softly, "If you want me to." Amelia nodded her head in agreement and looked at Chris with wet, broken eyes.

"I'm sorry," she mouthed quietly. Chris could feel his guts beginning to twist into acidic knots.

"She's pregnant Chris…" Sam said and suddenly found that he could not finish the sentence. Mike stepped up behind his brother and forced himself to deliver the atrocious message that festered in his mind.

"She got bit man. Amelia got bit by a Shambler," Mike could feel tears burning in the backs of his eyes, but fought the emotions back; this was not his time to fall apart, his friends needed him. "I'm sorry man…I dunno…I'm just so sorry."

The world began to spin and the ground dropped out from under Chris. His knees buckled, but he fought to stay on his feet. Gozer and Zule whimpered softly, somehow sensing the travesty that loomed before all of them.

"When?" Chris choked, "When did it happen?" Amelia was reeling, but forced herself to answer.

"I found out I was pregnant after you got taken," Amelia sobbed, "The fucking zombie bit me a little more than a day ago." She pointed to the filthy bandage around her leg. "It happened at the Municipal lot when we went to get the guns."

"Why?" Chris said with tears streaming down his face. "Why didn't you just stay behind?"

"I couldn't," Amelia replied, "I couldn't leave you here. I had to know you were ok. I needed to see for myself." Chris and Amelia both began sobbing unable to speak, but Amelia was slightly relieved to have other shoulders to help carry the burden.

Bruno had been listening and quietly walked over. "Amelia," he said gently, "Can I look at your wound?" She nodded and he bent down to carefully remove the wrap. A ring of teeth perforated an area of flesh on the lower part of Amelia's leg. Bruno bent closer to investigate and looked confused.

"This happened days ago?" He asked, poking at the edges, "It looks like it's already beginning to heal."

"Why does that matter?" Amelia said despondently.

"Because," Bruno said, "If it were a virus or infection or whatever that was causing all of this, I should see some signs of it. It should be necrotic or inflamed, but it looks like you just got cut and are healing. Do you feel feverish or queasy? Anything weird?"

"Weird? I'm pregnant and standing knee deep in twice killed religious whack jobs," Amelia scoffed, "You mean anything outside of that? No, I guess not."

"Holy shit!" Bruno exclaimed, "That's gotta be it!"

"What?" Chris asked, unsure of how to feel or react, "What's it?"

Bruno grinned, "I'm not sure, but I think it's because she's pregnant man. That's gotta be what's making a difference here. The placenta must somehow have filtered the virus or whatever it is. I mean, it's not totally unheard of where a mother with HIV has a baby that tests negative, so maybe the reverse happened here? Maybe the baby and the placenta kept you safe somehow? And really, who the fuck knows how this thing functions and what it does to us, let alone, a developing baby?"

Amelia and Chris stared at Bruno, mouths gaping. Could it be possible that being pregnant saved Amelia's life? But if that was true, would there be any effects on the baby? These questions and a million more ricocheted through their heads, but they knew asking them was an exercise in futility. Bruno was going purely on assumptions and evidence. They had seen hundreds of zombies at this point and it was true none of them had been visibly pregnant, but then again, neither was Amelia. So really when it came down to it, Bruno was simply going off the two little pieces of evidence in front of him; one, that Amelia was pregnant and two, that she was still alive and appeared to be healing.

"The baby?" Chris said, his voice cracked and raw.

Bruno's brow knitted together. He wanted to offer his

friends hope and reassurance, but also felt compelled to be honest. "Honestly," he began, "I don't know. This kind of thing is obviously totally new and I'm not a virologist. I'm just a field doctor, more trained for bullet wounds than pregnancies."

"Stop making excuses," Amelia snapped, "Just tell us what you're thinking."

Sighing deeply, Bruno continued, "It's a crap shoot. There's no way of knowing, but what I can say is that you seem to be healthy, which means there's a good chance the baby is too."

Amelia began to argue with Bruno, unable or unwilling to accept the diminutive sliver of hope that dangled in front of her. There was no way of knowing, but that was true of most things these days, so eventually, she resigned herself to accept that their baby had the same fucked up odds as everyone else.

"Ok," Amelia said, letting the stress bleed out of her body. "I guess we have to go with what we have in front of us, right?"

"Yeah!" Joey chimed in, "I mean...well...yeah!"

Shaking his head and smiling cynically Mike laughed, "Thanks for that insight Joe."

● ● ●

"Get ready!" Crawford bellowed, "Looks like we got the last of the group coming our way!" Ronnie and Watts prepared themselves for the fight. Their nerves were completely shot, but they wanted to keep the gate clear for their friends' escape.

"What the hell is that one doing?" Watts asked, peering through the wisps of greasy smoke and early morning fog that had blanketed the entire camp. "It's waving its arms or some shit. Whenever I think it can't get any weirder..." But his words trailed off as he watched Gozer and Zule fly happily through the gate and begin leaping at Ronnie.

Moments later, they stared in disbelief as their friends limped slowly through the gate. Mike, Chris and Bruno looked like they were beat to shit, but they were on their feet and moving; always a good sign.

"Hey there princess," Bruno shouted to Watts, as Sam and Joey helped him past the chewed pile of Shambler remains that clogged the gate. "What's up with you big, bad, soldiers sending in a group of kids to save my ass?" He said sarcastically.

"Kids?" Mike said raising his eyebrows, "I should've left your dumb ass in the zombie pit."

"Please," Crawford scoffed, "You're salty ass is probably only here because of them. Me and Watts would've fucked it up some how. Wait, did you just say zombie pit?"

"What the fuck happened in there?" Watts demanded.

"Later Watts," Sam said, "We got time for all that later. For now, let's just go the fuck home." What Sam had just said struck a chord long since forgotten. A strange look passed between everyone. It had been the mention of the word "home." With everything that had occurred over the last few months, everyone had unconsciously and in some cases consciously, come to the decision that "home" was a feeling and place that had died when the dead had risen; that it was as distant a memory as all of their loved ones who had been taken. But Sam was right. They were going home; even it was a school, a place many of them had griped about going to. Because now, in this moment, surrounded by death, hatred, and despair, they knew that those things would be left outside the gate, and that could eventually push the boundary further out into the world, creating a place worth living in. They had a family to return to; a home and finally something that gave them hope for the future. Finally, they had found a fight that was for something greater than just surviving the day.

# EPILOGUE

The winter passed painfully slow, but everyone within the Montville School Complex managed and happily bore the challenges of the season. The cold weather seemed to slow the movements of the Shamblers and few gathered around the gates as the snow fell. With the Pillar of Zion Church nothing more than a blackened ashen memory, everyone was able to focus on repairing and securing the school. There were plans to plow the back soccer fields in preparation for spring plantings, and supplies gathered to extend the perimeter fence out, reclaiming more and more of the desolate town.

Even with the ground frozen and a heavy chill in the air, everyone's thoughts were on the future and new life. Amelia was moving through her trimesters with little trouble, and somehow, to everyone's relief and amazement, had not succumbed to the illness. Chris greeted her every morning as if he had not seen her for years and as if every moment they had together was a gift. Holding his hand to Amelia's protruding belly, Chris would smile from ear to ear as he felt the gentle push of a tiny foot and stare in wonder at their baby. Gozer and Zule were never far from Chris and Amelia and seemed to have taken a cue from their owner. As the weeks stretched, Zule's taunt muscled stomach developed a small paunch and soon she too would be caring for babies.

Elsie, Emily, Erick and Ms. Koslov had become obsessed with transforming the gym teachers' office into a private suite and nursery for Chris and Amelia. Erick had meticulously stuffed a corner with towels and prepared for Zule; everyone knew that pregnant or not, there was no way the dog would leave the side of Chris and Amelia. List upon list of supplies, clothes and toys, were created to be looked for when the others went on scavenging trips. Everyone happily gathered the items and more in preparation and welcome of the new life.

Hector and Ronnie had spent the cold months scavenging auto parts from the parking lots and had worked tirelessly to replace the vehicles lost from their fleet. A continuous echo of loud metallic clangs resonated from the auto shop room as Ronnie and Hector repaired and modified the cars and trucks. Having seen the success of his catapult and worried about the availability of bullets, Ronnie had become convinced that they needed more siege weapons and began to spend hours combing through medieval history books and codices that he had amassed from scavenging trips to the public library. In no time, he and Hector had devoted nearly half of the auto shop for the construction of a myriad of strange weapons.

Ronnie's trips to the library had also given Alice and Bruno a wealth of medical manuals and text to pour through. Alice devoured every book that Ronnie returned with, making notes to herself and asking numerous questions, and as the ground finally began to thaw, Bruno marveled at how quickly Alice had taken to the field of medicine and become an excellent healer. Bruno and Alice were never far from Amelia, and continued to hover, doting and checking the baby, even when she cursed at them and commanded that they give her some space.

● ● ●

The first signs of spring hung auspiciously in the air, drafting warm touches and smells through the crisp early morning air. Sam and Mike sat on the roof of the school, wrapped against the cold, but they had both unzipped the neck of their heavy jackets to allow some of the pleasant promises of an early spring to waft in. They watched as a lone Shambler, blistered and leathery from the winter months banged feebly on a section of the school's wrought iron fence. The zombie appeared as if it could barely manage to raise its wilted limbs, but somehow, continued to insipidly rattle its skeletal fingers against the thick iron bars. Sam raised his SR-25 rifle and sighted the disgusting, yet pitiful creature, but then thought better of it and relaxed his weapon.

"They're kind of sad looking when you see one alone. Don't

you think?" Sam asked Mike.

A dry laugh erupted from Mike's lip in a cloud of condensation. "Yeah," he quipped sardonically, "Until you try and hug it and it takes a chunk out of your shoulder."

Sam rolled his eyes. "Don't be a douche," he rebuked his brother. "You know what I mean."

Mike nodded, a thoughtful look on his face. "Yeah man I do," he said, "Seeing them like that is a pretty nasty reminder of how much we've lost. Like a walking billboard for the end of the world or something."

"You really think it's the end?" Sam said tentatively, "Like that the world is just slowly dying and we're along for the ride?"

"Nah," Mike answered quickly, "Death has always been around. That's nothing new. I mean, don't get me wrong, the world *we knew* has definitely died, but *the* world isn't dead. Just think of Chris and Amelia ya know?"

Sam thought for a moment. "You mean the baby?"

"Yeah," Mike said, "I guess as long as people keep having babies then the world isn't really over, so I guess you and Alice better get on it." Mike shook with the laugh that only an older brother can conjure, after having made a joke at the expense of his younger sibling.

Sam blushed. "Shut the hell up," he seethed, but could not deny that the thought had passed through his head more than once over the last few days.

Clapping a hand on his brother's shoulder, Mike continued, "And when their kid is born, this is going to be the only world they know, so in some weird way, all this, the zombies and stuff, will be normal for them."

Sam nodded, "In some strange, sad way, that does make sense. They'll never know anything different. This will be their world, no matter how screwed up, so we need to make sure that it's as good as it can possibly be. Which I guess, means we have the responsibility to make it a place worth living in, right?" Mike nodded as Sam raised his rifle and dropped the lone Shambler on the outside of the fence. "And I guess it starts right here."

• • •

The waning, afternoon sun, shone brightly off the cracked blacktop and in the distance, barely visible wisps of heat danced and twirled above the road. The stretch of road had once been a busy, maintained black vein connecting the vibrant east coast, providing an easy route for city dwellers and suburbanites to escape to the warm climates and sunny beaches of the south. But that had been close to a year ago, and nature had quickly begun reclaiming the stolen stretch of land; roots cracking and twisting the pavement so large tufts of coarse grass could take root. Now the interstate looked like little more than an abandoned junkyard. Twisted hulks of wrecked vehicles choked the road in jagged rusted heaps, making them impassible. Every so often, a dull moan would rattle loose from one of the misshapen orange and red mounds of metal. From somewhere behind the twisted metallic angles and waist high grass, a Shambler struggled unsuccessfully against a frayed, blood-stained seatbelt, as a small girl happily skipped past.

The strong southern sun had tanned her skin to a golden brown that glistened with the perspiration of a long day's walking, but did little to change the bright pink half moon scar that ringed the flesh between her thumb and index finger. She causally looked at the freshly healed scar, as she heard the hungry groans of the creature trapped within the wrecked car and smiled. Readjusting the thick, padded straps on her shoulders, she continued on her way heading further south.

As she got farther away from the entombed zombie, another sound drew her attention, but this was one she knew well; something pitiful and hungry, caught somewhere between a death rattle and the wail of a child. Judith smiled proudly and removed the pack from her shoulders, to set it gently upon the ground. Moving a soft blanket, adorned with smiling yellow ducklings, Judith gazed lovingly at the small body underneath. The child struggled against a tangle of blanket, but stopped once it saw the tender stare of its mother. Its alabaster skin, streaked with dark viens, seemed to glow in the strong sun, but never tanned. Two eyes, one clouded and milky, the other a vibrant hue of green flecked with gold, widened as its mother gently shook a bottle, mixing a sickening meal of baby formula and blood. The child hungrily took the rubber nipple into its mouth and greedily suckled the pink liquid.

"That's right," Judith cooed, "Drink it all up and get good and strong darling. We'll need all our strength. There is still so much of the Lord's work left to do."

## Acknowledgements

There is a long list of people to whom I owe thanks for assisting in one form or another and without whom I never would have written *Zombie Youth: Playground Politics.* I want to thank my family and friends for their unyielding love and support. Mom and Dad, thank you for your love, support and for encouraging me to start writing and keep writing. Dennis, Katherine and Glen, thank you for welcoming me into your family and supporting my endeavors. I would be remiss if I did not thank Nugget, Douglas and Maxwell, who have all contributed in their own way.

Thanks also to Gary and everyone at Severed Press for answering my endless emails and helping to bring this book to life.

Finally, a huge amount of thanks is deserved by my beautiful wife, who has suffered countless hours of zombie movies, pointless debates and who tirelessly carried on through a never-ending amount of nitpicking and word choice deliberations relating to this novel. Your infinite love and support have not only made this possible, but so much more.

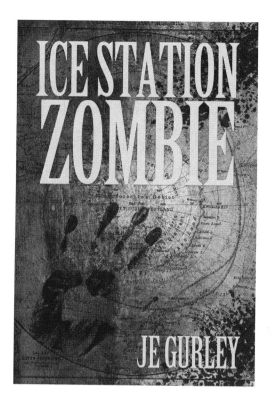

# ICE STATION ZOMBIE
## JE GURLEY

For most of the long, cold winter, Antarctica is a frozen wasteland. Now, the ice is melting and the zombies are thawing. Arctic explorers Val Marino and Elliot Anson race against time and death to reach Australia, but the Demise has preceded them and zombies stalk the streets of Adelaide and Coober Pedy.

www.severedpress.com

# The Coalition

When the dead rose to destroy the living, Ron Cutter learned to survive. While so many others died, he thrived. His life is a constant battle against the living dead. As he casts his own bullets and packs his shotgun shells, his humanity slowly melts away.

Then he encounters a lost boy and a woman searching for a place of refuge. Can they help him recover the emotions he set aside to live? And if he does recover them, will those feelings be an asset in his struggles, or a danger to him?

**THE STATE OF EXTINCTION**: the first installment in the **COALITON OF THE LIVING** trilogy of Mankind's battle against the plague of the Living Dead. As recounted by author **Robert Mathis Kurtz.**

www.severedpress.com

# RANCID

Nothing ever happens in the middle of nowhere or in Virginia for that matter. This is why Noel and her friends found themselves on cloud nine when one of their favorite hardcore bands happened to be playing a show in their small hometown. Between the meteor shower and the short trip to the cemetery outside of town after the show, this crazy group of friends instantly plummet from those clouds into a frenzied nightmare of putrefied horror.

Is this sudden nightmare related to the showering meteors or does this small town hold even darker secrets than the rotting corpses that are surfacing?

"Zombies in small town America, a corporate conspiracy, fast paced action and a satisfying body count- what's not to like? Just don't get too attached to any character; they may die or turn zombie soon enough!" - Mainak Dhar, bestselling author of Alice in Deadland and Zombiestan

www.severedpress.com

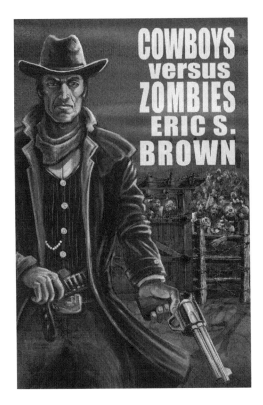

## COWBOYS VS ZOMBIES

Dilouie is a killer. He's always made his way in life by the speed of his gun hand and the coldness of his remorseless heart. Life never meant much to him until the world fell apart and they awoke. Overnight, the dead stopped being dead. Hungry corpses rose from blood splattered streets and graves. Their numbers were unimaginable and their need for the flesh of the living insatiable.

The United States is no more. Washed away in a tide of gnashing teeth and rotting, clawing hands. Dilouie no longer kills for money and pleasure but to simply keep breathing and to see the sunrise of the next dawn. . . And he is beginning to wonder if even men like him can survive in a world that now belongs to the dead?

# TIMOTHY
## MARK TOFO

Timothy was not a good man in life and being
undead did little to improve his disposition.
Find out what a man trapped in his own mind
will do to survive when he wakes up to find
himself a zombie controlled by a self-aware
virus.

20873686R00187

Made in the USA
Charleston, SC
28 July 2013